# IMMORTAL ACADEMY

## YEAR ONE

### S.L. MORGAN

# CHAPTER ONE

I grabbed a handful of chips from the tray my best friend was about to empty into the cafeteria trash can and shoved them into my mouth.

"Geez," she curled her nose, "you can be such a pig!"

I flashed her my usual grin as kids shoved by us to dump their trays in the trash and report to training exercises.

"Nice try." I patted her back, "I'll see you after school. We need to prep for the ceremony."

She followed my hurried pace and grabbed the inside of my arm as we walked out of the cafeteria and into the courtyard.

"What if…" her eyes darted around the bustling students, some nervous, some excited, and some like me who were ready to be done with all of this.

"What if what, Vannah?" I asked, sensing her frantic emotions.

I shouldn't have been able to feel *any* emotions. I was a shifter. A wolf shifter to be exact, and damn proud of it too. I had a mouth that got me in trouble all of the time, especially with my witch friend, Sahvannah. The arch of her eyebrow already told me she heard my prideful slang ring through my thoughts.

"What if they split us up?" she asked. "I'm dreading this ceremony."

"Why don't you grab a peek into the future with your little witchy ways and find out for us?"

"Jenna," she countered with an icy glare, "you already know they blocked our mage powers since the testing started. I couldn't see into the future even if I conjured my ancestors."

I widened my eyes in humor, "Conjuring the dead, eh?" I smirked. "Really, Vannah, don't worry about it. We're going to be okay."

"Fine. See you then, little miss confident," she said as she walked off, leaving me in the massive courtyard of Dark Water Academy.

I walked to a stone bench and sat down, needing some time to gather my thoughts. I was totally pretending not to be freaked out, and I certainly didn't want to think about what the ceremony was going to be like. Times like this made me wish I knew my parents. Like me, everyone I knew had been taken from their parents at age five and brought to one of these institutions for supernaturals and magic users, the only difference was that they saw their families again...I didn't.

I'd been to a handful of those places before I got to Dark Water, but the time had now come to find out whether or not I'd have to move on to the elite Immortal Academy, which was, just as the name said, an academy for immortal beings who went on to serve and protect all life forces. Supernatural or mortal human.

Vannah had it easy. She came from a long line of powerful witches. Woodson witches were like royalty, and she was, without a doubt, going to be one of the students accepted into IA. She was one-hundred percent immortal, and that made her enrollment mandatory.

I, on the other hand, had no friggin clue who my parents

were. Was I a full-blooded immortal, or was I just your average half-breed shifter who kicked ass and took names?

I had no idea. Part of me had always wished that my immortal blood percentage would be under the required eighty percent necessary for IA to *grace* you with their acceptance. If it would be 79.9 percent or less, I'd be well on my way to blending in with humans and getting on with my life.

My only hope in believing I had to have had diluted bloodlines was the fact that when I shifted into my wolf, her fur and eyes were a different color than mine. That was something that I'd never seen in any other shifter. My brown hair and brown eyes should've produced a brown wolf with brown eyes; instead, my wolf was silver and black with blue eyes. I could only hope that meant my genes weren't strong enough to carry over into my wolf. A girl could dream, anyway.

I wouldn't find out if my blood had fallen short of the eighty-percent requirement until the ceremony where they were to announce IA's new students based on our blood analysis. That put me in the same boat as most other people. The only difference between us was that, unlike everyone else, I didn't want to go. I was intrigued by human nature. The places I'd read about and pictures I'd seen in books made me long to live amongst them for as long as I could remember. I wanted to experience a new life, a different life, and if I were accepted into IA, that wasn't going to happen.

There were pretty steep rules for immortals to follow, and I was not one for following the rules. Obviously. My use of *offensive language* got me thrown in the night watch almost every other week. The night watch was a rigorous physical training that lasted from dusk until dawn, and when it was over, you were expected to show up to all of your classes. No excuses. My inner wolf loved the all-night workout, and I loved it too. It pushed me to be a stronger and more resilient wolf amongst the shifters.

Regardless of how tough I thought I was, I wasn't a fan of

living hidden away from the human population. For centuries, all the supernaturals and magic users had been forced to grow up in an enchanted realm that no human could find.

These realms were located in areas that humans couldn't travel to even if they were aware that we existed: inside frozen mountains, in the middle of a desert, a deserted island, at the bottom of the deepest part of the ocean, or in the thickest, darkest *haunted forest* in rural mountain communities. We lived— or so we were told—in one of the latter. It was a forest that humans had thought to be haunted for ages, but even the bravest ghost hunters wouldn't have had any luck if they wandered right up to the hundreds of thousands of acres we populated. Magnetic forces made it so no mortal could ever break the barrier of the veil that separated the supernatural from the human.

We knew about the humans, but they knew nothing about us. Certain immortals in the surveillance council were tasked to keep an eye on all supernaturals who lived amongst the humans. If someone shifted into their animal form, or if a witch tele- ported in front of a mortal, the surveillance council would send someone to erase the human's memory, and then deal with the offending immortal.

The punishment for revealing ourselves to the mortals was severe. Anyone foolish enough to get caught was given a one-way ticket to Rockfill Dungeon to live out their life as a servant to the Immortal Academy. Not an ideal scenario, and yet it was one that more than a few had to live out.

I knew if I'd ever told Vannah that I didn't want to go to IA, she would've been devastated. She couldn't understand why I had a tendency to act up in class or get myself in trouble all the time when all I had to do was follow the rules, and truth be told, I didn't necessarily understand it either.

All I knew is that I was different from everyone else, and I liked that I wasn't a *go with the flow* kinda girl. Hell no. I would much rather be known as the girl who has an opinionated, smart mouth than the pushover bimbo who is obsessed with what other people think about her. I was nothing if not strong-willed and determined.

"There's our sassy gal!" Tanner proclaimed as he walked over to me. "Let's go. We have the twenty-mile obstacle race." He ruffled my hair, "You think your cute little silver wolf can keep up?"

"As if my wolf hasn't whooped your cheetah every single time. Aren't you supposed to be the *fastest* animal alive?" I teased with a smug grin as I stood.

"Ouch!" he responded with a loud laugh. "Fighting words before a race only fuel me, you know."

"Oh, God," I heard Lacey grumble to the other female fox shifters as they strolled through the courtyard. Foxes were so cute in their shifter form, but this bitch made me hate the cute little critters. "I'm going to laugh when she and her little friends get split up at the Immortal Academy," she taunted. "Just because Jenna can run with the guys, that won't put her high up on any group there."

"What makes you think *any* of us are getting in?" I shot over to her and her blonde, ponytailed friends.

"It's obvious we will. This is an important school."

"Says who?" Tanner asked. "No one knows anything except for what they want us to know in these institutes. So shut your trap."

"Did you really just say *shut your trap?*" I said to Tanner with a belly laugh before the girls rolled their eyes and walked off in a huff.

"Hey, it's a timeless burn," he laughed in response.

"You crack me up," I said. "I'd rather not think about what Lacey said. I'm stressed out about the selection ceremony enough."

"Yeah, I know what you mean," he said. "It's not really a cere-mony, though, you know that. No need to dress little Jenna up."

"I know. They're gonna call some names, shuffle us outdoors and all that BS, but," I looked at Tanner's pointed features and bright green eyes, "Tan, this might be our last race if we get split up, you know."

"I get that." His mood was changing, and I could tell I was putting a damper on what should've been our last fun race.

I nudged him and laughed, "Well, what are we waiting for? Let's make the most of it."

"Lady wolves first," he said, stepping out of the way and stretching his arm out for me to lead the way.

I knew that one way or another, my life was going to change very soon, and I couldn't think of a better way to burn off my anxiety about that than to give my wolf a nice, hard run.

# CHAPTER TWO

I shifted out of my wolf form in the girls' locker room and dressed quickly in my leggings and tee. Dark Water Academy wasn't as strict as some of the other academies when it came to dress code, but from what I'd heard, IA was definitely the most rigid. I just hoped that if I was made to go there that it wasn't going to be all skirts and polo shirts, but it was the most prestigious academy of all supernatural time, so chances were that chicks were going to be in dresses, and dudes in those lame blazer jackets.

Before I left my locker, I reached in for the slice of pie I had stashed in there earlier. Most people love coffee, bacon, cake…I had a fetish for pies. Don't ask me why, but I'd never met a pie I didn't absolutely love. There was something about the sweet goodness inside a flaky pastry crust that made me salivate. It was definitely the food of the gods.

I crammed the slice in my mouth and sped out of the locker room—running late again—swallowing down and savoring the apple filling. I came out of the tunnel to see my shifter pals waiting for me while other students walked in large groups up to the auditorium.

Tanner, who I'd friend-zoned our freshman year, grabbed me and threw me over his shoulder.

"Dang it, Tan!" I put an elbow into his brawny back. "Put me down! You're going to get us in trouble...again."

"Nope," Tanner said with a laugh.

"Chill, Jenna," my friend Jon, a panther shifter, said. "If everyone hasn't figured out how we roll yet, then that's their problem."

I lifted my head and caught the tall, black-haired shifter in my sights. "Easy for you to say, Jon, but you know since all the academy ambassadors are here, they don't put up with this crap. Some academies hate—"

"When shifters act belligerent and stereotypical?"

*Damn it. Vannah was here to bust us all.*

"Save the language for if and when we get split up, Jenna," she said with her arms crossed and reproachful eyebrow. She never missed a single curse word that entered my thoughts.

Tanner set me on my feet in one smooth move, and I smiled at my bestie. "You're going to be cool if I lose it in there after they send you to that academy and send me somewhere else?"

"You know how I feel about all of this." She eyed my crew and me, "Come on, guys. You're all late, and I'm pretty sure we're going to be stuck in the back."

"That auditorium can seat at least a thousand people, Vannah," Jon said as we walked up to the double door entrance. "I'm sure there will be extra seating for you and your cute—"

"Shhhh," Vannah shut down the one shifter who actually fell for a witch. It drove her insane too, but she put up with Jon and his constant flirting with her. "Let's *try* not to make a grand entrance."

"Fantastic!" the dean of our school said, bringing his attention to all six of us shifters and our witch friend as we tried to sneak into what we *thought* was the back entrance. "Not only late but entering right in front of the entire auditorium as well," Dean Hagger said with an annoyed tone.

Dean Hagger was cool, but he was a vamp, and vamps thought they were royalty among all supernaturals, especially the shifters. So even though he had a level-headed personality, he could be a jerk most of the time.

"Sorry, we just—"

"Take your seat, Miss Woodson, and make sure your shifter friends mind their manners."

There it was. The prick side of the vampire. He'd be cool to a full-blooded immortal witch because she could probably smoke his ass here and now, yet he couldn't help but be condescending to the shifters. Dear God, if I got into this elite Immortal Academy, would it be the same friggin way there too?

"I'm not the only one who can read your thoughts in the room," Vannah hissed at me. "Seriously, Jenna, help me out a little here."

I rolled my eyes as we climbed up to the second landing of the auditorium and found our seats.

"Before the selection ceremony begins, I need to make an announcement. Some changes have been made to the graduation process of all supernatural academies," Dean Hagger started. "No longer will we be sending eighteen-year-old supernaturals straight out into the world if they are not chosen to attend Immortal Academy. Those not selected for the honor of attending Immortal Academy will attend a different university for supernaturals, and these distinguished ladies and gentlemen seated behind me are here from those institutions," he said as he motioned to a panel of people seated behind him. "If you aren't selected by your bloodline to be welcomed to Immortal Academy, then you will be assigned to one of these many other institutions by your achievements—or non-achievements—where you will stay for no fewer than two years in order to better prepare you for human interaction."

"What the—" I stopped myself and turned to Vannah. "He's freaking joking, right?"

"It's not a joke, Jenna," Dean Hagger shot me a dark stare from where he stood at the podium. "I would appreciate it if you would remain quiet, or I can assure you that the school you'll be heading off to is one you won't like."

*Asshole.*

"Jenna!" Vannah nudged me. "Knock it off."

"The reason this decision has been made is that we have had way too many disruptions from students who were ill-prepared for what awaited them in the mortal world. Too many have been punished, and even worse, too many humans have had to have their minds erased of memories because of it. It's time that stops, and this is our best answer." I went to speak, but the dean looked directly at me as if to halt me with his vampy stare. "I think our sweet shifter, Jenna, is reason enough to understand why you all must mature more through strict training before being released into the human population."

My eyes filled with tears, and it wasn't because the d-bag was making an example out of me. If for some reason I didn't go to IA, I had to wait at least two or three more years to find out who my parents were. God, I couldn't even remember what they looked like. I didn't know if I had any siblings. Nothing. Now, I wouldn't know the only thing I was so excited to learn after getting out of this joint.

"Without any further announcements, we will proceed with the ceremony. To make this easy, we're dividing this ceremony up into two parts. It will be easiest to have the esteemed ambassador from Immortal Academy, Miss Alicia, announce the selected students who will be attending their institution this year. Once she calls your name, please stand and excuse yourselves through the *back* doors as quietly as possible. You can wait in the students' admissions park for the ambassador to meet you and," he smiled at all of us, "I wish you all good luck, and I do hope you represent our academy well at the Immortal Academy should you be chosen. This will be your last hour here as there is a private escort arriving to bring you to the academy. The rest of you who remain will be admitted by each one of the ambassadors behind me to your various schools." He turned back to some blonde chick in a tight, sparkly dress. *Fairy. Awesome! Not.* "Miss Alicia, you may announce the students who have been chosen to attend the Immortal Academy."

I felt my palms sweating, and then Tanner gripped my shoulder. "No matter where we go, we'll all meet up in two to three years."

"Still Montana, right?" I said in a shaky voice.

"That diner I told you about brags that they make the best pies." He winked. He was always the positive one, but I could now see the trepidation in his eyes too.

"Well, that's me," Vannah said when her name was called.

*WTF.* "They're not calling names in order? How un-academy-like of them."

"That's not a word, and no they aren't, so pay attention," Vannah said. "I love you, Jenna."

Okay, she was bidding me farewell. What school would I be attending after the Immortal Elitists got their butts out of here? After always getting in trouble, totally pissing the dean off today, and my stubborn attitude, I was probably heading off to the supernatural school of fallen angels or some crazy crap like that.

"Jenna Silvers," Miss Alicia's song-like voice rang out, looking right at me with her bright yellow fairy eyes. "Jenna?" she laughed, trying to make it seem like fairies could actually be sweet.

I couldn't freaking move. My butt was glued to my cushioned chair. My wolf...she wasn't happy about this either. When my inner Jiminy Cricket seemed to hide in her cage, not liking this at all, I knew something wasn't right about going to this school. I just didn't know exactly what.

It would've helped if my wolf gave me some reason why she was hiding deep within me, but nope, I was on my own. This royally sucked. My wolf made better decisions than I did, and yes, she was pretty much my alter ego. I thought differently than she. We were two separate minds but still one and the same. It's how all shifters and their animals within them were.

"Jenna," Tanner whispered. "Get your butt up before the fairy moves it herself."

I looked at the horror on Tanner's face. "I love you," I told him. "God, I hope you get into this place, I don't know what I'll do without you."

"Two to three years," he reassured me. "Go. I know that Vannah is going to flip when she sees you!"

I found my feet and unglued my butt from my seat. I left quietly through the back doors, not even having the desire to shove it in the fox girl tribe's faces.

Once the bright sun touched my face, I glanced around, completely lost for the first time in my life. I should have run off to where Vannah was waiting and assured her she'd have her bestie at IA with her, but I couldn't. I was seriously heartbroken. How the hell was I over eighty percent immortal?

I heard the door shut behind me only to see another witch who'd made it into IA. I had to get out of here. I had to calm down. I was so screwed. I was going to some elite academy, and with the way my manners were, you'd think I was a rat shifter instead of a wolf. How was I going to manage this?

My wolf perked up at that, and I drew on her strength and shifted instantly. I took off toward the woods, leaping over the rapidly flowing creek and kicking up dust under the pads of my paws. I don't know why I thought this was a great idea, it's not like running away was going to solve my problems—it would just screw me worse.

I stopped at the edge of the veil at the thick forest line and sat down, facing a black paved road out in the middle of nowhere. I curled my tail next to me and stared through my wolf's eyes at the temptation just to step out of the veil and into the human world. Maybe I would never shift back.

"Stop it, Jenna," I heard Vannah say.

My wolf whimpered, how was she in my head?

"I'm always in your head." I felt tender hands run along my silky coat, "I brought you some clothes, you need to shift back. They're almost done loading everyone into a fancy-looking charter bus headed for IA."

I shifted back, feeling comfort in my best friend's strength. She tossed me some gym shorts and a hoodie. "It's all I could find in your locker, and we don't have time to get our stuff from the dorms."

"What?" I said, pulling my gym clothes on. "I have personal stuff. They're taking everything from us? What are they going to do to us at this place, transform us into robots?"

"Quit being so dramatic," Vannah said. "You're overthinking. Why did you come out here?" Her eyebrows shot up in humor, "to run away?"

"I don't run away unless I sense a threat."

"You don't even run away from threats, Jenna," she said dryly. "You face that stuff head on. What's your problem? I wanted to hug you and be so excited that we're off to IA together, but your aura is dark and depressed. What's happening?"

"I don't know. I wanted to see my parents again. Now, not only am I going to be three years deep into this lame academy that everyone treats as the best place on Earth, but I'm going to be split from my guys too."

"Making new friends isn't the end of the world." She hugged me, "Don't forget, we all made a pact to meet up in Montana after the IA releases their students. So let's go."

"Three years isn't that long," I said out loud, mainly to myself.

"No. It's not."

"How'd you know I was here?" I asked her, my mind settling

down and beginning to wonder how my bestie teleported to my hidden escape spot.

"Well, Tanner's over eighty percent immortal, and when he saw you missing, he knew you'd be here. So I teleported here, and voila...here you are."

I hugged her tightly. "This isn't going to be that bad after all. Tan's gonna be there, and so are you."

Exactly.

"Don't tele—"

Too late. My witchy friend dropped my stomach when she did her stupid teleporting thing, and the next thing I knew, we were in line, facing the large charter bus and ready to load. Tanner was at my other side in a flash. I smiled at my best dude, knowing if I had at least these two with me, we'd be in and out of this academy in no time. This was actually going to work out well.

At least that's what I told myself over and over and over again.

# CHAPTER THREE

I remained quiet as we loaded the bus, watching a tall, lanky man with long silver hair carefully assessing the newly-selected students as they attempted to board. I had thought I'd seen everything growing up in supernatural schools until one fairy girl was caught trying to sneak onto the bus without the exclusive *immortals only* permission.

A cloud of gray dust kicked up right as she walked toward the man. At first, his eyes turned creepy white, then the dust came out of nowhere, and in a whirlwind, it snatched the girl off her feet, and...*poof!*...she was gone. No one said another word after that.

I knew the girl who was whisked away only because of the snobby friend she tried to sneak onto the bus with. They were two obnoxious fairies who forever got away with everything just to get good grades and stay at the top of their class. They charmed their professors with their fairy dust and by kissing their butts at every turn. Now, the stuck up duo was split up, and God only knew where Destiny's sidekick, Kira, was whirled away to.

At this point, I clamped my mouth closed and shut off my

mind. These immortals didn't put up with crap, and it was already showing. I was betting the hardest part of being at this academy for me would be keeping my mouth shut, my head down, and just getting through the next three years without a whirlwind of dust taking me off to the unknown.

"You're best to think that way too, Miss Silvers," the tall dude said as I approached him. "Yes, we are a very strict academy, and for a good reason."

This dude was mysterious...and weird. *Aghhh, stop thinking, Jenna!* The man smiled and held out a long arm, motioning for me to enter the bus. I leapt up the steps, seeing some students I'd never seen before were already seated on the plush seats. It was evident that Dark Water wasn't IA's first stop on the way to gathering all of their new students. I had no idea where the others had come from, but we were all headed to the same destination.

I took a seat next to Vannah. I let out a breath and rubbed my forehead as I noticed that the dark windows from the outside of the bus were a facade. There were no windows on this thing at all.

"I guess they're afraid we'll giveaway where the school is if we actually see where we're going. Why do all academies feel they have to do this to us?" I whispered to Vannah.

"You know that reason," she answered, reclining some in her oversized seat. "If you knew where Dark Water was and you were successful in your escape, then you could give away the school's whereabouts to the first human you felt like confiding in."

"That's lame," I said, sinking further into the comfortable seats.

"Why were you out there, anyway? You're not one for running away from things."

"I know. At first, I think I really did want to run away from it all, but the more I think about it, I think I'm just curious about my family. I really thought this would be my chance to get out."

"Why, though?"

The bus jerked without any prompts and then gravity pinned us to our seats like we had hit warp speed.

"Good grief," I said, gripping the armrests, feeling a wave of nausea overwhelm me. "I'm going to need to shift just so I don't barf."

"Here," Vannah said. She rubbed my arm, and a purple and pink swirl of energy seeped into my skin and headed straight to my bloodstream. My nerves instantly calmed with her relaxing spell. Sometimes it was awesome to have a witch as your BFF. "Feel better?"

I smiled. "Yes. I could fall asleep right now."

"I know you want to meet your parents, and I back you on that. I just don't understand why it can't wait."

"I don't know, either. I feel like there is much more to my life, and it will never be complete until I see them again."

"Do you remember them?"

"No. Maybe that's why. I'm crazy, I know, but I do and say things that make me wonder if I got certain mannerisms from my parents. If I did, what were they like? Am I an only child? Maybe I have some human in my bloodline, and that's what makes me feel this way."

"If you had an ounce of humanity in your bloodline, you wouldn't be heading off to IA. You know that any human who procreates with an immortal will produce a mortal child one-hundred percent of the time. They can still be supernatural, but definitely not immortal. That's common knowledge."

"Well, then, there's the first clue. Ma and Pa aren't human, and my ancestral line was never crossed with human blood." I yawned. "What the heck did you do to me?" I rubbed my arm, realizing I was more tired than I should've been.

"I released a little more punch to that spell. You were fidgeting like crazy after I brought you back from your planned escape, and I'm not going to let you show weakness by needing to be in wolf form just to travel on a bus."

"That's moving a thousand miles an hour, by the way."

"Funny how you feel the gravity pulling you," she said with a smile.

"Shifter. One with the earth, my friend."

"Attention students, we are arriving at the outer barriers of Immortal Academy. Please pay attention as these rules must be followed after you are dismissed from your seats." A chime of a voice came over the intercom.

Sounded like another freaking fairy. It was looking as though IA was a fairy-ran school, which was totally going to suck. Fairies were ruthless, and you couldn't trust them for anything. Well, some were cool—the elves and leprechauns, primarily—but the rest? No.

"Once your rows are dismissed, you will follow one of the masters to Brickhall Theatre where you will then be given your uniforms, dorm room information, and schedules. In exactly two hours you will report back to Brickhall where you will be admitted into the auditorium for introductions. Thank you, and welcome to Immortal Academy. You are our future."

"Here we go," I said, glancing over at Vannah. "New school, same crap."

"I'm sensing that you should probably tone down your attitude until you get your bearings here. Look what happened to Kira. I'm pretty sure this school isn't messing around."

Our row was next, and so I patted my bestie's hand and stood up. "That's what worries me. Who knows, maybe this school is the best thing that ever happened to us." I glanced around the bus, seeing Tanner had found some cute chick with bright pink hair to mingle with while on the magic bus ride to never never land. "Looks like Tanner already fits in," I said with a laugh.

"That boy will wind up busted before he knows it. A shifter flirting with a pixie? Sort of stupid if you ask me."

"At least all eyes will be on busting him and not me." I nudged my friend and followed her down the aisle and off the bus.

When we stepped off and our feet hit the glittery, lime green grass, I felt like we'd been brought to supernatural paradise. My eyes—which had excellent sight thanks to my wolf—took in the most majestic place I'd ever seen. This place shimmered, sparkled, and swelled with beauty underneath a brilliant white sun.

From where we stood, all I could see was a colossal, silver brick building. Next to the golden entry gates were two brick columns that swept up and created a vibrant archway that students were walking through and toward the steps to the open doors of this place.

Brickhall Theatre was being written—and I mean being written over and over with some invisible magic pen with glittery gold ink—on a black plaque that was placed on each column that the archway was built up from.

"This is where we go."

"You think?" I answered my best friend's soft voice. "Is my witchy friend shocked for the first time in her life?"

"This place. The magic. The talents. It's so…" She gazed up at the shimmering white steps we were headed to. "It's unreal."

"Yeah. Don't let the looks deceive you. Part of me thinks this place is pretty on the outside and probably freaking black as sin on the inside."

"So we have a pessimistic new student. Wow. Most students are enamored at our beautiful school," a raspy voice said as we entered into a luxurious atrium.

I glanced over to see a woman in an elaborate gown offering a warm smile that literally forced me to smile back. "I'm just acting new," I rattled off, not knowing how to answer.

"You'll catch on." She winked, nodded, and then we followed the group down the large floor to ceiling window-filled hall.

"You okay?" Vannah asked, snatching my arm, and flooding my body with warmth from her energy. "That was a vampire, and she just made you look like a bumbling idiot. I'm sorry, I should have snapped you out of the soothing spell I cast on you before we got off the bus."

Coming to, I looked over at Vannah's dark and flawless skin, seeing pink touch her cheeks. I could tell she felt like crap that she put me at the mercy of a friggin vamp.

Humans had a funny idea of what vampires were. They weren't the bloodsuckers that all of the books and movies portrayed. Most vampires fed off of the physical energy of their prey instead of their blood. Once they sucked out a person's energy—supernatural or human, mortal or immortal—they could do a real number on their victim's mental state, making them do almost anything they wanted. I shouldn't have been surprised that a vamp didn't resist the first opportunity it got to make a shifter—one of their most hated supernatural rivals—look like an absolute dumbass.

It wasn't Vannah's fault she threw me at the mercy of the haughty creature, but I couldn't have her protecting me to the point of hurting me at a new place like this. I needed control of all my senses.

"I promise to behave and keep it cool, so long as you promise no more spells unless I'm dying. Cool?"

"Dying? She laughed. "Girl, we're immortal, and unless I missed something in Professor Mark's class, immortals can't be killed, but I know what you mean. No spells, period. I feel horrible for putting you at her mercy."

I glanced over my shoulder to where the vampire once stood. "Don't feel bad, I'll get my revenge."

"That's your first mistake," a deep voice said from out of nowhere. "Revenge is not a word you want to use at IA," he said, walking at a brisk pace.

"Great, you're already getting busted," Vannah said as I studied the robust guy with pitch black hair walking past the line of new students marching in the hallway.

From behind, the dude was gorgeous. You could see his back

muscles flexing in his tight, navy polo shirt, which was tucked neatly into his slacks, and the shape of his...

"Jenna," Vannah said as I almost ran into the line of stopped students. "Pay attention."

The dude who interrupted my conversation had stopped and stood off to the side. His hair was tamed and smoothed back on the sides. The top was cut short, but you could see where he had some wave to it. He glanced our way with his dark brown irises, and the girl chatter kicked up like that gray dust that hauled Kira away from her best friend. I couldn't say I blamed any of them.

This guy had a perfectly symmetrical, utterly gorgeous face. Strong jawline, biceps stretching the short sleeves of his shirt—must have just worked out—this guy was perfect, and it was all probably going to be for nothing because he was a warlock or something.

His brooding look made his jawline flitter with apparent frustration. I watched as a beautiful, leggy, raven-haired girl, who surprisingly matched this dude's tall height, approached him from the side, and a smile lit his face when he spotted her. As if he needed any more help on looking like the most gorgeous specimen I'd ever seen, that smile sealed the deal.

"Quit gawking. You look like every other helpless girl waiting in this slow-moving line," Vannah said with annoyance. "Sheesh, you'd think a school like this would have their admissions part down. Let the witches do it or something. This is ridiculous."

"I'm not gawking. I don't *gawk*, especially at guys that look good. As far as I know, he's a complete jerk, so why would I give him a fraction of my time?"

"Good question. I get you back into reality with a waking spell, and after he put you in check, you're checking the dude out."

I craned my head, looking pointedly away from the guy. "It's obvious that chick is his girl anyway. I'm not into him, so chill. I'm with you." I turned back to see the line slowly moving forward. "What the hell is with this school and their admission process? A freaking witch could snap her fingers and move us right into our dorms."

"Let's just hope this is the only flaw I see in the school."

I glanced over and smiled at my judgmental witch friend. "You and I both know you're going to complain about anything unless you find out an ancient witch is running this joint, and you know it. You witches are all the same. You judge others pretty harshly."

"It's not my fault we have impeccable standards," she said with a wink. "I'm just ready to move along."

"Me too."

It felt like an hour before we were given our schedules and dorm room numbers, complete with an enchanted map. Vannah and I were obviously split up. New students were paired up with existing ones.

We were each given a mystical map, complete with a magical bug icon that walked on the map, leading us to where we needed to go. I couldn't help but laugh at the adorable little thing as it trudged down the hallways of the second floor of the Manor House building where my dorm was located. The bug's tiny legs were scrambling on the map, trying to keep at the same pace as me and not get too far ahead. If the magical bug turned right down a hallway, I needed to turn right. Simple as that. My curiosity couldn't allow me to follow the critter without wondering what would happen if I went the wrong direction though.

I laughed out loud when the bug shook like it was having a breakdown because I was going to get lost. It started to turn red, waving its front legs in the other direction as if I was going to fall off a cliff if I didn't go the other way. I decided to turn right again before the bug had a heart attack and keeled over on my map. It finally led me to Dorm 307.

I walked in to see two twin-sized beds on opposite sides of

the room and two French doors that were opened, leading out to a balcony. Glancing around the room, I was impressed with its size. Two large dressers to match the white, metal bed frames were against the wall just beyond the foot of each bed. Two doors, each leading to bathrooms, were next to each bed. *Personal bathrooms? Nice touch.* The wind blew in through the French doors, and along with the white chiffon curtains, the girl who was with the hot dude from earlier blew in too.

Just my luck. I get to share the room with a girl who was obviously a vamp. Thank God this room was big because Miss Vampire Pageant was going to need to give me some space. This wasn't going to make sleeping easy. If this chick so much as winked at the thought of draining my energy and using that to compel my shifter butt to get busted, she was in for a big surprise.

Knowing myself, she'd be wasting her time. I was probably going to do that all on my own. Either way, I was going to have to sleep with one eye open. Shifters and vampires were polar opposites. To put it nicely, we hated each other, and I was stuck bunking with one of them.

# CHAPTER FOUR

## HOUSE OF BRAECLAW

## SCHEDULE OF CLASSES
FOR OUR HIGHLY ESTEEMED SHIFTERS.

WELCOME TO IMMORTAL ACADEMY:

## ORIENTATION: DAY ONE

*At Immortal Academy, we strive to make your first day your best day. Today is our introduction day where you will meet professors and learn of the various activities that Immortal Academy has to offer. Please make sure you are on time and in uniform upon arrival to Brickhall Theatre. Classes will start tomorrow.*

### PERSONAL SCHEDULE FOR JENNA SILVERS:

*Immortal Shifter: Species; Wolf.*

**5:00 a.m. - 7:00 a.m.**

Training in natural forms

Attire: Combat uniforms

Instructor: Master Dominic Rossi

Location: House Braeclaw lawns

**7:00 a.m. - 7:30 a.m.**

Shower and dress in universal school uniforms

**8:00 a.m. - 9:00 a.m.**

Breakfast

Location: Brignell Dining Hall

**9:15 a.m. - 10:00 a.m.**

First Session

Class: Shifters of House Braeclaw

Professor: Sir Samson Candor

Location: House of Braeclaw building, unit 501

**10:00 a.m. - 12:00 p.m.**

Second Session

Class: Vampires; The immortal history of

Professor: Mistress Sirena Masorne
Location: House of Draguar building, unit 632
**12:00 p.m. - 12:45 p.m.**
Lunch
Brignell Dining Hall
**1:00 p.m. - 3:00 p.m.**
Third Session
Class: Fairies, the immortal history of
Professor: Dr. Winston Goldwater
Location: House of Fae building, unit 717
**3:00 p.m. - 5:00 p.m.**
Fourth Session
Class: Witches, the history of
Professor: Madame Helen Von Tassle
Location: House of Mage building, unit 890
**5:00 p.m. - 6:00 p.m.**
Dinner
Location: Brignell Dining Hall
**7:00 p.m. - 8:00 p.m.**

### *Shifter forms:*

This is considered *Shifters' free time and agility workout* with your assigned Braeclaw Master. Your assigned Master is *Dominic Rossi.*

This is the **ONLY** time your animal may be present unless otherwise specified at this academy. If any shifter is found in their animal form without proper permission from your professor, you will be reprimanded, and repercussions for this offense will be decided by the dean of the school. This is taken very seriously, and we advise you to comply with these rules. Dean Darius Edgewater is rarely involved in matters such as these, but for this, he will make exceptions.

*(IMPORTANT: Your assigned Master has the right to revoke your shifting privileges at their discretion).*

**8:00 p.m. - 10:00 p.m.**
  Free time/Study Hall
  **10:00 p.m. - 5:00 a.m.**
  Retire to your dorm for sleep

"CAREFUL, or you're going to tear that schedule in half if you grip it any harder," a sweet, almost too nice voice said from across where I had absently sat on my bed.

"This is crap," I said, unable to peel my eyes away from the paper. "We can *only* be in our animal forms for an hour out of an entire day?"

"A lot of us vampires felt the same our first year in too. Being limited to our vampire abilities—our true selves—for only an hour felt like an eternity. It was almost like a detox process," she finished with a contagious, kind laugh.

My eyes slid up to see her sitting in her cute pleated skirt and white polo shirt, the crest of this overly strict and overbearing school glaring right at me. The girl was definitely all legs on top of her vampire goddess beauty.

I slapped the paper down over where I had thrown my map of the dorm building at the foot of my bed. "This is bullshit," I grumbled, watching her perfect features highlight with humor.

"Careful of your language," she said with an arch of her brow. "If some Master or professor catches you cursing, it's not a good consequence."

"Is it as bad a consequence as me shifting outside of the hour they give me a day? My freaking wolf is part of who I am. If I keep her caged up like this, she might blow a fuse and come out like the wild animal she really is."

"My twin had a mouth the school didn't approve of, and he washed a lot of dishes, so much so that his hands and nails started to become softer than mine." She laughed, but I just stared at her in confusion.

"Why are you of all supes—a vamp—being nice to me? We both know our kind don't exactly have good blood in the supernatural realm."

I could see something behind her vampy, light blue eyes, but she wasn't going to give *that* away. "It's what this school is for, Jenna. That is your name, right?"

"Yep, Jenna. Your wolf shifter bunkmate."

She nodded. "Good. It's nice to meet you. I'm Lusa."

"Well," I conceded with a smile, trusting the vamp for now, "It's nice to meet you too. I guess I'd better suit up in these lame uniforms and head off to demonstration hour."

"Demonstration hour?" she asked with her forehead wrinkled in confusion.

"Yeah. Where they tell us everything we need to know and all about how we're all lucky to be at this school?"

She giggled. "I'll be with. Since I am a second-year student, we get assigned to newcomers. I hope you're cool with a *vamp* joining you. Besides, I'd like to get to know you better."

I tugged at my bottom lip with my teeth. "Yeah, I'd like to figure out how a vamp is cool with sharing a room with a shifter myself."

"There's going to be so much you'll learn and love at Immortal Academy. It may seem like other schools to you, but it is very different. The first of its kind to merge all supernaturals. We all get along and work together."

"That's definitely something I'm looking forward to figuring out for myself." I smiled. Crap, I was actually playing nice with a vamp. My guard wasn't down, I wasn't tired, she wasn't draining me and compelling me to like her right now. This was freaking weird.

She stood up and glanced down at my schedule. "Careful of your map."

She eyed the papers on my bed. "The little critters who guide you through the campus buildings are called Scio." She smiled, "They're brilliant and very much alive and part of this school."

I pulled my schedule off the map, and when I looked at *the bug* that was in the paper that crawled its way around the halls getting me to this room, I covered my mouth. The thing was upside down, its hair-thin feet curled up.

"I killed the poor thing!" I said, feeling awful. "How was it even alive? It's just some magic on paper!"

"No," Lusa said with humor. "I mean, yes, they are of House Fae's works, but your little guy is still alive. He's only playing dead. They're mischievous little things."

"I would imagine so if the thing was created by a fairy." I moved my finger on the paper, trying to disturb the bug. Nothing. "Well, guess my bug's dead. I'll just throw the thing in the trash and figure my own way around campus."

I watched as the stubborn thing remained in its *dead* state, and I decided to challenge the fairy-created turd. I took the paper and headed toward the shredder, and I was shocked when the thing stayed dead, knowing it would've heard me turn on the machine. "I think it really is dead," I said with a soft voice to the vampire.

She shook her head. "Stubborn." She smiled, her lush pink lips glittering with her eyes in humor. "It would actually let you shred it to its little magical death before letting *you* win for insulting it."

"Oh, this is fantastic. I have a paper bug pissed off at me."

"Upset," the vamp corrected me. "I think if you give it an apology, it'll pop up and be back to work in no time."

Immortal Academy lesson number one, don't offend the freaking bug on the paper. Stubborn bug, 1 point, Stubborn Jenna, 0 points.

"Well, I don't have time for this. Hey, little dude. Sorry about not realizing you're a living thing. I won't insult you again."

Nothing.

I closed my eyes. I had the same temper as my wolf right now. She was perked up and in on the whole schedule reading from earlier too. She knew she was shut down to an hour a day at this place for the next three freaking years, and she wasn't pleased. I didn't have time for a bug with hurt feelings. I tossed the paper on the bed.

"Well, hopefully, the bug forgives me, or I'd better figure out all the buildings at this academy and quick," I said, kicking off my shoes and rolling my eyes at shiny black loafers that completed this ridiculous academy ensemble.

The vampire smiled. "I've never seen someone react with annoyance at one of the Scio. Usually, new students are enchanted by them."

"I'm not enchanted by anything right now. I'm serious, I can't cage my wolf up like this," I said, feeling panic run through my veins.

"Trust me, you'll get through it. I promise." She glanced over at my paper. "Look, I think your Scio forgives you."

I pulled on my new crisp cotton polo shirt and looked over to find the fairy map bug fluttering its wings, tiny particles of blue dust lifting off the paper and into the air. "What the…"

"It's offering you something to help for your wolf, I think," she said. "I've never seen a Scio offer dust to its owner."

"This is insane," I answered.

Lusa cupped the dust the bug sent off in the air and reached her hand out toward me. I instinctively stepped away from my natural enemy in the supe world.

"It's okay," she smiled. "Take it or leave it, but I think the little guy feels sorry for you. You should name it and become friends."

"Friends with a vamp, then a fairy-created bug. Are we sure that *IA* doesn't really stand for *Insane Asylum*? This is wrong on every level."

A ring came over the intercom in our room. "I need to go. I'm part of the presentation and the introductions today. Don't be late."

Lusa floated out of the room in fantastic and flawless vampire form, leaving the dust the bug offered me on the map. I stared at the bug, the dust, and the map. I had to take a breath and stop reacting too harshly, or I was just going to keep feeding my wolf hostility and paranoia. I learned a long time ago we are the masters of our animals, and we could never let that turn the other way around on us.

If I fed my wolf, she would eventually take over, and the only place for a shifter with their animal in full control was an institute. I needed to calm down. I inhaled, swiped my finger over the bug dust, and instantly felt its gift calming my nerves down once I welcomed the bugs sympathy.

*Jenna Silvers, this will be three of the most essential years in all of your existence,* I said to myself.

At that moment, I decided I wasn't going to nitpick this school, but instead, I would open my mind up to it. Learn from it. Heck, my best friend was a witch, why not have a best friend in the vamp department too?

I smiled at my new bug friend. "I'll name you Bug," I smirked. "Like that, little dude?"

The bug flitted in circles of what seemed to be happiness, and I let out a breath of sheer disbelief. "Alright. Let me get this lame outfit on, and then you and I are off to the races, Bug."

I was looking forward to seeing Vannah again, but I was also intrigued by this introduction thing I was headed to now. Would there be any more surprises, or was this going to be the highlight of the academy? A shifter, a bug, and a vamp roommate. Almost sounded like the beginning of a bad joke about walking into a bar.

# CHAPTER FIVE

I followed Bug, who seemed to be excited to walk through the wing that my dorm was in. The dorms were part of the main building: the silver, sparkling building we were dropped off in front of when we first arrived. The dorms were on the third floor, and from watching Bug, we were headed down a flight of stairs that must have been where this Brickhall Theatre place was.

Glancing over the map of this main building, I could see that its beautiful main entrance wrapped around some courtyard with a huge fountain right in the middle. It was one of many structures on the property. I had no idea how many facilities there even were.

I wondered if I would be given a new map at the introduction assembly and a new bug to help me figure out my way around all these particular and *new to me* house names for each supernatural at the school. Maybe Braeclaw House, my shifter house, had its own map and my Bug wouldn't be a part of navigating me around that building or whatever the place was. Or maybe Bug would jump onto the new map and carry on. I'm sure I was about to find out soon enough, and if I didn't stop worrying about it and paying more attention to Bug, I was going to accidentally run into a wall.

"Right this way. You're here with two minutes to spare." I looked up and saw Lusa smiling as she approached. "And tuck in your shirt. No bare skin in the mid-drift department."

"Tuck my shirt into this skirt?"

"Just do as I say, or you'll be singled out by Mistress Sirena," she said with a roll of her eyes. "She's extremely strict and highly intelligent."

"Let me guess, if I remember reading correctly on my schedule, she's the head vamp professor?"

"However did you guess?" she winked.

"The highly intelligent part was a dead giveaway." I smiled back, knowing how vamps felt about other vamps. The lady could be an absolute bitch, and her vampire students would still think highly of her and never find flaws. Why? Vamps stuck together like that.

"Jenna!" I heard Tanner's familiar voice shout.

I strained my eyes—and shifters don't strain their eyes—to locate my buddy in the direction where his voice came from. The place was dimly lit, and velvet, red-cushioned seats all in rows rose up from the stage where lights were shining down.

*Why is my vision sucking right now?* I thought, then I felt my wolf was still agitated and pretty much ignoring being part of any of this. This is something she and I needed to get a handle on and quick. Even though she couldn't have her runs as often as we had at my other school, she'd have to remain focused with me. I needed her as much as she needed me. Also, I couldn't let my wolf throw these temper tantrums, I had to keep her in check. I didn't want to run the risk of her rebelling and sending us straight into a real insane asylum for supernaturals.

I internally reprimanded the wolf, and it was as if I saw her silver snout twitch and then her eyes close in absolute boredom.

*Listen, we are one and the same. I don't like this any more than you*

*do. So get in the game, and help me out so we can get through this crap!*
I hated internally talking to my wolf because I was pretty much
talking to myself and subconscious. Though we were separate,
we were the same being all in one. It's how we shifters were.

"Please find your seat, young lady in the back," a raspy voice
came from the speakers, singling me out in front of the packed
auditorium.

The wolf gave in and gave me my superior vision back,
lighting this room up like they hit the lights just for me. I walked
down numerous steps to the friggin front row because I seemed
to be the last to arrive. What happened to all the smart, suck-up
fairies who always wanted the front rows so they could start
kissing their teachers' butts? I paid zero attention to the scene I
was causing as I found an empty seat on the front row.

"Sorry, kiddo," a deep voice said seriously but with a touch of
humor. "These seats are reserved, and they're not for new
students."

I glanced over at a bearded man who appeared to be in his
mid-twenties, which wasn't a surprise since all supernaturals
stopped aging around that time. From the vibes I got off the
dude, he was a vamp. Dressed in a sharp, tailored suit, his hair
slicked back and plastered with gel. His skin was fair, letting his
green eyes glint with an emerald sheen.

"Any ideas where I should sit? This place is sort of small from
what the map shows, and it's jam-packed in here."

"There's a middle seat in the row behind us that's not taken."
He was curt and it just re-ignited my annoyance with the
vampire race.

I stood and gave up on not making a scene with all the new
students. I'm sure Tanner was trying not to burst out into a laugh
that would echo in this small, yet elegant theater, and Vannah
was most likely covering her eyes, unable to watch me continue
to embarrass myself.

*The freaking fairy row!* I plastered the friendliest smile I could manage as I sidestepped my way in front of the stupid fairies. I was really trying *not* to hate this school, but it was like the school itself was putting me into scenarios I hated. First, a vamp roomie, now I got the pleasure of sitting awkwardly right smack in the middle of glittery-skinned, annoying fairies. Any shifter in my position would agree that Jenna's ticket to Immortal Academy really sucked.

"Welcome!" A chipper voice came over the speakers and belonged to a short man on the stage. "I'm Sir Frederick Darium," the short man with fiery red hair exclaimed. "I'm the assistant to Dean Edgewater, and I am pleased to be one of the first to welcome you to our beloved Immortal Academy. I hope your first few hours have been just as exciting as learning you were selected to attend our prestigious academy. You all should feel delighted to learn that you are amongst the 1% of all immortal supernaturals throughout the world. It's an honor, and you all should feel privileged.

"Please allow me to introduce you to our first speaker and the dean of our academy. His family founded this much-needed academy for Immortals, and he's very pleased you all are finally with us. Everyone, please welcome Dean Edgewater," he said as he turned to his right and started clapping.

A tall man with long, smooth black hair crossed the stage, and I couldn't have gotten a read on the dude's supernatural heritage if I went into mediation. Sheesh. What the heck kind of supe was he? Tall dudes like him usually belonged to the elf family of fairies, but this dude didn't have pointed ears. He couldn't have been a vamp; although, he was certainly dressed like a pompous prick, but he didn't have vampire eyes. The only other supe that could be as tall as he is would be a shifter. *Please, God, let the dean of this school be a shifter!* Dang it, I noted his gangly features... shifters were way too muscular. Crap. What was he?

"Welcome Immortals!" he tugged at his waistcoat. Yeah, this cross of whatever supernatural was in a tailcoat and everything.

"We at Immortal Academy are looking forward to all of you having a fantastic first year. I'm sure you found your maps intriguing. We have our pixies to thank for creating such fun little creatures to help you enjoy learning your way around campus. They're pesky little things," he said in a corny voice that he seemed to find amusing, "so don't upset them too much."

His smile was broad, and his teeth were glistening white, but the vibes coming off Dean Edgewater weren't good. My wolf bared her teeth, and that told me this guy wasn't going to help us if we needed it. I got the feeling we were all his little sheep, and he was the big bad wolf, waiting to pounce on the prey he held captive and eat when he got hungry. The thought made the hairs rise up on my arms. There had to be some dark stories hidden in this *prestigious* academy that he was running.

I shut my thoughts down immediately and fought off my wolf's instincts. She backed off too, yet remained at full attention. At least she and I were on the same page again.

"Enough from me," he laughed, prompting the auditorium to laugh along with him. "Let's get to your professors."

The vampire who had managed to make me stumble over my words when I first arrived seemed to float across the stage in a long, red gown. Dean Edgewater extended his arm out toward her, "Please welcome, from House Draugar, Mistress Sirena."

He walked briskly off the stage, and my eyes followed him, not failing to notice his quick glance out at the auditorium and the sinister expression that came and went faster than I could blink. Yes. Something was up with the dude, and it was my responsibility to stay out of his office and not get busted.

"Very nice to see all of you promptly arriving today," she started in her vampy, musical voice. "As I was introduced, I am Mistress Sirena. There is no need to ever refer to me by my surname, as that was the name of my father, and I despise him. I killed him long ago."

The room all sucked in a breath at once, including me, until a mischievous grin appeared on her face.

"I guess we have no jokesters in the audience today? Forgive my attempt at a bad joke. Please," she covered her heart, "I prefer Mistress Sirena."

I grimaced. A vampire apologizing for a joke? Never. A professor vamp apologizing about anything ever? Double never. I was feeling uneasy, but it was a new school. New schools were like this. Right?

One by one, the different professors came up and introduced themselves. They explained the meaning for each supernatural house name. Apparently, we were all descended from these immortal ancestors, and these houses were the longest lasting in the history of immortal supernaturals. We were to learn more about the houses and their supernatural heritage through the first semester, which pretty much summed up my class schedule.

The professors all had their own weird sense of humor. It was almost like they were trying too hard. My wolf stayed with me, even during the boring parts. She knew I needed her as much as she was going to need me at this school. Instead of being excited by what I was hearing, I felt more of a sense of haunting coming off of this introductory presentation.

No one ever mentioned why shifters weren't free to be themselves and shift more than only one hour a day. Maybe Professor Samson would explain that part when I got to his class tomorrow. I left with more questions than answers. This whole thing just seemed like some big show—a charade—to keep us intrigued. I gritted my teeth in frustration with myself when I realized I was the only one walking out with a confused expression.

I wasn't a negative person. A bit set in my ways, yes, but not like this. I was getting some seriously bad vibes off the walls of this place, and I didn't like it.

At least one great take away was I learned that my magical

pixie-made map that carried Bug on it would transform to the map of whichever building I was in at the school. I was definitely going to take care of Bug and the map, or I would get lost. This place's structures seemed to go on for acres, and as far as I could tell, there didn't seem to be enough students to fill it.

It was dinnertime, and I was starved. Unfortunately for me, I got the feeling that unless Bug could guide me to a bakery in this realm, I wasn't going to be getting my precious apple pie—or any pie for that matter—any time soon.

# CHAPTER SIX

F inally! Finally! Finalllllyyyyyyy...this place had the dining
area of my dreams. At first, I was excited to get into the
Brignell Dining Hall building—yes, an entire building—just to
catch up with Vannah and hopefully run into Tanner, but when
the aroma of steak, chicken, and smoked pork hit my nostrils, I
thought I'd died and gone to food heaven.

I glanced around at the steam gliding up from the many
serving areas, loving how it was all divided up into sections with
neat little fresh market signs above where people were walking in
front of the counters, selecting their specific food variety for
dinner.

I closed my eyes in euphoria when bacon hit my nostrils, and
my stomach howled in delight for what was to come. The marble
walls had large white pillars lining them and archways carved
with intricate detail. The large windows that spanned the entire
wall to my left made the gold carved into the marble walls on the
opposite side of the room shimmer.

I was food swinging—my word for having a mood swing
when I was hungry—and I loved everything and everyone right
now. I practically waltzed to the meat section, picked up two

plates, and placed them down in front of the chefs designated to carve meat. Steak chef was my boy, even if he appeared to be from House Fae.

"Serve it up, and don't be bashful," I said as I watched him slide his sharp knife into the juicy prime rib roast.

"One enough?" he asked with a knowing smile. "I know the male shifters have appetites, but female?"

"Call me a dude then because I want three of those steaks, bud." I smiled at him.

He grinned and carved away. His orange hair led me to believe he was most likely an elf. Elves always had vibrant hair colors, and they were actually nice to the shifters. I didn't know if I just liked the dude because he was contributing to my feast, or if he really was a friendly elf.

After piling both plates high with meat, some carbs, and hesitantly, vegetables—strictly so I wouldn't have to hear Vannah's objection to my unhealthy eating habits—I turned and walked through pillar archways where everyone was sitting.

The room was completely different than the bright, shiny room I'd come from. This room had dark red brick walls, ornately-carved wood ceilings, and what seemed like hundreds of candles flickering along the walls and hanging from large bronze circular fixtures floating—midair—and hovering overhead. I wouldn't have been surprised if a few gargoyles were lurking around, but who cared. It was time to eat.

"Jenna!" I heard Tanner call from across the room. "Over here in the back."

I spotted Tanner at a thirty-foot-long wooden table to my right. He was with a group of chicks, and Vannah was sitting across from him with a blue-haired dude to her left. She turned and smiled her usual *only Jenna* smile when she noticed me weaving my way over to where they sat, balancing both plates of food as I eagerly made my way to their table.

"Glad you're not trying to impress anyone," Tanner grinned.

"Good grief, Jenna, you could have toned it down and at least broke the school in easy on your eating habits," he said before he took a bite of the ham on his plate.

I smiled, set my plates of delicious food down on the table, and reached across to steal a piece of bacon from his plate and took a bite. Tanner laughed while I let the flavors erupt in my mouth.

"Oh, my gawwwwd." I savored the bite like it was a piece of hot apple pie, "Maplewood smoked bacon." I sighed and shoved the entire strip in my mouth, closing my eyes in food paradise.

"Jenna, people are watching," Vannah said in a whisper. "Get a grip on yourself."

I nodded after slicing into my prime rib, admiring the perfect pink center before sinking my teeth into it and beginning to devour my food like I was the only one in the room.

If anyone ever wanted me to join the dark side, bribing me with this delicious food would've totally done the trick.

"Fresh desserts are prepared for those of you with a sweet tooth," a voice came over the intercom.

I waved my knife in the air. "I can already smell the heavenly scent of baked goods hitting that food utopia in the other room. Hopefully, it will still be warm by the time I'm done with all of this delicious meat."

"And vegetables." Vannah giggled. "Girl, you never cease to amaze me. You know your wolf needs the nutrients from vegetables too, and still, you think eating proteins alone will help you and your shifter strength."

"I'm eating carbs too, mom, chill out," I said, stabbing my fork into my fully loaded baked potato. "See," I held up my bite and made sure to put a chive on top, "I'm getting in my greens too."

"Here, Jenna," Tanner slid two wedges of warm apple pie in my direction. "You can have my slice. I still don't know how you can handle all that sugar. You've got to be part fairy or something. Shifters hate sweets."

I eyed Tanner with an unapologetic expression. "If you're trying to make me lose my appetite, it's not working," I said. "And besides, what a perfect way to ruin a shifter."

"Not to mention, that cross has never been accomplished before," a girl with shimmery white skin and shiny platinum hair said, watching me curiously. "Although, I would imagine if a fairy and shifter were able to procreate," a smile lifted on her opalescent pink lips, "this might be what their child would eat like."

"Hi," I shoved my empty, stacked plates to the side and pulled the pies closer to me. "I'm Jenna," I said to her. "Shifter. Pretty much full-blooded shifter, but who knows."

Tanner smiled. I could tell my guy was already crushing on this chick. "Jenna, this is Emma." He ran his finger over a silver rune that shimmered on her forearm. It was some kind of symbol, a circle with swirls that continuously illuminated.

"You're a sprite?" I asked, knowing that rune represented air.

All of the different Fae had runes to distinguish which element they controlled. Sprites controlled the air, though I'd never met one or seen their rune before. The only runes I'd seen up close were the pixies' runes, thanks to Destiny and her friend Kira, the one who was whisked away in the dust cloud for trying to sneak on the bus.

The pixies had blue runes with a swirl of a wave in the middle. They controlled water with the power of their runes, but you'd think Kira and Destiny were sprites with their stuck-up attitudes. Of all the Fae, the sprites walked around like they owned the place. They were the vamps of the Fae, I guess you could say. They thought they were the most important of their species.

"Yes." She smiled and then looked at Tanner, batting her white lashes over her purple irises. "I have to admit I feel like I know you already. Tanner talks a lot about you and the witch, Vannah."

I lifted my chin, gulped down the pie I had been chewing on, and looked at her. "You don't have to call her *the witch*, you know?" I felt my voice growl in annoyance.

"No need to defend me, Jenna, Emma is chill. She just did a project at her previous school about my family's heritage. She knows a lot about the power that came from my ancestor."

I turned to Vannah. "You're cool with a sprite that Tanner is probably going to love and lose in a day calling you *the witch*? It's rude." I looked back to see Tanner glaring at me, and the sprite's eyes were wide with whatever the hell she was worried about right now. Tanner cheating on her? He was a frigging player. Everyone knew that, and little miss air element should've been smart enough to pick up on that too.

"I'm sorry to have offended you," she finally said.

"Don't apologize to her," Tanner grumbled, mainly to me. "Jenna is Jenna, but it's probably best to stop referring to her best friend as *the witch*."

"Good call," I added. Tanner could be pissed at me all he wanted, but the fact that he was defending me after I popped on Emma told me this chick was gonna be old news quick. "So what do we do until lights out tonight? Seems they made it perfectly clear that we only get one hour a day to shift into our animal forms. I'd kind of like to give my wolf some time to sniff this place out for herself too."

"If you paid attention, you'd know after dinner we are to report to our designated houses for further introductions. That's probably where you'll find out when you get to shift and get out of your crazy mood," Vannah said.

I sucked in a breath. I couldn't confide anything to my best friend with all these fairies and new people around, so I had to try my best to play nice.

"Who's the guy?" I lifted my chin to the blue haired, pointy-eared elf sitting next to Vannah.

"This is Nikolas," she said nicely. "He's with my bunkmate, Isabelle. They've been together since they first got here."

"Nice to meet you, Nikolas." I lowered my voice, "Why are you hanging with your roomie's guy and not her? Is she an elf too?"

"Call me Nick," the electric-blue-haired boy exclaimed. "And Bella is with Lusa. They're friends."

My eyes widened, and I smiled at Vannah. "You got a vamp as a roommate too?" I laughed.

Vannah grinned. "Bella isn't a vampire. She's actually a shifter."

"Wait. The shifter is best friends with a vamp and is dating an elf?" I looked at blue hair and back to Vannah.

Tanner laughed, "Crazy world. Awesome school."

"You said your bunkmate is Lusa?" Nick asked.

"Yes," I answered. "Should I be worried?" I arched a playful eyebrow at him.

"Never worry about the students," a stammering voice came to my left. He had just sat with a plate filled with vegetables and fruits. His hair was cut short and was a white, platinum-blonde color.

"Hi there," I said to the guy who had chimed in. He seemed to be just as enthralled with his plate of veggies as I was my steak earlier. "Why would you say that? You know them all?"

"I know what I feel," he answered, eyes never leaving his plate of food.

"What's your name?" Tanner asked the guy.

"Ethan Carter," he said, finally looking over at me. His silver eyes told me he was a shifter, but not a ground shifter. A winged one. There was no freaking way I was sitting next to a bird of prey. I loved this kid already and didn't even know who he was. He was slender and had soft features, but there was something more to him. It was like he could pick up on anything and everything. This guy was unique, and I hoped he and I could get to know each other.

Usually, the winged shifters didn't like the ground shifters.

Ground shifters were more obnoxious and annoying to the elegant and intellectual winged shifters. The fact that he would come to sit next to me was actually a compliment, seeing as though I just absently licked apple pie from the corner of my mouth instead of using a napkin like he would have.

"Well, Ethan Carter," I said, feeling the importance of his name alone in just the way he said it, "It's really nice to meet you. I'm Jenna Silvers."

"From House Silvers," he questioned after he dabbed each corner of his mouth with a napkin.

"House Silvers?" I asked. "Do you know about my family? How would you know anything about a House Silvers?"

My prying seemed to make him back way off. He gripped the sides of his tray and stood. "Nice to meet you, Jenna. Sorry, I must go to get a good seat."

With a rush of wind, Ethan Carter bounced on us all, leaving our entire table speechless. I looked at Tanner and Vannah in disbelief.

"Jenna, don't get too excited," Tanner was the first to speak. "He may have known your name from something else. I mean, I'm pretty sure *your* name is being gossiped at every table in this place by just the way you walked in with enough food to feed an elephant shifter."

Vannah placed a hand over my suddenly cold one. "Tan is right. Please don't let this Silvers House thing get your mind going in a hundred different directions. Maybe he knows something, maybe it's nothing, but don't go down this road."

"I've never heard of ancestral, monarch-type supernatural *house* names until I got here and read my school schedule. What if I came from a family that was important enough that someone might know who I am...someone might know my family."

"Dang it, Jenna," Vannah released my hand, "Please, don't do this to yourself. Just take it one day at a time here, okay? Let's make friends and try and have fun."

Vannah was right. I was going to spin out and spiral down for the same reasons I didn't want to come here, but to hear my last name was probably part of a shifter monarch house? There was no way I wasn't a full-blooded shifter if that was true. Vannah was right, I was already doing it. I needed to stop and focus.

"Alright, so back here at 5:00 sharp, everyone," Tanner said, standing from the table first. "Then after that, it's chillax time. See you all then." He looked at me and smiled. "Well, let's go. Time to head off to House Braeclaw."

Thank God I had Tan with me. I was in a strange new school, but to have a familiar friend at my side was just what I needed to help keep me grounded.

# CHAPTER SEVEN

The cobblestone path Tanner and I walked on illuminated in brilliant hues of different colors, something intriguing if you didn't feel the fairy magic at work beneath your feet. Being a wolf shifter, I loved to feel the earth beneath my feet—whether I was in an enchanted, hidden place on the planet or not. Shifters felt the magnetic pull and were one with nature the closer our feet were to the soil.

This fairy-enchanted stone walkway kept a barrier between that, and I was really starting to long to be in my element again. This academy felt like it was stifling me. I might've been breathing fresh air, but I still felt like I was suffocating.

The stones led us to two stone pillars with lions carved on them. All gray, no glitter—no magic. That was nice because it felt like home. The pathway turned into a regular gray brick walkway that matched the brick of the building House Braeclaw was crafted from. With dark green ivy sprawling up and all around the building, you'd believe it was abandoned for centuries, but to me, it was the most beautiful place I'd encountered at this school so far.

We stepped up into the building, following Tanner's bug on his map. His was bright green, where mine was brown. Hopefully, Bug wouldn't be pissed at me for following another bug on a different map. I suddenly got the feeling that I was going to have to make up for this massive betrayal. I'd make it up to Bug later by giving him some paper shavings to eat or whatever these fake navigating bugs ate.

The room we sat in was reasonably large, and rows of seats curved around the podium where this professor would teach us. There were no desks, just wooden chairs, and nothing was on the walls to distract us. Everything was situated to stare straight ahead and listen to lectures.

"Afternoon students," the brawny shifter professor from the introduction assembly said, taking his place at the podium. Behind him were five chairs, with four people sitting in them. The first was a muscular female with short, choppy brown hair, and to her left sat three robust dudes. All three guys had buzzed heads and typical, ground-shifter type bodies: they were shredded with broad shoulders, and long, muscular legs. A chair was empty, so someone was late, and thank God it wasn't me.

The four sat behind the professor and nodded when he gripped his wooden podium and looked back at them. Strangely, none of them were dressed in the ridiculous uniforms the students wore. They wore ninja-like fighting attire, all black. They looked hardcore, and I couldn't help but wait to find out who exactly they were.

"As you may recall from earlier, I'm Sir Samson Candor. Once we all get acquainted, maybe I'll let you call me Sam." He chuckled. "That was a joke. Call me Sam, and you'll be in the kitchen scrubbing pots while the others are out in their shifter form."

*Never call the dude Sam!* I made a strong mental note.

"Moving on. It's a pleasure to have our nonshifters with us at House Braeclaw. We hope you enjoy learning the history of who we are and why shifters are so important to the supernatural universe. Especially the Immortal Shifters." He held his hands up just as I wanted to internally curse the fact this wasn't a shifters only class. "Trust me, you may someday be in a position—if you haven't been already—where you'll find your talents fail you, and a shifter will be the one to save your life."

"The shifters will always be more powerful," I heard a familiar voice come from beside me.

"Ethan Carter?" I whispered to the kid.

He nodded without looking at me. He was intently focused on Professor Samson. I followed his lead, feeling the wisdom pouring off the shifter.

"Behind me are the masters for the shifter classes. I'd like for you all to meet them because they are the best in their classes and have been promoted to master for a good reason." He motioned for the shifters to stand. "Finley is the only female thus far to ever have been awarded this most prestigious of titles, and she earned it by the end of her first year at IA too. No other shifter has ever been able to achieve such a high status at such an early stage at the school before. Shifters, if you are assigned to Master Finley, you might just get the workout I'm sure you're craving." He smiled, prompting her to loosen up and smile at him in return. A devilish smile to be exact. "Next up, we have Master Scott, and to his left, Master Ian. Unfortunately, Master Dominic is not with us as he is on a special quest with a few shifters at this time. Shifters assigned to Master Dominic will report to Master Scott for your training until your assigned master returns."

"None of those shifters look like a winged master. Do you know who you'll be with?" I quietly asked Ethan.

"The winged shifters have no master," he immediately informed me.

"Weird," I said, prompting him to look at me with questioning, yet stern blue eyes. "But super cool." I lifted my eyebrows with a smile.

Ethan half-smiled, and up until that point, I figured this kid was stiff and too smart for me. Truth be told, he had been starting to intimidate me with the authoritative way he spoke and the way he could cut into any conversation with the hard facts he delivered.

"So, let's get started." The lights dimmed, and a holographic screen appeared, going over the details of the many different shifters out there.

After what seemed like four hours of learning about how the first shift for any shifter can start at age thirteen and how it is an agonizing experience, the class finally dismissed. Shifters were to meet with their masters, and for the first time since getting here, shift into our animals and turn them loose.

"I never felt the pain that he described the first time I shifted," I said to Ethan, trying to conjure up him mentioning House Silvers from earlier. "You think that's normal?"

"Only one percent of shifters don't experience any pain with their first shift," he stated factually.

I grabbed his arm, and he immediately reacted like I had just electrocuted him.

"I'm so sorry," I said. *Okay, Jenna, boundaries! Dude likes his space.* "You mentioned something about House Silvers—"

"All of Master Dominic's shifters please follow me. The faster we shift, the more time we have in our animal forms."

"Bye, Jenna," Ethan said politely before he turned and walked out of the room.

I was shuffled over to where Master Scott and his green eyes probed through all of us like we were bottom feeders and way beneath him. Seriously? Why did a shifter have to act like a friggin vampire? We were all on the same team.

I glanced around and saw my buddy Tanner heading off with Master Finley's group, and I laughed, imagining how Tanner would try to charm her. From the look of the scowl on her face, Tanner was in for some tough training, and hitting on his master would be a really dumb thing to do.

We followed Scott out of a side door that led to lush green lawns and another building.

"Ladies to the right, gents to the left," he said. "You may shift in your locker rooms, and then meet out under the white oaks."

I wasted no time getting into the locker rooms, stripping down, and shoving my clothes into a bottom locker. It was the first time I was pleased to be short and not all legs like everyone else. My wolf was practically leaping inside and clawing to get out. It was time to set her free and have a good run or go through an obstacle course. Anything. She needed to breathe too.

The obstacle course was an intense and excellent one. I was right behind Master Scott's large brown wolf, my wolf so eager to be out and doing anything aggressive. We sailed over large creeks, raced through paths in the white woods, and lunged over large brick walls set up higher and higher the further we got into the forest. By the time we'd hit the largest obstacle, my wolf should have slowed and contemplated, but she didn't care if we both slid off the rock face and fell back into the small pond we had just cleared to climb the face of the granite rock we were on.

I was blown away that I was flanking Master Scott's wolf, and my wolf still wanted more. Good grief, I didn't even realize my wolf could knock it out like this. She was certainly taking full advantage of her time.

After the rejuvenating hour of the run, I trotted hesitantly back to the locker rooms. My wolf was hungry, so that was a good reason to shift without having an internal argument with her. Once dressed, I left the lockers, looking for the Master to be dismissed.

"You're pretty stealthy," Master Scott said, studying me as I walked to him. He was definitely a looker, but not my type with his arrogant demeanor.

"A lot of practice," I answered.

We were joined by more in our team under Master Scott. "You one of mine?" he asked, planting his hands on both hips.

"No, I'm assigned to Master Dominic."

His face crinkled in humor. "Nice."

"Did I miss something?"

"Take my advice on this, don't show off like you did for me today. Master Dominic isn't into that. He's into—"

"Hold up," I said, mirroring his stance, "I wasn't *showing off* for anyone. I was just running the obstacle course."

His face grew more serious. "You are free to do whatever you want, but trying to beat out your master isn't a bright idea—especially with Master Dominic."

I clamped my mouth shut. I wasn't going to get into it with the asshole of a master shifter, but this place was making even less sense now. Usually, the shifters all had each other's backs, especially their trainers—at IA they were called masters. Either way, we all got along. Not here, apparently shifters were cool being douches to their own kind; and apparently, vamps, fairies, and witches were all cool with each other.

This place was upside down and inside out. I was trying to do this, God knows I was, but this first day felt like I'd already been here for three years. I was ready to decompress or internally combust with everything being so out of sorts for me.

I stopped the negativity as soon as we were dismissed, and I decided to walk over to a white oak tree that looked centuries' old. I slumped down next to it and pinched the bridge of my nose.

Why fight the system when this school was working to unite all of us? Why be afraid of changes? They served awesome food here. The vamp I was bunking with was cool. The fairies all seemed chill, so that was good. Maybe it was just me and my attitude. Maybe I was trying to prove to Master Scott that I was a pretty killer shifter wolf, and that was a lame idea. I had a lot to learn, and my attitude was the first thing that needed to change.

I was acting like a spoiled brat, but I had to be careful, my inner wolf could prey on this weakness and take over. She would dominate, and I would sit backseat all because I was afraid of change. I didn't want to come to this school but guess what, I was here. I needed to be all in or all out, and there was no way out—at least for three years.

# CHAPTER EIGHT

After a solid week at this new school, I was finally getting it all down. The morning drills with Master Scott were invigorating. I only wished that the two-hour time block consisted of turning my wolf free and letting her go. By the time her hour arrived and I took on my wolf form, my wolf took off and acted like she'd been set free in the wild.

Master Scott had shown his annoyance with my wolf keeping up with him, even to the point of veering off one of the courses and forcing an injury to poor Jessica, the fox shifter. She was too slow to make the jump, and he accidentally broke her hind leg in the process of climbing over her. Shifters heal very quickly, so I thought it was weird when it took her an entire day in the infirmary to recover from that. Maybe she was a weaker shifter, but dang, the chick was an immortal—you'd think that would help her out a little bit in the speedy healing process.

All-in-all, Scott was a complete dick, and I despised the punk. He was a sore loser and was definitely glad to be rid of me by the last drill we ran tonight. Truthfully, it sucked to have a wolf shifter get pissed that you're an asset in being great in what you do. I was just not normal. With an attitude like that, Master Scott shouldn't have been a master at this place at all; instead, he should've been doing the freaking dishes with the fairy crew because that's pretty much how he acted—like a freaking pixie who didn't get his way and was throwing tantrums over it.

I walked in with my usual two plates of meat and sank down at our usual table. Vannah did the typical eye roll, but I think she was getting used to the fact I wasn't here to impress anyone.

"How are you feeling, keeping your cheetah locked up for twenty-three hours a day?" I finally had a chance to ask Tanner after his new girl, Emma the sprite, took off to get a bowl of fruit.

"Meh, it's fine," he said, chomping into his bacon burger.

"Really?" I asked in confusion. "My wolf is mad as hell about it."

"You shouldn't use profanity." Ethan's monotone, quick-to-the-facts voice made me smile.

I loved the mystery of this kid. He was an owl shifter, one of the rare, winged shifters, which pretty much meant not many people bothered him. He could probably run this joint with how intuitive and how in tune with their surroundings the owls were.

Owl shifters in their *person* form saw everything through different eyes. It was like their brains functioned at the highest possible capacity, whereas ours were pretty much average...well, less than average in some cases. To put it plainly, Ethan was unique, ultra intelligent, and very intuitive, and my wolf and I perked up and loved the energy he exuded any time he was around us.

Sadly, winged shifters stuck together, but the owl shifter, being the way he was, didn't go with the flow of his kind. For some strange reason, he was my lunch buddy who had *adopted me* and corrected me every time I screwed up—like now.

I looked at him and smiled. "Sorry if that offended you, old wise owl," I teased.

A smile lifted on the corner of his lips. "You understand the rules. You know better, Jenna Silvers."

"I know, Ethan Carter," I poked back. "Anyway," I brought my attention back to the others in my group, "What about you, Vannah? You cool with having your witchy powers limited, using them for only an hour a day? Don't you think this is weird?"

"What's weird about it? They want us to learn outside of our supernatural abilities in case something were to happen while living in the human realm, and we are unable to use them. We're learning to survive with and without our supernatural abilities."

I had shoved a huge bite of steak in my mouth, listening to her BS, perfect-student of IA answer. I swallowed and sighed, poking my fork into my meat. I shoved my plate away, and Tanner's eyes widened.

"Dude. Jenna, it's all cool. What's with the questions? The vamp in your room giving you trouble?"

"Why would you bring her up?" I asked. "Lusa's sweet, but she's a freaking chairman or something of the Committee for Entertainment. She's arranging this stupid *Ageless Ball,* and we all have to have a pixie help us dress up for it, so that's taking all her time I guess." I leaned my elbows on the table. "I just think it's all weird. We're at an academy that I imagined would help us hone our supernatural skills; instead, it feels like they're trying to take it away."

Just then, my eyes roamed over to a familiar dude with his pitch black hair, dark brown eyes, chiseled face, *and* biceps. He was standing in all black clothes—like our shifter masters—talking with the jerk, Master Scott. He was soon surrounded by a few other shifters, and the girls—pretty much every girl in the dining hall, including me—took notice of him.

The difference between me and everyone else was that I wasn't trying to cover my smile, whisper to my friends, or throw my hair wildly over my shoulder to gain his attention. The dude had an air about him that drew all eyes to him like God himself walked into the hall.

"Who's that dude?" I asked Ethan, knowing he'd probably

picked up on the energy of the room shifting toward the perfect, muscular specimen.

"He's not a dude. He is a shifter, Jenna Silvers. You will see."

"Do you always have to talk like your foretelling some crazy story that's yet to play out?" I asked in frustration.

That was the wrong way to approach my new friend. He half smiled and left the table. It was fifteen minutes before dinner was over anyway, so that was his usual timing of ditching us and always leaving me guessing about what he was going to do.

The smell of warm pie wafted over to my nose, and suddenly everything melted away. No worries about Ethan, the hot dude was a distant memory...pie was here, and that was all I cared about.

"Thanks, Tanner," I said as four more wedges of pie were placed in front of me. "Where'd these come from?" I asked, looking up and seeing the smile on my friends' faces. Nick, the elf with blue hair—who I think might've had a thing for Vannah—smiled at me.

"While you were gawking over there at that shifter and his groupies, we snuck you some pie. You don't seem to be in the best mood tonight, Jenna."

"I'm just annoyed," I said, inhaling my first slice of pie and heading to the second. "The dude over there is with Master Scott, and Master Scott is a freaking jerk."

Tanner and Vannah laughed in unison, "Kicking your wolf's butt finally?" Tanner winked.

"No, and that's what's weird. I'm keeping up with his wolf, and he doesn't like it. Usually, you're coached up and rewarded for doing well when you bust your butt. That guy doesn't see it that way, and that's not how you teach people," I said.

As soon as the words came out of my mouth, I made eye contact with the mysterious, statuesque shifter guy, watching his smile fade as his deep brown eyes focused on me, shoving pie into my mouth as if I were a pig shifter. If this dude could hear me over all the commotion in the room, his hearing must've been hardcore.

His expression was more authoritative than I'd ever encountered, even with my alpha wolf friends at my other schools. My inner wolf woke up instantly. She was at attention and wanting to give me her eyes to meet his with.

Oddly enough, since I had stifled my wolf down to an hour a day, she and I seemed to be losing a bit of our intense connection. A chill ran down my spine as I remained locked with this dude's gaze.

"He's one of the masters," I said, feeling my wolf give me better insight and something I should have easily known. "Dude's *our* Master," I said in a soft voice to myself.

As soon as I said it, the guys chiseled features that were hardened with his death gaze at me, relaxed and his closed lips lifted in a knowing grin. I chewed on my bottom lip, trying to figure this shifter out, but the shifter was blocked off to me.

"You gonna drool over Dominic Rossi or eat the pie?" Emma said with a chuckle.

"I'm not drooling, I'm trying to figure him out is all," I said, pulling my gaze away from him completely ignoring the fact he tried to pull some mental alpha crap on me, and it didn't work. I should've been trembling with some fearful feeling right now, but instead, all I wanted to do was march up to him and slap him across his arrogant face for thinking he could try an alpha move on me.

"You look upset," Tanner said. "Did that dude do anything to you? I swear—"

"You swear, and you're busted," I said sarcastically. "Rules of this stupid school, remember?"

"Just because things aren't the way Jenna likes them, doesn't mean you have to act like a spoiled brat," Vannah said.

I turned to my best friend, who I seemed to be growing more

and more distant from thanks to this school managing to completely separate us. "You know that's not it. This place is weird, and after today, I'm feeling the vibes that something is just off. I mean, look at us. We're not supposed to be eating dinner from seven to eight, yet here we are. I swear this place changes like those magical little maps do when you enter a different building."

"You're overreacting. They changed the hours because they had shifters returning from a quest training."

"Explains why my master over there is back, and apparently every girl is crushing on the guy," I answered Tanner's girl.

"Dominic Rossi has a name at this school. If he's your master, it's a good thing, not a bad one."

"Well, seeing that he is in a joking conversation with his jerk friend, Master Scott, I'm not too sure it's a good thing. I think these guys aren't mature enough to be in positions to take on new students and train them."

"Master Finley is great with us. She's over there chumming it up with Master Dominic and Master Scott," Tanner stated.

"Whatever. I guess I should be glad I have some nice eye candy as a master instead of the complete dii….." I stopped, if I said it, I'd probably get a hard elbow to the ribs from Vannah.

"Complete what?" Tanner taunted me.

"Ding-a-ling?" I said slowly, finishing with a confident grin.

That stupid comeback cracked us all up, but now, it was study time, and what would you know, Dominic was in the massive library and surrounded by women. Lusa sat for a few minutes with Tanner and me—Vannah was gone, as usual since witches really didn't have to study. I needed to remind myself to head off with her during our free time tomorrow. I was curious as to where my best friend kept heading off to, leaving me alone with just Tanner. She split with the fairy crew, and it was like the shifters were the ones always in here studying because even though we were fast, fierce, and feared—brains on history really weren't our thing. So the library was mainly the place for shifters.

It sucked, Vannah was always my study buddy, and now— gone. Whatever.

"Hey, girl!" Lusa brought my attention up to her radiant smile. "Sorry for ditching out on dinner again. Planning the Ageless Ball has been taking up all my time."

"It's cool," I responded. "You here to study?"

"No, no time for that. I need to catch up with Dom, then get back to work. I'll see you at lights out."

She waltzed over to the guy who I knew wouldn't be able to resist her beautiful looks and charms, and when they laughed and hugged at their reunion, they were officially the most beautiful couple in the room.

The severe and bad-ass look of Dominic faded as soon as she walked up to him. Their conversation was short, and it was no time at all before he was back to looking at the floor to ceiling bookshelf again.

Later that night, I was in bed, staring at the ceiling. All the lights were out, but I heard Lusa exit her bathroom and sigh with exhaustion as she sat on the edge of her bed and braided her long, black hair.

My vampire friend was exhausted? Come to think of it, shifters didn't typically wake up feeling like they needed a pot of strong black coffee to get their day going, but I had been dragging butt every morning. I was drained of energy, and it took doubling up on carbs to try to stay energized.

Who knew what that was about. All I knew was that tomorrow was my first day with Dominic as my master, so sleep needed to come and quick.

Just as I was drifting off to sleep, a cold burst hit my room. I spotted a shadow figure out of the corner of my eye, and it felt like it was checking in on us. The dark energy I felt was bone-chilling, but I got up to check the hallways anyway. Freaking ghosts didn't exist, but dark, created beings did, and if something like that was going to try and come for the vamp and me, I was definitely blowing the whistle on someone using blood magic at this school.

The halls were clear, but the cold energy remained. What the heck was going on? I climbed into bed, not letting my guard down, and pretty much screwed myself by staying awake all night. Maybe Ethan could shed some light on this. If there were dark magic around, an owl shifter would immediately pick up on that crap.

Either way, the clock was ticking, and in no time at all, it would be time to meet Master Dominic. Well, if Master Scott told him I was some crazy chick shifter that kicked his butt at every exercise we did, then Master Dominic would learn tomorrow his friend was a liar because I would be lucky if I could do three pushups when it was time for physical training.

I was screwed, but with this energy still looming in my room, I knew I would be more screwed if I shut my mind off and fell asleep. I knew something was up with this place, and I was probably going to go insane, trying to figure it all out.

## CHAPTER NINE

I didn't sleep a wink and was totally freaking annoyed because I shouldn't have been *this* tired, but the fact that I was stuck at this prison academy and forced to learn to survive without my wolf probably played a factor in that. Regardless of my wolf, I was a supernatural being. My wolf wasn't my only source of energy so...what the hell was going on?

"You're up early," Lusa said as I finished pulling on my combat boots.

"Didn't sleep much and now I have to train with my new master." I stood and tightened my low ponytail.

"Why not?"

"You were too busy snoring to notice," I started as I planted my hands on my hips and stared over at the doorway, "but some shadow creature was creeping on our room last night."

Her eyes widened. "Dark magic?" she questioned. "Jenna, if something like that is happening, you know we have to—"

"Report it, I know," I answered. "But I'm not really sure anymore. Maybe I'm delusional at this point. I mean, don't you think the dorm master or *someone* else would have noticed?"

"Dom and E are on this floor, both would have noticed," she said, curious. "Jenna, you look horrible."

"Thanks for the compliment, Miss Immortal Academy!" I teased with a yawn.

Lusa was cool, but she and I didn't really know each other well enough for me to confide in her about my concerns with this place. We were roommates, and that was it. Even though I was learning to understand that the other supernaturals weren't my enemy, I went with gut instincts and clamped my mouth shut.

I rubbed my forehead and sat back on the bed as soon as I got super light headed. *Gah! I need some freaking energy, or I'm not going to last today!* I seethed to myself, practically begging my entire being to snap out of this state.

It wasn't a moment later that I suddenly felt what I can only describe as a jolt of energy. It was as real as if Vannah had juiced me up with one of her witchy spells, and it couldn't have come at a better time. The haze of exhaustion lifted, and I was ready to go. I glanced at the clock, seeing I only had five minutes to spare.

As I started to dash out of the room, Lusa's slender fingers caught me by the bend of my arm.

"What just happened to you?" She stood in front of me and took each of my shoulders in her hands, studying my face. "You look like..." she swallowed hard, interrupting herself. "It's like you're glowing. How did you do that?"

"I have no idea, but trust me, I'm really going to need it because I have to sprint to Braeclaw lawns. I can't be late for my new instructor."

*AKA: Your boyfriend.*

"Maybe we'll see each other at lunch?"

"Yeah, we'll see what happens with your party planning," I said, rushing out the door.

She always seemed to try and meet up for lunch, but she never made it. Lusa and a few other second-year students had been busting their butts to plan the Ageless Ball. It seemed to take up every last second of her time. The ball wasn't just one of your run of the mill school dances, it was a gala, it was an IA tradition, and unfortunately for me, it was mandatory.

"Silvers," my new friend, Justin, said as I slipped in the back of the group. "You're late, not cool. You already upset Master Scott, now you're starting off on the wrong foot with our real trainer."

We were in our formation—four rows, ten shifters wide—waiting on Master Dominic to bring his muscular butt over here to start running drills with us. I could use a good run after the energy burst I'd conjured up earlier, which I was definitely telling Vannah about when I saw her.

"I called an order, Silvers," a deep voice resounded through my head, snapping me out of my train of thought.

*Crap!* I instantly dropped and started doing push-ups with the group.

"Now, get up. Jacks!" Master Dominic snapped.

We were up and loosening up our muscles, jumping legs in and out, arms up and down. Master Dominic walked with his hands behind his back, examining his group. His face was expressionless as he monitored us.

Once we got our warm-ups done, I was expecting Master Dominic to call me over and chew me out for not pushing when he called out the order. A shifter with a wandering mind wasn't a freaking shifter at all. I was prepped for whatever lecture he had or grueling exercise punishment he was going to deliver, but instead, nothing.

Then, as if that wasn't strange enough, Master Dominic didn't have us take the usual ten-mile run; instead, the brawny dude ran his hand through his loose charcoal locks on the top of his head and studied us as we stood at attention.

"Get into battle mode," he commanded. "We'll do fight drill rotations. No one stops until I say. Now, get to it."

We started with our partners next to us. This was a fun exercise, and I definitely enjoyed it. We went through each partner, running fight drills with each of them. Master Dominic used this drill to study us further, correcting those who were out of form with their jabs, uppercuts, or any other move.

The fox shifter, Jessica, was in the middle of drilling with me when I planted my back foot, locked my leg, and went to do a surprise high kick for her to deflect. Foxes were stealthy and fun to spar with, especially Jessica. Her eyes drifted down to the leg I was going to use for a high kick, and that's when I felt a heel against the side of my knee.

"Lock a leg out like that again, Silvers, and I'll break it," Master Dominic's low smooth voice ordered. "Get back to it."

I didn't have time to look, but I could sense that screwing around wasn't going to be on the agenda today. Not even having the tiniest bit of fun. Master Dominic was checking out his group, and although we'd all had gotten to know each other, he hadn't had a chance to learn anything about his trainees.

"Step outside of your fight circle. You're going to push until the exercises are over," Master Dominic singled me out.

*Way to go, Jenna, you've got his judgmental eyes on you, and he's watching every stupid mistake you make now.*

My eyes met the dark shades of the black glasses Master Dominic wore.

"You would have been killed at least seven times fighting a fox shifter," he said as he looked me up and down, unimpressed. "What's with the sloppy formation and fighting technique? You *are* a wolf shifter, correct?"

I squared up, pulling my shoulders back to stand at attention. He tightened his hands behind his back, practically taunting me. My sleepy little wolf—for the first time—decided to perk up and peek through my eyes, sizing up his wolf.

"Take a run," he ordered the group, his eyes never leaving mine. I went to take off with my class. "Not you, Silvers," he said in a commanding tone.

"You know what, I'm having a rough damn day, so if you could cut me some—"

A smile played on his full, tightened lips. "Profanity directed at your instructor?" He cocked his head to the side. "Not starting off the right way with me. I'm curious," he took his glasses off, "why didn't you respond to my command to start pushing earlier?"

"My mind was drifting off...long night," I answered truthfully.

"No, I called an alpha command that you should have instantly responded to whether or not you were daydreaming."

"With all due respect, Master Dominic," I lifted my chin, "I wasn't daydreaming—"

"I asked you a question, and I want an answer. Why didn't you —as a wolf shifter—follow my alpha command?"

My wolf was snarling inside me now, wanting a piece of this jerk for herself.

"I don't freaking know. I have no idea. Maybe because this stupid school is snuffing the wolf side of me out?" my voice rose as I spoke.

"Listen, insult the school on your own time and outside of my presence, but know this," his brown eyes were beautiful, but terrifying in their severity, "I am not here to bend you, Silvers, I'm here to break you. My unit will be the best, they always have been and always will be. That wolf inside you that doesn't want to find its place with an alpha, I'll break her too. Don't expect this to get any easier between you and me."

I pinched my lips together tight in frustration. I felt the rage ripping inside of me, and my wolf was battling to come out and have it out with this Dominic guy. I didn't know why I didn't follow an alpha's orders. That sort of thing never happened. If he said jump, I should've asked how high.

The most troubling part to me was that shifters never became alpha or beta until we reached our full maturity at age twenty-five, so how was this joker able to give me an alpha command?

He was a master. Masters were students. Honestly, I wouldn't be able to tell if the guy was twenty-five or a hundred and twenty-five, but his role with this school didn't fit his ability to give me an alpha command in the first place.

Then his words came hauntingly back to me—he's going to break me? Break what? What the heck was this school really after?

"You can push until the others get back," he said after both of us finally ended our stare down.

I dropped and started hitting the pushups, faster and faster. I needed to get this anger out of me and keep the wolf silent. I had no idea why I was filled with rage. I pushed the dude to pop on me, so I knew I had it coming.

Lunchtime was going to be spent in a corner with Vannah. I needed to know if her witchy senses were picking up on stuff going down. There was no way this was happening to me and no one else. I had a shadow creature in my room last night and now an alpha wolf up my butt—oh, and let's not forget the surge of witch magic that soared through me this morning too.

I had to get a grip because if I didn't, I felt like reality would start slipping right through my fingers like sand. I wasn't going to lose my mind in this place, if anything, I was going to figure out what the hell that thing was last night and what *exactly* was going on.

This alpha thing had to ride back seat, but Dominic was right about one thing: an alpha command should have made me immediately obey, and it didn't. Now, my inner wolf was pissed, and I was about to go straight into my shifter class, completely spun out like a wild animal.

# CHAPTER TEN

It was a crappy day, to say the least. Even shifting into my wolf form didn't help get my irritability out, and that was saying a lot, but that was most likely due to not being able to get Vannah off alone at lunch or dinner.

All of my friends were acting like they were high on academy life, and I was starting to question these stupid fairies they befriended. The sprite that Tanner was officially calling his girl had me wondering if she was sneaking her rune magic on him. It seemed like the only logical answer for him not being in his usual *love 'em and lose 'em* mindset. The sprite could've been using her ability to manipulate the air on him because, from the way he was acting, it was almost like his brain was starved of oxygen. It's not like I wanted the poor girl dumped after the next supernatural cutie came around, but I knew my friend, and to put it bluntly, it wasn't like him to keep a girl for over a day much less the two weeks we were going on.

Then there was Vannah, my steadfast and authoritative friend who seemed to be all in at this school and thanking the elements of earth, wind, water, and fire that this school of horrors existed.

I strained my eyes on the words of my textbook, trying to go over the material for the exam we had tomorrow for House Fae. The class was tough enough to focus in, being that it was all magical and majestic here.

Each supernatural house had its own touch. House Mage was more like a witch's dungeon, but it was really cool with the way the candles floated in the room, and we got to sit on couches instead of the stadium seating of the other supernatural classrooms.

House Draugar was precisely what I expected from the vampires. It was too extravagant. Everything was gaudy and overdone, pretty much showing how the vamps were. Their house practically screamed they were above all of us, and nothing less than luxurious with everything they did. I imagined if a vamp were in the human realm, you'd spot them a mile away by how they put on a display of being in positions of power and having boatloads of money.

Then there was House Fae, which gave me a headache every time I sat in the brightly-lit room. Vivid colors, glitter, and everything mystical thrown into one place...it was way too much for the shifter mind to take in.

The fact that Braeclaw was completely plain showed how much shifters cared about any of this. All we wanted to do was shift and be one with the earth. So, all in all, each house represented each supernatural at the school pretty well.

*Focus!* I strained my eyes at the history book. Since it was of the Fae realm, each word was printed in a foily, glimmery color of the rainbow, and then if that wasn't enough, they mixed colors up, so one page that had a thousand words meant there were a thousand different glaring colors to read.

"Jenna," Vannah's voice rang through my head like it was my imagination. "Jenna!" she said with a laugh.

I looked up, and I was so happy to see she searched me out *alone* that I couldn't help but turn to my side where she sat next to me and hug her like I hadn't seen her in years.

"Oh my gosh, I'm so happy you showed up," I said, filled with excitement.

"Relax," she brought her lips close to my ear, "Master Dominic is watching you right now."

"I couldn't give a crap what he thinks. I've missed you."

"You're showing weakness." She pulled back, and her familiar smile was so settling. "Knock it off," she mouthed with a knowing arch of her eyebrow.

"We need to talk, but I swear I think these walls are probably eavesdropping on me already."

She frowned, "My gosh, it looks like you've seen a spirit. Are you feeling okay?"

"What if I told you I saw a shadow figure come into my dorm last night? It got cold, and then in the morning my energy didn't replenish like it should have after being up all night."

"What!?" she practically shouted. "Here," she looked around the room and then back to me, "I have to do this quickly and hope I don't get busted."

She took my arm, closed her eyes, then released it.

"Well? Anything?"

"You don't have any energy that tells me you've been altered or have been exposed to dark magic like that," she answered. "Are you sure you saw this? Did Lusa?"

"She was knocked out when her head hit the pillow. I saw it out of the corner of my eye, but it vanished, although I felt the damn thing in the room—"

"Shh," Vannah rolled her eyes. "Great, here comes your master. Could you at least try not to cuss?"

"Don't you dare leave. I need to talk to you."

"Do you find it amusing to taunt me?" Dominic's—dare I say it—sexy smooth voice questioned as he stood at the edge of the table.

"Sorry, I got a little excited, and to be honest, I didn't know you were in the room. Sorry about the language," I said, wanting to get him out of here so I could catch up with Vannah.

"You know the repercussions of your disrespectful language won't be something enjoyable for someone like you."

His deep brown eyes glittered, but the jerk wasn't charming me. He was baiting me, and I wasn't going to fall into any of his stupid *Master Dominic* traps and get stuck tomorrow doing pushups instead of being able to shift into my wolf.

"I know. I'm sorry if it offended you. Or this school, sir," I added, just to throw a cherry on top of the butt-kiss comment so he would leave.

He smirked, and dammit if the dude didn't have some dumb effect on me, making me feel like one of the groupies who seemed to worship every ounce of the robust and perfect physique he strutted around with.

"Trust me, it doesn't offend me, but you are one of my trainees, and I won't have any of my crew saying or doing anything out of line with Immortal Academy's school policy."

"Understood," I said hurriedly, seeing Vannah looking up at him like he had her locked up in his charm of perfected beauty too.

"Trying to dismiss your master, Silvers?"

*Oh. My. God. Really? Just go!*

"Why would you think that?" I asked, my stupid inner wolf now panting at what she was picking up on from his wolf. This was a freaking battle of emotions I wasn't prepared for, and now my wolf was betraying me. She'd had one run with Dominic while he was shifted into his massive black wolf, and now my wolf was in *love*?

"Well, you just rolled your eyes at me." He crossed his arms. With my luck, his wolf was probably picking up on what mine was doing.

"You give yourself too much credit." I ran my hands over the Fae book I was studying. "If I rolled my eyes, it was probably at the fact that me and my friend, Vannah, were trying to get through this rainbow that threw up on these pages so I could pass my exam tomorrow," I answered.

"I'll see you tomorrow." He turned to leave, "Oh, and maybe if your wolf was at ease, you could look through its eyes and study." I met his knowing smile with heated cheeks. "You know, flip on the black and white sight for reading the fairy lore books."

I closed my eyes in absolute disgust that this dude picked up on my wolf who was practically prancing around for him to notice her. At least he was sorta cool about it, and I was definitely taking his advice, that's if my wolf would calm down and focus when I needed her.

"Wait!" I called out to Dominic. "Stay here," I said to Vannah, jumping up to catch up to my master.

He turned back with a different demeanor, Master Dominic demeanor.

"Yes?" he questioned as if I had already taken up enough of his valuable time.

"You mentioned seeing through my wolf's eyes."

His brow knit together. "Yes. Why wouldn't you do that?"

"Because I'm losing her," I said, truthfully.

Dominic shockingly laughed at that. "Why would you assume that your wolf is a separate being from yourself? I think you're losing your mind."

I bit my bottom lip and refrained from instinctively snapping at him for insulting me. "It's how I've always seen my inner wolf. She's sort of her own, and we work together."

He leaned his six-foot-four frame down to me, "Keep talking like that, and they'll lock you up."

"You think I'm crazy," I stated.

"I think you've dangerously allowed your inner wolf to carry on a life of her own. That's something that could get you into big trouble. That's something I'll fix if I have to, but trust me, you don't want to go through that routine."

"You're a real dick, you know that? I'm not crazy."

He took my arm and pulled me off to the side. "Listen, Silvers, there's something different about you, I've already picked up on it." His eyes darted around us and then zeroed in on me. "Now, you're talking about being a shifter who basically gave her inner creature its own life force. That is dangerous. If that wolf decides it wants something different than you—and bad enough? Trust me, Jenna Silvers will be nothing but a name we all remember."

"You're saying I have no control over my inner wolf? The part of me that this place is trying to kill off?"

"I think *this place* is the safest place for you and your shifter abilities. When did you give this wolf of yours that much power?"

"I haven't given her power!" I whisper shouted back.

His eyes grew severe, and my wolf was intently snarling at him now. "Oh, my little trainee, yes, you have. I sense her wanting to shift and come at me as we speak. Do you even feel her wanting the shift outside of the rules set forth?"

"I feel her wanting to kick your ass right now," I answered.

"Take it easy on your language," he glanced around with concern. "Listen, if you piqued my curiosity about who you really are, then others have taken notice too."

"And who are the *others*, Dominic?"

Hard lines of anger creased his flawless face. "Just trust me. Lay low, and stop feeding that damn wolf," he said in a low growl before he walked off like nothing ever happened.

I watched him meander over to where the other masters sat at a table with some shifter chicks who instantly looked down at their books, acting like they hadn't been watching our interaction. Dominic casually joined them and shook off some shifter girl who touched his shoulder.

When Master Scott said something, I watched Dominic look back at me, then to Scott before Scott strangely went right back to reading his book.

*No.* I pinched the bridge of my nose in frustration. *No. No. No.*

I wasn't going to let this school change me further. Dominic was wrong. If my wolf wanted a life of her own, she'd have done that by now. There was a reason I saw her as my strength outside of myself. If Dominic saw that as giving my wolf power to take over who I was, then he was sorely mistaken. He was as delusional as everyone else seemed to be at this school in obeying what this school wanted.

"I need to get back to my dorm. We're going to finish this conversation later," Vannah said, walking up to where I stood glaring at Dominic's study table. "And you're going to explain what Dominic was worried about just now. I've never heard an instructor use foul language to any student. If what he said was right, then we need to work on that."

"Can't you see it, Vannah?" I said through gritted teeth. "Something is completely wrong with this place. How are your witch powers not picking up on it? I'm *not* losing my mind."

Her eyes widened, "That's why we're going to find time to talk this out. I have no idea what's going on with you, but I can tell you right now that I don't like it. All I'm picking up on are your intensely negative vibes and your rebellious nature. This isn't like you. You've changed. I have to go. I'll see you tomorrow."

Her voice was stern and yet filled with concern. I was stiff, rigid, and ready to combust with anger. *I've changed?* No! This place is changing *all of us,* and we're somehow its victims inside this enchanted realm. I wasn't okay, not one bit.

I walked over to my book, slammed its rainbow words shut, and dropped it in my leather satchel. I deliberately walked in the other direction, needing out of this library and knowing I was going to fail the fairy exam tomorrow. I had no time to study and more crap was swirling in my brain again.

For the first time in my life, I wanted to break down and really have a good hard cry. I hated this place, and I was stuck here for three more years.

## CHAPTER ELEVEN

I threw my covers off the bed in a panic. The room was black, but the hallway flickered like it was illuminated by candles on the wall. I licked my lips, trying to calm down and get my bearings. I pinched myself to make sure this wasn't a nightmare—I never had dreams, so this would be a first.

I felt a cold rush of energy wash over me, paralyzing me, then leaving as quickly as it came. My eyes shifted to the door where a tall shadow wearing a fedora hat floated by as if it was patrolling the halls.

"Lusa!" I knelt by the side of her bed, rousing her awake. "There's something out in the hall. That shadow thing that I saw..." I paused, noticing the once flickering light in the hallway getting dimmer.

"Jenna?" She sat up, rubbing her forehead. "Calm down a bit." She said, trying to wake up. "What are you talking about?"

"Remember last week when I said I was awake all night with that shadow thing?"

"Yes."

"It's back." I tugged at her arm, "I'm going to check the halls, but you need to stay awake. That weird, cold energy was in here again."

"I'm coming with you," she said, pulling a silk robe over her nightgown, the total opposite of the tank top and gym shorts I slept in.

"You awake enough? I'm just going to check."

She stood with me. "If there are shadow creatures out there, you and I both know you're not going alone. It's best to have a vampire at your side who can ward that stuff off."

She was right. Darkness never really came after the vamps. They had a way of taking that energy and destroying it if their black magic creator wasn't strong enough to make them dangerous.

"Let's go," I urged.

I left my goddess vamp back in the room, rushing out and almost running straight into Ethan. Ethan's eyes were all white, something I'd never seen before. He was pacing and rubbing his hands together in what seemed to be agitation, or it was the fact that he knew exactly what was lurking on the floor of this dorm.

"Immortals don't die," he started repeating to himself.

"Ethan!" I tried gripping his shoulders to calm him down, his energy was making my heart race. The owl shifter picked up on something, and his chant was creeping me the hell out. "Ethan, come on, buddy, snap out of it."

"Immortals don't die." His eyes were bright silver-blue when they met mine for a split second and went white again.

"Oh my gosh, E!" Lusa said, rubbing his back. "E, sweetheart, what are you saying?"

"What the hell is going on?" Dominic's voice came up from behind where Lusa and I were trying to calm Ethan down. He absently jerked me away from Ethan and took both his hands and placed them on each side of Ethan's head.

"Immortals don't DIE!" Ethan yelled as he tried to pry Dominic's hands from his head.

"E," Dominic's voice was lower and authoritative. "E, come out of it, man. It's okay, we know," he said, trying to coax him.

Dominic and I hadn't had a conversation since that night a week ago when he jumped my case. In fact, this last week went by like a blur. It was like someone hit fast forward on time, and here we were.

"What happened to him?" Dominic seethed to Lusa like this was her fault.

"I don't know." Her eyes were wide with fear but set with sadness. "Jenna saw some shadow out here. We came to check and found E like this."

"E!" Dominic brought his attention back to the poor shifter. "Ethan Carter, don't you dare shift on me!" he demanded.

Ethan's eyes came back, and he looked directly at me. "Immortals *will* die."

"What the..." Dominic started, but the next thing we knew, a large white owl was flapping its enormous wings, and Dominic ducked just in time for the owl to soar sideways down the hall and out of the building. "NO!" Dominic growled, then looked at Lusa and me with anger. "Both of you get in your rooms. This never happened. Lusa, kill the lights. I've got to find him."

"But, Dom, he might..."

"Do what I said, now!" he demanded and ran down the hall where Ethan's owl flew off.

"What a jerk!" I said in disgust.

"It's fine," Lusa said in a soft voice. "He's gotta find E before one of the school authorities do."

"You know Ethan pretty well, don't you?" I asked, following her into the room after she hit the hall lights and they shut off.

"Yeah, we do," she said, distracted and looking out the window. "No. This can't be happening...Dom is in his wolf form. This is not good," she said, bringing her perfectly painted nails to her teeth.

I watched the large wolf disappear into the woods, knowing

that Dominic and Ethan just busted two rules this school apparently didn't take lightly. My wolf, on the other hand, wanted to be a part of the search and rescue mission, but she laid low. Thank goodness.

"You think someone will understand after we inform them that there was some shadow person in our hall? Owls should get a pass on something like that. They can't be around the darkness."

"The administration won't understand. Both of them will be punished harshly if they're caught."

"Well, after your boyfriend yelled at you like that, I think harsh punishment is a good thing." I tried to lighten the mood with a goofy joke, knowing this really was bad.

Lusa burst out laughing at my comment and shook her head as she walked over and shut our door. "Dom is not my boyfriend," she said as she lit a small candle and closed the curtains to our room before she stretched across her bed. "He's my twin."

"What the hell?" I answered. "I mean, I only thought that because you're the only person I've seen him smile at or hug, I guess, but I don't understand. A vampire and shifter can't be twins—that's not even fathomable. What's going on with that?"

"Dom and I are brother and sister," she said, studying me. "We are twins. I grabbed my mother's genes, a vampire...and Dom got dad's, a shifter. Both full-blooded supernaturals. We come from a very unique family line."

"No shit," I said.

"Stop with the cussing," she said with a smile. "I think we've raised enough red flags for the night."

"Yeah, okay, but seriously, I've never heard of anything like this," I said.

"You come from a very sheltered world, it's understandable, but you're right, it normally doesn't work that way. When two supernaturals procreate—a vampire and shifter in my parents' case—the stronger supernatural DNA is the one that determines what the child will be."

"I would imagine the shifter is stronger than the vamp," I said, trying to give my shifter side a win.

She laughed. "Well, you have learned tonight what the elites of Immortal Academy know, the shifter and vampire have equal power or else both Dominic and I would be the same species of supernatural being. We are one of seven sets of twins who have ever experienced this phenomenon. We were told that it was most likely because of our parents' heritage that this happened. My mother is a full-blooded direct descendant of House Draugar, and then my dad's side—the side Dom takes after—is House—"

"House Braeclaw?" I questioned in shock.

"Yes," she said the word with a sigh. "It's why Dominic is the strongest shifter here and why his alpha behavior developed early." She looked at me with a question in her eyes, "You're a mystery to both of us, you know? E won't leak a bit of information—it's like he's guarding you or something—but all we want to know why *you* are the only one that Dom's alpha commands have zero effect on."

"I'm still trying to process a vampire and shifter popping out of the same person, much less that Ethan Carter—a winged shifter—is your cousin, and he is protecting me from something."

"Yes," she smiled as I sat back on my heels in front of her. I was glued to the floor with all of these revelations. "I noticed it when I saw him attach to you from the moment he sat with you that day at lunch."

"I thought it was pretty cool a winged shifter would even have a conversation with a ground shifter, then I was blown away he was an owl shifter of all things."

"He's a gem to all of us. His parents were poached and killed in the human world when he was little. That's when mom and dad took him in, and he grew up with Dom and me."

"His parents were owls too?"

"Yes," she said.

"And they were related to your parents?"

"My dad's sister was an owl."

"Now, you're really tripping me out."

"I know, but you can't share this with anyone. Especially your friends. You have to promise me."

"I can't even process it, how could I share it. So let's just say you hook up with a shifter, you could have a shifter and vamp as twins for kids? Maybe pop out an owl?"

"We have no idea for certain what kind of offspring will come from us, but we don't think about that too much. Trust me, Dom isn't here for the girls. He's so into being a wolf shifter that I think he'll grow into some old professor here with no offspring to carry on the crazy family line." She laughed.

"He's probably afraid. He's so into the whole alpha wolf crap, he'd probably die if his lady birthed an owl or vampire."

Lusa's face frowned, "I hate that you know him as Master Dominic. He really isn't *that* person. Dom has a heart of gold, he just doesn't plan on giving it to anyone."

"And there you have it. Master Dominic or not, he's kind of a selfish jerk. I feel sorry for the girl who falls for him, or if he actually did happen to fall in love, he sounds like a dude who'd be into what makes him look good and that's it."

For the first time ever, I saw the dangerous vampire come out in Lusa's expression, "And that's where you're wrong, Jenna, and rude. You don't know him. You sound more judgmental than a fairy."

"I didn't mean to upset you, sheesh. I just call it how I see it."

"Well, if you think he's into things that make *him* look good, then why is my brother risking losing his status as a master and getting himself thrown into the dungeon for at least a month to go help save our cousin? If E gets caged into the dungeons for this, Dom won't let him go alone."

I saw the sincere sadness on her face, and it broke my heart.

"You're right," I said. "I'm sorry I took a shot at him like that. He's your brother, I was out of line."

"You know what? We'll find out what happens tomorrow," she said in a shaky voice. "We need to go to sleep and hope for the best. Please, I beg of you, don't tell anyone what I told you. The academy doesn't want a spectacle made out of us, which is why Dom and E will both face the same punishment as any other average shifter if they get caught."

"You think they will?"

"I think Dom is stealthy enough to help E and get back without anyone noticing, but you will quickly learn that there are eyes on everyone at this school constantly."

"That's hard to even conceive since it looks like we have a dark spirit on our hall, and no authority has said a word about it."

"Sometimes I question those in authority here. It's not the same school it was when my parents' ancestors founded the academy. I try to keep an eye out for when and if bizarre things occur. After the way E acted tonight, let's just say something isn't right, and it might be him picking up on it sooner than Dom and I could have. He's been acting differently ever since he got here, and Dom and I have both noticed it. This school has him very unsettled."

I pulled my covers up over me as I laid down on my bed. "He's not the only one. I'm feeling something too, and my friends walk around like nothing's wrong and Jenna is the crazy one. Well, that's what I notice in the minimal interaction we're *allowed* to have. The school has sort of separated us."

"You're fighting the school, they're not. You need to be careful."

"Or I'm thrown into the dungeons?" I closed my eyes, feeling tired. "Lusa, you better not be draining me of energy."

"I wouldn't dare," she said. "Why would you say that?"

"Because my mind should be reeling with questions and I

should be worried about Ethan, but I'm ready to fall asleep like I haven't slept in a week."

"Someone is doing this to you. It's not me." She looked over at the door. "Can you fight it off like you do with Dom's commands? Can you resist it?"

I yawned. "No." My eyes felt like they were burning, and my lids were so heavy I couldn't keep them open to save my life.

I fell back into my comfortable pillow, trying to fight, but I was going out. The same deep sleep that had been washing over me every night was taking me off to restful bliss. It was a vampire draining me.

"What!" Lusa's voice rang in my head in shock. "Mistress Sirena?"

The name of House Draugar's headmaster rolled off her tongue in disbelief, and the next thing I knew, my mind was shut off, and I was out.

CHAPTER TWELVE

I woke up the next morning, my head killing me and my lips parched. *What the hell happened last night?* I thought, stepping into my shower. My thoughts were scrambled, and it was frustrating. My inner wolf was sound asleep, and that wasn't normal, so something must've happened, but I couldn't remember what.

"How you feeling, Jenna?" Lusa's voice was filled with concern as were her clear-blue, gemstone irises. She and I walked out of our bathrooms at the same time, and I was beginning to think she had some fairy in there with her, doing her hair and makeup and making her shine in half the time it took me to blow dry my medium-length hair.

"I feel hungover or something. I don't feel right at all." I rubbed my forehead, then looked at her, recalling some of the events. "What happened last night?"

She swallowed hard. "Well, E shifted, Dom went after him, and I gave you a little history lesson on our family heritage after you thought Dom and I were dating," she softly said.

"That's right. The wolf and vamp twins and I'm not to say a word about it." I suddenly remembered the deep sleep I was put in. "Tell me you didn't drain my energy last night just to knock me out!" I snapped.

"No," she covered her heart, "But I know who did, and it won't happen again."

"You're going to tell me who got a hold of me right now," I demanded, losing trust in the girl by the second.

"Jenna," she reached for my hand, but I pulled back, "Okay. I get it. Do you remember E and Dom shifting last night?"

"Yes, what happened to them? Do you know yet?"

"Yes. They're fine, and they'll stay fine if we both just forget about everything that happened, including the person who put you to sleep."

"This is so monumentally messed up. You do realize a vamp doing that is a complete violation, right? You know in the *real world* of schools where shifters can shift at any time without getting busted for it?"

Mumbling out my frustration, made me recall Lusa saying Mistress Sirena's name last night.

"Jenna, please."

"Please, what?" I snarled. "I heard you say her name. Why is Mistress Sirena involved? What the hell is going on in this school?"

"Here, sit," she said, forcing a smile on her face. "Listen, this is mine and Dom's second year at this school. We're aware the professors can take advantage of students they don't trust, and neither of us likes it, but there's nothing we can do about it."

"Nothing you can do about it?" I snapped. "So we're all their victims?"

"Not if you follow the academy's rules. That's all. From what I can tell, you're the only student here who questions everything and fights the system. They're all watching you—waiting."

"Waiting for what? What am I going to do, call the supernatural police on them? From what I've learned in my classes so far, this place trains those in supernatural authority, so what exactly can I do, and why do I have a target on my back for thinking this place is messed up?"

"I don't know. Honestly, I don't." I could see the truth in her eyes. She was an innocent victim of this place too. "All I know is Mistress Sirena warned that if you said anything about what she did to you, she would reveal what happened with Dom and Ethan last night."

"Doesn't add up or make sense. Why would she threaten them?"

"Because she wasn't the only professor that saw them. Professor Von Tassle saw it too—felt it, really. She's the eyes and ears of this school."

"House Mage's headmaster? A witch is secretly spying on us here?"

"It's not like that," she said sternly. "Dean Edgewood relies on all his professors' talents to keep his school running like a well-oiled machine. If there's a bad apple, they kind of throw it out before it affects the entire school. Students who rebel tend to go away, and no one knows to where. All we know is that the ones who've been a problem never come back. He can't have discord when dealing with the strong blood of an immortal."

"So…" I paused for a moment. For the first time in my life, I was absolutely speechless. "How can he expect us all to just fall into place? What if the students—like me—were forced to come here? I didn't ask for this."

"The school will make you a better shifter. I'm already a stronger vampire myself, and that's just a year in. Look at Dom, he's thriving here."

"I don't know what to say," I said, feeling like the poor girl was brainwashed as bad as my friends were in this place. "I'll keep my mouth shut."

"If Mistress Sirena asks you anything?"

"Well, the only way she'll get it out of me is if she does her vampy energy drain and compels me to tell her the truth."

"Which she will. I know her." She bit on her thumbnail in thought. "Can I try something on you?"

"No. No way, I'm not going under compulsion."

"You're right." Her eyes pooled with tears just as my wolf was rousing. The wolf seemed to whimper as soon as she felt the energy of the brokenhearted vamp. "It's just—Dom can handle the dungeons, but Ethan can't. He'll never be the same if he's locked up. He's so pure and innocent, but no one will understand."

"What he said last night—what he was chanting. Do you know why he would have said that?" I asked, remembering his *Immortals don't die—Immortals will die* chants.

"I have no idea, and Dom said after he got him to shift back and talk to him, E didn't recall saying it. It was like he was in one of his dream trances. He does that sometimes."

I let out a breath of frustration. "Before you drain me and compel me, please tell me first what you're compelling me to do, and then tell me you have the talents of the stronger vamps to give me my strength back when you're done. I imagine today's workout with Dom is going to be like any other day so long as we're all keeping secrets, and I'll need my energy."

"You're right about Dom. He'll act like nothing happened. As for the rest, yes, I can restore the energy I drain from you after the compulsion. All I will do is have your mind go blank only if Mistress Sirena questions any of this."

"I'm trusting you. I have a witch as a best friend and I will—"

"There's no need to worry," she smiled. "I owe you, we all owe you for this."

"Let's just get it over with."

"Miss Silvers," Mistress Sirena's high-pitched voice stopped me dead in my tracks. "I need a moment of your time."

I stopped, and Nick, the elf, looked at me, almost knowing I was busted for something. "I'll be fine. Just let everyone know I'll be at lunch later. Guess I flunked my quiz from yesterday."

He nodded, but I could see the concern on his face. Good. Finally, someone else was catching on to the weirdness of this school.

"Yes, Mistress Sirena," I said.

"About last night," her eyebrow arched so high it practically went into her forehead. "What do you recall, darling?" Her smile was snake-like—if snakes actually could smile before they struck you and pumped you full of venom.

"I recall getting woken up and..." My mind literally went blank. "Um, I don't know. Maybe it was a dream?"

"Shifters don't dream." Her thin red lips pulled up on one side. "Be truthful, dear."

"I honestly don't remember anything. Should I?"

"You question everything at this prestigious school, and Dean Edgewood is starting to ask us about your rebellious streak. You've been heard vocalizing doubts about what he's done to better the immortals at Immortal Academy. We don't need students who think they know more than ancients."

"No, ma'am," I said, feeling entirely at her mercy.

"Good." The silver streak in her dark brown hair set off her hazel irises, but her gaze was severe and her smile threatening. "Enjoy your lunch then; hopefully, your attitude will change, and you'll learn to appreciate your heritage and why you were privileged enough to come to this amazing school."

"Yeah," I stammered. "I mean, yes." I plastered on a smile, wanting to get as far away from the woman as possible.

"You're dismissed."

I turned to leave, feeling like I was caught in the middle of something dangerous and way over my head. My friends would be no help, they were too brainwashed into this system too. I had to wonder if Dom—ugh, I just called him Dom—Master Dominic and Lusa felt the same way, or if they felt exactly how I felt right now: serve the three-year sentence and then get the heck out of here.

"About time," Vannah said, and for the first time, she looked at me like something wasn't right. "Everything okay? Did you pass the quiz?"

"Flying colors."

"Have you decided who you'll go to the Ageless Ball as?" Emma asked.

"I'm sorry, what do you mean? *Go as?*" I asked, confused.

"I'm not surprised you missed that part," Vannah said. "We have to dress up as a mortal that we wish would have never died —pick someone we wish was immortal. A favorite monarch, people like that."

"I haven't had a wink of time to study human history to find someone I want to be," Tanner said with a laugh.

"First of all, Tan," I said, stabbing my meat like I had a vendetta against it, "What's with the *wink of time* dropping out of your mouth. I swear," I chomped on my steak, "you've spent so much time with your pixie girlfriend, you've started to talk like a damn fairy."

"She's a sprite. She controls the air, remember?" Tanner glared at me. "Keep insulting her, and she might just snatch the air right from your lungs."

I gulped down my steak instead of choking on it. "Oh, like she snatched the air from your brain? I swear all of you aren't the same anymore. I really don't give a crap what you think about me, this school has changed all of us. It's making me cranky and crazy, and all of you prance around like you're on some kind of fairy crack."

Nick put a piece of pie in front of me, and I looked over at the dude with a lethal stare, "Trying to shut me up?"

"It would be smart to trust your friend. Eat your pie, Jenna Silvers. You must calm down, they're watching you."

*Ethan. Thank God.* "Well, if it isn't my favorite guy. How you doing, buddy?"

"Don't call me buddy. I am your friend, Jenna."

"Sorry, Ethan, it's just a name I call my friends."

"You mean it differently with me. Sympathetically. I don't need sympathy for who I am."

He was right, I was treating him like a kid, but in reality, he acted older than I and had ten times the brain power I could ever dream of having.

"You're right. I'm sorry. Alright," I nudged him and was happy he was getting used to me teasing him like this, "You're my dude." I smiled over at Tanner, "Since I lost Tan to a fairy, it'd be nice to have a guy pal again."

"You're such a brat, Jenna," Tanner grumbled. "Eat your pie and cheer up. Do they have therapeutic massages for shifters who get all worked up because they can't shift whenever they want and have to follow the rules?" he asked Emma his girl.

She looked at me and then quickly recoiled from my death gaze. "Probably shouldn't be too eager to answer that. I'm not going in for a massage, sprite."

"Now, you're the rude one," Vannah said. "What is *wrong* with you?"

I pulled my pie in front of me, stabbed my fork into it, and shoved the pie in my mouth, hoping it would soothe my wound-up nerves. "Okay, okay, sorry. I just need to eat my pie, then I'll be *go with the flow* Jenna again," I said.

That's when I made eye contact with Dominic across the room. He was flanked by a hot chick on either side of him, his bro club sitting all around. The table he was at always drew attention—the one table everyone wanted to be a part of and not just because four Master Shifters were there in their black ninja attire, looking hot and unashamed that they were all gorgeous. It looked like the fun, party table—the VIP section.

Dominic's eyes were locked onto me, and I knew exactly why.

I raised my eyebrows up at him and smirked, prompting his facial features to soften some. He subtly raised his glass to me, and I could tell it was a silent gesture, thanking me for shutting up about him and Ethan. The only person who was really screwing herself right now was me. That had to stop right now.

"Hey guys," I said to the group, "I'm sorry about my mood lately. Tan is right, I'm having a hard time getting used to the fact that I can only shift once a day. I don't know how any of you took to not using your gifts whenever you wanted like we could before we all got here."

"You sorta just get used to it," Emma said. "I'm sorry it's tough for you."

"Thanks," I grimaced. "I'm just struggling. Maybe there's a support group for people like me."

"Jenna, be for real," Vannah laughed.

"Either way, I guess I should figure out who I want to go to this Ageless Ball as." I looked at Ethan, "What do you think? Want to go as a pair? You can pick my dead human of importance. Maybe they had a good friend or something you could be?"

"I'll think about that," Ethan smiled. "I need to get my seat."

He rose up and disappeared through the doors. I smiled at the clock. Fifteen minutes until class—right on perfect *Ethan* time.

I returned my attention back to my group of friends and decided to keep quiet and finish my pie. My thoughts drifted to what happened the night before. I was seriously going to crack the code on this place if it was the last thing I did. That's when it hit me. Ethan is an Immortal, so how exactly did his immortal parents die? Immortals don't die.

I gripped the sides of my head as Ethan's chants came rushing back into my head from last night. Immortals really don't die unless someone figured out how to kill one. I know for sure that a human couldn't take one out, so that's a line Lusa's parents wouldn't have fallen for, would they?

*Immortals will die!* What did all of that mean? That wasn't a bad dream. What if poor Ethan saw his immortal parents killed and that's what his nightmare was about? It made perfect sense that something so traumatizing would force him to shift into an owl. My gosh, poor guy.

I couldn't stop my curious mind from wondering what nonhuman thing would want to kill his parents and why? Maybe this school was the safest place for Ethan. Maybe the immortal killers were out there, and that's why Dominic and Lusa were doing everything they could to keep Ethan safe and under control at the school.

One thing at a time. I knew that I had a week of exams in front of me, and I had to pass them or I'd be on lawn mowing duty or something for failing classes. Then, from what I was told, the school would be transforming in preparation for the Ageless Ball. Solving this mystery was going to have to sit on the back burner for the time being.

# CHAPTER THIRTEEN

Throughout the week of exams, I was intently focused on each of my courses and studying until my head hit the pillow each night. It helped take my mind off the craziness that seemed to have surrounded me since day one at this academy. The atmosphere of the bizarreness of this place silenced during this week, and I was grateful for it.

My friends seemed to be acting normal enough again, and we even started studying together. Just when I needed it too. Dominic was a different story altogether. He seemed to have singled me out whenever we trained—primarily when we fought.

There were plenty of other shifters in our group, like the weak male wolf who was continually getting his butt whipped by the two female foxes and the lioness in our group. Even though that wolf needed some major correcting, Dominic seemed to have turned a blind eye to that. It's like he had a vendetta out for me.

I didn't let it bother me, though. I needed the beat down—so to speak—it only made me get back up more fierce and strong. There were plenty of times I wanted to just punch him in his commanding face, but I held off. I knew his little secret—about his family and that night he shifted to help Ethan—and in some strange way, he and I both were on the same level, whether or not he wanted to admit it.

None of his training or drills were abusive toward me, he was just pushing me much harder than the others. I had to admire him for that, it's exactly what I knew I needed. And since turning my aggression into strength for our physical training and when we shifted and ran obstacle courses, that's when I started finding peace at the school.

That's when everything changed for the better.

"I can't believe I let Ethan decide that Gorga—or whatever her name was—should be my costume for this ball," I said, mortified with the outfit the elf seamstress had created for me.

"Her name was Gorgo, and she was an amazing queen over her people. In those times, queens usually sat under their kings while their kings had many wives. The Spartan queen you are honoring stood at her king's side, and he consulted with her." The sweet elf smiled as her sprite assistant blew into her hand, manifesting a shining silver comb. The elf finished pinning my braided hair up and secured it with the comb somewhere in the back of my hair. "She was known to be a very wise, intuitive, and witty woman. A king would not have listened to a wife who gave bad advice."

I stood up and shook my head at the material of this dress, sliding back and exposing my leg. "You don't think he listened because his wife walked around in revealing dresses like this tunic-looking ensemble, do you?"

"I'm sure the Spartan king enjoyed the company of his wife. The Spartans—men and women—had their independence, and I wouldn't be surprised if the queen trained rigorously alongside the men of Sparta, though it was never recorded in human history."

The sprite, who was using her air elemental gift to blow items of jewelry for my costume into existence, seemed overly excited to help the elf make me look more revealing than if I showed up to this ball naked.

"So," I looked at the two fairies who spent a total of twenty minutes from the creation of the too revealing gown to polished perfection of the jewels I now wore, "Are we done? Can I head out?"

"Oh my gosh!" Vannah came into the dressing area where I was the last to come in, get ready, and head off to this Ageless Ball. "What are you wearing—if I dare say you are wearing anything at all."

My dress seemed to be created from one long piece of soft, white fabric. It was pinched together by leather straps at the tops of my shoulders and fell all the way to the ground, bound only around my waist by more leather straps so the fabric wouldn't slip out of place and expose any of my important bits—which seemed to be the only parts that were covered. My sides were completely bare, my neck to my navel was exposed, and the slit of this dress came all the way up my entire leg.

"Well, it seems like school policy allows it since this is what the Queen of Sparta wore, or at least it was documented that she and the other female Spartans dressed like this in their day."

Vannah covered her mouth, "I'm shocked you even are going with this."

"I promised Ethan I would. I guess I should have researched past the part about how she was the one to give counsel to an amazing and fierce King Leonidas before he bravely died defending what he believed in, but whatever. Who are you? I thought you were going as..."

"I'm Queen Victoria of the English monarchy. Nick and I decided to make it official that we are a couple by going as Prince Albert and Queen Victoria."

"Well, what better way to introduce yourselves into *society* of Immortal Academy than to go as a royal couple." I smiled. "I love this crown with the emeralds on it too."

Vannah touched the emerald jewels at her ears and the brilliant stones of the diamond and emerald necklace she wore. All of it matched, and it shone so beautifully against her dark, flawless skin. "The sprite who designed it made an exact replica of the set that Prince Albert had made for his beloved Victoria."

I weaved my arm through hers, "You look radiant, and though I don't know much about the monarchs, I'm glad you chose to go as a monarch couple."

"They had their trouble, but Victoria learned as she grew. She assumed the throne at the age of eighteen, you know? A lot of responsibility, but she was fierce even though most around her waited for her to fail. She proved them all wrong, and Albert, so innovative for the human culture at that time, reminds me a lot of Nick. He has so many amazing ideas as an elf. I look forward to one day bringing both our powers together and doing great things for the supernatural and human worlds when we leave Immortal Academy."

"Sounds like a bonding might happen in the secret halls of House Fae," I teased.

"Bonding? We aren't shifters to be mated for life." Vannah giggled, "One day, maybe though we will commit to each other through a ritual from both Mage and Fae that will lead to a bright future together."

"Bright is the word for it, my friend," I laughed as we followed the lit pathway to the Edgewater theatre. "I imagine you'll have flashy and sparkly little sprites—the offspring of a witch and elf procreating."

"Stop." Vannah rose an eyebrow at me. "You're just jealous."

"No," I smiled warmly at my friend that I finally had back. "I'm extremely happy for you. Who'd ever think I'd be happy my best friend was in love with a flipping fairy of all things?"

"After almost a month of dealing with your mood swings, I never thought you'd approve. It makes all of this so much nicer, and," she shivered with excitement, "I don't know. I'm just happier than I've ever been, and now I can share it all with you."

"I'm happy too. Nick's cool. So is Emma. Funny how my two best friends ended up with fairies," I laughed.

"Oh, keep it on the down low, but Emma and Tan aren't really getting along right now," Vannah said.

"What? Dude's dumping her right before a *ball*? I kind of feel bad for her. If she is anything like every other student here, this is to be the *night of all nights*," I exclaimed dramatically into the air.

"No," Vannah lowered her voice. "Tanner caught her messing around with some pixie dude."

"Oh, man. When?"

"Nick told me about it before I got dressed. Tanner is going to take her tonight, but they're busting up after tonight's event."

"If you ask me, from what I learned about Henry the Eighth, Tan should have gone as him. Off with the sprite's head for betraying him."

Vannah grinned, "You did do a little research on this whole thing, I'm proud of you."

"Don't be too proud. If I did the proper research, I would have not accepted Ethan's idea of me going as the Queen of Sparta."

"This outfit still," she laughed. "So not you, Jenna."

"Yeah, well, it is tonight."

# CHAPTER FOURTEEN

The entrance to the theatre was elaborately decorated. It wasn't swallowed up with the magic of the Fae, but everything seemed to have been taken from historical aspects from different periods in time—supernatural and human.

Long blue velvet drapes were falling from the wood carved ceilings, flowing like velvet waterfalls to the ground. We walked past neatly carved statues of people and beasts of power that were placed displayed on pillars with a vibrant blue light shining down over each figure. We passed through halls of glass, separating the artifacts from us in the hall and the golden, silver, and wooden pieces on the other side.

Dean Edgewater seemed to have his way of showing all of us how he supported the humans and the supernaturals coexisting from the dawn of time until now. It sort of brought to my attention the real reason for the academy, and training us immortals to not only revere the humans but also coexist with them without our supernatural side needing to be present.

My wolf was much tamer these days, or I'd imagine her snarling at the fact this school was teaching the immortals to learn to live like humans instead of by our true nature. It was peculiar that we immortals would be prepared to live like mortal humans, but I was starting to believe it was better for all of us in the end.

It was in class that I had learned IA had helped to stop immortal vamps from drinking blood altogether. They put together the Immortal Forces—something I was quickly becoming more and more intrigued by. If a vamp was caught drinking blood, Immortal Forces stepped in at once and put an end to it.

Immortal Forces kept all the races in check. In my opinion, the shifters were fine for the most part, but some shifters didn't have full control. Those who couldn't control their animal could find them in a position where rage forced a shift, and innocent people could get hurt in the process. A shifter in animal form acting blindly out of rage was a wild beast and out of control.

They kept an eye out for witches who were dabbling in the dark arts. I imagined they probably got the most work from these ladies and gents because having the temptation to go to the dark side for a witch wasn't something many new witches could resist. Vannah had even almost accidentally meddled in dark magic, and if anyone would've found out—even though she didn't know what she was dealing with at the time—she could've been in serious trouble.

The human race benefitted most from the fairies being policed. It wasn't beneficial for anyone to have those who can control the elements running wild. Leprechauns could set fire to anything they wanted, pixies could cause a flood, elves could bring about an earthquake, sprites could whip up a tornado...all of them could bring about mass destruction with their element just because they were bored. The debt of gratitude owed to Immortal Forces was immense.

As we walked down the hall, I saw the progression through history as more and more supernatural forces became more civilized and better policed. What was once barbaric had become peaceful. The only thing that made me frown was seeing the area where humans were destroying Earth.

*Why wouldn't anyone police that?*

"Free will," a voice answered my thoughts from beside me as I stared at a picture of a war zone. "We may be able to control what we do and do it for the better, but the humans haven't seemed to figure that out for themselves."

I turned and saw the tall, dark-haired man next to me was Dean Edgewater. "Why can't someone do something to stop it?" I pointed to a figure where it showed a snowy area and the holographic scale showing it practically melting to nothing. "Or here. Why don't the elves and the pixies work together to stop this? They're elementals. This is what they do."

"We can't stop humanity from destroying gifts given to them." He smiled at me, and even though it was a kind smile, I felt a dark energy present behind his glimmering white teeth. "We can only control ourselves. I am glad you're finally accepting this school, Miss Silvers. I was worried about you for a while, but I was hoping you'd come around."

"Yeah, I just needed time to adjust I guess."

"That's usually how long it takes for our supernaturals who are set in their ways." He looked back at the display. "You come from a family that you'll learn about one day, and when you do, you'll understand why you accepting this school weighed heavy on my mind."

I went to speak, but he cut me off.

"For now, celebrate the fact you survived your first month. It's all uphill from here." He winked and then was gone in a blink.

*Teleporting.* He was a witch. I knew that ability from a mile away since it was Vannah's favorite thing to do before this academy shut it down. Maybe they'd let her use it once she proved she would use it for good. I had no idea. I really didn't know what years two and three brought the supernaturals at the school. Lusa was in her second year here, and after she used compulsion on me, she still had to keep it in check. Same with Dominic. He shifted and could've suffered severe consequences for doing so outside our allotted time when Ethan freaked that night.

"Are you coming?" Vannah tugged on my arm. "Let's go. You're going to die when you see this massive dancing area and then another room that's just as big as that, filled with desserts." She looked at my dress and smiled, "Be careful ravishing the pie station, you're wearing all white...well, the parts that are covered, I should say."

"What am I doing wearing this stupid thing?" I said with hesitation, realizing this was over the top.

"Wear it like the Queen of Sparta you are tonight, my sweet and crazy friend."

We walked into music that even made *me* want to dance. It was a mix of fast beats with classical instruments keeping up, creating a rhythm that set the stage for an eventful night. I smiled and ignored every single person dressed in lavish clothing—all monarchs and royalty—and focused on getting to the pie station. Awesome music combined with my favorite food? I was totally down for this night I'd been dreading.

Vannah was right, bright crystal chandeliers hung from the ceilings, and students lined the white porcelain pillared walls. It was an intoxication of beauty, but the only thing I was about to get high on life with right now was the pie that was calling me into the magnificent dessert room. The black and white checkered floor made my eyes so thankful it wasn't a bright multicolored fairy floor. It was simple, and beams of light fell on the desserts as if they were just as special as the artwork and sculptures in the entrance of this building.

I was in the middle of cramming a piece of pie in my mouth when some tall chick who hung with Dom and Company—my new favorite term to refer to Dominic and his crew —approached.

She was dressed in a chiffon gown with some ribbon and crest adorning her shoulder, and before I could swallow the bite of pie, she was flanked by a panther shifter I liked to call *red lips* because of her ostentatious makeup, and a lioness shifter with thick, golden blonde hair.

The chick in the chiffon stood in front of me, arching a brow almost as high as Mistress Sirena. Her leathery skin was evidence that she spent too much time in the sun or something. This chick had charcoal black hair, emerald green eyes, and pouty pink lips. Her eyes would have been something of beauty if they weren't always sending daggers in mine and my friends' directions.

"Did you hear what I asked?" She stomped her foot like a four-year-old throwing a tantrum.

"No. Sorry. Don't speak bitch. Gotta go," I said and left the mean girl tactic that had me singled out at my weak spot—the pie station.

"You should watch your language," I heard the high pitched trill of red lips shout out, "the dean is present tonight."

I ignored the trio and headed reluctantly out of the dessert section in search of my friends.

"Jenna!" Tanner's eyes were as wide as saucers and smile stretching from ear to ear. "Dang, girl, it's a shame you friend-zoned me a long time ago."

"Mind out of the gutter, dude." I pointed into his chest. He wore coattails and a strange hat with a bizarre looking white wig. "Who the heck are you?"

"George Washington." He pulled on his blue tailcoat, "First president of the United States of America. It's a place I think I want to live once I'm out of here."

Tanner rattled off about the president while my eyes fell on where Dom and Co. stood. I'm sure my eyes were as wide as Tanner's when he first saw me when I saw what Dominic was wearing—or lack thereof. The red burgundy cloak that hung from his back should have drawn my eyes away from the veins in his bare arms, and the abs of steel that were shredded and more than tempting.

*Holy mother of shifters*! The dude was in some kind of early year regalia for a warrior, I just had no idea what. The shield he carried made my throat go dry. That's when Dom and Co. saw me standing there, jaw open and probably looking like I was drooling over the guy who was carrying the...

"Shield of Sparta?" I seethed out. "Tanner, tell me I'm wrong. Oh my God, I'm going to *kill* Ethan for this."

"Sorry, ma'am," Tanner touched my lower, *bare* back, and I jerked away from him. "You are looking at your king, my lady. Leonidas..."

"Shut." I held my hand up and closed my eyes. "Up."

"You both make a fine pair." Tanner chuckled.

"Alright. Where's the group hanging? I'm standing in an area for everyone to witness this, so let's get out of here."

"We're actually over there by the King of Sparta and his monarch bros."

"What?" I said, trying to duck behind the slow dancing crowd. "Come here," I said, grabbing President Washington Tanner and looking at the people dancing in some fancy way. "Tell me you practiced in the one hour they taught us some of the dancing we'd be doing tonight?"

"I believe you're dancing with my queen, Washington."

I wanted my head to fall into Tanner's sturdy chest and rescue me from the mortification to follow, but it was too late. Tanner—like every guy at this school—gave Dom his space, and now I was looking up into humorous brown eyes that spoke to my soul somehow, and my hands were caught in rough, warrior hands.

"Well, if we didn't want anyone thinking we were a couple, dancing together like this isn't helping us," I said, pulling my eyes away from the guy I'd hardly said a word to since he'd shifted that one night. "Every. Single. Person. Is. Watching. Us."

"You know, some words aren't made to be complete sentences," he teased as he led our dance.

*Watch his feet, Jenna.* I was determined to keep my eyes off the crowd and off his enticing brawny olive toned abs—*gah! Crap, he's in sandals, and his feet are even beautiful.* In the art of pulling it together, I stared boldly into his eyes. Dude's rigid and muscular body was too tall and his shoulder too wide for me to glance around. I had to face this monster head on. How could Ethan think this was cool? Pairing me up as Dom's queen for the night? Bet Dom and Co. and the fangirls were enjoying this. It certainly explained why three of his groupies wanted to kill me at the pie station a few minutes ago.

Well, at least I crossed a line with the students this time—and not with the school. Now, I was just left to wonder if this song was ever going to end.

## CHAPTER FIFTEEN

I resorted to glancing around at the audience Dom and I had created while dancing. It was much easier to look at their gossiping expressions instead of falling mercy to the Greek god of a body in front of me.

Dominic's hand slid to my exposed lower back due to the nature of this dancing ritual. Yeah, I said it, ritual. There was nothing dance-like about this. It was me and my fierce, no BS master dancing like we were somehow meant to be. I had to fight everything off at this point—everything as in *my soul felt drawn to the power of this guy, and I couldn't explain it.*

I'd never been *this* close to any guy in my life, much less someone I was inwardly admiring for his commanding air, strength, and the power that poured off him in waves. It also didn't help that he was easy on the eye, which was putting it mildly now, having seen him half-dressed in these warrior clothes of the Spartan King.

My throat was dry, my palms balmy—which I knew he felt— and my heart trying to fall out of its normal rhythm. It wasn't fair that he had this much control over me, and I was growing frustrated that I was turning into one of the groupies who gawked at him.

"You shouldn't worry about what others think, you know," Dominic said, and I heard a smile in his voice.

"Just trying to find Ethan. This was his idea." I finally looked back into his beautiful brown eyes, noticing his thick black lashes that highlighted them. "It was his idea..."

"That you be my queen for the night?" he rose an eyebrow of humor at me. "So, tell me, *my queen*, what intelligent advice do you have for a king you love so desperately who is about to head off to war only to die to protect his people."

"I really didn't study up on this couple, so you got me there. Like I said, I asked Ethan to find a character for me to dress up as, and he told me I fit this person very well."

"You do." He smirked. "You also wear the clothing very well too."

His expression became sincere as his thumb absently rubbed the area where his hand rested on my lower back. It glided over my spine, giving me an internal shiver. My emotions were destroying my confidence, and I was losing control of the front I was keeping up in front of Dominic.

"Yeah, the sandals look great on your feet."

Dominic chuckled and drew me in closer, his lips were at my ear now. "Are you getting flustered by the appearance of my feet?"

That's all I needed, some dumb, arrogant remark, and suddenly, the warmth of his breath that should have raised goosebumps all over my body had no effect on me. "I hate feet. They're ugly and weird."

"But mine are attractive. You just said it."

"Dominic, please. I'm just trying to get through this dance. Your groupies are going to give me hell for this, and I'm not in the mood to be the topic of this school's conversation over the next few months."

He grew more serious. "What if I told you I was glad Ethan told me I reminded him of the King of Sparta? Except for the death part, of course; although, I would fight to the death and go fiercely into battle to protect my people—if immortals actually died, that is."

"Then I'm glad you're glad. You kind of run at the top with this school, so you're not going to get crap about this, but I am."

"Like I said, who cares what they think. Let them talk."

"Easier said than done."

"I have a proposition for you." He cocked his head to the side, and just as he was finally starting to pique my interest because the look on his face resembled more of the master I had grown to know, the music was ending. "It'll have to wait, but for now, please don't hate Ethan too much for doing this. Will you trust me when I propose we do something together to help Ethan, something that I really need your help with?"

"What are you talking about? I mean, I'll do anything to help Ethan. What's going on?"

We broke as soon as the music stopped. "That's all I needed to hear."

He threw his crimson cloak back, did some weird bow, and then turned back to where Dom and Co., the groupies, and the snobby trio had all remained in conversation, watching me and Dominic make some kind of a dumb statement in the center of the room.

"You guys actually make a cute couple, even if Dom stands a head taller than you." Lusa met me, wearing a simple dress, so very un-vampire-like of her. She winked and smiled, and I let out a breath of relief that never-ending song had ended.

"Nice. You and Ethan? Were you both in on this together?"

"Ethan is wiser than you give him credit for. He smartly paired you two up, though all of us are only amazed because it seems like you literally despise my brother." She laughed.

"He's my training master, I'm supposed to hate him." I laughed.

"Well, let the gossiping gals start in. You're both sure to have made Immortal Academy Ageless Ball history tonight."

"Speaking of which," I eyed her simple white gown, "who are you dressed as? A queen in her nightgown?"

Lusa laughed, but before she could respond, she was pulled away by Mistress Sirena. "Talk later, gotta go." She smiled and then floated through the crowd as flawlessly as only vamps could do.

"Holy crap," Nick said with a laugh. "I can't believe you and Dom match historical characters. The only people who show up as matching partners are couples here. You and Dom secretly dating?"

I glared at him and folded my arms. "No. I really wish this Queen of Sparta was alive because apparently, she was super fit, trained like the Spartan warriors, and more importantly, she was witty and smart, and I could use her advice right about now—or her brains."

"What are you talking about?" Vannah smiled at me. "You're all of those things. I mean, you're not really Dom's queen, but you're everything else you just listed about that queen. Just go with it and have fun. All those girls with painted faces who act like they're in Dom's tribe only wished they'd thought of this."

"I need some fresh air. Seriously."

"Take the back door through the refreshment area. That's if you can make it past all the desserts," Tanner smiled.

I noticed he and Emma seemed to have made up, which made me happy for Tan. Part of me wanted to jerk the dumb fairy up and chew her out for hurting him, and the other part made me think that Tan finally got a taste of his own medicine.

"Alright. I'll be back in a few," I said before my skimpily-dressed butt crisscrossed through the dance floor, trying to go take a much-needed breather.

I walked out into a dark courtyard and saw a path that caught my attention. Less time in there with judging eyes, and more time out here close to nature is what I needed. I took off my sandals and meandered through the archway made of vines out to an area that we'd never had the privilege to explore on the school grounds.

It was dark, and my wolf lent me her night vision to navigate behind all the buildings to an abandoned building where I heard angry voices off in the distance. My wolf hearing engaged right then, and I was able to hear the sounds of men grumbling and arguing with each other.

"Get rid of it by getting it out in the Dark Woods where none of the students go. The lake will be there, you idiots know this. We'll figure the rest out later, just dispose of the body now."

*I did not just hear that.* My wolf's ears fell flat back, and she bared her teeth as I snuck behind bushes that weren't trimmed into all shapes and sizes like the ones on the front lawns.

"Here, come with me," a deep voice growled out. "Just leave it, and we'll handle this first."

My heart was racing when I saw a bag that was obviously cinched up with what could only be a *dead body* inside. Did a vamp drain a human and the school was trying to cover it up? Why was there a dead body at this school behind the supernatural barriers?

I inched forward, hearing the voices fade farther into the building. I made it to the bag, and I should have feared the sight of a dead human, but I wanted this to be my first lesson in why we protected them. My major at this academy was leaning even stronger now in the direction of the Immortal Forces who policed this crap.

The bag was made of very rough cloth, and my shaking hands reached for the one place that wasn't tightened by rope. This poor human's head.

I froze when I pulled back the cloth and saw Jessica. The fox shifter's hollow eyes were dilated, staring into oblivion. I covered my mouth quickly, biting my tongue hard so I wouldn't scream right then and there.

"She shouldn't have been asking questions. Besides, we need to feed her."

"It's just sad, the way she fought."

"You know it's our job. If you can't take it, then get out of it."

I covered sweet Jessica's innocent and *immortally dead* face, whispered I'm sorry, and stealthily hid behind bushes that concealed me from the evil men I heard talking. These guys weren't part of the school, though I could scent in the air through my wolf that they were *very much* part of this school.

I sank down in the bushes, knowing I needed to get out of this place quickly, but I couldn't believe what I had seen. Jessica, my friend, was not only dead, but she was a dead immortal! No one cracked the code on how to kill an immortal—or at least I had never heard of an immortal dying.

An inner voice—my wolf and her wisdom—broke through the trembling nervous breakdown I was about to become victim to. I had to get out of here and tell no one about what I had witnessed.

If I wanted to get to the bottom of this, I had to act like I'd never seen it. I couldn't trust anyone at this school.

Ethan's words came back to me at that point. *"You can trust the students. Immortals don't die. Immortals will die!"* All of which made me trust the owl who saw life differently than the rest of us. I had to stick close to my guy. That's how I felt as I scurried off unnoticed from Jessica's body.

I couldn't be suspicious. I needed to act normal. The dean made it clear he was worried about me not accepting his school tonight. He was number one on my list of people not to be trusted. I had been drinking the happy punch lately with all my friends because it felt good to be talking to them again, and I had to keep doing that.

I wanted so badly to confide in the *old* Vannah again, but I wasn't sure she was all there anymore. She wasn't one for guys, and here she and a fairy were planning their future together after the academy. No, Vannah wasn't Vannah anymore. Tanner might buy this, but the relief when I stopped fighting everyone and everything was so apparent with him that I really didn't think I could trust him either.

*Dominic?* I thought, walking into the dancing area, bumping into kids dancing in front of me. Could I trust him? I couldn't carry this burden by myself, but the truth was, until tonight, Dom was a hit and miss with me. I couldn't trust the dude, he worked for the staff that, one-by-one, I was quickly putting on my suspect list.

The only person I could trust was myself and my wolf instincts. I would be a lone wolf, but that was fine, a lone wolf could be more dangerous and fierce than one who ran with a pack, needing their efforts for her survival.

I thought back to what the men said about Jessica asking questions, and I tried to remember my last interactions with her. She seemed a bit frazzled I guess, but she was a bit flighty to begin with, so I didn't think anything of it. Had she started to see through the façade at this school the way I had? Did she see the shadow creature?

She was asking questions, and now, she was dead. An immortal had been killed.

## CHAPTER SIXTEEN

I managed to make it through the Ageless Ball, but my mind was so consumed with the death of innocent Jessica that it was difficult. After what I'd seen, it took all I had not to spin out of control. Putting on a fake face and getting through the rest of the stupid dance was probably the hardest thing I'd ever had to do.

I was numbed to everything right now, and if it weren't for my wolf sitting in the driver's seat of my mind, I would be trembling in fear and risking my life to shift and bust out of this place.

The school succeeded in brainwashing my friends into loving this place, which now might've been a good thing. They were safely alive because of their devotion to this menacing place, but on the flip side, that meant I couldn't confide in my best friend about this horror that, quite frankly, was utterly impossible.

I had to play it cool and find a way out of here. Selfish, I know, but how was I supposed to get help from inside this nightmare of a place? Maybe it seemed like a stupid choice, but I certainly didn't want to end up like Jessica, and I was on pretty thin ice at this place in the first place. One wrong word from me and that could be the end.

I took a deep breath in the shower after a restless night. I had to play fake, and I had to plan a way out. I had no one I could trust. Period. Not Lusa or even Dominic...definitely not Dominic no matter how much my wolf kept forcing his handsome face to the front of my mind right now.

My inner wolf might have picked up on something with him, but she made her mistakes too. She was practically drooling over his wolf while we danced. His wolf was larger and more fierce than any shifter I'd ever encountered. I needed his strength, that was for sure, but how was I to know this school wasn't using one of the most powerful shifters for their evil work?

I had to get my fake face on, pretend to love this evil school, and go through the motions while I tried to figure things out. I wished with everything that was in me that I could snap my friends out of their apparent trance so we could all escape together, but as the wolf continued to remind me, I needed to leave them alone. They were all safe.

I would do whatever I could to get answers, but I also needed to make sure I stayed alive. I couldn't do much to help if I were a ghost. All I knew was that my wolf and I were on a survival mission, and that mission began with playing the game.

I WALKED OUT and ignored the dark clouds that blocked out the sun. It's like the atmosphere was disturbed over what happened last night during our dance.

*Stop thinking. Spies. Mind readers!* It was me talking inside my head, but my wolf was the one reminding me. I appreciated my wolf being more engaged, but she needed to take a back seat ASAP because Dominic dressed out in his all-black training attire was definitely perking my wolf up. He would sense that a mile away, and I'd be totally screwed.

As if my wolf knew what we needed to do, she mellowed down and gave me my head back. I felt the weakness fall over my body, but I overcame that immediately.

"Where's Jess?" Freddie, a coyote shifter, asked in confusion. "She's usually the first one here."

Dominic nodded and stood in his usual posture: legs apart and hands behind his back. He always hid his gorgeous eyes behind dark glasses, so no one ever really knew what was going on in his mind. Smart on his part, annoying for someone like me.

"Jess left school. That's all I know. I was informed before reporting to the fields this morning. No questions, it's time to get busy. Things are changing up a bit after today's workouts. The dean wants to use this week to determine who will be moving under different instructors." He smiled at Master Ian, who had his group lined up closer to ours than usual. "First, you're all invited to watch me, Master Ian, Master Scott, and Master Finley take the leadership challenge. If you were paying attention in class," his dark sunglasses and strong jawline looked directly where I stood, "you would know that after a month, the masters go through a challenge to see who will take on the strongest to weakest shifters in their groups." He started pacing through the lines. "A quest awaits us, and before we take any of our students on that quest, your masters will do it on their own. When we return, we'll choose who we believe can handle the quest and bring you on it after some smaller exercises. The reason we don't bring just any student on a quest without training is simply that they are grueling, and this school has a different outlook on succeeding in them."

"Master Dominic?" red lips, the panther shifter, called out.

"Yes, Kat?" he answered in his commanding, dismissive tone.

"When you and the other masters leave, what are we supposed to do?"

Dominic smirked, of course, he enjoyed the fact that her

whiney little question proved she was going to feel lost without our badass master for who knows how long.

"We trust that you're all responsible enough to follow the lead of the students we put in charge while we are absent."

"Yeah, that's going to be a problem," I shot off.

Dark sunglasses whipped in my direction as Dominic cocked his head to the side. "Why, so, Silvers? If you can't respect your peers who've been selected to help instruct you, then you should be off with the sprites, blowing air up someone's butt."

I tightened my lips in frustration, ignoring red lips—Kat—practically losing it in laughter with Dominic shutting me down.

"I think Kat is proving my point." I decided to go for her immature reaction. "If you were to pick a shifter who can't control her laughter after the master decides it's cool to insult a student and a fellow supernatural's talents, then how is someone like her supposed to run your unit in your absence?"

"I owe you no explanation, but I will tell you that I see and hear everything. We've never had a problem putting a student of our choosing in command. Let's just say that the expression on your face tells me you would immaturely make Kat do a grueling exercise because of her immature reaction. So that rules both of you out on leading this unit in my absence. I have chosen who I want running the unit already, and I think you all will be grateful." He turned his back to me and paced up another aisle, "Let's get our workouts going. Tonight will be a fun night if you would like to see the different masters fighting for the top spot on the shifter regiments. The shifter who wins tonight leads the mission, and when we choose our new students, the lead will pick the ones he wants, leaving the rest to continue to build up to being in the top master's class."

*Good God. Dude's talking like he has this in the bag.*

"Do not forget, the top master will be bringing his students on the quest before the others after the masters return. That's all in time, but for now, enjoy the new changes that will be underway for House Braeclaw's shifters. This is when it all gets fun."

The morning routine pretty much stayed the same, kept my mind busy, and that was a good thing. The worst part was getting through class and keeping my memories and mind silent about everything that happened.

Finally, it was lunchtime. I used my steaks, ham, and smoked pork links to keep my mind happy and my stress levels down.

*Time for pie!*

"Sheesh, Jenna," Tanner laughed. "You inhaled your lunch, which was half a cow and pig. You're already going for dessert?"

"What can I say, intense workouts today, and the C I got on my lame Vampires Through History exam has me stress eating. Everyone's lucky that they wait to bring the pies out, or I would have skipped proteins and went straight for my comfort food."

Vannah caught my hand. "Hold on, don't make it look obvious."

I looked into her stern eyes. Maybe she did a witchy thing—popped out of her trance—and knew something wasn't right. She was part of one of the most powerful witch families in history. Maybe my bestie came back to me?

"Obvious? I want pie. I smell it." I decided to test her.

"You're showing weakness." Her eyes were severe, "Don't want to do that in front of Dominic, especially all his little groupies who have been glaring at you since you got here. That Kat chick and her two friends are at the table next to the entrance, watching you, and who knows what they'll do now that they think you and Dominic planned on dressing as the Queen and King of Sparta last night."

I straddled the bench seat at the wooden candlelit table where we always sat. "First of all, I don't give two craps about what *they* think. Second, you're stalling me, and there are kids already in there. Third, everyone knows pie is my weakness. Boom." I smirked.

Vannah rolled her eyes, "Go get your pie. Quit talking like that. You sound so lame when you come up with excuses to eat your stinking pie."

"I hate to hear your new way of muting a cuss word," I looked over at Nick, her boyfriend in her new delusional life at this school. "You sound like a fairy with your new terms now too. So *stinking* lame." I shook my head.

"Hey," Tanner said, bringing my attention to him gulping down his water, "Emma and I are doing great, by the way."

"Glad to see that." I looked at Emma, "Other dude too boring for you, or did you actually realize losing Tanner was a stupid idea?"

"Jenna!" Vannah snapped. "Go get your pie and quit being so awful."

"Exactly, if you fairy-loving friends of mine would have let me go when I was ready, my dark side wouldn't have come out. Sorry, Tan," I apologized to him, but I didn't miss the opportunity to eye Emma whose cheeks were painted pink with embarrassment. *Good. Don't cheat on my friend, bitch fairy.*

I walked past the high-pitched trills coming from the *Dominites'* table—Dominite was my new word for the three groupies who followed Dom around as if he was gonna wake up one day and give them the time of day. The trio acted like they were part of his harem or something, utterly ridiculous.

I balanced a plate of banana cream pie and a plate of blackberry pie in one hand and held a piece of apple pie in the other as I walked past the Dominites' table.

"Do it!" I heard a whisper just before one of the mean girls slid her foot in front of mine, tripping me. It all happened in slow motion. My precious apple pie crashed on top of the banana cream pie, and both splattered onto the floor. God only knew who had the privilege of wearing my blackberry pie.

I sprang to my feet, furious, and turned back to see the trio laughing, and the entire lunchroom was either laughing under their breath or waiting for what I was about to do. What I wanted to do was punch Kat in her pointed little feline face.

"Jenna," Tanner grabbed my arm, knowing I was about to lunge. "I'll get you some more. Get back to the table before you get busted for starting a fight with a jealous cat."

Kat rolled her eyes and brought her red nails to meet her lush red lips. "Sorry about that," she said in some stupid fake voice.

"Yeah, I am too," I managed.

"Get back to the table," Tanner said.

I followed his instructions, and my eyes met Vannah's stern ones. She smiled, and her witchy gaze literally spelled me out, and I walked like a numb robot to my table.

"Unbelievable. If Dom had control over the chicks who clung to him, I would still have my apple pie."

Vannah's eye's widened. "I don't think Dom was part of that. Can't blame him for jealous girls."

"Screw that and screw Dominic. Damn it, I have pie all over this lame uniform now." I turned back to the table when Tanner smiled and slid me a piece of rhubarb pie.

"Here, Jenna." He smiled and had some weird, dumb look on his face, "You love to try new things. I think you'll like the rhubarb pie."

I placed each hand on the table, mad at the pie that did nothing wrong. "If I wanted to try something new, I would have gotten this disgusting pie in the first place, Tan."A strong hand covered my balled up fist to the left of my plate. My lethal gaze left the pie and went to the familiar hand. "What the hell are you doing?"

"Taking your friend Tanner's advice," Dominic's humored voice rang through my head. Now, my wolf was up and ready like it was her freaking wedding day. Dom's wolf was present, I could feel the power of it and him. "Trying something new."

I turned to see his smile. God, he was beautiful. It was like the floating candles of the room highlighted the dark five-o'clock shadow on his face, enhanced his beautiful irises—*focus, Jenna.* Wait. Let's forget about the fact I just lost the last piece of apple pie, Dom and Co. were all at our table now, and not at their *anointed* table. Where the hell was my boy, Ethan? After last night, this was an unsettling feeling for me. Did *they* get him too?

# CHAPTER SEVENTEEN

I sat there, contemplating Dominic holding my hand with a gentle, yet tight grip. My eyes roamed over to the other two handsome guys in the Dom and Co. universe who were conversing with the annoying female shifter trio, three fairies, and one witch that migrated with them from the other tables.

"Yeah, Sahvannah Woodson," Vannah answered a question from a tanned skin, dark-haired, green-eyed witch who seemed to act extremely interested in my formerly normal best friend.

"Of the Woodson coven?" she asked as she leaned her chin on her fist, giving Vannah her full attention.

"Yes." Vannah perked up.

"A very powerful coven. Tell me, have you been able to teleport yet?" green eyes asked. Her brown hair was pulled up into a messy but cute top knot.

"Yes," Vannah met my shocked gaze with a cheerful smile. "I've been able to teleport my friends whenever they've come close to crossing a line here and there." She laughed.

Green eyes looked at me and displayed her polished white teeth. "Jenna, is it?" she asked.

I played along, ignoring Dominic clutching my hand as if he

and I *had* been a couple for months. The wolf in me was pacing nervously for my reactions and also because her dream wolf was sitting right next to us.

"Yep, Jenna. Wolf shifter, one of Master Dominic's students."

"I see that." She looked at Dom's thumb rubbing the side of my hand. "Has Sahvannah teleported you?"

"Nice underhanded way of asking if she's caught me out of line." I smiled and tried to take my hand back from Dominic, but he held it tighter.

I glanced at him and saw his bright eyes practically begging me to play along with him. My inner wolf was acting like she wanted to bust out of her cage and jump all over this muscular man that had an inner beast she'd blindly fell for.

"I wasn't trying to be like that. Just wondering if being friends with a powerful witch got a wolf shifter like you some fun rides, that's all."

"It makes me want to barf." I looked at Vannah, remembering the good old days when my friend teleported my butt out of the trouble I seemed to find at every corner of our other school.

"That's amusing," green eyes said with sarcasm dripping off her lips.

"What coven are you from, and why would you bring up things that are forbidden at this *awesome* academy?"

"Just trying to figure you and your friends out," she said.

"There's nothing to figure out. Obviously, my friends date elves, and I love pie." I looked back to see a beet-red face from red nails, the sweetheart who tripped me and destroyed my precious apple pie. Chick must've been fuming that Dom and Co. elected to sit at our table.

"Speaking of pie." She giggled and looked at the other nosy mean girls next to her. "You must be mortified taking a fall like that. Clumsy shifters don't do well at this school," she said condescendingly.

"Why don't you keep your insults to yourself, Misty," Dominic spoke up before I did. "I can tell you first hand that my girl can hold her own, and she will tomorrow when she takes on Scott's best shifter."

"Wait, what?" I looked at Dominic, making a note to hit him later for what he just said. And where the hell was Ethan? What was this charade all about? I went to pull my hand out of his and go off, but something told me to knock it off.

*Just trust me.* That's what he asked after we danced last night. Something about doing something for Ethan. Okay, we had a situation, maybe Dominic knew more, and he would let me in after he explained our new boyfriend-girlfriend dilemma in private.

"Yes. Scott is choosing his top shifter, I chose mine. You go into the challenge tomorrow. You seem to be the type who would want to go on the first quest of the year."

"Yes."

"Then you better kick some serious butt tomorrow."

Lunch dragged on for a lifetime, and that was even after Dom slid over his apple pie to me—and I ate it, obviously. I needed answers for this strange turn of events, like, right now.

Lunch finished, and where it was usually Tan and me walking to our next class together, it was Dominic who was escorting me there. His arm was draped over my shoulder, and I was as stiff as a board.

"Thanks for doing this," he said under his breath, nodding at a group of girls giggling as they passed.

"I don't understand what the hell is going on right now. You need to give me something."

Dom stopped our walk next to a building. "I'm simply acting on my wolf's instincts. He's leading me to be more attracted to you."

"Shut the hell up," I practically shouted.

Dominic took my arm and led me closer to the building. Now, the staff was in the area, heading and scrambling to their classes.

"Cool it with the language," he ordered in that stupid alpha voice that didn't work on me. "I need you to go with me on this, can you do that?"

"On what and why? I'm not good with secrets, and I'm even worse at pretending to be fake. Where's Ethan? He always sits next to me at lunch."

"Don't worry about Ethan," he dismissed me with his jerk tone.

"I can do whatever I want." I pushed him off me. "I'm not good with this. My stupid wolf is acting like this is all A-Okay, and it's not. Tell me where my friend is."

"If you remember correctly, he's my cousin, and I'll handle him."

"You're a jerk," I seethed. "And trust me, for Ethan's sake, I didn't cuss. Please, tell me what's going on. For all I know, you idiot, arrogant masters are playing games before your big challenge tonight. None of this makes sense."

"Why would you think I would play silly games like this?" He grew more severe, and I got a peek at the wolf he kept hidden in him while he was in his normal form.

The black, enormous wolf was fierce. It made a chilling feeling shoot down my spine, and it made my inner wolf lay down and whimper in submission.

"I'm not submitting to an arrogant, piece of crap like you and your immature friends. You want to throw your wolf in and freak me out, then I'm not playing your dumb game. You, Dominic Rossi, can go find some other groupie of yours to pull this nonsense off with. I'm out."

In less than a breath, Dominic had me up against the wall, his firm body towering over mine. "You need to relax. If anyone is acting like an immature fool right now, it's you."

"Get off me." I went to shove him away, but the surprising act of him bringing his hands up to my face and lowering his eyes to meet mine, paralyzed me.

"It would be nice if your biased mind didn't jump to conclusions about me," he said in a low growl. His lips were at my ear, hands tenderly caressing my face he had framed in them. "I would never play games with a girl, and I would definitely not play games with you, Jenna Silvers. I'm asking you to go along with this for reasons that I can't discuss."

"You don't trust me," I exhaled, my body betraying me in every way possible. "Then, I don't trust you."

"You'll learn, and then you'll understand, you stubborn brat."

Before I could snap back at him, his eyes darted toward what I assumed was Dean Edgewater's long and lanky figure. I couldn't see or even think for that matter now because my lips were silenced by Dominic's firm lips on mine.

My body went limp, and my heart was set ablaze with some flame that ignited out of nowhere and sent it beating at a pace that should have given me a stroke.

His lips found my bottom one, and I swear I heard the dude softly moan like he actually was just as taken by this simple kiss as I was. Officially, Dominic had become my first real kiss.

Instead of pushing the attractive guy off me, my hands slipped under his arms and pressed into—holy crap—the taut muscles of his back. He was all power and strength. Oh my gosh, I was getting lost in the Dom spell over a kiss.

"Hey. Hey," Dean Edgewater's voice broke through this oddly connecting moment that was starting to bud between Dominic and me. I couldn't get the woodsy, rich fragrance of his masculine scent out of my head that was completely spinning right now.

Dominic chuckled and pulled my weak body up and next to his in a tight embrace. It was apparent he knew I was limp as a noodle right now. "Yeah, Dean Edgewater?" Dominic lifted his chin and smiled at the Dean's mischevious stare.

"A master dating his student?" the dean arched a brow at Dominic. "You know I will have my eyes on you both. I expect no favorites to come out of your mastering her amongst the others, or you will lose your title."

"I have no intentions. In fact, I have her going up against Master Scott's finest shifter tomorrow."

Dean Edgewater studied me, "You both agreed to this."

"I didn't," I said, angrily and truthfully. "I have no idea what Dominic is doing. Trying to get the love of his life killed?" I said, not really realizing I used the word killed.

"Immortals killed?" Dean Edgewater laughed. "That'll be the day. I'm watching you," Edgewater said to Dominic.

"Yes, sir."

"Both of you are late to your classes, not a great way to impress teachers as a master dating his student at Immortal Academy. Before you know it, you'll have the entire school watching your every move."

Dominic smiled, "We wouldn't want any distractions, would we?"

Edgewater laughed with his weird smile. "Too late for that, Dom," he said with a smile. "Get your shifter selves to class before I throw you both in the dungeons." He winked creepily, then vanished.

"Get to class. Mission one...accomplished." He kissed my hand like he was some dude who fell out of the time when young men actually behaved like gentlemen. "By the way, that kiss," he let out a breath and gave me a devastating smile, "next time, I'll take you to your limits, Silvers." He licked his lips and grinned at me, "I'll never forget how that made me feel."

"Quit being disgusting. How long do we play this game of yours before you explain what's going on?"

Dominic turned back, and a smile played on his closed lips for a fraction of a second. "For as long as I need it to. And don't say you and your eager little inner wolf didn't enjoy that simple peck either. It felt like more, didn't it?"

I watched his curious expression, his wolf still shut off to me.

"Felt like you assaulted me to get the dean's attention. That's it. This better be worth it."

Dominic smiled, "I knew you felt something more. See you after class, Silvers."

"I think I can manage walking to House Mage on my own."

He threw a hand up, walking away, "After class."

He dismissed me and then took off.

*What. The. Hell.*

If someone wanted to distract me from more pressing issues at this school, Dominic kissing me was obviously more effective than a piece of pie. A freaking peck had my knees buckling? I had to ground myself.

It would've been nice to have my best friend and a grounding spell right now. Too bad, she was drinking the fairy juice, and I was sitting here as one of Dominic's victims, getting played to probably make the jerk look better. God only knew, he probably had some stupid bet going on with his friends. The big challenge was tonight, maybe they all pulled some sick joke on each other like some weird initiation to being the champion and lead master.

Sounded about right. Scott and Ian had stupid smiles on their faces while Dominic started the whole boyfriend-girlfriend status between him and me at lunch. So there's that. The most obvious choice, and tonight I would be rooting for Finley to kick all their arrogant asses.

I walked into my Fairy class and scanned the room for Ethan. I hadn't seen him at all, not even to chew him out for dressing Dom and me as matching King and Queens from Sparta. Did he take off? Did he see what I saw last night? Now, he wasn't in class.

My heart was racing in fear for my new friend. I practically shouted *thank God* when I saw him sitting in a different place in class. Unfortunately, there was no space to sit next to him, and the usual glaring headache I had in this brightly-lit, colorful fairy room hit me harder than Dom's lips earlier.

At least Ethan was cool. Maybe I was starting to think the worst because I saw the worst. I wanted to ask Ethan if his owl picked up on anything weird, but he was out of the class before I could catch him, and as promised, my new fake boyfriend was leaning up against the archway entrance like a shifter god sent to take me to my next class.

Good God, if this was some joke—at my expense—between him and his lame friend, I was going to literally knee him in the balls so hard they'd never drop down again. This was BS and even worse than what the mean girl trio could conjure up with their jealousy.

I was officially their target, and the fact that Dom just drew me in and planted another kiss on me—instigating a chorus of gasps and whispers—wasn't good if I wanted to stay under the radar.

My life was going to change at this school because of this charade Dom was playing, and if it did, I was going to make sure Dom's life changed for good too.

# CHAPTER EIGHTEEN

Bright lights overlooked the grass field which had been turned into some kind of an arena for the challenge of the shifter masters tonight. I sat with my friends who were insistent on finding out how and when *Dom* and I got together. Dom's little charade put me on just about everyone's radar...the jealous girls, the headmasters and professors, and creepy Dean Edgewater.

I wanted to believe this was some lame challenge the masters put on each other, and Dominic Rossi was proving to them he could snag any girl at any time, knowing my wolf wouldn't let me back out of it if I tried.

I was more angry about becoming the girl who was instantly hated and judged for dating a celebrity who deserved better. It was hard enough to keep my mind clear of thinking about what I'd seen at the Ageless Ball, now I had to make doubly sure I didn't let my mind wander to that night because all eyes were on me, and anyone who had the ability to read minds wasn't going to pass up the opportunity.

I narrowed my eyes down at the arena where Finley and Ian were in a match of skill. Scott had been eliminated for taking a hard shot and dislocating Dominic's shoulder, which if I was honest, I enjoyed watching even if it was a cheap shot, but Dom didn't even flinch. The pain made him smile. He reset his arm and acted like nothing had happened. In fact, the only thing that annoyed him about the cheap shot was the fact his friend broke the rules by causing an injury to win a match. He stood, arms crossed, intently watching Finley and Ian go at it.

The match between the two masters was short lived when, even though Finley was sharp and agile, she was taken down by Ian's stealth move and large frame that had her pinned for trying to take him down from behind. The guy ducked her attack, spun her around, and pinned her to a point to where she tapped his arm, forfeiting the match and losing. *Bummer.* I was rooting for her to kick Dom's butt next. I took note of the move I would have naturally used to save my own butt from someone bigger and stronger than me, seeing that it leaves you more open and vulnerable than I would have imagined.

"Five minutes, and we'll have our final match between masters," Professor Samson's voice ordered over the speakers.

I was shocked at how this event attracted spectators of each supernatural race at the academy. Maybe they were intrigued by how shifters fought in their natural form without shifting.

"Why'd you even come out to this?" I looked at Vannah, who was holding Nick's hand as if this was date night for them.

"Extra credit." She smiled at me. "Besides, I was curious if your new boyfriend would achieve the esteemed role of Master Shifter."

"Give me a break." I glanced back down at Nick holding her hand, "You two just wanted an excuse to be out on some weird Immortal Academy date together."

"True." Nick laughed and pecked Vannah on her cheek.

I inhaled deeply, I couldn't get mad at their open display of affection. Dom had practically made a new rule at the school that it was okay to grab your girl and kiss her in front of anyone at any time.

"We're going to get some punch, want some?" Vannah said, standing up with Nick.

"And miss Dom getting his butt whipped by Ian? No, thanks," I said with a laugh.

The two waltzed off like newlyweds, leaving Tanner and Emma down the benches from me, smiling in my direction. I rolled my eyes and crossed my arms, watching Dom take his shirt off, leaving only his black workout pants on for the final fight. *Oh, God. Give me a break.* I wanted to be annoyed, but good Lord, this guy's body was cut, chiseled, and perfect. I would have thought this was Dom acting like a peacock shifter and strutting in front of everyone, but Ian followed in the new shirtless fighting match that was about to happen.

Unfortunately for Ian, Dominic made Ian's ripped, muscular body look scrawny and like he missed a few workouts while Dom was a devoted student of chiseling out the perfectly-carved, manly body.

"God, Jenna, stop!" I quietly scolded myself. "Dude's a joke," I reminded myself.

"He protects the ones who are in danger." Ethan's familiar voice almost made me jump four seats down to where Tan and Emma were sitting.

I looked at him and shut my mind down right then and there. "Where have you been?" was all I could manage to ask.

"He didn't know about her, or he would have—"

"Ethan," my heart started racing, "About her? Who? Do you know something?" Then a thought that should have hit me a while ago slammed into me hard and fast, and I couldn't clamp my mouth fast enough to not ask. "What did you do to her? Did they use you? Was it you?"

"You ask a lot of dangerous questions." Ethan's blue eyes met mine. "Don't. You will be next if you question things."

"Are you threatening me?" I looked at him in disbelief. Everything in me knew that Ethan couldn't hurt a fly, but maybe that's the vibe the owl was giving off. A freaking owl shifter. Maybe that's the trick to killing immortals.

"I could not threaten you. You threaten yourself," he said in the matter-of-fact Ethan tone.

"Listen, Ethan," I grabbed his arm, sending his blue eyes to glance down at my hand with some fiery gaze, "you need to tell me the truth. Stop talking like this. You weren't at the dance. You were nowhere to be found when your dumb cousin made a spectacle out of us today—to protect you. I went along with it because I—"

"You talk too much. It's dangerous. You have to stop thinking about what happened."

"How can I ignore what happened to Jess?" I said, brokenhearted that Ethan must have done something and Dominic seemed to have been covering for him and using me in the process.

"If you want to survive, you'll stop asking questions. Forget what happened and live."

And just like that, Ethan stood and left. I went to follow him, but all eyes were on me right now. *Thanks, Dom!* My new fake *use Jenna to cover up his cousin killing someone* boyfriend was walking into the middle of the field with a sparring stick. Dean Edgewater's eyes were practically looking through my soul, mindreading, or listening to everything Ethan and I had been talking about.

*Focus on Dom's abs!* I inwardly told myself, knowing my mind would get distracted and stop thinking about things that Edgewater could call me out on later.

The two masters stepped out, and my eyes went to Dominic. He oddly drew me into how he was finally going to fight. His eyes were focused, his body was flexed, and he was parading around like Ian was, twirling the sparring stick he held. Ian had a stupid grin on his face while Dominic had a calculating look on his. Dom's stature was rigid and ready for attack once Ian stopped showing off for the audience. Dom could have taken the dude out so quickly, but I could tell Dominic wanted the fight, not the easy victory.

Ian's smile deceived us all when Dom spun to the side, and Ian jumped over the stick Dom used to take him out by the back of his knees. Ian squared up to Dom, and now the fight was on. Back and forth, the two sticks matched each other's attack. Ian was faster than Dom on sudden strikes with Dom taking a hit to the lower back, his arms, and now his waistline.

I wanted to call the winner then and there, but I sensed what Dom might have been doing. The dude apparently could turn off his pain receptors and take a hard blow with a sparring stick. He was wearing down his opponent. The two friends didn't once smile or smirk, they were now in full combat mode.

Dom stepped toward Ian's sparring stick, which would have hit him in the chest if he hadn't leaned to the side in a blur of speed, and then he pulled Ian by the stick past him. He quickly turned, ducked Ian's weapon as it swung toward his head, and jumped Ian's follow-up move that was meant to take Dom down with a blow to the back of his knees.

Their sticks made a loud cracking sound each time they came into contact with each other, and the sounds resonated through the area as the fight grew more fierce.

Dom dropped Ian, but Ian rolled and sprang to his feet to counter Dom. I watched Dom's feet, they weren't moving super fast; instead, they were grounded and ready to counter any attack that came his way. He moved slowly, and when he did, he seemed to move in a direction I would've never expected. Just like the wolf he kept hidden from me—and most likely everyone else at this school—Dom's fighting moves were a mystery. A natural, calculated counter-attack or lead attack wasn't how he fought. Instead of taking the obvious shot with his weapon, he took a simple yet smart shot against his opponent.

Ian was doing precisely what Dom seemed to want him to do, wear down. Dom wasn't sucking in air fifteen minutes into constant strikes and blows, but Ian was. Smart, but stupid. Sometimes you need to move quickly to save your life, not sit there all day taking time to wear down your enemy. If this were a vamp, Dom would be toast. Vamps were faster than a gust of wind, and if they threw you off mentally, they drained you and could kill you. If anything, Dom was going to lose this match by points. It was apparent Ian was faster, made more contact with Dom— even if Dom didn't react to the blow—and was still going.

It wasn't long before—in true Dom fashion—dude changed the game. Dom went after Ian, moving so fast I could hardly see his stance, his position before he struck Ian, or how he made three moves in one all while countering a sudden attack.

Dom was now using his feet to strike Ian, knock the dude off balance, then a follow-up with his sparring weapon to Ian's back. This happened five different times before Ian's frustration was apparent on his face and in his fighting technique.

The crowds cheering or gasping—all of that was background noise to me as I tried to learn from the two masters as they fought.

Dom was sent to the ground after Ian delivered a few quick and violent blows. Dom lay there and just when I thought the dude *wanted* to lose the match, Ian jabbed the point of his stick down toward Dom's chest. Instead of rolling out of the move like Ian had done with Dom, Dom lay there. To my shock, the dude caught the jab with both hands, gripped the stick, and used Ian's weapon to hold him. Ian's face was red and tense, fighting to get the stick to touch Dom's chest for the win. Dom kept the tip inches from his chest, then used a leg to sweep Ian off his feet.

Ian went to roll out of his vulnerable position when he was stopped by Dom, pinning the dude to the ground, falling on his shoulders with his knees. I watched, and couldn't keep up with the stealth move to figure out when it was that Dom broke Ian's sparring stick in half, pinned him, and was now holding his victim in a deadly position with one stick over Ian's heart, the other jagged, broken end under Ian's neck at his chin.

"Dominic Rossi," a voice came over the speakers, "Congratulations on your new title as Head Master Trainer over House Braeclaw shifters."

To my surprise, Ian's angered expression softened and he smiled after Dominic sprang to his feet and reached down to help his friend up. I was sure the two would hate each other for life after Dominic kicked into that new gear and they both practically went to war until Dom ended it.

I had to give my fake boyfriend some credit. Even though he didn't officially wear the master shifter down, he changed up his game when that tactic didn't work and kicked his ass. In the end, I learned that physically and now mentally, Dominic was a mystery in everything.

When he gave me a glance at his wolf, I had no idea what power it really had. He and his beast kept that under wraps. It was obviously a bad idea to underestimate the guy because he obviously used that to his advantage. In fact, that's exactly how he was beating Ian, allowing Ian to believe he'd jab or counter a certain way, yet Dom hit him with an entirely different attack. I couldn't even calculate Dom's next move. He was an enigmatic fighter, and nothing was predictable about him.

I couldn't help but wonder about him. Who was this guy? Why did he pick *me* to fulfill whatever agenda he had planned? Did he have something to do with what happened at the dance? The outfits, Ethan missing, Jessica—all of it. It had to be connected, and as I studied Dominic as he received his congrats from his master friends and pulled his black shirt back on over sweaty muscles, I knew he must've had something to do with it. If dude thought he was going to pull me into what he and his cousin had done to the fox shifter, he was sorely mistaken.

I couldn't talk to Lusa about any of this because she was gone doing some vamp quest, but I was determined to get answers one way or another, if not tonight, then tomorrow when lover boy stepped out of nowhere and our fake dating day began together. Something was up, sadly, my inner wolf didn't agree with my judgment.

I made sure I was gone after quick goodnights to my friends, in my dorm room, and going to bed. Five minutes before the final announcement of lights out, heavy footsteps brought sharp knocks to my door.

*Dominic.*

Yeah, not dealing with him while crowds were greeting him and praising him outside my door. I wasn't getting locked up and put under a Dom kiss spell. I was going to get answers. I didn't know exactly how with my wolf pretty much snarling at me for ignoring him at my door, but I'd figure out how to get past her controlling me like this. Somehow, it felt like my life depended on it.

# CHAPTER NINETEEN

The next morning consisted of me trying to put myself in a different mindset about everything. I had no idea what today would bring, but the impatient knocks on my door, while I was trying to get my combat boots on, was pretty much telling me my fake boyfriend was here to take me to the first challenge of the day.

I stomped my laced-up boot into the floor of the room and swung the door open.

"Tan?" I questioned in confusion. "What the heck are you doing here?"

His smile reminded me of the old Tanner—the non-fairy charmed Tanner—and it was nice to see while dealing with this menacing school of horrors.

"I'm here to pick up the girl who's going to kick some major butt today." He gave me that crooked *Tan-Man* smile.

"Yeah, we'll see about that. Who knows who those idiots set me up to fight against."

Tanner rolled his eyes, "Come on. I'm excited to see how this all goes down. Finally, Jenna gets to show these other shifters what she's worth."

"Mm-hm," I said, stepping out of the room with him. A wave of nervous energy washed over me, making my stomach nauseated, and I wanted to barf right then and there. "Oh, God," I said gasping for air that just didn't fill my lungs quite right. "I'm gonna barf."

"You serious?" Tan said, looking at me when I broke away from him. "Are you *actually* nervous about this?"

"I'll meet you out there," I said, running back to my dorm.

I threw myself over the toilet and heaved. This wasn't good. I needed breakfast, I needed carbs for energy, and that was part of the challenge. Seeing who could beat their opponent without the fuel of food to keep our stamina throughout a grueling match. I was screwed.

I was going down if I couldn't find a way to get past everything against me at this point. This wouldn't necessarily be a battle of strength and endurance for me. It was going to have to be a battle of mental power instead. If I couldn't get my mind to overcome this psychological defeat I was suffering from right now, I was going down as the weakest shifter at this school.

I glanced at the clock, fifteen minutes until I had to report. I was up early—obviously because I never entirely fell asleep—and I'd spent the last hour trying to clear my mind. I couldn't have Dean Edgewater in my head. I couldn't have anyone at this school in my head at all. I had to become just as mysterious as Dominic Rossi was.

I sucked in air, feeling my nerves rumble at the thought of my fake boyfriend. God only knew what was going to go down with that guy today. He was now head master of all the shifters, and I was apparently *his* girl.

I walked out onto our balcony, desperately craving fresh air before I walked back through the halls where I had ditched Tan. Our view was surprisingly peaceful. It overlooked the woods that we trained in and the woods where all of the obstacles were.

"Holy crap! That's it!" I said to myself. I need Dom to get me on that quest with him and the masters, and I would plan my escape from there. I could ditch the masters on their run through on their quest, and get the hell out of here. My mind hit another gear that I was sure I wouldn't be able to stop now. There was so much to plan. I had to find my way around the human world once I breached the barriers of this place. I had to find someone high up in our supernatural world—whom I could trust—and blow the whistle on the Immortal Academy.

I rubbed my forehead. *One thing at a time.* I had to slow my brain down. I studied the forest of my new escape plan. This time, I was going to be the one using Dominic freaking Rossi, not the other way around. Good thing dude was playing the fake boyfriend-girlfriend game, and our *ship* was the most talked about thing by every person at this school.

Good call, Dom. I'm going to use you, this fake ship of a relationship you created, and blow the whistle on you, your vamp sister, and your cousin they're using to kill immortals.

*I'm going to barf again. Breathe—Jenna—Breeeeaaaaathhhhhhe.* Okay, let's stay away from the one thing that hurt me the most: Ethan being the one who took out Jess. I wanted to say he was under the same spell my friends were all under, but he wasn't. Owls could not fall under any spell or hypnosis. Their minds were so sharp that nothing could alter them. Ethan made a choice to work for the dark school—it was the only reason he would do this for them.

*Stop it right now, Jenna. Stop thinking about him, it, all of it.* Dammit, I worked hard to get this crap all cleared out of my head. I could hear the bustling out in the halls to confirm that everyone was thrilled to see who would win these matches.

Seven shifters total would go on the very first challenge quest of this school year, but that's not the one I wanted on. I mean, I needed to win just in case my fake boyfriend wouldn't squeeze me in with him and the others when they went on the trial run of our big quest, that would be my backup escape plan.

With my luck, the dumb dean would be watching us through the winged shifter's eyes. I wouldn't put it past him to be able to possess a shifter and be able to look through its eyes. It wouldn't be the first unexplainable thing to happen at this school.

I hadn't seen but one other chick at this school who was a winged shifter—the rumors were out there that there was a girl who sat amongst the Dom groupies who was a hawk shifter.

I didn't have time for this nonsense to keep rushing through my thoughts. It was time to win the match, then beg my new boyfriend to take me on the masters' trial run. I had to get on the team with the masters. I had to convince them to do something new. Take a newbie who could kick some butt on a master's only quest.

Jenna's new loverman was going to make this happen. I was determined. My weak body ramped up with the strength of what my mind knew we needed to do.

Oddly enough, my wolf was not speaking with me, and if I had to paint a picture and show everyone how my stubborn wolf-side was behaving, it would be her sitting arrogantly with her back facing me. She has an ear flicked back, listening in on my thoughts and plans, but she was not in agreement with them. I wanted to trust the wolf in me and her not wanting to be a part of my new plans, but for all I knew, she was just pissed off because we would be betraying and using her big black *dream wolf*, and so she wasn't playing along. Period.

She'd come around once I got my way and got in the game. She had to understand we were doing this to get help for all the kids at this school who could be killed. If my stubborn wolf could get her brains past falling head over heels for the dominant wolf Dom shifted into, she would be jumping at the idea to help people.

"Immortals don't die, freaking stubborn wolf!" I tried to remind my inner wolf. "Though, we might be next on the hit list, so get your stubborn butt in the game. We have to help these kids."

Nothing. As expected. Maybe she'd perk up once I got our first hug of the morning from the fake loverman of mine. She loved Dom, so seeing him again was what I needed to get my inner wolf moving and grooving with me.

I needed this win. I needed on that Master Shifter quest, and I was about to play the *Dom N' Jenna* game to get on that mission. Hopefully, Dominic Rossi was ready to receive his cheery girl-friend with open arms because it was officially game on for me now.

# CHAPTER TWENTY

I rubbed shoulders with practically everyone on the floor of our dorm room. Everyone was ready to get their extra credit, watching us newbie shifters find our ranks and new masters after today's fight challenge.

Because of my new status as the head master's girl, I had mostly judgy and questioning eyes examining me as I tried to stay focused on what lay ahead. I had to stop thinking about the spectacle that Dom had raised by snatching me up as his lady and focus on using that to my advantage. First up? Kick the butt of whoever Scott's best shifter was.

I ditched the muttering crowd of witches, vamps, and fairies when I made it to the pathway that cut along the side of House Braeclaw's main building. It was our private pathway that we took every morning to report to our vast training fields.

Walking out onto the dewy, freshly-cut grass, I noticed that nothing had changed since they set this whole arena up the previous night. All the different groups were sectioned off and doing their usual warm-ups and stretches, prepping for the day. As soon as I arrived at my group, I started with some ballistic stretching to get my wound up nerves and muscles to loosen up.

While I swung my arms across my chest and bounced a little on my feet, I saw all the masters across the way, discussing something. Their eyes were on the groups and clipboards in hand, most likely choosing different match opponents. Even though he was head master of all the shifters now, Dominic seemed to stay humble as our master for the time being. He didn't appear to hold himself higher than the others, he just intently studied each shifter warming up.

I brought my attention back to my crew as they warmed up, and I had to ignore Jessica's absence. She had been my warm-up buddy, and I was not doing well, trying to get her out of my head. The freaking dean was going to be here any second, and I had to have the thoughts of a murdered immortal out of my head.

"Who's ready for Jenna to kick some serious butt today?" Freddie, the coyote shifter, asked. His yellow eyes met mine with a knowing grin. "You know Master Dominic wouldn't have picked you if he didn't think you could take on Scott's strongest shifter."

I shrugged, "We'll see. I have no idea who I'm going up against. After watching the masters fight last night, I learned a couple of things I've been doing wrong."

"Like what?" Julia, the lioness shifter, asked. She had her thick blonde hair braided tightly and out of her way. "Jenna, you're awesome. I have no doubt—"

"Shhh," I smiled and stretched my arm across my chest, pulling my tight muscles. "Don't jinx me," I said with a laugh. "I really am hoping to win this."

"Well, if you win, you don't have to challenge anyone else. You stay under Master Dominic. The loser will have to fight other shifters and work their way back into his group—that's if they go undefeated in each match."

I let out a breath. I did not want to have to battle all day long to stay in Dominic's group to convince him to take me on the master's mission. All of it was a far reach for me. Winning the toughest match of the day, suggesting Dom take me with the masters if I win...that was something I was sure had never been done before. He owed me, though, for going along with his cover-up.

I reached my hands behind my straight legs and gripped the back of my ankles. This stretch was my favorite, and after I saw Dean Edgewater approaching with the professors of each house, I had to drop my thoughts about everything *again* and immediately.

"Alright," Dom's voice broke through the chatters of our group. "Silvers!" he said in Master Dominic fashion.

I rose up and met his commanding gaze with the best flirty smile I could muster up. Bad idea, Dom was in combat mode. I dropped the fake smile and jogged up to him.

"You're up against Seth Waters," he said, writing something on his clipboard. He lifted his dark sunglasses to the top of his head, brown eyes boring through mine. "Have you witnessed him fight while you were in Scott's group?"

"He's a fox shifter," I said. "He's got some tricks, but nothing I can't handle."

"So you're going to take him down? No excuses now."

"And if he manages to get the drop on me?"

Dominic's eyes took on a completely different and highly severe look before his gaze left mine, and he looked at the group. "Everyone, huddle in," he said with an exasperated sigh. "Come on," he demanded in his jerk voice.

"Listen, I'll take the dude."

"Quiet," he barked. "I want all of you to understand one thing, and I'm only going to say this once because I shouldn't be wasting my voice on it at all." He glanced at me and then back to the group giving him full attention. "I thought I trained all of you to have a positive mental outlook on everything. Even if the challenge was frightening, too much, or you felt defeated when we did our practice combats with each other, you were to always believe you'd win, no matter how large, quick, or smart the other opponent is. That's how you win. That's how you defeat your enemy. Going into today's match with an *iffy* frame of mind is not an option. Period." He glared over at me, "I'm sorry that our leading fighter feels she might lose the first fight of the day because she's not confident enough in herself to give me a straight answer."

"You know what?"

"I'm not finished speaking, Silvers," he snapped. "Listen up, if Silvers loses the first match, fine. Let this be your lesson learned from our underconfident shifter: Don't second guess yourself, and know that this day will be your victory. Know that *all* of you will remain under me, not just as your first master, but the head master of all units."

*What a freaking douche bag.*

Dominic making an example of me acting like a chicken shifter only fueled my rage. I instantly transferred that rage into my balled up fists and contained it there. Then, because I was obviously pissed, I took a wordy shot back at the arrogant SOB.

"You know, Jess was a lot like that. She should have been your top choice, but I guess—"

"Jess left the school," he retorted with a glare. "Leave the ones who can't hang at Immortal Academy out of this."

"So you know why she left?" I planted stiff hands on my hips.

"Doesn't matter. Get your head in the game. I swear if a wolf shifter loses to a fox, you'll be the running joke for a while at this school. Don't let that happen, for your sake and for mine."

The *for mine* part wasn't worded as in *our relationship*, he didn't want me to make him look bad in the end. I saw Dean Edgewater intently watching us...*thought change ASAP*. If I didn't have plans for Dominic Rossi later, I would've planned to lose just to make him look weak and dumb now.

Dean Edgewater's thin lips pulled up on one side. Dude was

in my mind, I could feel it. Looks like Jenna is going to make some magic happen today.

"Silvers," Dominic shouted. "For the third time, get in the ring, we're ready to start this."

The look of utter disgust on his face was so freaking annoying. What—was he pissed I didn't praise his holiness last night? Was this our first relationship fight? Give me a damn break.

"Jenna," Freddie pulled on my arm, "You've got this. I have no idea why Master Dominic is acting like this with you, but we all know how he is. He pushes us hard to have confidence."

I shook the coyote shifter off. "I've got it. I answered one of his stupid questions wrong. I'm over it. I just need to beat Seth, and then I'll sit the day out on the sidelines." I smiled at Freddie, "Listen, we're all going to kick some major butt today. As much as I'd rather be in Master Finley's group because I like her fighting style, I want us all to stay together and be the best shifters at this school."

"Besides the quest will be so much fun."

"Silvers," Dominic's voice was now grating on my nerves. I never hated my last name so much until right now. "Over here."

I walked next to Dominic and clamped my mouth shut. The words I had for him wouldn't help me later when I made my request of him for the quest. "You need to lock it up mentally and right now. Fluffy talk about BFFs staying under me as their master and cheerfully going on a grueling quest like we're going sightseeing isn't what I want to hear from any of you."

"Got it," I said.

"Good," he answered. "Now, get to it and get it done. Make that shifter work so you can appreciate a good victory."

"Yes, sir," I said in a subservient student tone, but the truth was, I was mocking the jerk and the only people who really knew that were any of the idiots intruding on my mind right now.

"First up will be the highest scoring and ranked shifter from Master Scott's unit, Seth Waters. He will be challenging Head

Master Dominic's choice for his top shifter, Jenna Silvers," the announcer started as I walked into the arena and sized up the red-haired shifter. The kid was scrawny but agile, sneaky, and quick. Foxes were like that. They weren't built big, but damn they could move and take you down with a cheap shot you never saw coming. I watched Seth's green eyes, and the usual friendly dude had a fierce expression—like a *ready to rip my freaking throat out* expression—on his face. "This is the one and only challenge that the winner will not have to challenge any other shifters. The loser will be forced to challenge Master Finley and Master Ian's top-ranked shifters." The crowd booed because it was stupid. Why would the winner challenge another top shifter? It made zero sense. Scott didn't even win last night. The two top shifters were Ian and Dominic. Shouldn't their top shifters fight and that could determine a single winner? Or more than that, shouldn't each master's top shifter fight each other for the top position? Dumb.

"Alright, let all of your extra credit points begin. Today will be an all-day event. Concessions are open and House Braeclaw thanks all of you for attending our shifter face-off," Professor Samson said.

Now...the fight was on. I couldn't lose. I had too much to gain if I won. Sadly enough, I felt like I had to gain Dominic's freaking trust again. My lame, fake boyfriend, Head Master Dominic.

Well, pressure was the name of my game, so peace out, little fox shifter. No hard feelings, but you're about to go down.

# CHAPTER TWENTY-ONE

In true fox nature, Seth's first shot was a cheap one. We had been in somewhat of a stand-off, pacing in a circle, and we eventually started drawing in closer and closer. As soon as I took a leading step forward, Seth attacked with a misleading punch, giving him the ability to sneak his heel around my straight leg, and he buckled my knee from behind. I regained my balance, but it came at the price of a soft punch to my chin.

The rules went like this: Everything was fair game, even cheap, sneaky fox shots. The only things that could get you penalized for or could possibly end the match were kicks or punches to your opponent that could lead to serious physical injury. It was basically like a soft-touch fight challenge, which was tricky in and of itself because it wasn't natural to hold back any form of strike, jab, or kick. If I injured the dude—which could happen with the current mood I was in—I would be disqualified.

I had this working against me because I was fighting like a total idiot...like I was afraid of the opponent, and if I was honest with myself, I was. I was scared of knocking his butt out, wishing it was Dominic's face I was punching right now. I had to direct my anger into stealthier moves, not powerful combat.

*Damn it.* Another blow to my chin because my brain was elsewhere. *Focus Jenna!* I spun around, ducked, and sent a sweeping leg under Seth's feet. Fox shouldn't have planted both feet at once, that move put him in a crippling fall, but I did what Dominic requested. I let the fox get up instead of using my maneuver to pin him and force him to tap out, allowing me to win the challenge. If I wanted to seem trustworthy to go on quests, I had to prove I had stamina, could follow the rules, and win a long match, pretty much showing off every defense and attack move I had in me.

Seth threw a jab to my face since that was becoming his most successful attack, but this time I dodged it, slid past his lunge, and lightly struck his lower back. Instead of a hard straight arm into his lower back, me succeeding in that soft strike was just the confidence I needed to get through this without being disqualified for injuring Seth.

The match became a fun game at that point. I baited Seth with certain moves to study how he would react to them. I threw some punches and low kicks, observing his defense and counter strike techniques. He was a fox through and through. He moved like one, snuck up on you like one, smiled before he struck— giving himself away—and danced around a lot. This could be easy now because I had his style down and already knew how I'd win this match.

The fox would go down by me tricking him into believing he had the final position to deliver the winning takedown. So as we danced around, pivoted, and ducked each other's punches, I slowly gained more points by beating out his obvious strikes and counters to mine. This dude loved to fight on his feet, so letting him take me to the ground was where I'd beat him.

Fighting on the ground was the most difficult since your opponent could overpower you if you got locked up the wrong way with them. This was something that took me a while to learn, and having had Tan's muscle and larger frame to practice ground fighting with in the past, I'd gotten pretty good at it.

Fox and I had been at it for at least ten minutes, and I could tell we were starting to repeat things. That was boring for spectators and boring for me. The fox was boring, period. They loved to be on their feet and weren't very *creative* when it came to fighting. It was turning into the same old stuff, which made me question how this dude could have been Scott's best.

Time to end the fight.

I locked my back leg out, knowing *Head Master Dom* hated when I did that, and let the fox slide his way in and take me down after putting all my weight on my back leg for the high kick. Seth took the bait, my leg buckled, and I fell to the ground. Seth remained on his feet and sent a foot to my face while my eyes were closed. I heard and felt his back foot dig into the ground— without the help of my wolf, she was still not talking to me—and the wind swooshed behind his heel as it headed toward my face. Freaking foxes and their face strikes.

With my eyes closed, I caught his ankle just before his foot touched me. An attack like this, while I was on the ground, was known as a finish attack. If we were in hard combat, this would've knocked me out, and that's exactly how they scored this attack. Catching the foot before it touched me saved me from losing and threw the fox off. I watched his eyes widen then felt the force behind his foot as he pushed with all his strength to get that last inch, touch my face, and win. Seth's face got red and started shaking, putting everything he had into this and not realizing how vulnerable the rest of his body was.

This was how Dom baited his buddy Ian in last night, except Dom had a sparring stick he was holding off, and I had an angry fox's foot I was holding off. I pulled the foot up and away from my face, rolled, and dragged my outer leg behind his stiff one. Seth fell and crashed so hard I heard something crack. *Not my fault!* Dude set himself up for an injury not being prepared to go to the ground. I felt bad, but I had to get him to tap out and end this. Oddly enough, the crowd got excited again over someone getting hurt. Messed up.

I rolled behind Seth, who was trying to get up, brought an arm under his shoulder, and locked it with my other hand, clutching them together behind his head. He was now in front of me, and I wrapped my legs around his waist, sliding them between his legs and slowly stretching and spreading the fox apart.

"Dude, tap!" I struggled to say.

"No!"

"I've got you pinned. You let me take you in the worst way, you can't get out of this," I said, confused.

"NO!" he tried to claw at me, but I had all his limbs stretched and locked. Any more pressure and I would be disqualified.

"Tap!" I ordered him.

"What are you doing?" Scott's jerk voice screamed out. "The wolf is hurting my shifter. Disqualify her."

"Call it now," Dominic ordered the idiot that was refereeing us. "She's got him down. He can't get out of that move. Scott, tell him to tap before she does hurt him."

"He's still in this."

"Nonsense," I heard Dean Edgewater's voice say smoothly. "He's about to be disqualified for provoking his opponent to injure him."

"Winner. Jenna Silvers, wolf shifter of Head Master Dominic Rossi," the idiot scoring us and watching our every move finally shouted.

I shoved Seth off me. "You're a real jerk, you know that?" I stood up and brushed the grass off me. "Stupid foxes. Predictable and stubborn."

"It's what keeps us on top, wolfy," he snarled, springing to his feet. "I was getting ready to make my final move on you before they called it. You're lucky you have Dominic as your boyfriend, and that's why the dean had your back."

I went to punch the idiot in the face, but my arm was caught. I turned, expecting it to be Dominic, but it was in the icy grips of Dean Edgewater. He smiled, "Don't want to do the wrong thing after finally working so hard to win, now do you?"

It was the way he said it, the stupid fake smile on his face, and the tone that had me thinking behind my smile and fake thank you that the dude was onto me being concerned about his precious little Immortal Academy.

"I've got her. I'll go over some things and then she can join her friends in the stands," Dominic said, nodding to me. "Let's go, Silvers."

I walked by his side silently, eyeing everyone who thought I won this because Dom and the dean were on my side. I was pissed but still thankful I beat the slimy fox shifter. With the mood I was in, I was about to challenge the dude outside the arena and show him that this *wolfy girl* could knock his ass out tonight with no audience.

"You held your own. Great job," Dominic finally said.

"Yeah. It looks like you and the dean won that for me, so thanks for the fake relationship that screwed me over today."

Dominic's lips tightened, and he exhaled. "I'm not going to baby you, Silvers, but I will instruct you that it's wise to accept your victory, knowing personally how you achieved it. To allow opinions of the weaker shifters to rule your attitude is foolish."

"I am done talking about it," I said, knowing he was right, but still pissed he put me on everyone's radar like this.

"I am too. Go find your crew and hang with them. You don't have any more challenges today, but the team still has more competition to finish."

He split after making sure I understood that I needed to continue to support the others on his team. I did, they all deserved to be rewarded for going into challenges today. I needed to get over myself and focus on the real plan...going with the masters on that quest.

Dean Edgewater smiled that eerie smile again, and I shut my thoughts off

immediately.

"Hey kid," the voice belonged to Master Finley as she approached from behind me. "Gotta sec?" she asked after I turned back to her. "Whoa, you are upset, aren't you?" she asked with a smile.

"I won that match fairly. If all of you want to think it was Master Dominic and the dean helping me, then I'm sorry."

"I know you beat that fox fair and square. Pretty tough not punching a sneaky fox in the face, isn't it?"

She smiled. I felt like maybe I finally had someone on my side, but my guard was still up. This was the first time this chick had said one word to me, and I was curious as to why she came after me, leaving her unit in Ian's care. She had a look on her face that was more than just being in solidarity with another girl shifter, there was something behind her smile, her studying me, and her now clapping me on the back and encouraging me to continue walking next to a tree, off and away from everyone.

Maybe this chick knew something about Dominic and his cousin and was going to give me the big reveal? Could I even be that lucky? She definitely had my attention. Even if this girl talk had nothing to do with what I knew about Jessica's murder, at least I could kiss her butt; hopefully, she'd then convince the other masters to take me on my *escape* mission...their quest. This might just be the *real* win I needed today.

# CHAPTER TWENTY-TWO

S he stopped at a stone bench, sat, and patted the empty part next to her for me to join her. Following my secret kiss-butt plan, I joined her with a slight smile.

"So how'd you managed to hold that fox in a choke without being disqualified for him not blacking out?" Master Finley asked.

"Keyword? Disqualified. I'll take him out when no one's watching," I softly laughed. "Dumb foxes will do anything to outsmart their competition, so I wasn't shocked he'd sit there and ride out the chokehold."

"True," she stated factually. "Although, if he were truer to his nature, he would have slowed his vital signs down and acted like you blacked his sneaky butt out."

"And stoop to the level of an opossum shifter? Doubt that." I rubbed my hands over my legs. "Is there something you wanted?"

"Straight to the point kind of girl, huh?" She smiled, lighting up her rosy face. "I like you better already."

"I didn't mean that to come off rudely," I quickly recovered. "I'm just wondering why you left your group to talk to me?"

"I'm curious as to why Dom has taken an interest in you, and you seem to hate him. It's all bizarre, and people are watching you both."

I held in my exasperated sigh. "I don't hate Master Dominic, he's just an alpha, and it's obvious my inner wolf is a beta wolf who allows his command to follow him."

I had no idea why I'd just said that, but it definitely felt like my inner wolf was now speaking on my behalf. Naturally, this crap would happen because I'd let my guard down with my wolf while I was kissing Master Finley's butt.

She laughed in response and shook her head. "You're lying to me. I don't appreciate being insulted."

I heard her command voice come out instantly, but I wasn't backing down. "I don't know why anyone cares what goes on between Dom and me …and I'm not lying. He just has that effect over me and my wolf."

"I could see him having that effect over your wolf, but I also can see how you behave a little differently than any other shifter I've ever met. Your wolf is your most dominant force, but I sense more than that."

Now, I was confused.

"What the hell does that mean?"

She smiled, her eyes narrowing at me. "You curse like it's accepted at this school. A beta wolf—especially one under the command of a powerful alpha—would not bend or break the rules. She would stay true to her alpha's command. Dom wouldn't allow himself to be aligned with a female shifter who was," her lips tightened, "let's just say, *out of line* when it came to following rules."

"I don't know what you want me to say. Master Dominic has never given me an alpha command not to cuss. Sorry I let the word *hell* slip out."

"You are feisty."

I met her questioning eyes head on. "Listen, if you have a

point for this conversation, I really need you to get to it. I'm pretty sure you're not here just for chit chat."

"I'm trying to figure you out is all," she answered more sternly. "Not just the fact that Dom singled you out, but also why you seem to have your own alpha personality. You can try and say you don't, but I sense it in you. Your wolf can't be controlled, so either you've got more going on than a regular shifter or something else is up. Two alphas would never be attracted to each other, yet Dominic Rossi is with a shifter who displays alpha traits. It makes no sense."

I stood, "It's probably best you ask *Dominic Rossi* what he sees in me then because I was just as shocked as anyone else at this school that he plucked me out of the crowd, and the next thing I know..." I stopped, closed my eyes, and forced myself to say it. "The next thing I know, the one dude here I find irresistible is now my guy."

"Yeah, Dom won't whisper a word about relationships or his personal life to anyone. Even when we were in a quite serious relationship our senior year at Broken Bend Academy, he never allowed me in enough to catch a glimpse of that wolf he hides deep inside."

She had my attention now. "You two dated? Is this some jealous ex-girlfriend conversation?"

"I'm the one who moved on from him if that helps answer your question."

"Not really."

"Listen," she finally stood and eyed me, "I know Dominic well. I finally gave up on him after learning his heart was more involved with advancing here at Immortal Academy. He trained me while we were a couple, and I saw some of his skill in your fighting today. I also see how you're doing things with him that I was never able to achieve."

"Like what? I'm just a wolf shifter, no more no less. It's not like we're getting married tomorrow. He may dump me today, in a week, or a month. Who knows?"

"And that's what makes this even more of a mystery to all of us."

"All of *us*?" I urged.

"Don't worry about it. I kind of have a feeling why Dom would single you out. You're unique. There is more to you, and if you want to keep your secret safe, that's fine." She crossed her arms and smiled, "Just understand that if I'm picking up on it, others at this school will too."

"Well, you're picking up on something I have no idea about. I also know that Dom brought more attention to me than I wanted. It's BS, but I guess it's the price you pay when you're with a guy like that."

"It is. Trust me, you can handle the jealous queens at this school, but you won't be able to handle the others who might see you as a threat." She became more serious, "It's probably smart if you keep your free, wolf spirit low until your three years is up at this school."

*Is she part of this murder crap too?*

"Or else what? What! Immortals can't be killed, so I think I'm safe."

"Why would you suggest such a ridiculous theory?" she laughed. "I'm just warning you of the ones kept in the dark rooms underground, chained up, and starved to supernatural desiccation. That's where you'll end up, kiddo."

"Then I'll heed your advice."

"It's probably the best advice I could offer you." She clapped me on the shoulder, "Good luck with Dom, and no, I'm not the jealous ex-girlfriend. I just know that Dom has no intentions of being with anyone until he selfishly gets what he wants. Don't want your heart broken by thinking he would actually want you. There's a reason for the game he's playing."

"Well, when he's done with his games and ready for *true love,* I'm sure he'll find his way back to your arms."

"No," she laughed. "That ship has long sailed."

She walked off, leaving me to think about how bizarrely that conversation went and how weird she was to have it with me. I was more confused about everything now, and especially on her picking up on more than me being a shifter. Why, because I wasn't the perfect little humble beta wolf?

I had to make a note to punch Dom in his face once I got him alone too. He literally set me up to be watched by this stupid school, masters, and staff. Now, if this chick was right, I could be a threat and possibly thrown to starve and live a life in the dungeons?

Finley acted like she knew more than she was letting on, but after she thought I'd be thrown into the pits of this school, it showed that she was possibly on the fairy crack too. She was just as delusional as everyone else here, or she did know about the fact immortals have died at this school, and Jess was one of them?

I rubbed my forehead, feeling a headache nagging at me. I was exhausted. I wanted to scream at everyone to get the hell out of here, but I couldn't. My temper was the number one reason for my bad decisions, and I could sense my anger was trying to run my plans. I wanted to feel normal again. I wanted to laugh and joke with my friends like I did before coming to this place of horrors.

Elite Academy my ass. This was a school that had a lot more to it. It was something dark, and I didn't know who it was or why this was happening. Good grief, couldn't we just have a standard three years here, move on with our supernatural lives, and be done with school?

No, I was at the school that seemed to breed nightmares for fun, but I wasn't giving up for Jess's sake and for my friends' sake. I felt like I was their only hope.

A strong feeling slammed into my chest, sucking the wind out of me instantly. This school would take them too. This school would take me. This wasn't an ordinary school at all. It felt like we were all here to be harvested, not schooled to live with humans.

I had to get on that mission. Damn it. I had to kiss Dom's ass and get this done. I wasn't stopping until I was out of here.

# CHAPTER TWENTY-THREE

I sat numbly next to my overzealous friends, their personalities completely changed now. I didn't want to act like this, but the truth was, I didn't belong around these people. Tanner was acting like he was on something while feeding berries one-by-one to Emma, and Vannah was nonstop, high-pitched squealing while slapping her boyfriend Nick's hand away from her knee.

"Stop it," she said in a daring voice. "Not in here." She kept it at a low whisper, but being a wolf shifter, I heard it like it was in her regular voice.

I honestly didn't care that they were both over the top *in love* with their fairy friends, but this wasn't like either of them. It was making my skin crawl, and I knew it had something to do with this school casting them all under some spell. A spell I was obviously immune to.

"How ya doing?" Dominic asked, placing his food tray down in front of me. "You did well today."

"Didn't she? OMG!" Vannah said, prompting me to gag down the piece of steak I had shoved into my mouth.

I looked at her like she was one of Dom's groupies. Vannah

never talked like that...*OMG?* When did that term make its way into Miss Grammar Police's vocabulary?

Dom smiled at her and started cutting into his steak as all the masters filtered in around him and joined us at the table. New girls graced us with their annoying presence, and part of me wondered if they were under the same spell as my friends.

My eyes were drawn to Finley, who sat at Dom's left. She carefully slid her knife across her steak and ate it like it was a delicacy. She's the one who noticed something was different about me. Actually, Dom seemed to be the very first to notice the first time I didn't follow his alpha command.

Even if I had alpha blood in me, I already had a peek at his wolf, and that wolf was more alpha than I could ever dream of being. I should have heard his commands like a siren in my head, but instead, I heard nothing. I did nothing after he tried to pull more alpha moves on me, where I should have done whatever he said like a robot being controlled by someone.

Now, it seemed the school of terrors had no effect on me with this weird spell it had all my friends under. Freaking weird.

"Jenna?" Dom questioned. "You seem upset."

"She should have heard you the first time, Dom," Finley said, studying me now. "He just used an alpha tone. Odd how you didn't hear that."

I glanced at her. "I heard it," I answered. "I was just..."

Crap, I had nothing.

"I didn't use an alpha tone on my girl. That is rude, and you know it," Dom said to Finley as he bailed my butt out. He winked at me and went back to his food, giving me a break.

"That's strange because I felt the alpha call out," she said.

"No, you just hear what you want," Dom defended me again. "Eat your lunch before I really do pull an alpha command on you," he teased her with a smile.

"I'm getting some pie," I said, standing up.

"Oh, man, I forgot you would want that," Tanner said.

"You forgot?" I looked at my friend, his arm draped over Emma's shoulder. "Well, I guess true love would do that to someone."

I wasn't about to alert Dom and Co. to the weird mannerisms I was noticing with my friends who were on Immortal Academy crack right now. I didn't want to bring any unneeded attention to anyone at this point.

I let the aromas from the dessert area soothe my nerves like a tranquilizer. It felt like my favorite comfort food had been withheld from me for months, that's how bad I needed the two slices of fresh apple pie I snatched up.

"You should try that with vanilla ice cream, Jenna," Scott, the jerk master, said from behind me.

"And ruin it? Yeah, no," I said, walking out of the dessert room.

I was shocked when I saw Ethan sitting next to where I had been. He was back, but was he normal again?

"Son of a—" I was stopped while I recovered from red nails who decided to go for the grade-school bully tactic and trip me again.

I managed to keep my feet under me, but the pies met the floor with a resounding crash.

"Oops." I turned back to see the panther bitch covering her smile. "Sorry."

I went to scrape up the pies, but Dom was already there and beat me to it. He rose up and pinched his lips together. "I'll grab some more," he said nicely.

"I've got it." I took the slop of pies Dom had plated.

Dom looked over at the girls who silenced themselves, and their red cheeks were brighter than this chick's stupid painted nails. "What are you, four years old?" Dom said to Kat, the one chick who had it out for me since this whole fake Dom affair began. "You know you make yourselves all look more ridiculous when you bully up on someone, right?"

"I was stretching my leg. Kicking her friend Tanner's butt today really—"

I went to smear my pie slop in her snobby face, but Dom cut her off.

"Since you're still in my group," he narrowed his eyes in Master Dominic form at her, "It looks like you'll be doing push-ups and physical training while we're all in our animal forms. I won't tolerate any form of bully behavior. In fact, I think I'll have a talk with Headmaster Samson and Dean Edgewater and get you transferred to Finley's unit. It takes more than just skill to be on the head master's unit."

"What?" She placed her hand over her heart, "Seriously, it was an accident."

"You're off my unit. Lying doesn't help." Dom looked at me, "I'll get you some more."

Dom disappeared into the dessert room. I started to leave with my two smashed up pies, but the chick had to take another dig.

"Must be nice to have the hottest, strongest, and now Head Master on your side. I knew that's how you'd pop out number one today," she shot off.

I wanted to punch her in her perfect face, I was that freaking mad. Instead, I opted for the less hostile option and dumped my busted up pies over the salad she was eating. "You should probably eat more than a salad." I shook off the last of the plastered pie over her food, "You eat like a damn rabbit shifter."

"Cursing?" she glared at me, and her closed lips pulled up in one corner. "I wonder if your boyfriend will hold you back with me now. You know, cursing is not accepted at this school."

"Listen, *bitch*," I pressed both hands on the table, "A lot of things aren't accepted at this school. I would think bullying would be a stronger offense than a curse word here and there."

"Oh, please," her annoyed friend said. "You feel bullied up on, precious Jenna?"

"No," I smiled at her pissed off expression. "My pies were victims today because your friend can't keep her emotions under control. Trust me, at this point there's honestly nothing you could do to make me feel bullied. You just succeeded in pissing me off, and now I have to go before I act on my anger and am forced back to do PT today instead of letting my wolf run."

"Let's go, babe," Dom said a little too loud from behind me.

I walked toward my table and slid next to Ethan, forcing a smile to Dom for snagging some more pie to replace the others.

"Thanks." I smiled at him, then took the needed bite. My taste buds were singing praises for the oversized piece of pie I crammed into my mouth.

"Dang, you do love your pie," Dom said, smiling down at me.

"Always has," Tanner met my eyes with his stoned-out ones. "You're a great guy to take care of her like this."

"Tan!" I snapped, mouth half full. "Please?" I swallowed, "We're not like you and your fairy girl. Keep the mushy wedding day stuff to yourself."

"I'm headed off to have a talk with the dean and Samson about the incident. I don't mess around when it comes to stuff like what Kat did," he said in a low voice before he looked at Finley. "I want her on your unit starting tomorrow. Make her work for her skill."

"Never a problem. You know me, I love the troubled ones."

"The troubled one is in love with your ex," I advised her, only to get a questioning stare from Dom as he sauntered away with his usual stature of perfection.

"Even better," she smiled warmly at me. "I saw what she did. No call for it. She'll earn her status the hard way with me."

"I really don't care," I answered.

"That's the thing," she crossed her arms and stared into my eyes, "You say you don't care, but I find people who use that phrase really do care. It bothered you."

"Fine." I swallowed another bite of pie. "I was upset she took her problems with me out on my pie."

Finley stood up. "Very funny," she mused.

I looked over at Vannah who was utterly oblivious to anything going on around her but Nick. This was just bizarre.

"I have to get out of here and on the masters' quest," I whispered to myself.

"The only way out is death," Ethan startled me with his obscure response.

I looked over at my friend who I knew in my heart had to be innocent of what I felt he was part of. "What does that mean?"

"You are noticed. Don't go on the quest," he stated.

"Ethan, what do you know?" I whispered in urgency to him. "Let me help you."

"I don't need help." His matter of fact voice returned. Then his stark blue eyes met mine. "You do. You won't escape. Death is the only way out."

"Immortals don't die," I said, remembering his chant from the night he shifted in the dorm hall.

His eyes never left mine when he recited the same cryptic words he used when he was spun out and shifted. "Immortals do die. Immortals will die."

I felt my stomach cinch into knots. What the heck. This school had a hold on my friends, stoning them out on something. Now, it had an innocent, sweet owl as its victim—doing its freaking bidding. I had no idea why Dom and I were still pretending to be an item, that was the next explanation I needed. If Dom was onto this crap too, then we could work together.

Did I trust my fake boyfriend enough to bring up what I thought this place was doing? I mean, we were in a fake relationship and Dom was playing the loving man part well. Crap, dude was probably on the fairy dust too.

# CHAPTER TWENTY-FOUR

It seemed as though weeks had flown by, and yet, I had little recollection of them. I didn't know if something was happening to me at this place, but try as I might, I couldn't fill in the blanks of my memories. Days blurred as fast as vampires' rapid movements, and I didn't know what to make of it. All I knew was that it was making me more and more suspicious of this place.

Lusa had returned from whatever quest the vamps had been sent on, and no matter how hard I tried, I couldn't for the life of me remember the day she returned or her telling me anything about it. One thing I did know was that her state of mind seemed completely different than it had before she left. Something was off.

The small talk we shared previously was over, and overall, she seemed annoyed with me. Even after a month of this charade of the Dom and Jenna showmance, she still wasn't a fan of it. In fact, she was actually a bit hateful toward me for thinking I could *distract* her brother from his goal of becoming the ultimate Master Shifter.

"Lusa." I stopped her from her usual morning routine of

throwing me a half-smile, chin nod, then vamping in a blur out the door. "I need to talk to you about Dom and me," I said, standing up, boot laces still untied.

"You need to finish getting ready," she flatly returned. Crap, even her beautiful irises were zoned out.

"Lusa. Come on. This wasn't my idea. Dom asked me to…" I stopped myself, I couldn't trust Lusa in this Immortal Academy drugged-up state.

"Asked you to what, Jenna? You're holding him back. How can you not see that?"

"I get you're his sister, and you care about him, but I'm not doing anything to hold him back. Where are you getting this stupid idea from?"

"He's not the same. Something changed from the moment I left for my blood-thirst quest until I walked back onto this campus."

"Where'd you guys go anyway?"

"You already know I'm not allowed to share that information with a first-year student."

"Fine. I'm getting nowhere with you again. Just know that I would never do anything to hold Dominic back."

"Whatever you say."

And just like that, I got nowhere with my dorm mate who seemed to have grown to despise me. This freaking sucked. I went out, did my training, went through all my classes, and as usual, the day vamp-sped by and the next thing I was doing was getting ready to shift into my wolf form.

I pranced out to where Dominic waited in his huge, black wolf form for the last of his shifter unit to join him. Tanner had replaced Kat after Dom kicked her out of the unit for tripping me and murdering my precious slices of pie. Even Tan was more messed up than the day he was feeding berries to Emma like newlyweds at their wedding reception. This place managed to get progressively weirder.

Dom was the most massive wolf on campus. The sight of his wolf made mine cower, but she still claimed him like that strong freaking wolf was hers. Unfortunately for her, she was up for a heartbreak pretty soon because I was done playing Dom's games. Who knew, I probably tried to dump him and question him a million times about why we were doing this crap, but hell if I remembered doing it. The black holes of memory loss were obvious and annoying.

Dom took us on a punishing run with challenging cliffs to leap, long trees to balance on over rushing rivers, and steep, slick rock faces to climb. The feline shifters and foxes loved this challenge. They were so agile and steady with their paw pads that they usually soared past the rest of us while we struggled to keep our momentum to make it up the rock faces without sliding down and failing the obstacle courses.

Dom, however, wasn't beaten by anything. His wolf seemed to thrive the harder the challenge. Today, I forced my wolf to stay on his flanks. I had to prove myself. In the month of blur, I did recall asking him to take me on the quest they were leaving on in a week, and his answer was the obvious *no*. So with that in mind, I let that drive me. I had to get out of here.

Dom lunged up and up like he was on a flat surface while leading up the face of a smooth, wet rock. I was on his flanks and could swear my wolf was going to kill me for this later—if I could walk. Dom was more fierce today than he'd ever been, and I was shocked I was right there alongside him. I could faintly hear the others behind us. They should have been closer, especially the feline shifters, but this seemed to be a personal challenge between Dom and me now.

Once we hit the end of the course, Dom trotted us all back to the changing rooms.

I stood under the hot shower longer than usual and was the last one to be dressed and presentable to leave the rooms.

Now, it was free time. Free to do what? Study the things I

couldn't remember learning in my classes? Hang with my friends who seemed to forget my freaking name now? I was lost and confused, to say the least.

I walked out of the dressing area, numb and pissed.

"Gotta minute?" Dom's voice was flooded with authority.

"Who knows? I probably won't remember anything you're going to say, so shoot!"

"Follow me," he ordered.

"I'm not going anywhere with you," I said, thinking he was hauling me off to do this school's dirty work. Maybe my time was finally up.

He turned back, and his wolf eyes were staring sternly at me. "Trust me."

"No," I said, challenging his authority. "I don't trust you. I don't know what the hell is going on. Your freaking wolf eyes haven't even shifted back to normal. You gonna take me to Ethan and have me killed?"

Dom's hand was on the bend of my arm, and he was stomping away, dragging me as I protested his hostility the entire way. His biceps, the size of my freaking head, had more power than tiny little me, but I wasn't going down without a fight.

"Quit fighting me," he said, looking back at me like I was crazy. "I'm not going to hurt you. Just shut up, and quit causing a scene."

I relaxed some when I felt my wolf begging me to go with him on this. "Fine," I jerked my arm out of his firm grip. "Just tell me what you want and why we're out here."

He led me to an area I had never seen at the far east end of the back of the vast school lawns. *Freaking fairy trees.* He stopped and turned back to me, his hand now gripping the back of his neck while his eyes focused on the blossoms covering the ground. Oddly enough, the painted rainbow bark of the trees and the sprinkled flowers blanketing the ground like moss covering rocks weren't glittery as if a fairy had created them. Not even illuminating either. The moon was our only source of light, and it reflected the silver that surrounded Dom's brown wolf irises. His eyes met mine with sorrow, but they were still stern. He blinked, exhaled, and when his eyes met mine again, they were the brilliant copper brown I was used to seeing.

"Tell me what the hell this is all about. Why am I out here, is this how they killed Jess?"

His forehead crinkled as his thick black eyebrows pulled together. "What are you talking about? She left this school. Her parents demanded that she come home."

"You're delusional. I saw her corpse!" I said.

Then I covered my mouth. *Crap!* "They can hear us. Why are you baiting me for them to have reason to take me out?"

"No one can hear you. These trees aren't enchanted like the trees the fairies and witches have touched with their magic and dust. They're eucalyptus trees, rainbow eucalyptus to be exact. The school kept the human trees and left the magic away from them since its opening centuries ago. It's the only place no one can use their talents to get into your mind. We shouldn't even be able to feel our wolves in us right now, but I do.

My wolf pranced around as if to say, *I'm here too.* Freaking wolf!

"You feel your supernatural self, don't you?" he asked. "You feel your wolf."

"How would you know that?" I asked.

"Because I feel her—my wolf acknowledges her presence," he said slowly.

"Okay, fine. We're special. We feel our wolves around the rainbow trees. Why did you bring me out here?"

"I had to talk to you—warn you," he said.

"About?"

"You're being watched, and it's partly my fault." He sighed. "At the time, I did it to protect my cousin. I had to keep their eyes off him. Ethan won't let it go about immortals dying at this place, and his interest in *you* is validating what we're all picking up on."

"And that is?"

"There's more to you than your wolf shifting abilities. Jenna, this school will lock you in the dungeons. We'll never see it coming until it was announced you violated a school policy or whatever excuse they will come up with. I couldn't live with myself if that were to happen. I was already drawn to you, wolf-wise, and so I trusted you could help play along with protecting Ethan while not being hurt that the relationship was fake. That only took their eyes off E and put them on you. I've made you a target, I'm so sorry."

"How do we fix it then?" I asked through gritted teeth.

"I need you to stop pushing your wolf as hard as you are. Stop asking questions about the school. Now that they've all bought us as a couple, just follow my alpha commands like a normal beta wolf."

"I am following your stupid alpha commands."

"Really?" he sighed.

"Yeah, I sense it like the rest do."

"Start pushing, now!" he ordered me in the Master Dominic command.

"What?" I said, not liking his abrupt change of mood.

"See, there you have it. I toss out an alpha command at you—one I would use against another alpha—and it goes right over your head."

"Damn it." I rubbed my forehead.

"Please, you have to find a way to trust me and work on this. I have to get their eyes off you."

"You know what. Since starting this school, I've officially lost my two best friends, gained a hate fanbase for all the girls who seem to be in love with you, your sister can't stand me anymore, and now you want me to trust the one person who has put me in a position to be locked away for eternity? Screw you, asshole!"

Dom threw me up against the tree, and my wolf loved the dangerous alpha who was nagging at him to shift into her lover wolf. He wasn't hateful or hurtful, he was exuding his power, and my wolf loved the closeness of the power she felt coming off the wolf in him.

"You have no idea who I am, Jenna Silvers," he said, eyes locked on mine, woodsy aroma complementing what female shifters loved in a male alpha. "I do not want you hurt. I'm not that jerk your wild imagination has made me out to be. Ethan needed my protection. You seemed to adore my cousin, and I found that extremely admirable of you since most tend to run the other way in fear of the wisdom coming off an owl shifter. You didn't. You embraced his nature, and no one has ever done that before. My wolf sensed more, but I ignored the wolf and went with how you seemed to care for my cousin. I figured if I could ask you, you would have said yes to going along with getting the school to stop watching him. He's unlike any owl shifter they've encountered. He's rare, and they don't want anything out of place here at this school. I could sense Ethan was in danger the night he shifted. I had to do what I could to help him. I figured you would be fine with that once I got a chance to tell you about it."

"Fine," I conceded, my wolf going insane at the thought her fated wolf was opening up to us. "Show me your true wolf if you want me to start trusting you. For all I know, you're on the crazy cocktail of loving this school too."

"What? My mate is the only one who's getting a look at my wolf." He looked at me like I was insane. He smirked as his eyes darted back and forth intently studying mine. "I see. You think we are wolf mates?"

"I don't think anything like that, and if you're picking up on my wolf, then stop. She and I haven't agreed on a lot of things lately. Mainly you and your dumb motives."

"Hold very still," he said, his lips close to mine.

I ducked away from the kiss of death. Screw that. He was able to get in and see my wolf, but I couldn't see his? Lame.

"No more," I said. "No more games. We show the school you dumped me, since that story is believable, and then to repay me, you insist I go on the mission with the masters."

"Absolutely not," he answered.

"You have my ass in a vulnerable position. The best you can do to make this up to me is get me the hell out of here for a couple of weeks when you four leave."

"If you fail any of the obstacles on this quest, you're instantly teleported back to the school, and a grade is docked from your shifter finals. It won't work. You won't survive the mission."

"Screw you."

"Stop being so stubborn. You will fail, at least on the first obstacle. The fairies and their tricks are all over these quests. The witches have spelled anything and everything against us. I might not even succeed."

"You're not being honest with me." I was shocked that came out of nowhere. I had no idea why I even said it.

"What about? You will get whacked and teleported back to the school. You won't make it. That's as honest as it gets."

"Everything. You know more than you're saying," I insisted, wondering if my wolf was speaking for me again.

"Maybe I do. Maybe you should just listen to me and stay here where you're safer. You go on this quest, then they'll have their way with you when you get transported back to the school."

"I'm willing to take my chances."

He smiled and shook his head. "You are something else, you know that? You're right, I owe you for helping me with E. I'll get you on the mission, but if I have to break you out of those dungeons and risk getting thrown into one myself, then you owe me your immortal life for that." He laughed, and I was shocked when he took my hand in his. "Under different circumstances, maybe my wolf would be drawn to you. You said you wanted to see him?"

"Yes." My heart picked up, knowing his mood had shifted.

He brought his hands around my waist and drew me in. With our bodies molded together, he let his forehead rest against mine. "Here."

I felt immense power, unstoppable energy, a wolf that should have never been tamed, yet it was created to run a pack of his own. I felt loyalty I had never known could exist in someone. It was an excellent explanation for why he was trying to protect me now, and for what he did for Ethan. Most of all, I felt confusion and, oddly enough, fear toward me.

His wolf didn't like what it sensed off of me because it couldn't harness whatever it was I carried outside of my own wolf. I felt his wolf drawn to mine, but I couldn't determine if it was drawn to my wolf's power or the mystery of her. His wolf definitely liked that my wolf was *madly in love* with his, but out of self-preservation, it restrained itself from the attraction I was sensing both these wolves felt for each other.

It wasn't happening, though. His wolf would never entirely give my wolf what she needed and wanted from him...his love and devotion. My wolf needed to understand that Dominic's wolf was not her true mate, but maybe it was her protector. I was turning nineteen in two weeks, most shifters would never sense a mate until they were at least nineteen or twenty.

Dominic pulled away, leaving me breathless. "There. I think you have all you need to trust me now."

"Then I'm on the mission."

"I'll get you on it, but you better stay with me and not fall behind. This won't end up being a search and rescue, got it? There's a reason the masters test these things before we lead a quest of students."

"And we're broken up now too?"

"A great reason for me to take you to the trees where they can't hear our thoughts or lurk with an invisible spell."

"Good. When do we leave for the mission?"

"Next week. Now, think of something sad and start crying. Lusa would be more likely to believe our story if you played up some tears about it."

"You mean for her to believe we actually *had* a relationship and broke up."

"Yeah," he oddly stammered.

"Why doesn't she know you did that to protect E? He's her cousin too. She loves him as much as you do. That would've made my life a hell of a lot easier."

His expression went blank. "Come on, let's get back. You need to study, and they're going to question if we were out secretly mating."

"Answer me," I urged. "Why didn't you tell her?"

"She wouldn't have let me use you like that."

He said it, but I knew that's not how he felt. I also knew that Lusa would have at least played along and been more apologetic than he was.

"She's changed since she's been back," I said. "She's acting as crazy as my friends."

"You have no idea what the hell is going on, Jenna. Stop asking the damn questions, or you'll be in the dungeons before we can get on the quest."

"Oh, he cusses."

"You have a way of pulling that out of me."

"Let's go. I'll get my answers my own way."

"For the love of God, stop it! I'll deal with my sister. Vamps trip out after coming off a blood-thirst quest. Leave it alone, for your sake, hers, and mine."

"I'll just focus on the quest then."

"God dang, yes. I asked that the first damn time. Just chill and stop it with the risky questions."

"I'm with you. Time to go through some old books and research."

"I'd focus on your House Mage studies if I were you. Word has it you're about to fail out of that class. You want help?"

"I think you've helped enough. I've got it."

"Alright. Let's get back before questions start floating around, and we really end up as wolf mates...in a friggin dungeon beneath this school."

I followed him out. All that mattered now was that I was getting on this quest for the masters and getting out of here. Freedom and finding help was finally possible. My wolf was crushed, but she'd get over it. He wasn't her true mate. It was all a physical, lustful attraction toward his wolf anyway. Her fault for falling for a wolf without really knowing what that wolf was all about.

# CHAPTER TWENTY-FIVE

Dominic made the break-up dramatic, and everyone seemed to buy it. Thank God! I was relieved to be out of that ridiculous spotlight, but it came at a different price now. It wasn't the rigorous drills Dom practically ran me into the ground with—I knew that was on his agenda given that I had demanded to go on the quest—but it was how much the others loved him seemingly *picking* on me.

Now, here I was, sitting alone—again—in the library, studying the foiled pages of the fairy realms. My head was killing me, and my immature and depressed wolf wouldn't lend me her eyes to cancel out the brilliantly colorful words of the book. She would most likely be the reason I would fail the quest and couldn't bust out of this joint. She wasn't the nagging issue though. Since Dom and I broke off our fake relationship, my stoned-out friends were officially no longer my friends. I tried my hardest to fit in with them and look like I was drinking the fairy juice they were on, but no matter how hard I tried, my friends—my best friends who I missed so much—wanted nothing to do with me anymore.

It was weird and heartbreaking all at once. Literally overnight, it went from Tanner hand-feeding Emma and Vannah giggling like an immature little school girl to them blatantly ignoring my presence while I sat with them at lunch. I couldn't fix it, none of it. I wanted to blame their love interests, but I knew those fairies well enough. Nick and Emma weren't doing this to them. It was this damn school.

Without my fake boyfriend, all I had now was my Ethan who sat next to me at lunch and interacted with his quick, hard, and cryptic facts. I couldn't take this anymore, and I still had five more days until I got to break out of here and go on the Master's Quest.

I had come to the point where I couldn't nail down what was the most frustrating, losing my friends or the fact that I wished Dom and I were still in our fake relationship just so I had someone to talk to at lunch. At this point, I'd talk about anything. Fairy stones lighting up on the way to House Fae, I was down for that. The weather, why the heck not? Unfortunately for me, it wasn't only the simple conversation that I felt I wanted from Dominic. More than once, I caught myself staring over at him with the other masters, the chicks who made sure they sat at his table, and whoever else was with Dom and Co. at lunch.

I had to continually put myself in check, especially when I was fixated on him. His smile, his commanding yet fun personality that seemed to humor everyone who sat around him.

I had no idea why, but I longed to be close to him and in his presence since the night he took me out to the eucalyptus trees. Was it because he showed me more of a glimpse of his wolf? I had no idea.

I watched Ethan get up from the table he sat alone at. I would have joined him, but Ethan always made it known he didn't want company while studying in the library. I glanced at the clock. Twenty minutes before lights out. I followed a gut instinct that came from nowhere and shut the fairy book I had barely read a sentence from.

"Ethan," I said in a soft voice, knowing the owl in him would startle, being that he was still processing whatever he'd studied. Owls were like that. You never snuck up on one.

He had just reached the last step of the library when I called his name, and he stopped. His head craned up to where I stepped lightly down toward him on the path that led out to the front lawns of the school.

"Yes, Jenna," he answered with a partial smile. "I am going to my dorm."

"Wanna take a detour?" I smiled at his pleasant demeanor.

"I don't understand. Detour. I will walk my usual path to the dorm. Everyone knows they—"

I hesitantly and slowly linked my arm into his. He stood tall like Dom, but he was skinnier and not as robust in his build. "I know, I know. I just wanted to take a walk with you. It seems like you're my only friend at the school these days."

"Not true." He glanced at my hand in the bend of his elbow. I waited for him to alert me to not touch him, but instead, his soft blue eyes met mine. "Your friends are here, you're the reason you can't reach them anymore."

"Wow, that was pretty harsh."

"It is the truth."

"And that's why I love owls. Nothing but facts and truth spewing from your mouths," I teased. "Come on, let's walk."

He conceded with a stiff nod. "We have eighteen minutes, I cannot be late for bed."

"I know, and I can't be either."

"No, you can't."

"Come on, my favorite owl," I said as I encouraged him onto the path that led to the trees where no supernatural could hear us.

"Why the silent trees?" Ethan asked as we approached the rainbow bark of the eucalyptus forest.

"Silent trees? Why do you call them that?"

"They aren't like the other trees that have been spelled by

witches and enchanted by fairies at this school. Leaving these trees was an oversight the school never believed students would take advantage of. The other trees listen and inform the administration of student behaviors."

"Oh, so the trees are the tattle-tale bastards of this place, huh?" I covered my mouth, "Sorry. Didn't mean to cuss."

"You use your strong, unnecessary language too much. You can make better points without profanity."

"I know. You're right. I'm working on all of that."

"Why are we at the silent trees?" he pressed.

"Ethan, I saw something. Something that you've stated to me about immortals dying at this school. I need to know if you had anything to do with it."

Ethan broke free of my friendly hold on his arm. "I know what I need to know. I also know that you don't need answers to that. You already know I would not harm anyone."

Thank God. "Yeah, I know that. Why is this school killing immortals? How is that possible?"

"I can't answer these questions. Please don't put these questions in my mind."

Being desperate, I ignored Ethan's warning. "Ethan, immortals don't die, but you said they do. Did you see Jess? I saw her."

"Immortals will die." He started fidgeting and chanting, and that's all it took for me to know I'd freaking blown it.

"Ethan, please, calm down. It's okay."

"You're not safe. Immortals will die."

His feet stomped hard into the ground, and he paced harshly back and forth. *Crap!* He was going to shift, and Dom was going to kill me for this. All his efforts to keep his cousin safe, and I ruined it by trying to get info from the one person I believed knew what I knew.

"Ethan. Please. Calm down. It's okay. I'm following the rules. Please," I pleaded with his frantic spirit.

"You are not safe. House Silvers was not safe."

What the hell did *that* mean? I was so dumbstruck by what he'd proclaimed that I couldn't say another word to stop him from shifting. He burst into a glorious Great Gray Owl, blasting me with strong winds as he climbed the air with his wings to the top of one of the trees. That shouldn't have happened. Including Dom and me, Ethan made the third supernatural who could use their talents around these trees. Dom made it seem like he and I were unique by feeling our wolves while being around the trees that somehow diffused supernatural magic.

I was glad he was safe up there and not flying away, but we had fifteen minutes before lights out. I was about to bite the bullet and go get Dom, but he was already racing up to us, his expression black with anger.

"Why?" he growled at me. "What the hell are you doing?"

"I just had some questions."

He looked up to where Ethan was perched on a high branch. "Jenna, I told you to stop with the questions about everything! How hard is that to follow? Why Ethan? Why would you use him to answer questions that I told you needed to stay unanswered."

"Because my life depends on it, and you know it."

"Now, his life is in danger. I can't protect both of you at once. Damn it, Jenna."

"I didn't do this on purpose." I felt my eyes pool with tears of frustration and regret. "I tried to stop him."

"I have to get him back. Go! The last thing I need is for Dean Edgewater to find us out here and see Ethan has not only shifted during non-shifting hours but also that he's shifted under the trees that should mute that ability."

As soon as I started to leave, I saw the large owl soar out toward the forest of glittering purple blooms of the wisteria trees. This was not good.

A huge wolf thundered past me, and before I could shut my wolf down, I went into protective mode and shifted too. Officially, I had just screwed all of us. I knew better. *Damn it.* I dug my paws into the hard soil, and my wolf followed the trail Dom's wolf was making through dense bushes. We were a mile into this dense forest of glitter when Ethan landed on the ground. The wolf dropped his head and stalked toward the owl. A whimper came out of the wolf as it went into a submissive pose, lying down, snout resting over his front legs stretched out before him.

Ethan's owl blinked a few times, then I could sense his natural form returning. I turned to leave when I realized my unexpected shift had destroyed the clothes I was wearing. I had no idea how to get back to my dorms naked and evident to everyone I had just shifted back from my wolf. It was either walk the halls naked or prance my wolf right in. Neither of those options was acceptable.

While walking back to the dorms in wolf form, I was met by Dominic's wolf. He was pissed, and I was screwed. The wolf snarled at me as if I were its longtime enemy. I dropped my head and crept forward, challenging Dom's wolf further. Oddly, I wasn't afraid of the wolf like any wolf shifter would have been.

I bared my teeth at the exact time he did, but not being as trained and fierce as his wolf, I was stopped and taken down. I was pinned, and in natural submissive behavior, I cowered under the wolf's massive paw. He brought his snout to my neck, letting me know he could rip my throat out faster than my heart could take another beat. My wolf took over at this point, and I let her. Never in my wolf shifting life—training or tests—had I been in this position before. I knew I was the weaker of the two, and Dom was the dominant one.

In typical wolf form, Dom continued to sniff my neck until my wolf conceded to the submissive position we were in. My wolf licked his snout, his neck, and along his face—tail tucked and all. This was worse than kissing someone's butt, this was full submission and allowing Dom to be my dominate wolf. My tail was tucked, and legs curled as my wolf continued to give Dom her power. The only reason I didn't fight this off was that I knew I was wrong to shift, and now Dominic had to risk his own butt in shifter form—another rule broken because of me. I was about to owe this dude my life because I lost it and shifted out of guilt for what I did to Ethan.

That guilt only made things worse for the three of us now. Dom rose his head up and looked on, bristled, yet pleased I had submitted to his authority over this matter. He eventually backed off of me, and his silver lined brown wolf irises met mine with some understanding that I wasn't fighting him and making a horrible situation worse. He stepped away, and now I was royally screwed. What did we do now, wait in the freaking forest for a pair of clothes? All of us see each other in our birthday suits and waltz back onto campus for all eyes to take in the naked body of the three who shifted outside of school guidelines?

Hell, I was ready to just prance my stupid butt right into the dungeons and let the jerks have me. I was so confused, and mostly because I gave everything up to Dom right now. I had to follow his lead. He yelped, prompting me to look over at him. Ethan was clothed, and I had no idea what the hell made that possible.

Dom let out a soft growl, and it was an order to follow him through the trees. I did. He led me around a tree stump and through bushes covering the base of it. He eyed me once before nosing the bushes and pushing his head into them.

I came over and sniffed and scented the area. I smelled the cotton of clothes behind the greenery and poked my head through the thick shrubs covering the stump of the tree. It was a den, I could smell the fresh dirt. Dom's wolf nudged my shoulder, and I walked through the bushes. Inside the den was a small cave. Clothes scattered, all Dom's clothes. This must have been where he hid stuff for emergencies.

I shifted back, hearing his wolf outside the den. I pulled on black pants that I had to cinch around my waist, and a black long-sleeved shirt that was lying on a pile of other ones. This was all of Dom's training clothing. Dude was definitely looking out for himself, and this stuff was planted for protecting Ethan. I could tell the clothes hadn't been here long. It all seemed to be an area set up because Dom knew Ethan wouldn't be able to control his shift at times with the strange rules of shifting only once a day at this academy.

Drowning in his clothes, I could smell his fragrance again. He was to be trusted, and I was the one making it worse for him. The loyalty I caught coming off his wolf was riddled through the weaves of his cotton shirt material. His heart was purposed to keep those he loved safe at all costs. My gosh, what did I do? The guy would probably hate me now, and he'd most likely use my submitting to him to discipline me in our training. Not that I didn't deserve it, but it was totally going to suck.

All that mattered was that Dom was saving all three of our butts with this little closet he'd made a den for. I owed him again and again. I mainly owed him an apology for misjudging him. He could have easily left me screwed, and God knows what this school would do to me for shifting like this if I was caught. He didn't, though. Instead of leaving me to fend for myself, he helped me cover up the fact that I shifted.

I crawled out of the den, and his wolf swiftly disappeared into it. "You okay?" I asked Ethan, who was wearing Dom's black clothes too.

"I am fine. We must go back. Dominic will protect you," he stated.

I wasn't going any further in conversation than that. I wasn't risking anything at this point.

Dom came out as quickly as he went into the den. He ruffled his black hair, clearing it of any debris and then turned back to cover up his hidden clothing area.

"Ethan. Head back now. When and if you're asked, you will answer you were looking for Jenna and me. Do you understand me? You must lie."

"I was looking for you and Jenna."

"Who were you looking for?" Dom questioned Ethan, who was acting nervous again. Owls didn't lie. This would be one for shifter history books if Ethan could pull it off. "Ethan. Why were you in the woods past lights out?" Dom urged his pacing cousin.

"I shifted."

"NO!" Dom growled. "Ethan, why were you in the forest? You must protect her. You have to lie, or they will hurt her."

Ethan's eyes fell on me, and he stiffly nodded. "I was looking for Jenna. I was worried about her."

"You keep her in your mind going back. If they find out we all shifted, I can't help anyone anymore. Lock that in your owl mind. You're doing the right thing, E! You're protecting her." He crossed his arms. "Ethan, why were you in the forest?" he asked again.

"I was looking for Jenna. I was worried."

"No hesitation. Hold on to that and get back now."

Ethan ran swiftly out of our location and back to the school yard.

Dom looked back at me. "When we're stopped, you let me do the talking."

"I'm not letting you take the hit for what I did. This is my fault."

"I'm not letting you go down because my cousin can't control a shift when he's agitated. Now, when they ask why Ethan went looking for you, *my* answer will be that I took you off to the woods alone. I wanted to scare you off the masters' quest."

"They're not going to buy into that."

Dominic shocked me when he smiled. "Oh, they'll definitely not buy into that lame story. They'll think I was out here getting a good night kiss from the girl I just got back together with."

"*What?* That game is over."

"You just revived it and raised the stakes. You're lucky the dean is all about his students finding their true mates at this school, or it wouldn't work. Welcome to being my girl again."

I rubbed my forehead, "Will it all ever end?"

"I asked myself that question when I watched you lure my cousin out to the trees to get info from him. It's all I ask myself about you these days, Silvers."

"Something isn't right at this school. How can't you see that?"

"I think you know I know something is up, but I'm not dumb enough to drag everyone around me down as I try and get through these years. You have got to chill, and since your wolf submitted to me," he eyed me, and I sighed...*here we go,* "you're going to follow my lead and at least try and last three full years here. God dang, that's if you can last three more minutes. I swear you're going to ruin me, Silvers."

He finished and silenced me by snatching my hand and resuming the new fake Jenna and Dom relationship status again. This new relationship should really be awesome now—Dom and Jenna out making out in the woods and getting caught. Maybe being starved in the dungeons was the better option for me at this point.

# CHAPTER TWENTY-SIX

Being submitted to Dominic actually seemed to help tame my senses and erratic feeling. It was serving as the grounding force I really needed. I felt it the moment we were approached by Dean Edgewater at the front entrance of our dorm rooms.

Instead of panicking and feeling like I had to jump in and speak for Dom, my mind shut off to the creepy dude, and I let Dom do all the lying. Thank goodness Ethan held to his lie of *looking for me in the woods,* and Dominic took it from there.

Dean Edgewater excused me with his usual half-smile that gave me an internal shiver every time he flashed it, and Dom followed the man back to his office. I would've naturally assumed he might be in danger, but something told me he would be safe, and he could pull this all off.

"So," Lusa smiled at me from her bed, "You and Dom are pretty serious about each other then?"

I looked at her in confusion, "Um, what makes you ask that? Rumors can't possibly spread that quickly. Do you and Dom have a crazy mental twin connection or something?"

There was no way Lusa could have found out that our fake

relationship was back on. It just happened last night, and when I snuck into our dark dorm room, princess vamp Lusa was snoring louder than a bear shifter.

She walked over to me and hugged me, her flowery fragrance filling my senses and calming me. She stepped back and folded her arms, glittery blue vamp eyes staring into mine.

"I'll admit it, in just the short time knowing you and all the years knowing Dom, I never thought it would happen." She laughed.

"What happened? I don't know what you're talking about." Confused was a mild word for how I felt.

"I can sense him in your aura."

"That's a bit trippy for me. Can you keep the witchy phrases out of this, what the heck are you sensing?"

"His wolf calls to yours, and he's allowed his wolf to accept that. Alphas will not do that unless their wolf is certain it's found its true mate."

I wanted to collapse onto my bed. What the heck happened to me after that submissive situation last night?

"Lusa," I licked my now dry lips, "trust me, it's not what you think it is." I studied her eyes, and I could see she was still a bit stoned on whatever this school did to twist up the brains of the supernaturals here.

"It's exactly what I think it is. Dean Edgewater is going to be thrilled to learn that under his leadership at Immortal Academy, two wolves found their true mates. These sorts of things are huge. Shifter mates don't come easy, and when they are found at an academy, it makes the academy look that much better than the others."

*Okay, she's back to worshipping the creep dean and singing his praises. Go with it, Jenna.*

"Yeah, it was crazy how it happened."

"So you do admit it. He's your true mate!"

"You've been pissed about this since you came back from your quest. You know, me holding your brother back and all?"

*Not to mention shifters don't necessarily find their true mates until they reach their maturity and stop aging at twenty-five,* I internally reminded myself.

She giggled—the fairy-juice annoying giggle—and sighed. "You know as well as I do that when shifters find their one true soul, they bond first," she smiled again, "then mate. The bond itself is enough to make you two very powerful, but bringing your wolves together by sealing the bond through mating?" Her cheeks tinted red, "My gosh, with the power Dom has alone with his wolf, you both will be a powerful force. It will be amazing."

Yep, she was on the juice bigtime, and I was done with this mating ritual weird conversation. "Yes, but let's take it one step at a time. Dom and I aren't mating, I hardly know the guy."

"But you trust him. He's already helping you and your wolf right now. Why wouldn't you want that?"

"I don't know, maybe because I'm young and I'm not ready for an intense bond and relationship. Can we just sideline this conversation?"

"You both waiting until you graduate from Immortal Academy for the ceremony then?" She paced the room, "It will be gorgeous. We'll have it at our family's estate. I'll help the designers with the décor. Outside or inside ceremony?"

"Slow it down." I felt a growl erupt from my throat, then sucked in a breath to calm myself down. "Seriously, Lusa, I'm more happy that you're not pissed at me. The sealing of mateship bonding will be something we talk about if I can get through the next three years at this academy. My grades suck, and I'll be lucky if I even get out of here." That was actually true.

"You'll see how your grades will change now." She smirked. "With your wolves joined, he will excel, and so will you. You both will complement each other in ways you never saw coming."

"How do you know this crap? I didn't even know this would happen after I let my wolf submit to him."

"Second year here, Jenna. All the basic learning is in your first year. Between our second year and having a father who is a direct descendant of House Braeclaw, Dom and I both know how it all goes down."

I started feeling anger bubbling up in me. "So Dom knew this would happen after he forced me to submit to him?"

"Dominic didn't force you to do anything." Her eyes were questioning. "Why would you say that? What happened between you two last night?"

"Hell if I know," I said, truthfully. "We kissed." I quickly lied to cover up my confusion of Dom and I somehow forming a bond I wasn't ready for.

"No, it was more than a kiss. What happened?"

I was searching for my next lie, but I had nothing. *Damn you, Dominic Rossi!*

"I submitted to his wolf. That's all."

"Why, though? What would make you and your wild little wolf spirit submit to him?"

"I have no idea. One moment we're kissing, then the next I felt his power…" I felt the bile creeping up in my throat, knowing I was screwed, hating *this* version of the story, and having to speak it all out loud.

"And?" she urged.

"And it was like a drug. I felt his strength and let my wolf take the lead. That's when I knew he was my true alpha, and my wolf was drawn to him."

"That's exactly how it all goes down." She whirled around and laughed. "Dom is a great guy, he'll always be loyal to you and protect you with that power you felt. There isn't a shifter out there who wouldn't be over the moon to have such a fierce wolf as her alpha."

"Yeah. I'm one lucky gal," I choked out.

If Lusa was picking up on this, then every supernatural who sensed these things in shifters were going to pick up on it too—especially the shifters.

*Oh. My. God. Hope it was worth it, Jenna. Now, you have your alpha.*

Screw this, I wasn't a fully submissive wolf to an alpha. Dom may have been a stronger wolf than I was, but I didn't need him alpha-running my show. I didn't need to answer to him for anything or be controlled by him. It wasn't in my nature to be locked down under any alpha. I felt that in my wolf. She was strong, and she didn't need some alpha dude taming her spirit under him. Dom and I had to reverse this thing somehow. I wasn't his to claim, and that's exactly what I let happen last night by submitting to him.

While running our fight drills that morning, I was kicking ass and taking names. *Thanks, Dom!* My steady mindset had me thinking clearly with my fight moves and countering with better maneuvers than I'd ever been taught. Our sprint in normal form had me leading the pack, and not sucking air with burning lungs. Okay, so this part of whatever happened between Dom and me was impressive. I could do this. It's like I took his clear mindset and his physical endurance and was able to function at a higher level than our entire unit. This was awesome.

"See you later, when we all shift. Today we start pushing ourselves to limits. I want you all to pass the quest in two months. No one dies on it. To make that possible, I'm making the morning drills more challenging and afternoon shifter routines will require stealth on your part. Now, get out of here. Nice work today, all of you," Dom said as he dismissed us.

Dude was to be congratulated for not playing favorites with me or even acting like anything happened between us last night. Part of me wondered if there was a way to mute the effect we had on each other because he definitely acted like nothing had taken place. His sister, on the other hand, was most likely recruiting fairies right now to help enchant the final bond ceremony between our two fated wolves.

I turned to leave and was caught by red-nails Kat. "I can't and won't believe you both are true shifter mates."

And so it starts…with this one, no less. "Well, don't lose faith just yet. It was just a kiss. Shifters split up all the time."

"Just a kiss." She rolled her glaring eyes at me. "You are putting off a lot more than *just a kiss* vibes today. Everyone is saying that you and Dominic found your true mateship last night. It's absolutely unbelievable to me. He deserves better."

"Really? How so, you jealous bitch?" I snapped.

Her lips curled up in a smile of bitterness, "Listen to your foul mouth, you can't even follow simple rules at this school. You don't behave like a normal immortal would. You act like a disgusting pig shifter with the way you smack down your sickening pies. Your manners are embarrassing to all shifters, yet you managed to snag the one we all would do anything to be bonded with. I guess his wolf must love bottom feeders."

Without thinking, I clenched my fist, and just as I was about to do what I'd been dreaming about since she tripped me the first time, my fist slammed into Dom's hand, stopping me from breaking her pointy little nose.

"Why?" I growled, meeting his dark expression. "Let me go!" I demanded.

"What's going on here?" Dom questioned me, then looked at Kat's amused expression.

"Well, if I recall correctly, you just stopped Jenna from a major school violation."

"You're a bitch, you know that?" I spat out.

"Jenna, calm down." Dominic used his alpha master voice on me. Ha. Dude didn't have the hold I thought he'd have on me with my submitting to him.

"I'll calm down when Kat takes her BS attitude and gets the hell out of my sight."

"Kat, you're dismissed. I will deal with you later."

"I did nothing more than ask Jenna how it was that she and you could be fated and practically bonded over some lame kiss everyone is talking about."

"What happened between Jenna and me is our business. If she doesn't want to fill you in on all the details, that's her decision, not yours."

"I don't want details, I want answers."

"I said you're dismissed. Get back to your rooms and classes."

Dom's alpha voice submitted her fully, and she scurried off, stomping like a three-year-old who didn't get a piece of candy.

"Can I go?" I looked at him, knowing this was going to be a more lengthy conversation than I wanted.

"I want to talk to you about what's going on. I'd be an idiot if I thought you weren't mad about it."

I planted my hands on my hips and looked into his dark sunglasses. "Yeah, what exactly happened after I let my wolf submit to yours? I mean, I only did that to keep us out of trouble. Why all of a sudden am I picking up on your strength, vibes, and crazy crap like that?"

"You're saying you don't like it?" He smiled.

"Don't play games with me. Tell me what the hell happened."

"Well, to rest your mind at ease, it's not a full attachment." He kept the kind smile on his face. "Obviously, or you wouldn't be throwing curse words around like you wanted to be on cleaning duty for the rest of the week. You're not following my alpha—which you promised you would to stay out of trouble—so there you have it. I'm not your true alpha, you—as complicated as you and your wolf really are—have somehow managed to take on some of my natural instincts like bonded shifters would."

"So, this is all my fault?"

He jerked his sunglasses off. "Yes, in fact, it is. Do I need to remind you about last night and what you did to startle E and make him go into a frenzy worrying about you? Maybe you forgot how all three of us shifted and should be in the dungeons right now."

"Fine, got it."

"Now, thank goodness you have this power of projection because it's helping everyone buy into our story. My punishment from the dean was nothing compared to what it should've been."

My mind went back to Dom selflessly taking the hit for Ethan and me last night, and I felt like crap for acting like this to him. Thanks to Kat pissing me off, I was irritated about everything in the Dom and Jenna showmance again. I had to give Dom some credit here, he was grounding my mental state back to where it should be.

"What did the dean say anyway?" I asked softly. "I'm sorry that happened. I'll keep my attitude in check, I owe you for saving my butt last night."

"Dean Edgewater was ecstatic about one of his strongest shifters bonding so early at his academy, but, of course, he had to bring down a punishment, or everyone would be heading off to the woods to share a romantic kiss—or worse—mate behind a bush or something completely out of line like that."

"That's disgusting," I added.

"Yeah, well, your friends all act the type to go off and do something like that." He smiled and laughed.

"They were nothing like this before getting to this school."

"Stop it with the school stuff, Jenna. I'm dead serious." His eyes were stern when he said the words, and that's when I felt it hit me. He knew something, he just wasn't telling me. "Anyway, he gave Finley my Head Master status, and after we get back from the quest, if you're looking for another *kiss* from me, you can find me on kitchen duty, scrubbing pots in the back."

"Are you kidding me? He pulled you from Head Master Shifter over a stupid kiss?" I practically shouted. "Why didn't he bust me for it too?"

"Because it was my responsibility to make sure you were

back in your dorm rooms and not out enjoying a kiss with the best kisser at this school." He pulled his lips up into some crooked smile I'd never seen before. My heart jumped out of rhythm in response to how sexy he looked with a smile like that. "See, I can see it on your face, you know I'm a great kisser." He laughed.

"Not fair. You can't hit me with some flirty *Dom* smile and think I'll be okay with that."

"Dom smile?" His irises lit up in amusement. "You are too much, Silvers. Sometimes I want to make you do push-ups until your muscles seize up with exhaustion, and sometimes I do just want to kiss you—or slap you on the butt."

"Dude," I looked at him in shock, "take it easy. We didn't kiss. Remember? And I feel horrible you lost the Head Master status."

"It was a slap on the wrist for what it could have been. We're all good now, and the dean is allowing you on the quest so long as Finley approves it." Unexpectedly, he intertwined his fingers with mine, and the showmance parade began. "Finley says it's cool with her, but I still don't understand you wanting on this mission so badly."

"I like challenges," I lied.

"Yeah, I don't believe that for a second. You have motives, I just don't know what they are. You're a puzzle I can't put together, and it drives me insane."

"Good." I smiled over at him. "Well, you ready for a day filled with hate tribes, judgy eyes, and stupid looks from everyone?"

He shook his head, his sexy smile playing on his lips as he walked at my side. "If I actually cared what anyone thought of me, I guess I'd actually be giving them all that power right now with being concerned about their opinions."

"That's a pretty smart way of looking at it."

"I know. If you hadn't noticed yet, I don't give anyone my power. Until last night at least. You and Ethan will probably be the death of me."

"Do you feel it like I do?" I felt my cheeks warm up with the question I was a little embarrassed to ask.

"Feel like you do what?"

"You know, um, the power thing? I'm thinking more clearly, and if you hadn't noticed, my fighting skill has enhanced since I submitted to you last night. It's the stuff everyone is picking up from us," I managed.

"I just feel a soft hand in mine." He glanced at me, then looked out away and off to his right, "Other than that, all I feel is relief that Dean Edgewater bought my story and your wolf managed to send off vibes to everyone to back it up and then some."

"So it's just me then," I answered, more confused.

"Not a bad thing. You kicked butt and looked sharp out there today. You should see it all as a blessing." He hit me with that irresistible smile again.

"You're going to love me having to kiss your butt over all of this, aren't you?"

"Until the day we leave this school, Silvers."

*That's if we all get out of here alive.* Something told me Dom knew what I knew, he just wasn't saying anything. This was a dangerous place, and I knew Dominic knew it too. So, he could blow me off all he wanted when I questioned what he thought about this place, I knew how he really felt...thanks to this crazy little submissive bonding connection we had last night.

All I knew for sure now, was that I was going to give Dom some credit here. I needed this new stealth and power to get the heck out of here while on that quest. I was grateful for that at least, and I was willing to put up with all the broken hearts at school today. It was going to be annoying, because seriously, Dom was a catch, but good grief, these girls treated him like he was a god or something. Whatever. That was their problem. I had four days, and then it was escape time for me to get help for everyone here. I needed to focus on that and be grateful for my newfound strength.

# CHAPTER TWENTY-SEVEN

The day was turning out quite well, whatever connection Dom and I had forged actually helped in my classes too. It's like I'd gained the ability to settle down and focus on my studies instead of focusing on the horrors of this school.

I got to my shifter class and sat in my usual seat, forgetting that our seating assignments had changed at some point. Confused, I looked around and strained my mind to remember when our professor mandated newly-assigned seating.

"Whenever you're ready, Miss Silvers," Professor Samson grumbled.

The class laughed under their breath as I made my way down to an open seat right smack in the middle of the room. I had a shifter snob to my right—Tamara, the lioness from Scott's unit, lover of all things Dominic Rossi—so that was awesome, and an over-zealous sprite with lime green hair sat to my left. At least this chick, Ella, was nice.

"Anything, Silvers?" Professor Samson asked.

"Repeat the question. I'm having a braindead kind of day, I guess."

"Braindead, huh?" he leaned on the podium. "Without embarrassing you, I can't imagine why you would be struggling. An attachment like yours should be enhancing your mind, not killing it." He smirked.

"Excuse me?" I shot back, absolutely mortified that my professor, of all people in this room, would bring up my personal life.

He stepped around the podium and addressed the class. "You all know that it really does take full maturity to form even the slightest connection as a shifter. What Dominic and Jenna have accomplished is something that only happens—well, it never happens. This is a first for Immortal Academy and something that just might be celebrated by the dean. Two shifters finding their bond so young tells us all something." He raised his hand up and turned on the large holographic screen, "Only great family houses—like House Braeclaw—have these abilities. Jenna, you must have descended from a great family."

My heart was racing and not in the way of excitement.

I spoke up while he clicked through pictures of shifters from decades ago, "That's all I've ever wanted to know, actually. It would be nice if someone could tell me anything about my family...my parents."

He turned around to me. "No one has that answer, Miss Silvers. All the administration knows is that a leprechaun from House Fae enrolled you into the supernatural school systems. It would be nice to try and uncover why none of us know your ancestry, though."

At that moment, my wolf's ears lay flat back, and she bared her teeth at his response. What the heck? I wanted to ask my inner wolf why she thought this was going in a direction she didn't like, but then, I got it.

I was a mystery to even him, and now I was being told that my family line just piqued interest with House Braeclaw's professor? This wasn't a good thing, and my wolf knew it.

As much as I wanted the professor to dig, I backed off and quickly changed the subject. The last thing I wanted was to be under a microscope, yet here I was, front and center...the star of the freaking show.

"Meh," I threw my hands up, smiled, but quickly cringed at evil, yellow eyes sitting to my right and looked back at the professor, "As unusual as it all is, I've heard of shifters forming these bonds before they reach maturity. It usually doesn't work out well for either one of them in the end."

Professor Samson killed the holographic image and did a casual side lean on his podium. "Really?" he questioned my lie. "Can you give the class an example of this wealth of knowledge you have that I'm not privy to?"

*Crap!* Lies upon lies. "Sure, one of my former classmates. It was their uncle's best friend's cousin who was a, um, I think he was some bear shifter. The bear bonded early, kind of like Master Dominic and me, and from what we all were told since it was outside of the usual laws of bonding for shifters, it worked against them. They broke it off right after they graduated from their academy."

I swallowed hard while Professor Samson eyed me, clicking his fingers one-by-one. "Do you remember this uncle's best friend's cousin bear shifter's name? Because I'm sure Immortal Academy would have had them in their attendance."

"Not sure and not really sure they were full blood immortals either. Just remember the story."

*Oh my God, Jenna, you are digging yourself into a grave right now.*

"Interesting."

"Is there something else we can talk about besides this? I'm bored," some guy shouted from the seats above and behind me.

"This is a unique situation. All of Immortal Academy is celebrating this coming from the school. First of its kind to happen."

I needed this class to be over. My stomach was uneasy and mine and Dominic's plan to save all three of our butts last night had backfired on us entirely. Instead of ducking the audience of this school, we gained a celebrity couple status.

As if this class couldn't be more complicated, Dominic walked in with the other three master shifters. I heard the lioness sigh next to me, and I got it. I just stole her guy off the market. How many shifter chicks were seriously this infatuated with him? Why of *all* the guys I would end up in some stupid spotlight relationship with did it have to be the dude *every* shifter chick wanted? Why couldn't it just be some regular, fun dude that no one cared about but me?

"If it's not the man of the hour." Professor Samuel leaned out and glanced over at Dominic, whose lips twitched in a smile to be respectful to his Headmaster.

Dom eyed me with a questioning look, then pulled his hands behind his back and stood at attention like the rest of the shifters. "We were just talking about how unique your and Jenna's bond is, and how it all worked out. You're what, twenty-one now, Rossi?"

"Yes, sir," he said mechanically.

"So intense." The room was silent, a smile played on Finley's mouth while Scott looked down, trying not to explode into laughter. Ian, thank goodness, also managed to keep himself contained. "Anyway," Samson sighed, and I swear the entire room let out a breath at the same time. "The masters are here to fill you in on what's to be expected while they're on their quest. They have documentation of the previous quest Master Dominic took at the beginning of this school year and wish to show you all what exactly these quests consist of. Rossi, go ahead and begin your video presentation."

My head fell back against my high-back theater seat when the lights dimmed to show us the quest presentation. It felt like I had just come off of some adrenalin high as my tense muscles unwound from being flexed. I watched the screen and video through a camera Dominic wore on his head while going on this survival quest.

The video changed to the cameras of the other shifters who were with him that had graduated the year prior. They had chosen a Hidden Elements Quest, so this one revolved around beating the different kinds of fairies at their own game. It actually looked fun up until the fire part. For the first time in my life, I feared an element of the fae, and I couldn't understand why. I cringed, felt my breaths shorten, and tears started streaming out of my eyes while I watched the shifters have to fight their way out of the fire as it consumed everything around them.

I had seen fire before, I'd freaking roasted marshmallows over a fire, watched someone cook me a dutch apple pie on a fire, so why the hell was I in complete panic mode over this fire that was eating its way through the forest? What the hell was wrong with me!

I stood up and rushed out of the back of the class. I ran to the ladies' room, cupped water into my hands, and splashed it on my face.

*"Get them out, Nikolas. Now!"* I heard a terrified woman's voice scream in my head.

*"Baby, stay with me. I'll be back,"* a deep male voice responded.

*"I love you all!"*

I looked up in the mirror, and my irises had the same silver as Dom's did when he used his alpha eyes on me. What the hell was happening? I gripped my head and had to escape the bathroom. I heard voices, I had Dom's silver alpha-wolf eyes.

I slammed into the hard chest of the one and only Dominic. His arms steadied me as I tried to escape him but couldn't. "Please, I have to get out of here."

"You're not going anywhere, what's wrong with you?" he pulled me back, and his eyes widened at the sight of mine. "Jenna, what happened?"

"I don't know. One second I have a panic attack in fear of fire from your quest, the next second, I hear terrified voices in my head. What did that bonding thing do to us last night?" I looked up at him, tears streaming down my cheeks.

He pulled me in for a tight hug, and I felt him rest his chin on my head that tucked neatly into his neck. "It's going to be okay. I don't understand how your eyes are in full-blown alpha attack mode right now, though."

I rested my cheek against his chest, letting the gentle rhythm of his heartbeat soothe my own. I let out a breath and collapsed into him, needing his strength to hold me up. "I can't explain any of this. Am I losing my mind? Even the professor said what happened between you and me, it doesn't happen…but it did."

"You need to relax a little." He continued to rub my back, "I don't know why it happened this way with us either. We just have to deal with it together."

I pulled back and looked up into his sympathetic eyes, and for the first time, I saw a different person in Dominic Rossi. I sensed a caring and loyal man, not a jerk or some punk at the school. I saw someone I think I'd totally misjudged. Maybe my wolf was right the entire time, and my stubborn, judgy self got him all wrong.

He smiled—making this revelation worse—and touched his thumb under my eye. "Back to your normal eyes again." He smirked. "We have enough crazy eyes on us already, we don't need them all asking about my alpha wolf bonding with another alpha wolf because *that* really does not happen in any sense of the shifter world."

"What's going on with me?" I asked him.

"Could the pie-loving gal I've grown a little attached to be falling for her one true mate?" he wiggled his eyebrows in humor.

I reached up and touched his face. The velvety soft stubble highlighted his strong jawline and gave a perfect definition to his cheekbones. He was perfect, but more than that, his lame joke just reminded me of my friendship with Tanner. God, I missed that guy, but it was nice to be around someone just as goofy as him even for a fraction of a second.

"You okay?" he became serious again.

"I miss my friends," I finally admitted to him.

"I bet you do." His voice was low as he caught my hand and pulled it off his face. "I'm not them, though. Don't do that to yourself."

I looked past him, knowing he was right. Then my head snapped back up, "You know, don't you? You know what's going on."

Dominic's eyes widened, and he glanced around us. "I do. It's crazy what happened to us. You will miss your friends because of our early bond."

"Damn you, Dominic!" I shouted. "Just when I was cool with it all too."

"Jenna!" he growled as I shot past him.

I was sick of this place, and I had to leave now. I wanted my friends back. I wanted this weird bond thing to go away, and most of all, I wanted to say every cuss word and then some just to piss this school off. I had to get my friends back and at least get us out of here.

I ran through the halls and was stopped when I darted out to House Braeclaw's lawns and ran directly into Dean Edgewater's creepy long frame. My thoughts cleared, and I felt sick. Like barfy sick. I mentally conjured up the emotion and then chucked it all up, sending a present right onto the creepy dean's suit.

"Good grief, Jenna," he said, repulsed by my butt-saving barf idea. "Dominic, get one of her classmates to bring her to the nurse. She needs to be evaluated. One might think you've mated, and that's why we're all sensing this bond."

"Are you effing kidding me?" I said, insulted. "Of course that didn't happen between us. You think I'm pregnant, you sick piece of—"

"I've got her. She's having a hard time taking on some of my strong alpha traits is all. She means no offense to you with her foul mouth or regurgitation. I did push my students hard this morning," Dom said, clamping his hand down on the back of my neck, stopping my mouth from sending me straight to the dungeons.

"You're right, and you have Dominic to thank for that too, Miss Silvers. This accident, your profanity, and your disrespect will be forgiven only once before you do end up doing some time and learning some hard lessons."

"Let's go, Jenna." Dominic's voice was severe, and I needed a freaking break. Seriously.

"I can't believe that jerk thought you and I actually *mated* last night." I glared back at the man who was acting like I ruined a million-dollar suit.

"Well, you are acting wildly crazy right now." Dominic looked at me, half annoyed. "Sheesh, calm the hell down, or we're done. Why did you barf all over the dean of all people at this school?"

"I had to come up with something. I thought that was my best excuse to get away from him."

"Stop being afraid of that guy. He reads into you better through fear, it's like he feeds on it," Dominic said under his breath. "This quest can't come fast enough for you, and I'm making sure you feel it on this too. You need to work out some crazy frustration right now. You're starting to make me nervous, and I don't get nervous."

"I need pie," I said, walking straight ahead and turning to head back to my dorms.

"I'll sneak you some pie. You're in Mistress Sirena's class next, right?"

"How the heck are you going to get your hands on a piece of pie?" I questioned.

"I have my connections," he shrugged with amusement.

I smiled. If this dude were willing to break the rules to get me some pie, I'd have to admit that he was a keeper. That offer was definitely the way to my heart.

# CHAPTER TWENTY-EIGHT

The day dragged on at the pace of a sloth, and I felt I was literally going to lose my mind. Dominic and I tried to douse the spotlight on us by acting busy with other things—that was easier for Dom than me. While he was off with the masters and forming the quest objectives, I was stuck sitting next to my *friends* who only acknowledged me if they accidentally bumped into me or looked over at me.

I was reminded of the emotions I used to pick up on at Dark Water Academy. Those were gone completely, and it was most likely because I wasn't on the same crazy juice as everyone else here. My wolf was pretty much my only companion at this point, but I wasn't going to get sent to the insane fairy assylum if someone caught me sitting here alone talking to her.

It was best I didn't talk anyway. I had four days until the quest. Edgewater told Dom he was looking forward to seeing how I did after this early bond thing between us. Score one point for me submitting to his wolf last night, other than that, the school was a walking nightmare for me.

"Quit tapping your fingers on the table!" Vannah said across from me while I was forcing myself to make the colors of the fae book black and white so I could read.

I glanced up at her, thinking she was back to old Vannah and giving me a hard time. My smile was met with an annoyed expression from her and her blue-haired fairy boy. "Sorry, trying to focus."

"It's annoying, Jenna."

"I'm sorry. Maybe if you were your normal self, you'd actually help me study instead of getting all pissed off with the way I study."

"Let's go, Nick. She's rude."

I stood up, "You know what, I'll leave. This grade-school BS is beyond my limits right now. I can't do this anymore."

"It's on *you*, Jenna. You're the reason it's all turning out this way. Remember that!" she snapped while her glittery-skinned, elf boy glared at me.

*Nice. Now, it's official. No friends, period. I hate this freaking place,* I thought, walking out of the library because I was in desperate need of fresh air. That chick in there was not Vannah. Not even on my worst day of acting like an annoying complainer was that Vannah. God, I missed her so much. What did this school do to her?

I walked around the back of the building and saw another body bag. The same one I saw that night I came upon Jess's body out behind the Ageless Ball. I slammed my body against the wall when I saw the bag thrown onto the ground by two men in dark clothes. The older, gruff voices from that night were back and handling whoever was in that body bag.

Once they walked back into the back of the dark building hidden in ivy leaves, I used large bushes as my cover to go find out who this school just took out. I was stopped halfway there when the voices returned. I spread my hands quietly through the ferns I hid behind and saw another bag being carried out.

*Holy shit! How many did they kill?*

The two men who had shadow-black faces with no definition to them—like freaking demon dudes—took back off into the buildings. My heart was slamming inside my chest, but I had to know who was in the bags. Once their voices faded off into the distance, I continued forward. I had plenty of cover so I could do this.

I reached body bag number one, uncovered the face, and my eyes widened when I saw who it was. My heart leapt into my throat when my mouth was covered by a firm hand. I was pulled into a sturdy chest, and two lips were at my ear.

"Quiet," Dom's low voice was barely audible. "Shhh." He worked to calm my heart that was hammering out of control while dragging me back and away from what I'd just discovered.

My eyes were filled with tears of fear and shock as Dom worked to get us both out of the danger zone.

"Follow me," he said, his eyes mysterious and silver-lined with his wolf guiding our way back to safety.

Once we were out in front of the closest building, the library, I stared at him with horror. "That was red nails—Kat! Wait, what were you doing out here? Oh my God, they killed her!"

Dom's hand covered my mouth, his eyes returning to his usual bronze ones. "You have to calm down, Jenna," he ordered in the alpha tone that never worked on me.

I shook my head, protesting and wanting to scream in fear. I had to knock it off, or we were as good as dead too. I started breathing slowly through my nostrils, holding Dom's hands that covered my mouth. I closed my eyes, feeling a tear slip down my cheek as my panicked state started to subside. I reopened them, and the brilliance of Dom's amber-brown eyes and the comforting expression of patience he held for me steadied me.

"That's it," he nodded, his eyes intently focused on mine. "Just keep breathing like that. I'm going to remove my hand, but you can't say a word until we get down to the eucalyptus trees. Got me?"

I nodded, and Dominic brushed his thumb over my wet cheek where my tears had slipped out one by one.

"I need you to focus, Silvers. They can't find you like this," he said softly.

I nodded and kept focused on his eyes. I started to feel more depth in them, comfort, and security. It was strange how it was washing over me, but I wouldn't dare fight it.

Dom's hand slowly slipped away from covering my mouth, but I kept my hands tight around his. I felt him readjust my clammy palms and cover both of my hands in his strong ones. "Still with me?" he whispered.

"Yes," I stammered. "Let's go."

Dom turned, keeping one of my hands in his, and we both went into stealth mode. We rushed off to the eastern part of the school, walked through thick brush, and made a new trail out to the rainbow eucalyptus trees.

Once we were deeper into the trees than he'd brought me the first time, Dom stopped. He walked ahead of where I stood, staring blankly at him. I watched him brace himself by leaning over, his hands gripping just above his knees, breathing slowly.

"Jenna, you can't breathe a word of this to anyone," he said, staring at the flowery ground in front of him. "You can't even think the thought. Have the fear. Nothing." He rose up and looked at me. "Lives depend on both of us being able to keep our mouths shut."

"Why?" was all I could manage to squeak out. I finally had someone to talk this out with, and *why* was the only freaking thing I could say?

"I don't know. I have my suspicions, but I don't know," he said, looking up into the rainbow bark of the trees. "What I do know is we have to stay quiet until I can figure this shit out."

"How many more will die before that happens? I saw whatever those things were. They had no face, all black like that shadow thing in my room that one night."

Dom's lips tightened. "It's a dark force that's working for someone at this school. I just don't know who or why."

"How long have you known? Did you know about Jess too?"

He looked at me in confusion. "Jess left..." he rubbed his forehead. "Ah, dammit. All I was told was she left the school, I swear it."

"I saw her," I choked out. "The night of the Ageless Ball. I saw her in the bag like I saw Kat."

Dom's hand slipped to the back of his neck, and he tilted his head to the side, studying me. "This school is determined that you and I merge our wolfs," he said in shock. "Jess and I had something of a moment, so to speak, and the dean saw it. We weren't getting together, but I think he thought that. God, it was just a stupid kiss, flirting leading to dumb things. I never had feelings for her, I think they killed her for that reason. It makes sense."

"How the hell does that make sense? So what if you and Jess got together? Why would they want to kill her for it? And Kat? The other body, did you see who that was? God, if you're getting chicks killed at this school—"

"No!" he shout-whispered at me. "Jess was a kiss, it was nothing more, but Kat? She wouldn't shut up about how much she hated you. How much she hated *us* being somewhat bonded like we are. She begged me to use my wolf and break our bond. It was the most insane conversation I'd ever had. I don't remember the name of the fairy who was with her, but she offered to toss in some fairy magic to make my wolf reject yours."

"Are you freaking kidding me?" I seethed. "What the hell?"

"Yeah, I thought the same thing when they approached me. Edgewater saw it and probably heard it. Ethan felt the hatred toward you and warned me to stay away from Kat and her friends."

"So Ethan is in on this?"

"God, no!" he let out a breath of frustration. "Somehow, Ethan is protecting you, and now me, from whatever in the hell is going on. Ethan picks up on things quickly, and he told me Kat will die if I don't stop her from hating you." He planted his hands on his hips. "It all sounded strange and harmless. E has a tendency to overreact, but he's in hyperdrive lately since meeting you and arriving at this academy. I should've been listening to him and following his lead. Instead, I worried over him too much. I still have to. He's in just as much danger if he loses it again. God, I hope he doesn't sense their death. He tripped out the night you saw Jess. I had to have Lusa compel him to calm him down. It worked, but every time something sparks up here, he flips. That's when I came across you and the bodies tonight. I was looking for him after he started mumbling under his breath. I thought I had him calmed down until he took off practically screaming *your* name."

"Can Lusa help him again? God, Dominic, no one else can die…and because of us? I'm so damn confused right now."

"One thing at a time. No, Lusa is lost to this school. She's under its spell. She's been different since coming back from the blood thirst quest. I can't even talk to my sister."

"Ethan. They can't hurt him. We can't let them hurt him."

"I know," he growled. "I have to think this out. Right now, you're the only one who this school hasn't affected. You and me. We're alone and in this together, Jenna. You have to focus on one thing right now."

"And that is?"

"Play the game. Let me take care of Ethan. I'm going to suggest to the dean that he let me take E on the masters' quest, but I have to keep him quiet until we leave." His eyes were somber when they met mine. "*You* have to keep it all under control until we leave. Can you do that? I can't help Ethan if I'm trying to keep you safe too."

"I don't need your protection. I've got this. I just want the hell out of this place."

"Play the game, Jenna," he ordered in the tone that didn't work on me, but my wolf practically nodded in response and saluted him too.

"Okay. Play the damn game. What game are we playing again?"

"You need to act every day like nothing is wrong. You keep your thoughts shut down, and let me try to figure out how we're all going to get through the next three years alive."

"You and Lusa are out of here in two years," I reminded him of his freedom.

"Looks like I'm coming back as a professor," he said with certainty. "I'm not leaving my cousin and you here. The rest of the students need help too."

"I don't get it. This is happening because the creepy dean wants you and me together? Stupidest thing I've ever heard."

"It's just an assumption. The dean was too excited about us having that connection. The dean must see something in both of us. Something that has him offing immortals at this school."

"Good God. I'm not okay with this crap."

"Doesn't matter. What matters is that we get on this mission and get you and Ethan away from the school. I will feel safe if E is with us and away from the school."

"How are they killing them?" I asked.

"No clue."

"Lusa mentioned Ethan's parents were owl shifters, both poached and killed. Since Ethan is an immortal, I'm assuming they were too. Immortals don't die, Dominic. So what the hell killed them, and what is killing the kids at this school?"

"Million dollar question, Jenna." He sighed. "Listen. We can sit out here all day and throw our theories around, it's solving nothing. Let's focus on one thing at a time. I need to keep Ethan calm, and you need to keep quiet and play along like everything is normal. Can you do that?"

"Well, since I lost my friends tonight, I'm going to have a bit of trouble."

"You're with me. You're my girl. I don't want you with your friends. I want you to myself." He looked at me like he was trying to impress on me what to say and do like he did Ethan the night we all shifted. "You following me?"

"Possessive, dominant boyfriend that I would never be cool with? This should be easy." I rubbed my forehead, feeling a massive tension headache coming on.

"Jenna, you have to do this. They'll buy that trash of a relationship. Your friends won't care."

"Fine." I stepped back, my head killing me now. "I'll do it."

"If we're going to keep everyone safe, you have to do it."

"We have to get on that mission," I said, getting ready to reveal my escape plan to him. I went to speak, but I was up against the tree, Dominic's lips tensely pressing against mine. His hands came up on my sides, and he pulled me into his body.

My nerves relaxed, my body reacted in a quick, violent shiver. Without thinking, I reached up to frame his face and urge him for more of this kiss that muted my sudden headache. I felt more secure, connected, and grounded than I had ever felt in my life. This was an overwhelming sensation that made me feel like we were connecting on an even higher level. I craved more from him, but the stubborn guy wouldn't give it to me.

I was floating in this strange kiss and in the euphoria that my inner wolf was experiencing right now. Good grief, what was he doing to me?

"You two," a cackle came from the creep's mouth. "Save it for later. Now, come on."

Dominic stepped back, and I watched his fierce expression soften before turning to Dean Edgewater. "Does this mean we're on dish duty?"

Dean Edgewater walked up to Dom, placed a hand on his shoulder, and looked at me with a smile. "I'll leave it at a warning between us three for now since no one in the school saw you two run off to these trees but for me." He grinned, his teeth reminding me of a predator, not the fake nice dude he was trying to play off right now. "As much as I enjoy watching the power of you two develop at my school, you're going to have to take it slower, or I might be forced to keep Jenna back from the mission." He arched an eyebrow playfully at Dominic. "Maybe I'll send Ethan on the trip to watch over his cousin. I know if that owl shifter picks up on you getting out of line like you did with Jess," he laughed wickedly, and it made me nauseated, "then he'll definitely come back and report you being out of line with my special little wolf shifter here."

"Yeah, I'm the one at fault. Dom tries to act like he's the one," my voice was shaky under the snake eyes of this creep, but I kept it cool, "but come on, I just can't resist him."

"Yeah, it's upsetting quite a few shifters here. Two more were sent out of the school tonight. Their parents opted to pull them out after we told them what their ultimatum would be if they continued to conspire against you two."

"What?" Dom frowned. "People have a problem with Jenna and me?"

Dean Edgewater fell for it, "Yes and rightfully so. Dominic, you are the strongest shifter here, and that lures shifters and all supernaturals to want to unite with you. Some stronger than others. Sadly, those who crave the mateship with you and have learned they can't have it? Well, they resort to extremes to get that. In Kat's case, using Abigail, the pixie, was a poor decision." He looked at me. "The plans they had to help steal your alpha away were not good. So we called their families, told them it was a violation of this school's policy to seek harm to another. They were either to be sent to the dungeons, or their parents could take them out. See, we're not all that bad here, it's not straight to the dungeons." He grinned. "Well, not if I'm having a good day."

"Thanks. I can't imagine what they would have caused if I lost my alpha mate."

"You're not mated yet, young one. That day is to come, and I'll be the first to say Immortal Academy will be even more esteemed above all academies when this reaches the elite supernatural councils." He laughed like this was all his doing, while I wanted to punch him in the face. "Ah," he exhaled, "Anyway, back to the school grounds for the both of you. It's nice seeing your relationship blossom."

"Isn't it?" I plastered on the best smile I could and reached for Dominic's hand. "Time to go."

We left in a rush. I had to focus like Dom asked. On the quest, I would find a way to tell him about my plans to get the hell out of this place and hopefully find someone to help us wipe out whatever or whoever was behind these deaths.

# CHAPTER TWENTY-NINE

The next three days were spent with Dom and Co., and it wasn't bad at all. The weird connection Dom and I formed —the connection that Dean Edgewater seemed to be killing immortals over—actually helped me sleep at night when my mind should have been reeling with fear, wondering if one of those shadow people were coming for me next.

I also felt his strength powering up my wolf, and she, in turn, was also helping keep my mind clear of the atrocities I'd witnessed at this forsaken school. Dom did pretty good with keeping Ethan chilled out too. I felt horrible knowing now that I'd jumped to the conclusion that Ethan was being used to kill immortals. I knew better—my wolf knew better—because owls never went near the darkness, they warned and protected innocents from it. Ethan was rare, though. He was an enigma."

I was ready to get out, get help, and most of all, get away from Dean Edgewater's cheeky, freakish smile that seemed to be lurking around every corner. Dude had his eyes on us more than Dom's fan club, and if only they could all control their hormones, they might live to see tomorrow.

"Hey, babe," Dom's voice chimed in a flirty tone as I hopped down the steps with a backpack filled with my clothes to change in after I'd shifted. Luckily, the bag had unique straps for my wolf form to carry on her back, so I didn't need to worry about how to get to it when I was in wolf form, it would still be with me. It wasn't the easiest maneuver to get the pack on while I was in wolf form, but my wolf managed to pull it off.

"You have to say that every time you see me?" I asked.

"It's sort of growing on me." He smiled and snatched my hand in his.

I had to admit, it was growing on me too, but I'd never tell another living soul. No random kisses were going down unless we felt the dean's scrutinizing gaze on us, or we needed to calm Ethan down. Those kisses were growing on me too, and it was a bit uncomfortable for me, reacting like I was a star-struck, Dom groupie.

There was something in these two simple, tight-lipped kisses that got my insides going nuts. I was sensing his protection, loyalty, and honor that he kept hidden away from all of us. His wolf was yet to make an appearance, but I think that's only because this was nothing more than Dom and Jenna trying to survive the school and Dom and Jenna turning into the saviors of this place.

I didn't ask for any of this crap, but innocent supernatural lives were at stake here, and now it was somehow tied to Dom and me. I really wanted to know who the heck my parents were to have given me some gene that would make sparks fly between House Braeclaw's golden son and me.

"Where's your mind at?" Dom asked after close to five minutes of silence while I felt his warm hand covering mine.

I squeezed his hand, sent a smile his way, and picked up my dragging pace. "Right where it needs to be, ready for the quest."

"Alright, you've gone through some strenuous exercises, and you performed pretty well. You need to keep your stamina going, though. This first part is not in shifter form. We'll probably lose the weakest out of the bunch. I've got Ethan calmed and collected, he's staying here in case you get transported back. I need his owl eyes on you if you get teleported back to the school for failing an obstacle."

I stopped and looked at him, "No. No way. You can't put him in the grips of the people—"

He covered my mouth with a finger. "Shh," he glanced around. "I know what I'm doing. Ethan is fine, if he weren't, he'd be going with us."

"I won't fail," I said through gritted teeth.

"Jenna, the mission is designed to force you to fail. Even me. It's the whole point of it. The big glaring lesson? Learning from your mistakes in the real world."

"That's the lamest thing I've ever heard."

"I know, but that's the quest we're on. If we survive it, then awesome. If not, Ethan is going to be back at the school for us."

"Lusa?" I said. "Can she help him while we're gone?"

"Lusa's too vamped out, she's useless."

"Same with my friends. Is there even a way to stop this?"

"If it isn't my two favorite kids," Dean Edgewater's cunning voice interrupted us.

"Ready to leave in about three minutes. Is there something you need?" Dom's voice was colder than it had ever been toward the dean.

"Nope." He slipped his hands into his usual black, billion-dollar slacks. "Just making sure the masters are all ready for the quest. Sorta wondering who's going to get axed first on the quest and sent back to us." He grinned.

"Axed? As in *killed?*" I asked the dean while Dom squeezed my hand to tell me to stop pushing the man.

"Yes, Jenna, killed. Master Dominic explained the rules of the quest, didn't he?"

"Yes," I giggled and hated the sound of that coming out of me. "I'm joking, goofy. Kinda hard to die if you're immortal."

"Exactly, right. Now, get on your way, and I'll be looking forward to hearing about all your scoring and how you did. I'm sending Brenda out, she'll be my eyes on the quest. She's a great hawk shifter," he said and turned to leave.

"Damn it," I said under my breath. "How do we get rid of the hawk chick?"

Dom looked at me and smiled, "Get them on the ground in their natural form and teleported back."

"You've done this before?"

"I hate the hawk shifters. They're arrogant idiots who think they're worth something because of their sight. The ones at this school are the worst, they practically live in a damn birdcage in the dean's mansion."

I laughed, "True. I haven't seen a Brenda yet or met one."

"Oh, she's here, you'll recognize her when you see her. She's rude to Ethan. She and I already have gotten off on the wrong foot, so that's going to make tossing her down a canyon that much easier for me."

"Sheesh, sort of violent, don't you think?"

"No one feels their death on the quest. In fact, she'll shift into her bird form on the fall, maybe I'll throw her butt into the campfire," he laughed. "Relax, we'll get her out of earshot. Finley will go soon after her. If you're still around, then Scott is usually the next to go, and Ian after that. Then we can talk out how we plan to take the school back and figure out what's going on."

"If I slip up and get teleported back?"

"Then I'll be pissed I just lost my partner, but you'll have to see what I planned out there when I get back and be ready to move to action with whatever I do."

"That sucks. It won't work. We need to plan together. Besides, I have something of my own that I think we should do."

"Well, if we're going to do this, then treat this quest like your life *really does* depend on it and don't die. Then we'll plan and figure it all out. They set the timing for the quests for two weeks.

After that, if we're not back, they come looking for us. Let's get to it and get this thing going."

I nodded, too bad in two weeks they'll be looking in the human world for us. I was definitely sticking with that plan. Plan A. If Dom didn't agree, he was insane. He was crazy to think that he and I could do this just the two of us. And no, mating to gain strength by merging the power of our two wolves was not an option. This fake relationship was already starting to do crazy things to my mind, so I wasn't about to go down the *committed to each other for life* road.

# CHAPTER THIRTY

We sprinted through the forest, leaping over fallen trees and bushes. It was energizing to get farther and farther into the dense trees, but I could still feel the grim atmosphere of the academy looming in the distance behind us.

Dom let Finley take the lead, being that she was appointed new Head Master of our shifter units. I was behind her, Dom was behind me, and Scott and Ian paced alongside each other. We followed Finley's lead in slowing our jog once we reached a shimmering golden rope bridge.

"Alright, we're getting close to the real deal," she said, turning back to us as we caught our breath.

"When will these fairies ever learn that highlighting their part of the quest and obstacles to take us out is a dumb idea," Scott said, peering over the cliff that the bridge spanned across.

"Don't get too cocky, Scott," Finley smirked. "Fairies set things up, and you never know when their element will take you down."

"I think it was the fairy that got you the last time!" Dominic laughed, only to get a playful punch in the arm by Scott. "Watch your step. This bridge is most likely part of the first trap."

"Good call," Ian said. He stood next to me and stretched his arm out, pointing up toward the shiny silver rocks. "See that?"

I strained my eyes to follow his finger. "All I see are bright silver, stupid-looking fairy rocks. God, I need some shades out here."

I heard the group laugh while Dominic held out his sunglasses to me. "I had a feeling you were still honing in your skill and letting your inner wolf have your eyes. Put these on, it'll help mute the fairy colors."

"As much as I don't want help on this, I hate the bright colors, and I'll admit, my wolf is having a hard time connecting with me since being at this stupid school."

"She curses the Immortal Academy?" Scott teased with a dramatic sigh and smile. First time I'd seen the dude smile. "How *dare* you, do you know how many supes want to be accepted here, and yet you hate it?"

"I have my reasons."

"And what would those be?" Finley eyed me.

Why did I feel like this chick was interrogating me since having our very first conversation?

"I hate the rules here. They're lame. Say one bad word and risk being on dish duty for a week."

"Which you've gotten away with so many times I've lost count. Seems like dean might like you, so that's actually a good thing." She smiled.

*Yeah, it only cost three innocent immortals their lives.* "Whatever. I think I've just managed to recover my foul mouth quickly, that's all."

"She hates that she can't shift whenever she wants. Can we get on with it before we end up waiting for a week to cross?" Dom said, ending the conversation by pulling his alpha card out on Finley and helping everyone refocus on more important things. "Don't forget, you're still in earshot of the school. We're only three miles out, and we have a hawk spying on our butts."

"Yeah, she's a goner as soon as I catch her hidden in these woods in her natural form," Scott said.

"She's mine," Ian said with a grin. "That's my girl, and she's hands off to all of you."

"I knew Brenda and you had a thing," Finley laughed. "Better watch out, Dom will kick your butt for going after a girl who despises his cousin."

"Can we get this going?" Dom said in annoyance. He came up and looked at me. "Put the sunglasses on and look up toward that rock with the amber trail running through the crack."

I pulled on Dom's shades, which were too wide for my face. They slipped to my nose, making me have to hold them up just to see through them at what Dom was pointing at. The glimmering bright lights of fairy illumination faded, and I was able to see a camouflaged rope wedged between the amber trail cut through the silver rocks.

"What do you think?" Ian asked me.

Dom stood in front of me, bending the wire frames of his glasses to mold them to fit me better. "What do you see?" Dom asked.

"I see a rope, and I think that the amber thing needs to get un-wedged from the rocks it's pinched between." I looked around, everyone seemed to be waiting on me to answer. "Somehow, we have to get the rope because that's the only way we're crossing."

"Sure about that?" Finley grinned. "What if the rope is the decoy to send you to the ground, and the bridge is the safest way across? You have to think like a fairy. More like a leprechaun, the tricksters out of all of them. The others add to the traps with their rune elements, the leprechauns design them."

"Shit if I know," I answered.

"Dang, you do have a mouth on you." Ian laughed and looked at Dom as if to say, *only you would date a rebel*. "Think."

"Why are you all leaving this up to me?"

"Because you're going first, and if you fall to your death and get teleported back to the school, we all know not to go that way," Scott smirked.

"You're an asshole, and I've wanted to say that since the day we met," I said.

"That's strike two. I wonder how many times we can get her mouth going to get her teleported back while just standing here and putting a little pressure on your girl, Dom."

"Keep annoying her, and you won't have your easy answer on this first obstacle," he joked back.

"Alright, everyone shut up and let me think." Besides the fact it annoyed me Dom was taking all of their *master status* sides on me being the tag-a-long inexperienced one on this mission, I had to really think, or I was toast.

I tried to get my inner wolf to rise up and scent the air, but she was taking a nap. Bless her apex predator little heart. Ugh, focus Jenna. *You can't fail this. Which one is the freaking way across?*

My mind went back to my leprechaun professor and a stupid joke he made in class at Dark Water Academy. *'Up is down and down is up! That's how a leprechaun always thinks, and that's why your quiz is written upside down, backward, and is missing words.'*

I remembered thinking that stupid quiz was pointless and the professor was as dumb as any other fairy I'd ever met. Useless ramblings from that man were now serving a purpose in my not dying in this quest.

Everything was backward and flipped inside out for a fairy. The obvious was their trick. They knew the wolf would scent out that rope—well, a wolf who wasn't sleeping on the job like my girl was. They also knew the wolf would expect the obvious to be a trap, and I studied the rope bridge. The boards and everything about the bridge was an illusion.

My eyes relaxed more, and some crazy inner magic hit me like Vannah had touched me and threw some magic in my system. It went straight to my head, almost making me light-headed until I refocused on the bridge. The top two rails of the rope bridge weren't really there. Illusion trap number one. The golden steps that served to create the bridge we would walk across disappeared. Illusion number two. The right side—the obvious rope to use—faded next. Illusion number three. I looked at the left rope that spanned across the ravine below us, it stayed, then faded to a standard brown rope color. It looked like we were either tightrope walking across this or hanging and working our way by using arms and legs to pull our butts across this thousand-foot drop below.

A cat shifter would love this, but I was not a cat. It was up to our own personal strengths and reaching outside of our boundaries to make it across. I glanced over at what we all thought was a swing rope and saw it was an illusion too. This was our only way across. I wasn't about to show my balancing skill, so hanging from the rope was my option.

I stepped out and heard a shout from Dom as I flung myself out toward that rope, catching it with one hand, quickly gripping it with the other, and hanging upside down with my ankles locked around it.

I was halfway across the two-hundred-foot span and moving quickly to get across. I pulled by reaching my arms ahead of me, and my ankles kept me inching forward. The nagging sensation of wanting to just run across the rope and get there faster hit me more than once, but I wasn't the tight rope queen, and I wasn't offing myself this early.

"She did it. Holy crap," I heard Finley say with a laugh. "I'll be honest. I was leaning towards the rope swing idea that would have kept us here an hour at least trying to figure out how to dislodge that sucker."

"Me too," Scott laughed.

"You guys are more amateur than she is," Dom said, and I

heard the laugh and pride in his voice. "She's hardcore, I like that in my girl."

I almost lost my grip on the rope when that fell out of his mouth. Yeah, Dom and I were fake dating, but that was the most real sounding thing I'd heard slip out of his mouth other than talking about protecting Ethan.

*Focus, Jenna!* I was almost there. The cliff was a slick rock and right behind me…finish mark. Now, I had to pull myself up and practically sit on this rope and plant my feet on it to jump to the flat surface.

I closed my eyes, searching for that magical insight energy I'd just had, hoping it would give me a little nudge of help. It surged through me once I thought of it again, and I unlocked my ankles, swung out and up, and now I was sitting balanced on the rope.

Without feeling the fear I should've, I swung my legs out and up, leaping onto the top of the rope. I stood bent over, holding onto the thing while it wavered. I focused on the energy I'd transferred into the rope, and then leapt from it, doing a duck roll and making it safely to the other side.

My pride in my accomplishment ceased when Finley walked the rope like she was on the ground. The other two followed in her actions, but Dom took the rope challenge the same as me. I pinched my lips and crossed my arms, watching the veins pop in his biceps as he glided smoothly under the rope, pulling himself without hardly any effort.

The other three patted me on the arm, laughed, and sauntered off further down the glittery path. Dom made some acrobatic move and was now walking over the final feet of the bridge. "Hey," he said, leaping off the rope and over to where I stood. "Nice call. Don't know how you figured that one out and so quickly, but that was pretty amazing."

"Listen," I lowered my voice for only him to hear. "I don't need your sympathetic way of doing this to make me look like

I'm not an amateur. You could have easily walked across that rope too."

"Yeah, I could have," he answered in the same low voice. "But you, you little judgemental, hot-tempered shifter, have no idea how I run on these courses. This is the boring part, and I like having a little fun. So chill and quit getting worked up over stupid crap or you will be the first one teleported out of here."

He walked off to join the others after putting me and my temper in check. The point I was trying to make was that I didn't need his help or sympathy, but that was in my personality. The minute I caved to this man I'd submitted my wolf to, would be my first and last mistake with him. He would use his alpha to forever dominate me, and I wasn't about that life.

"Any day now, Jenna," Scott said with a laugh to the others. Dom never once turned back to me, but who cared.

We traveled through the glitter fairy forest, darkness starting to claim the daylight now, and we dodged more obstacles along the way. I was now in the middle, Dominic most likely behind me to protect me, and was stopped when the sprite element came into play. We were in some sort of wind pattern that forced you to take small breaths, or your lungs would be overpowered with air and boom—there went your lungs—and a ticket back to the academy.

The wind was enough to blow the trees around us over, and when it hit head-on unexpectedly, I was thrown into Dom's chest. Annoying, but nice. I was reminded that my skin and body both loved being in close contact with him. The laugh that came from his chest, the gentle but strong way his arms held me close, they gave me a gentle push back to get my feet on the ground and steadied again. I liked his support and the friendly nature I picked up from him, but my mind fought him off like an enemy.

"Scott, don't!" Dom shouted.

Scott had just skipped a rock over the glass water lake that looked like red rubies, reflecting the sun setting to our right. The water instantly swelled up like a tidal wave, slammed over Scott. Before I could see anything else, my arm was jerked, and I was scampering off to the left, racing right on Dominic's heels, hearing the thunder of the water crashing down onto the path behind us.

Dom glanced back, grabbed my hand, and forced us both into a faster pace. "When you see a low branch, grab it and climb."

He ordered. Like magic, a branch appeared, and Dom jerked me under it to keep me from grabbing the thing. *Fairy trap*. We kept running and met with trees that had thick, low branches. I gripped one, the sound of the rushing water right behind us, sending Dom and me climbing the trees as fast as a bear shifter would. Once Dom stopped at the more brittle branches at the top of the tree, I stopped too. I leaned forward, gripping the smooth white branch, watching the water rush below us.

It flowed as if a dam had been opened, and I had to wonder if we were swimming our way to our next checkpoint. We were split up in the fae part of this quest, and it sucked. Maybe it was just me and Dom left now, or perhaps our whole quest was only slowed up by having to search for the others. All that mattered was I'd survived until sundown and was still here.

"We're still about a day away from beating the fae's obstacles. The leprechauns have placed all of the different fae runes around, so we don't know which element we're running into. It can be earth, wind, fire, or water, or it can be all of them at once. Anything."

"So think *end of the world* type stuff?"

"Basically."

"Do you know if they all survived?" I asked as he studied the water below like he was ready to dive out into it at any second and get to our checkpoint.

"Won't know until we get out of the fae realm. If they meet us at the next checkpoint, we'll know who won't be the laughing joke of all the fairies when we get back to the school."

"Are you serious?" I asked with disgust.

"What?" he looked at me, confused. "What are you annoyed about now?"

"Back to the school? You act like we're heading back to a normal place. I'm not going back."

Dominic's eyes widened, and he glanced around. "For all we know, that stupid hawk is perched in one of these trees listening in on us. Don't be stupid, and don't talk like that. No one is leaving this school, especially you and me."

I watched as he returned his focus to the water below. Fine. That conversation would have to wait. He sounded as serious as a freaking heart attack about not leaving. I would convince him otherwise, I had to. If Dominic wanted to help his own cousin, he would leave this place and go on a search mission to find the people that could shut this place down—or at least bust the people who turned it into a horror house for supernaturals.

Even if the dude was committed to his lame idea of staying here for the next two years, kissing butt, and coming back as a professor, I wasn't on that page with him. That idea wouldn't work out. For all we knew, Dom and I *would* end up somehow being forced into mateship at this school, empowering our wolves by merging them, and being the new higher force to help this school continue on its freak show ways.

I wouldn't put it past that stupid creep dean for already planning the big mating ceremony, then rewiring our brains with dark magic and turning us into dangerous wolf shifters, doing the academy's bidding—or worse—going out to do the dean's bidding and taking out enemies this jerk most likely made with higher powers than him.

That sounded like the more reasonable option. Dude probably was trying to climb the supernatural of dark evil ladder and needed me and Dom's powers to help him dominate the races. That wasn't happening, but it did level out the insane idea as to why he would kill off immortals for objecting or getting in the way of Dom and me having a relationship.

Edgewater was going to learn his lesson the hard way. For all I knew, these sensory reactions I was having around Dominic Rossi was dark-magic driven. I wouldn't know for sure until we got further away from the magical grips of the academy.

# CHAPTER THIRTY-ONE

I followed Dominic's lead since he acted like he could sense the House Fae obstacles a mile away. We remained silent as we rounded large, ancient-looking trees. We leapt over shimmering brick trails and stayed moving on the vibrant blue dirt trail that led through a dense area filled with red thorns shaped like spears coming off massive, blooming bushes.

When Dom jumped the vines on the ground, I did exactly what he told me by jumping things and following in his exact footprints.

We were on a steep climb now, my legs burning as we ascended the golden rocks to where Dom said was the trail to our first stopping point. I was exhausted. The first part of the mission was to journey for the first day or two without using our wolf form. It was a grueling exercise, but it made me start to appreciate why the school worked to keep us from shifting whenever we wanted. This served to give me more power in this form in protecting myself, and the lame school rule came in handy on the quest. Reining myself in from wanting to shift whenever I wanted this entire school year kept me from shifting overnight while making this journey.

"Don't touch the branches," Dom said as he leaned forward and used his hands to help him climb the steepest part of the cliff. "It's all arms from here."

Dom reached the edge of the cliff and gripped the golden ledge, letting his feet hang while using his arms to pull him up and over the edge. My arms were already burning, and I wasn't about to look down. I knew we were at least a thousand feet above the ground. Dom's face peered over the side, smiling that stupid smile that sparked electricity inside of me, then he extended his hand down toward me.

I wasn't about to prove anything to anyone. I took his hand without reservation and allowed the dude to help pull me up and over the side. I crawled out once on top and fell on my stomach, face down in the lime green grass. I was utterly bushed from running, dodging traps, and balancing on large logs just to get to this climb. I barely made it, but my determination to stay on this quest kept my mind off my body begging me to stop.

"You alright, babe?" I felt a pat on my back, and I rolled my eyes while holding a hand up to assure Dom I was okay.

A surge streamed through my veins when his hand clasped around mine. I turned my face to the left, where I knew he was and saw where he was knelt next to me holding my hand. This was just plain weird. Either Dominic was sending vibes to me because he actually cared, or what was more than likely true, we were still in reach of whatever spell that school might be holding over us.

Whatever. I was tired, and I was done thinking about it. This was nice, though. I loved the feeling of his warm hand gently holding mine and the soft laugh of humor when he asked me to get my lazy butt up.

"Come on, let's get something to eat. Finley's here, and we have our food rations. Trust me, you need some energy. This has been the easy part."

With a grunt, I rolled to my back, took his offered hand, and sprang to my feet. We walked over to where Finley sat in front of a stone circle, tossing branches into it.

"This fire isn't going to start, and we're going to freeze on this bluff. Everything is soaked from the water. Freaking Scott was acting like a moron, and he screwed all of us."

"Where's Ian," Dom asked, still holding my hand and leading us over to where Finley was. "Did he get wiped out by the water?"

"You know as much as I do," she said, annoyed. "You know, you both don't have to act like you're madly in love. Holding hands makes you both look like you're trying too hard."

"I'll do whatever I want. If Jenna doesn't want me to hold her hand, then I'll let her go," Dom said, looking out at the landscape of treetops that surrounded the bluff that seemed to overlook the world.

When I looked, I saw glittery, fairy landscape to the south and southeast. Everything to my left—the northern landscapes—was all dark forests with thick gray clouds swirling over them and through those treetops.

"Is that the witches' area we have to go through next?" I asked.

"Yep. It's most likely just us three...and the hawk shifter, Brenda, is somewhere around here too. She'll be cruising right alongside us. I can't wait to take her out."

"Where does it all end?" I asked Dom, ignoring Finley because her tone was bitchy, and I was too tired for her snappy remarks.

"What do you mean?" Dom looked over at where I sat in front of the stone firepit. "The quest ends after we have everything they can throw at us, and we survive it."

"I mean, where does the enchantment that hides this school end? I feel like there is no human population anywhere."

"Why would you care about the human population?" Finley asked.

"Just curious. I don't feel like this school is on the planet earth." I laughed.

Finley tucked her knees under her. "Of course we're on Earth, but where on Earth is the question. Some say Immortal Academy is hidden deep in the rain forests in South America, and some think we're in the Scottish Highlands. No one knows for sure until we leave, that's the whole point." She shook her head and looked at Dominic, "You sure know how to pick them. An immortal who actually wants to leave a renowned school just to go see a human."

"She has her reasons," Dom said, ignoring her rude comment.

"And those are?"

"None of your business," Dom quickly responded. "Quiet." He looked around. "You guys hear that?"

I listened, and all I heard was the soft rustle of the wind blowing through the yellow bushes that surrounded us.

"I hear it. Sounds like…" Finley paused, covering her mouth. "Oh my gosh, it's Ian."

"No one moves, or you'll smash him," Dom said, staring just past Finley who froze.

"What an idiot," she said with another laugh. "No, seriously dude, you must have drunk from water out of the wrong puddle dude. Good luck."

Dominic's lips were tight, but eyes crinkled in humor. It was the first time I saw a lighter, more youthful side to him. "Get on a twig, I can't see you in the grass, and I'm not shifting to find your stupid butt in wolf form."

"Yeah, you're lucky your hawk girlfriend didn't eat you, thinking you were a grubworm, Finley laughed and looked at me. "Can't you see him or hear him?"

"I have no idea what the hell is going on. Dominic is talking to the grass, and you're talking to Ian like his freaking ghost is here."

"It's a shrinking spell. The most embarrassing trap to fall victim to." He leaned down and pulled up a white branch where I saw a miniature version of Ian standing. "Dude, I don't even know what to say. This is the funniest thing I've ever witnessed."

"We can't even start a normal fire, you idiot. What makes you think we can conjure up fairy flames? You're so screwed. Might as well have your girlfriend eat you and send your butt back to the school."

Dominic started laughing, and I heard squeaks come from the branch he set on a rock next to the firepit. "Dude, you owe me so hard for this."

"You're kidding, right?" Finley rolled her eyes. "There's no way you have that fire starter, unless..." At first, her eyes were fierce, then humor lifted them in my direction, "Looks like your boy gets around at this school."

Dom ignored her and pulled a leather pouch from his pack. He poured some purple powder into his hand and threw it on the wet wood that Finley had gathered for a fire. Next, he struck two pieces of rock together, fairy dust applied to both of them, and bright flashes exploded from them. A spark floated up above the wood, and like a feather, it fell slowly to the dust covering the wood. Once it touched the dust, brilliant purple and blue flames exploded up with sparks exploding out of the flames like fireworks.

Dom reached over and pinched his fingers together, the next thing I knew, he was holding a two-inch-high fighting and squirming Ian. Dominic's laugh was enough to make me and Finley laugh together. "Dude. It sucks, but I got to light your butt up. It's the only way."

My wolf, the rebellious brat she turned into because it wasn't her turn to shift or whatever else was her freaking problem, finally lent me her ears and I could hear Ian's squeaky voice.

"Do it, and I will kick your butt when you get back to the academy," Ian warned in a high-pitched voice.

Dom laughed again. "Shut up, man. You're killing me right now. You're the fool that fell into a trap. This is your only hope."

"Fairy fire doesn't necessarily reverse a fairy trap, Rossi!" the squeaky voice tried to shout. "For all I know, that girl set you up. You did play her, and she didn't take lightly to it."

"Yeah, whatever. It was nothing serious, sorry she couldn't see it that way."

"I'm the one that's going to be sorry, you jerk." Ian threw a non-threatening fist up at Dominic, prompting him to continue laughing. "Finley, I'm not good with this. I don't trust the fairy Dom screwed over."

"Hopefully, Dom is right, and it reverses your cursed miniature butt," Finley said, entertained and waiting.

"What the heck are you going to do to him?" I asked Dominic.

"He's throwing me in that fairy fire. You're his girl, convince him not to."

"It'll be like ripping a band-aid off," Dominic said, tilting his head to the side, enjoying making his friend suffer a little for making a dumb move. "If it works, you're back on the quest. If it doesn't, then you were right about Amelia, I should have known she would try to get me back with her fairy temper."

"Do it." Finley laughed.

"Jenna, stop him!"

"I actually want to see if fairy fire does work to reverse fairy curses like this or not," I said, knowing this was a make or break situation for Ian. If the fairy fire didn't return him to his normal size, then it would teleport him back to the school."

"I can't go out like this," Ian urged.

"Yeah, I actually thought it would be Scott to go down the most embarrassing way," Dom said. "Alright. Three, two..." Dom was silent, Ian's scream sounded like a mouse screaming for dear life, and Finley lost it.

I was so consumed with waiting to see if the rumors were true. Fairy fire could reverse a fairy's curse—it was a purification, so to speak.

The flames were a deep blue now, white sparks shooting out of the top, making me and Finley scoot further away from the fire.

The next thing we knew, the full-size Ian was back, and not

one brown hair on his head was out of place. He walked out of the flames like he was the chosen one, then the fire died back down, and served to keep us warm. He went to punch Dom, but Dom caught his fist and smiled. "Don't think that's the only trick my little leprechaun ex-girlfriend gave me. I can shrink you, turn your butt into a pig, anything with the other pouch of dust I got from her."

"Dude, that was BS, and you know it."

"Would you have rather gone through the mission two inches tall?" Dom asked Ian's annoyed expression.

"No, but to trust a girl you screwed over—not just any girl, a freaking leprechaun—that could have totally screwed me."

"That's because you idiots don't know how I am in relationships. Probably shouldn't have judged that one. When I break from a girl, it's a clean break, and we're friends afterward."

"True," Finley added with a smile while Dom sat next to me. "I still have no idea why I don't hate you for the way we split."

"What can I say, I'm a likable guy." He laughed and draped an arm around me. He pulled me in close to his side, and I smiled at feeling like I was going to be able to take a nap here and now.

"You're pretty arrogant," I said with a yawn.

Dom's hand ran over the top of my hair—this was new—and I felt him laugh. "I don't see you having a problem with it right now."

"If I didn't feel like I could sleep for three days solid, I probably would. Right now, I don't care who or what you dated. None of my business. Everyone has a past. I live in the present."

"Interesting way of looking at it," Finley said. "I would think it would bother you that your man got around."

"Why don't you shut up, Fin," Dom snapped. "Leave her alone."

"I don't need your protection," I said in a hushed, sleepy voice. The fire was warming me from the inside out. The comfort of leaning into Dom's solid frame was pulling me faster into the sleep my entire being was aching for.

"No, you don't." I heard the smile in his voice. "But before you go lights out on me, you need to eat something."

I nibbled on some jerky while the other three bantered back and forth. Once I was done, Dominic stretched back against the tree we were in front of. The sun was sliding fast below the tree-lined horizon, and my eyes were burning as I tried to keep them open.

"Here," Dominic said, stretching his leg out and slumping back into the tree. His arm came up around me and pulled me into a comfortable position, leaning into his side. By some miracle, the guy seemed to become fixated with fiddling with my hair while he talked to the others. My face was buried into his chest as I leaned further into him.

He began gently pinching my hair through his fingers, soothing me, and that was it. Dom seemed to relax more, leaning back and letting me stretch further into him. I absently and carelessly draped a leg over his knees, craving the comfort of a bed. Poor Dominic, I probably was making him a tad bit uncomfortable, but I didn't care. Dude was playing with my hair, and that's as close to the soothing comfort of an apple pie that I could ever get.

God help me, I promised myself I would not think of a freaking apple pie this entire trip. I had my goals, I might've wanted my pie, but I would reward myself with that once I was on a path to helping the innocents at this school.

"Relax," Dom's lips were on top of my head, pressing into my hair. "You're tensing up. This may be the only sleep you get. Ian needs to recover to full strength, and I can tell your mind is starting to go crazy."

"I am relaxed. How would you know if I weren't."

His hand covered mine that was wrapped around his waist and clawing into his sides. "Because you're about to tear my skin off," he said with a laugh. "Relax, we have a while before we leave again. You'll want to be rested on this next part of the quest. We'll be shifting too, so let your wolf free up a little bit and get familiar with these settings."

"I don't even know how to do that."

"Simple." His voice had remained a whisper between him and I. "Close your eyes. My wolf is present, and I already know she enjoys his company. She'll be attuned to what's going on while your natural mind rests."

"I bet your wolf loves that my wolf is all about him."

Dominic laughed, "He's never been more annoying, that's for sure. Now, rest."

I wasn't even going to process that. It meant more, and I knew it, but then again, Ian, Finley, and the hawk shifter were all here. This was most likely a scene for all of them, especially for the dean to see through his little hawk's eyes.

Who cared, I was resting while I could.

# CHAPTER THIRTY-TWO

Our paws thundered on the hard rock surface of the eerie green forest House Mage had produced. We had things coming at us from every direction. I stopped looking anywhere but the tracks Dominic produced in front of me after a dark swirling wind blew through the trees and took Ian with it.

This was the fourth day of the quest, and things got bad fast. The fact that House Mage and House Draugar worked together on this part of the quest was something only Dom seemed unsurprised about. Keeping my wolf in his exact prints, kept my paws off the ground half the time. I was continually launching myself through the air, trying to keep up with him and off the hot zone where I could trigger anything to snatch me up and take me back.

It was me, Dom, and Finley now, and if I didn't know any better, it seemed as though we were practically running for our freaking lives—for real. Dom's ears constantly flicked back, most likely making sure Finley and I were still with him on this chase.

If my inner wolf was complaining before that she didn't have enough time in her form, then we were making up for it now. Before this started, the masters all told me it would be three solid days of our wolves running the course. No stopping unless we wanted to be teleported back to the academy. Sheesh, we were only at it for a solid day, and Ian was toast already.

Dom swerved to the right, leading us to a waterfall. We ran along the banks of it, seeing that the water was so murky it was almost black. My wolf crinkled her nose at the smell of sulfur coming off the river of poison to our right. Dom's wolf seemed to be searching for a way across because now his nose was to the ground, sniffing out tracks, and I was standing next to Finley, watching his frustrated wolf pace back and forth.

I stepped forward and sniffed the air, past the disgusting smell of sulfur. I could scent that there was a way across, but it was removed by something. The scent of witch magic, vampires, and another creature was in the air. I smelled fresh-cut foliage, sawdust, and tracks that led into the pitch black water. The farther away we got from the waterfall, the blacker the water was as it pooled into a large lake.

Dom's wolf was agitated because we were stopped and most likely, all three of us were trapped and about to fail the mission. I looked over at the agitated, ferocious wolf, and two silver and brown wolf eyes zeroed in on mine.

Finley's brown wolf cowered by the water, pretty much giving up. I looked up at the giant cypress trees, trees of death. We were screwed if we didn't go into the water. Through the water was the only way. We were surrounded by death, and the waterfall upstream wasn't promising either. Vamps and witches working together was definitely a hard one to beat. It was taking instinct now, and I was going with the water that was warding the other two off.

I stepped forward to see my wolf's reflection. The silver and brown wolf with blue eyes. How hadn't Dom and the rest picked up on this part of me? Entirely out of the norm. How did the brown-haired, brown-eyed girl turn into a wolf that didn't represent any part of who she was?

While I let my brain relax, I was grabbed by something in the water. A solid black figure pulled me in by my shoulders, and once below the water's surface, I bit and clawed the mass of a being that was clutching onto me, but nothing was helping. I felt an undercurrent pulling us through the tar-black water, and at that point, I was just waiting to wake up at the academy.

I couldn't breathe, and I should've been teleported by now. That's when I felt it. The weird energy pull. My hackles tingled, and my wolf relaxed. No! I'm not going back. I felt the grip of the thing holding me under the water loosen, and then I was floating. I saw a glittery paw—no, not glittery. It was a paw that was blurring in and out of focus. The water was pulling me down with each movement I made, so I let myself float.

Suddenly, House Braeclaw came into my vision. I was freaking dying and teleporting back. *NO! I will not die. I have to leave.* The vision faded, and all I could see now was the darkness of the water. I couldn't explain what was going on, but I knew I couldn't fight the water. I went with it instead. The current grew harder and faster, and I was being slammed up against hard objects. My lungs felt like they were punctured by the broken ribs I knew I'd sustained after the tenth hard slam into a jagged object.

I started growing frustrated every time House Braeclaw came back into my vision. I fought hard against that pull over and over, and the next thing I knew, I was slammed into something I could finally grip my paws on.

I pulled up, and my hind legs raked along the object, most likely a fallen tree since I felt like I was snapping branches to save my life from this place.

I was hurled out of the water, spat out onto blood-red sandy banks, my wolf form lying on its side and exhausted from the fight for survival. I wanted to shift back and build a fire because now I was freezing and shivering on top of exhaustion.

I did everything in my power to get my legs underneath me and get my bearings. I felt like I had been thrown eighty miles at least down the river and now I was on red sand and surrounded by white tree trunks...alone.

The fiery red leaves that shot up into the eerie green skies gave me no idea on my whereabouts or where the sun was since that was blacked out by dark clouds. I was screwed. Fortunately, I heard a wolf's howl in the distance. Dumb. Probably Finley all alone since Dom was right by my side when I fell into the water. Was she blowing the whistle that she was scared or was this what you did when you were the last one left on the quest?

The wolf's howl was more aggressive now, Finley getting brave? Who knew, I just knew I was going to follow the sound back to the other wolf that was still alive. The game wasn't over yet, and I was still here.

I leapt up a dark black jagged rock path, following the cries of the wolf. As I crept through the dead trees at the top of this trail, I softened my steps. I couldn't be sure if this were some sort of trick to trap me, so I proceeded with caution.

My wolf senses were on high alert. This was the call of a lonely, heartbroken wolf. This wasn't normal. If Finley had lost both Dom and me, we were just going to be teleported back to the school, or did we get caught up in some trap that this school seemed to function on and the wolf crying out was sincere in noting the loss—real death? Who knew.

I peered around to see Finley's brown wolf lying down, submitted to a black wolf that silenced as soon as I walked out to where the two were surrounded by dead trees. Totally confused by why Dominic was the one to do the howling and in this way, I lowered my head to greet the sad alpha.

Dominic's wolf spun in my direction as soon as I pranced out to him. The wolf's eyes were severe as they studied me, his lips curling up and baring his teeth. What was he seeing? I lowered my head farther, my tail tucked, showing the black alpha I wasn't his enemy no matter what vibes he was getting off my wolf.

Finley's wolf was up on her feet while Dom crept forward,

sniffing the air all around me. His nose met mine, then he jerked his head back as his wolf's snout was felt in my fur, picking up whatever scent was tripping him out. I stood still, seeing the hackles up on his back and knowing that one wrong move with his questioning wolf could have Dominic ripping my throat out and all this work was for nothing. I fought hard to resist dying in that tar water not to get teleported back to the school, I wasn't going out by startling an already worked up wolf.

As Dom came up along my right side, his nose nudged into my neck. We stood quietly and unmoving while Dominic's wolf whimpered and tried to process whatever he didn't like coming off my wolf right now.

I noticed Finley in her natural form now, dressed in her combat clothes. "There's no way that's her," she told Dom's wolf. "It's another freaking trap, don't fall for it. She didn't survive that water creature they conjured up. You know that."

Her eyes were intently studying me. Dom nudged me again, then his wolf licked at my cheek, under my jawbone, and around my face. It was his way of trusting it was me. Why Finley switched back into regular form if she thought I was some trick, was beyond me. That was just dumb.

Dom's lapping at my face was overwhelming and too much. The all-powerful alpha was acting like I was his new favorite toy and was practically knocking me over by wagging his tail and nudging me playfully with his face. I snapped at him, pushing him off, forcing the black wolf to snarl and go into attack mode.

*Oh, good grief.* I needed to copy Finley's movements and get my butt back into normal form. These two were acting like I had been dead for a week. The vibes I caught off these two was too much. We needed to talk about what happened.

I trotted off, Finley following me into the woods, and I shifted back. I forgot to drop my wet pack that my wolf had been carrying with my clothes in it, forcing me to pry the stupid thing off my shoulders.

"Here, let me help you." Her voice was a bit shaky. "Jenna, what the heck, man. You've been in that water for days. You were gone. Like really dead."

I turned back to her, snatching my black top she pulled out of my waterproof pack. I pulled it on, then the rest of my clothes she handed me. "Days? I was only in that water for like ten minutes tops. You're right, I should have been back at the academy, but here I am. Still with you guys. I fought crazy hard not to get teleported."

Stomping tore through the forest and the next thing I knew I was swallowed up by two large biceps, my face plastered against the bare and very firm peck muscles of Dominic's chest. I felt an energy wash over me that I couldn't explain. It was like a reunion of two souls that had been torn apart and then reunited. I couldn't explain it, I just embraced it because it was the right thing to do.

Dominic's hand came up and braced the back of my head. I pulled back, only to lose the smile that had been plastered on my face. Dom's eyes were somber when mine met his.

"Good God, what the hell happened to you two?" I asked him, looking over at Finley who was watching Dominic like she had no idea where this side of the alpha shifter came from. "Seriously. What happened after that thing pulled me into the water?"

"That water," Dom ran his hand over my face, "God, I can't believe you're standing here."

"I told you I was going to beat this quest." I smiled, trying to cut through the grim tension I was getting off both the master shifters.

"No, Jenna. That water should have killed you—*killed* you. It was laced with acid and sulfur. I almost went in after you, but I couldn't fight past my wolf's defenses of it. If you were going to *fake* quest die, I would have just been teleported with you. With my wolf literally stopping me, Finley's wolf almost losing a paw to the touch of that stuff, we knew something wasn't right. It swallowed you up, you shouldn't be here," he explained.

"You shouldn't," Finley said. "What kind of dark power do you have in you? And how did you find us up here? We're out of reach of the academy, and Dom got rid of the hawk shifter as soon as she came up to us and started chanting some weird shit about the school's *sovereign* being fed."

I looked around. "What the hell?" I said to Dominic. "Is this the crap they were using to kill the others? Does Finley know?"

"Once we got out of the grips of the school, I sent the stupid hawk girl back, and Finley came out of the control the academy had her under. That Brenda chick is working for someone at that school, we're not sure if it's the dean, but he has something to do with it. Fin's fine, she's cool like you and me."

"How did you find us here?" Finley demanded. "I'm not sure how to even ask how you escaped that water we should have never come across. Whatever is at the school wants *you*. At least that's what the hawk was spouting out like a damn mocking bird before Dom took her out."

"I heard the cries of Dom's wolf. I thought it was strange." I looked up at Dom studying me like I'd been brought back from the dead. "Why would you cry out like that if you're trying to stay hidden from everything?"

"He never cried out," Finley said with a look of confusion. "He never once howled. We were only in our wolf forms because dusk is here and dark shadows are coming after us. They aren't here to send us back to school. They're hunting us now, trying to kill us, we think. Our wolf forms have taken them out and sensed them better when they come for us."

"Then why are we not in our wolf forms?" I asked.

Dom looked at Finley, then me, "We had to be sure it was you before I killed you. I figured the shadows were manifesting what we wanted most now. I wanted you back, I can't explain it, but the belief that you died in that water ripped through me, and it was a void I can't explain." He reached for my hand, "you heard me howling?"

"Yes. You weren't? I heard it as plain as day."

He licked his lips, "Jenna, you heard the inside cries of my wolf. It was never audible. You shouldn't have heard that unless we were true mates."

"As in..."

"Yes," Finley answered, "As in *when are the pups going to arrive now?* sort of mates. You both shouldn't be this connected. Dom told me about the fake relationship to protect Ethan."

"Oh my God," I said. "What if the school is going to hell right now? Me, dead. You two out here being hunted...what if Ethan is in trouble?"

"Ethan has been following us," Dom said with some relief in his voice. "He's been fighting the hawk shifter off and secretly trailing us. When he shifted back, he led us here and flipped out, mandating we not leave for our safety. Now, I know exactly why he wanted us here. He wanted us to wait for you."

"Where is he now?"

"No one knows. He just watched over us from the trees," Dom said. "He'll be delighted to see you're here safe."

"What do we do now?" I asked.

"E told me to dig a den. I have, and with Finley's help over the last few damn days, we've practically have built a mansion underground. Come on, we have to start sorting through this mess. Ethan will show if he knows it's safe for him. They locked him in the dungeons, and he escaped them." Dominic laughed, "Apparently, they think he's still locked away, so he's safe out here and undetected with us. Let's get underground before the shadow hunters come, it's almost dark."

With that, I followed the two Immortal Academy fugitives underground and was blown away at what these two had accomplished to give us a hideout under the grounds of this sinister area. Now, I guess we all had to try and piece this part of the puzzle together. This was where I was going to recruit Finley, Dom, and Ethan to get the heck out of here. Now, I would have more people helping me search for someone to help stop the murders at this school…oh, and find the dark SOB who tried to murder my butt.

# CHAPTER THIRTY-THREE

I sat on a log that was close to the small fire pit where the fire that was built was struggling to stay lit. Dom dumped some twigs on it, and I watched as the smoke plume went up through a small hole in the den he and Finley had dug out.

The area was lit by the little fire pit, but I could tell that it was large enough to fit at least eight of us. Finley and Dom went for the packs, and we all sat quietly as we ate the jerky that was given to us as food rations for the quest.

"So how did this whole thing go dark on us?" I finally asked.

"We have no idea. After we lost you, Dom was in *save Jenna* mode since he instantly sensed this wasn't a fake death you'd suffered."

I looked at Dom, who sat protectively at my side. "Thanks for potentially risking your immortal life to come after me. While I was underwater, it felt like I was moments from being transported back to the school, but I fought that off."

"Why did you think you were being transported back?" Dom asked in confusion.

"I saw the school. I felt it pulling me back there, I fought it off, and then the next thing I knew, I was out of that black tar water. It seriously felt like I'd survived a trap."

"And you thought you were in the water for ten minutes?" Finley questioned. "How long did it take you to reach us?"

"As soon as I popped out, I knew the water had to have pulled me far away from where I fell in. I thought I kind of got lucky when I popped out of that and heard the cry of the wolf. I didn't really question my being lucky enough to wind up close to where you were, I was more curious as to why the wolf cry was what it was."

Dom exhaled and placed a hand over mine. "Jenna," he captured my eyes with his complex expression and amber brown eyes, "For you to hear my wolf…" He swallowed hard and hit me with the Dom smile. "You shouldn't have heard that."

"I picked up on your inner wolf emotions." I rubbed my hand over his. "Are you sure…" The words locked up in my throat just as it had Dominic's.

There was no way. If the dude were my wolf's true mate, no freaking way we'd be that connected. I shouldn't have heard his wolf, period, no matter what.

"There's something different about you, Jenna," Dom said, looking at Finley across from us before he darted his eyes down into the flames as they licked at the wood in the fire pit. "We may not be connected on a mateship level—we're not even in a real relationship—but you are unique. There is something that hides behind your wolf." He looked at me, "Can't you sense its power?"

"All I know is that I'm not your average shifter. I mean, my wolf is even different from my natural form. Her eyes are blue, and mine are brown. I'm sure you all noticed that a while ago."

"It was noticed by the masters," Finley smirked. "We just thought we had a half-breed shifter," she teased. "Seriously, though, that's when we all started watching you."

"And?"

"Well, we didn't have extraordinary abilities to sense what made you unique. We just thought we had a special shifter with us. When you joined Dom's unit and didn't answer his alpha commands, that's when we all really knew there was something different about you. You have no idea who you really are, do you?" she asked.

"I have no idea who my parents are. I wanted out of Dark Water Academy and out in the world so I could find them, but instead of graduating and being able to find out my lineage, I was brought here. All I know is I'm over the eighty percent immortal blood mark, and I was forced into this place."

"Ethan mentioned House Silvers when I asked him why he was drawn to you," Dom said. "I have no idea about your family's house. I don't know where Ethan got that information from, but he's a special kind of owl. He won't say any more than Jenna of House Silvers."

"Yeah, that one got me too. Maybe there is family history, maybe there's not."

"E wouldn't reference something if it weren't the truth," Dominic eyed me like he thought I knew more than I was saying.

"Jenna, we have to know everything. There's no way you survived that abyss for that long," Finley said in frustration.

"I have nothing. I'm just as confused as both of you."

"Leave it alone," Dom ordered Finley. "She has no idea, we have no idea. All I know is we have to get back to the school and figure out what the hell happened and why Jenna was almost killed out here."

"We can't go back to the school," I said. "We have to get help."

"Absolutely not!" Dominic's voice was stern. "Have you lost your mind?"

We were interrupted when we heard rustling come from the bushes that Dom used to conceal this hideout den.

"Stay here." Dom rose up and stalked over to the entrance.

"You have to leave." It was Ethan's voice.

"God dang, E," Dom let out a deep breath, "I could have snapped your neck."

"And I would have healed if you did." Ethan looked at his cousin's lethal expression with indifference. "You know I cannot be killed."

"What do you know?" Finley asked as she and I approached Ethan.

Ethan smiled at me. "I knew you would save yourself. Your power helped you."

I couldn't help but hug my friend. "I'm glad you're safe, Ethan Carter."

"I am happy you're safe as well, but right now in danger. You need to leave. I have found another area where they can't sense Jenna. She opened up something they're using to track her. You all must leave now."

"Lusa? Ethan, what about my sister? What's happening at the school?"

"The school is not harming anyone. The school hunts for Jenna. Lusa is safe."

"Alright." Dom looked back at Finley and me, "shift and get the packs." He looked at Ethan, "Get your owl to lead the way, we'll leave now."

"Your wolves must not stop. Follow me to safety."

We were shifted and on the move, using our wolf instincts to guide us away from the place where I'd found Dom and Finley.

Finley sprinted out in front, I stayed in the middle, and Dom was trailing us. Ethan's beautiful owl flew close to the ground as our wolves clawed through the thick mud to follow him to his new hideout.

I yelped when a large black mass swirled down and huge claws formed from it. It plucked Finley off the ground, and I knew she would be toast if she couldn't fight it off. Before I could leap up and try and attack the thing, Dom was in the air from behind me, and his sharp fangs sank into the claws that were deep in Finley's back. Her wolf wailed as soon as the thing disappeared and she fell to the ground.

She whimpered, barely able to move. Dom's wolf nudged her back to her feet, only to have her stumble again. *Oh my God, did that thing break her back?* I watched Dom back away as Ethan's owl turned and banked hard off to his left as it returned to us. The owl's massive talons extended and got Finley right behind her head at the scruff of her wolf's neck—the place that we felt nothing when carried—and Ethan screeched as if to yell at us to follow him.

The owl turned back and continued on with an injured Finley hanging from his claws. I felt horrible for her. We wouldn't know the extent of her injuries until we got to whatever safe place Ethan was leading us to. I hoped that he was leading us away from the enchantment of the school and into the human world.

After fighting off countless black shadows, we arrived at some massive cave. Ethan kept flapping his wings hard, so I knew we weren't stopping here. The cave opened up into daylight—maybe made it through a portal to the human population. It was daylight now, and Ethan was heading toward an enormous waterfall. The cliff the water fell from was hundreds of feet high, and tall trees lined the mountain range that surrounded this valley we were in.

We followed Ethan's owl as he banked to the left, then the right to fly in behind the waterfall. The cavern was wet and musty, and my wolf didn't like the damp environment, but it wasn't up to her. If this was the human world, then this is where we would plan to get help.

Ethan set Finley's injured wolf gently on a ledge that was on the other side of this cavern. Light peered in from a parting between two rocks, and I could scent the pine needles and nature outside that slit of an opening. Dom stayed in wolf form, trotting over to an area behind another group of rocks, most likely shifting back like Finley and I had to. We had to assess her wounds, and with Ethan here, hopefully, he had some way he could help her. He seemed to be blessed with some kind of special magic, and I was hoping healing was part of his unique owl DNA.

"Here," I said after shifting, throwing on my clothes and helping a slow-moving Finley. "Let me help you get your shirt…"

"Don't touch my shoulder." I looked, seeing a broken bone trying to pop through her skin. Her other shoulder was the same.

"God, both your arms are busted," I said. "Let me wrap your shirt around you, cover you up."

She let me tie the shirt around her chest because we knew Dom and Ethan were going to want to examine her.

"What was that thing?" I asked her.

"Same things we'd been fighting since hiding out at that other place," she said with a whimper. "Dang, this is killing me."

"The poison is in her. Her bones will be liquified soon," Ethan said, staring at her shoulders. "Jenna, you can stop it."

I looked at Ethan like he was insane. "Whatever magic you think I've got in me, it ain't healer magic."

"You can help her. Focus." Ethan's eyes were that weird white color again. "If you lose her. You will all die."

I glanced over at Finley who was kneeling in pain, gray veins showing her skin dying from the inside out. "I'll get wood for the fire," Dom said. "She's freezing. Do your thing, Jenna."

"I don't know what you guys are thinking, I don't have *a thing*!"

"Then, go! If I'm going down like this, I'd rather be consumed by poison alone," Finley lashed out in pain.

Her wails and groans and her body fighting the poison threw me into a strange trance. I felt heat surging in my bloodstream. I glanced at my palms as they turned fiery red—something that only happened to witches when they activated their magic. I heard Dominic drop the wood he was carrying to the fire, most likely stunned by what was happening to me.

I couldn't believe my eyes. I was part freaking witch now?

"Heal her. I must go back. The school needs me to watch it while they wait."

I ignored Ethan and focused the energy that was ready to explode like lava from my hands. Yellow—*fairy glitter* yellow—swirled around the bright red ball of energy that was sitting in my hand. A sparkling blue flame swirled around and through the energy ball. I felt like someone took my arms and guided them to where Finley was writhing on the cold, damp stone in the cavern. I pressed the ball of hot energy I'd created into Finley's spine. Like an x-ray, I saw two broken ribs, a punctured lung, broken arms, and dislocated shoulders as my magical healing ball went into her.

She collapsed over onto my lap, and her eyes shut peacefully with one soft sigh.

"Holy hell, what did I just do?" I said as I stared at my hands in total disbelief.

"There's some large leaves and straw out there. I'm going to fashion up a quick bed for her, and then we're going to figure this out."

I looked over to see the wolf in Dom's eyes. Whatever I had done had brought his wolf into the game either to protect Dom from me or to scent out who I really was. I just pulled a freaking witch-fairy-healer move all in one magical energy ball. What the heck was I?

As Dom worked fast to build up some bedding with leaves and grass in an alcove, I ran my hand gently over Finley's forehead. She was completely out, and I could actually feel the heat in her body, surging and searing her injured bones back together. Her shallow breathing slowed into relaxed, deep sleep breaths.

Dom took her and cradled her in his arms, walking her over to the makeshift bed he pulled together in vamp speed. He didn't seem to argue with Ethan flying back to that stupid school, so hopefully, E was safe, and we were safe out here.

It was easy to see that Finley was in a healing coma and would be out for at least twelve hours. Now, it was up to Dom and me to figure out what the heck I conjured up and just did to heal the Master shifter. This was insane, and I had never been more confused about who I really was until right now.

# CHAPTER THIRTY-FOUR

I took the logs Dom dropped on the stone floor and placed them together. I felt the heat still bubbling in my palms and remembered watching Vannah when she created these witchy magic balls. We were so amused when she first learned how to channel her magic, pull it into one place, and manifest these balls of light.

I could only assume I was part witch, and since I'd transferred off a witchy magic ball that I'd absently created to start healing Finley, I figured there was more energy left that I'd conjured up. I realized how cold the cave was, and how much Finley needed it warmed with fire, so I figured it was as good a time as any to see if I could do something about it.

I focused my energy into my hands, and when a fireball appeared, my heart raced in fear at what the hell I was becoming. I threw the ball of flames down toward the pile of branches Dominic brought in and watched flames erupt all around the wood.

I stepped back in horror of what I was, and I felt my eyes pool with tears. Dear God, what were my parents? Why didn't anyone prepare me for the fact that I would manifest witch powers one day? At least then I wouldn't be freaked out beyond belief. Vannah was thrilled when she accomplished one of the most amazing things a witch could do, but she *knew* she was a freaking witch. She wasn't a witch who suddenly started shifting into a damn wolf. This was insanity.

As soon as panic set in, I felt Dominic's presence next to me. I looked at him, and I knew I had fear written all over my face. Dom had the opportunity to pull his alpha card right here and now if he wanted to, or he could use his alpha strength to shut me down and take out whatever he feared I was. Instead, he looked at me like I was an angel sent to help us all.

His expression was set with curiosity, and I felt the warmth and pride radiating from him. He used the back of his knuckles to brush away the tears that spilled out of my eyes. I wasn't sobbing or ugly crying, I was standing there numb and scared of what was happening to me.

"Hey," he softly said.

"Hey," I managed. "Please don't ask because I don't know. I don't know what I am or what's happening with me."

"I know you must be scared out of your mind right now."

"To say the least."

He smiled, "I sense it."

"Please don't take advantage of this."

"You think I'm going to try to dominate you?" he questioned with humor in his expression.

"I don't know what you're going to do."

"My cousin told you he knew you could help her. E knows more than he says. I trust him, and you need to trust him too. You know owls, if this were a bad thing, he would have tried to hurt you himself. This is an amazing ability you have in you, Jenna. It's just new. Fear is natural, and the fact that I've never heard of a shifter being able to carry talents of witches and the fae makes it even more natural for you to feel uncertain."

"What if it turns me dark? This isn't normal, Dominic."

"Ethan would sense the darkness in you no matter how deeply it was buried," he countered. "This is a good thing. We have a fighting chance to take the school back and help the students because of you. This is the answer to all of it."

"We have to get help, Dominic. I have no control over this, it just happened."

"Who's going to help us, Jenna?" his voice was lower. "No one. We're on our own. You can use these powers and sniff out whatever is lurking in the walls of that place."

"Really?" I said. "Then why wasn't this power around when it came to saving lives, preventing murders at the school?"

"Maybe you were too late. It seemed like this happened with Finley when you were provoked."

I ran my hands through my hair and gripped my head in frustration. "I do not think it works that way. I have no control!" I shouted. "I have to go get help. You need to come with me. Finley will be safe with Ethan checking on her. Come with me to find someone with higher powers than what's going on at that school."

"We can't leave, Jenna," he said.

"Dom," I sighed, trying to collect myself. I needed to convince him. "Listen to me. We *have* to get to the human world. We need more than just Ethan telling me I have some power—of which I have no idea how to control—and your alpha wolf to take the school back from the evil thing that's looming over it."

"We're not going out to the human world. It's not an option."

I glared at him and shouldered my pack. "Fine. You stay here, I'll get help. We go back to the school like this, and we're as good as dead. I'm not wasting time arguing with you. I'll find Vannah's family. They're the most powerful witches on the continent. I'm getting us help."

I took off through the opening in the rocks only to see massive trees, bright foliage, and blossoms the size of my head all around me. This was paradise. I had to be close to the human world. This seemed to be far from the academy and closer to freedom. I was caught by the arm as I came around a tree.

I tried to jerk my arm free from Dominic. "Unless you've changed your mind about going, then let me go."

"Jenna," he said, his eyes glittering against the silver that lined his brown irises. "I felt it. I accepted it. Please tell me you feel it too."

"Feel what?" I asked in confusion.

"You, us—our wolves," he answered. "Don't leave me. You can't separate them."

"Whatever you felt, I didn't," I answered. "I have to get help. Why can't you see that?"

"Why can't you see this is a stupid plan?" he asked in a soft voice. "I'm not leaving my cousin and my sister to die. You say you have friends here?"

"Yes. Friends who are brainwashed because of that evil place."

"If you were a true friend, you would stay and fight."

"Can't you see," I glared at him, "I have no control over this!"

"They need our help right now, you have the help they need, but you're going to run?"

"You act like this is something I've had my whole life! I *just* tripped and fell into this…this…whatever magic this is. How can you act like I'm the answer when I literally have no clue what I am or what I can do? That's not fair at all, and you know it."

"You don't have to do this. Don't leave…" He paused and reached for my hands. "Don't leave me, stay and fight with me. Fight for all of them."

"Whatever you're picking up on me, I don't feel it, Dominic."

"Really?" he said unrelentingly. Then without warning, I was pulled into Dominic's firm body, his hand snaking around my lower back, and his other hand smoothly gliding along the side of my face. He bent, and his lips were on mine.

Dom's firm kiss and his hand caressing my cheek, encouraged me to tilt my head and follow the lead he was offering on his unexpected kiss. I couldn't fight him if I wanted to. I felt his wolf call to mine, the wolf he hid from me until now. Its strength and humility were exposed as his tongue slid along my closed lips, slowing prying mine apart. That's when sparks ignited in my body like firecrackers, putting my little magic energy balls to shame.

I felt a feeling of completion as our wolves met for the first time, not hiding anything from one another. Dom's wolf should have been trying to throw down an alpha on my inner wolf that was fully exposed to him and vulnerable to it, but his wolf didn't. His wolf practically bowed to mine while giving her everything he was.

Our wolves were finding each other like they'd been searching for one another their entire lives. Dom's kiss deepened and tasting the honey flavor of his warm and enticing kiss was bringing me to a higher level beyond our wolves connecting like they were.

I desperately ran my hands up his sides, pulling myself in closer, and I framed his face with my hands. The serenity, the passion, and the power we were both transferring to each other through a simple, yet daring kiss was overwhelming and should have made me pass out; instead, I climbed the ladder of strength and took in everything Dom was offering me. I felt it now. He was my counterpart. His wolf was the only wolf that I could ever allow in. He was the only shifter who could ever help me develop into what I was born to become. He was my other half. That's what true mateship was, and somehow we were experiencing this profound uniting of our wolves and souls in just a kiss.

His daring, strong wolf was holding my wolf up in high esteem and *love* instead of acting out in alpha form and holding her down to claim her. How in the world could someone be perfect inside and out?

The hopeless and helpless child in me who wanted to know who her parents were all these years faded. She found her place now, it was with this shifter. I didn't need to know who my parents were to feel whole anymore, I was whole right now.

I could feel what Dom was feeling too. It's how he was feeling. This entire time, he'd never considered having anyone at his side...until now. The welcoming of emotions by accepting a woman to be his equal to love and devote his life to overwhelmed him as much as it was overwhelming me.

The passion was moving us both in a direction we both knew we weren't ready for. We had to stop this now, or we were going to wind up out here acting like nothing else in the world mattered but him and me establishing our commitment of being together for the rest of our immortal lives.

This all hit so hard and fast. It was more than real, it was a complete union, and the next step would seal us forever.

I pulled away reluctantly. I licked my lips, seeing his perfect ones and couldn't resist bringing his face back to mine. Dominic groaned, and thank goodness he laughed at my abrupt return to our tasteful kiss because it snapped me out of the daze I was in.

"I have to get—" Crap I was light headed and tripped over my feet. "I have to go."

Dom caught me and pulled me into his arms. "You know it now. You feel what's been nagging at me since the day we first locked eyes. I couldn't accept it was you, so I fought my wolf off. I stayed focused on my job and treating you like the student you were. I'm so glad I let you in, Jenna."

"You can't use that to stop me. You know I have to go get help," I said softly.

"If only my alpha worked on you," he said.

"It can't work because your wolf will not dominate or do anything to change me. I felt him. I felt you."

"Then you understand why I can't let you leave," he said. "You know what this means."

"I know this just went from zero to ninety between us."

"Stay with me. We'll do this together."

"Why can't you trust that we need more than just you and me?"

"Why are you so damn stubborn?" he snarled.

"I'll be back as soon as I can. I feel your power in me. I feel like we're connected. We won't lose each other. Let me go, Dominic. Please. I feel like this is the only way."

"I can't leave with you. I can't leave Ethan or all of the other innocent students here."

"Then—" I was really going to say it, "if you love me, you'll let me do what is right on my end. You stay and watch over them. I'll go search out the help we need."

"If I lose you…"

I smiled. "Then you'll feel like you did ten minutes before we had that kiss."

"And so she takes advantage of me giving her what I've given no one."

"I'm just trying to focus. I don't want to leave you. I want more than that kiss. I think I have the bigger problem right now."

Dom reached for my hand and pulled me close to him again. He swept a strand of hair over my forehead, "Don't ever think for a second I'll be okay if something were to happen to you." He pressed his lips into my forehead, "I've never felt this way in my entire life, and trust me, I'm the one with the bigger problem. I want it more than you can imagine. I'm all yours. I never thought my wolf would submit to another being, ever, but here we are. The only reason I'm not demanding you stay is that it's not in my nature to pull this on you, though I wish I could."

"I'll be fine. Safer out there than in here," I said.

He let out a breath. "Go to House Braeclaw. If you have to go find help, find your way to Aspen, Colorado. There's a quaint little candy shop there, that's your connection. Mention Mark Rossi, he's my father. The workers will know where to take you from there."

"Colorado, Aspen, candy shop," I answered the man I didn't

want to spend half a second apart from. My wolf was pissed. If she had a mouth on her like I did, she would've been sending every cuss word in the book at me for leaving her mate right now. "Got it."

"Mark Rossi," he urged and then pulled me in for a lasting farewell kiss. A kiss that I would let help me get help fast and get back quick.

Dom left me with instructions of what to tell his dad once I found him. I ran through the forest in my wolf form, scenting the air and sensing I was getting close to another realm. This scent was fading, and the façade was slowly disappearing from the school grounds. A gap over a river sent me jumping through the air and rolling into….what the hell!?

I looked down to see that my hands weren't my wolf paws. I was wearing a pale yellow cotton dress, and I was in some crazy house with antique furniture. The smell of freshly-baked apple pie filled my nose, but for the first time in my life, it wasn't the fragrance I craved. I wanted Dominic's scent.

"Where am I, what is this?"

A wrinkled little lady with white hair tied up in a bun came walking out with a slice of pie. Okay, longing for my true love could wait. This pie was everything I needed and more.

"Wait," I said, holding my hand out to the meek little lady who was probably a sinister trap. "Nice try. Who are you, and why are you killing innocents at that school?" I demanded. I had to have just found our person of interest and fell right into their trap. Nice try, though, Dom and I may have not mated and joined our wolves eternally, but I had the man's power, and this trap was about to backfire. This little sweet old lady was toast, but she was going to answer some questions first—evil demon spawn.

"Sit down, child," she squeaked out. "I'm not a demon spawn. I'm not your enemy, Jenna Silvers. You may be rude, but you have grown into the beautiful woman your mother once was. She would have been proud. Especially knowing you controlled your hormones around your true mate too." She chuckled. "Sit, dear. I have to fill you in and get you on your way. Those students aren't going to help themselves. Young Rossi was right when he told you that you were the answer. For now, of course. Now, sit, eat your pie, and let's get you caught up and on your way."

# CHAPTER THIRTY-FIVE

I sat across an old coffee table that looked like it had seen better days—like five hundred years ago—and gripped the porcelain saucer the all too tempting pie was on. I eyed the pie, letting my wolf scent if there were some toxic elements to it, but my wolf was too involved with the lady sitting across from me.

"Go on, have a bite. I promise it won't bite." She giggled.

"Who are you, and how do you know about me?" I looked at the pie then the woman. "I think you'll understand if I don't want the pie, seeing that the only people who know it's my addiction are people I've known since—"

"Silence, child," she cut me off. "If you don't trust the dessert, don't eat it. Fine by me. We have more pressing issues for you than a slice of pie for my godchild."

"Godchild?" I choked out. "Who *are* you?"

"I know your parents, like I said, your mother would have been proud of you." She sat straight up, sipping on a tea filled with warm spices. "Care for the tea? You never did as a young one."

"How is this possible?" I stared at this woman, wondering who she was, how I got here, and how she found me.

"So many things are possible in the supernatural, Jenna. So many good and so many terrible things. Sadly, your mom fell victim to the terrible."

"She died?" I asked flatly. "Why don't I remember anything about her—or you? How do you know whether or not I like tea?"

"Twenty years ago, a beautiful, brown-eyed girl with a head of glossy, auburn curls was born. After five years, the shifter babe's exceptional powers began developing, but it was far too soon, and she was much too young, and so she was hidden away in the school system. Hidden from herself, and hidden from her family."

"Are you talking about me? I'm only nineteen."

"Like I said, she was hidden from herself." She smiled and arched a silver eyebrow at me. "Your memories have been with-held from you to hide you from the underground society of darkness. The coven is still searching for the child that Julia and Nikolas shared together. They haven't been able to locate her until now, until the age of twenty when I knew your powers would eventually overcome the memory loss."

I gulped. "Rebecca and Nikolas? My parents. Who were they?"

"They were the kindest people to walk this planet. Little did we know that your mother—being half fairy and half witch—would impart most of her genetics into you, and they would work with Nikolas' alpha-wolf shifter genetics to create a child filled with more power than any supernatural could achieve. We couldn't figure out how a child could shift into their animal form at just three years of age. Then, little by little strange things began to occur in your life. You began moving things with your mind," she covered a smile, and her eyes were distant, "one of the first being a piece of pie that your mother insisted you couldn't have. I'll never forget the look on your parents' faces when you concentrated on the piece of pie in front of your father. When it began to float and head to your highchair tray, I thought we all might faint. You moved that pie to you with your mind like it was the easiest thing in the world to do."

I smiled, almost seeing it with my own mind and realizing that I had a pretty serious pie problem at a young age. "So what happened to me? What am I? I pulled some crazy stuff off today. I saved a shifter's life, healed her, and I've bonded to another shifter *without* mating. I have no idea, and none of it goes along with what's normal for a shifter."

"You are a very powerful young lady. We do believe that the Maddison coven—the coven your mother was born into—wanted you as their own. They cursed your mother after she separated herself from them. The curse that fell on her is something abhorrent. It's been fifteen years since the curse consumed your mother. She is gone to the darkness, and she..." The lady's eyes were sad and brimming with tears.

"Go on."

"She is the one who is creating the sinister energy at the academy. So long as the Immortal Academy keeps her damaged soul fed with immortal blood, she grows stronger."

"Feeds her? What the hell did they turn her into?"

"Watch your language in front of me, child."

"Sorry. Immortal Academy is starting to cure me of the foul mouth part. I guess you'd like that part then. That place is a creep show, and I'm still not one hundred percent sure you're not a part of it."

"I am a part of it. The Immortal Academy was designed to create strong immortals, to bring the strongest bloodlines together in hopes they would procreate. More importantly, its students are groomed to go out and police all supernaturals to help them coexist with humans. The humans owe the Immortal Academy a debt of gratitude for ensuring vampires don't drink humans dry, or fairies and witches don't use their powers on the planet to serve themselves. The academy has seen brighter days. Those days subsided when your mother was placed there to consume, at first, only the strongest immortals—for the

Maddison coven. They were building her up to be what you are since they couldn't have you."

"Oh my God." I sat there, my mind flooded with emotions. "They turned my mom into a monster. What happened to this coven? How do we end them and get her back? Innocent people are dying at that school, we thought it was the dean. My friends are stoned out on something in the air there, people are being placed in dungeons…"

"Stop rambling. Listen, you've bonded with a powerful wolf from House Braeclaw. Mark Rossi's boy. This has triggered your powers, and you may or may not start getting the memories back that I had to block for your safety. You and that boy, Dominic Rossi, have the power to end this, but it will take time. This curse that has fallen on the academy has gone on too long with no one strong enough to stop it."

"You took my memories away?"

"Like I said, I had to hide you from yourself. All of this was done to keep you hidden, child. After they burned your house, your father barely managed to bring you to me so I could do a vanishing spell on the both of us. I took you across the globe from South America all the way to the States where I knew it would be the last place they looked for you. When your immortal blood revealed itself to the Immortal Academy board, I knew you were reaching the age where I couldn't shield you from them any longer. You have done well in allowing the bond to happen between you and the Rossi boy. The Rossi's—or the family better known for being House Braeclaw's founders—are a strong line of immortals. Their owl shifter has lent me his eyes and has offered himself as your protector, I see. Ethan is a very intuitive child, beloved to me. We owe a debt of gratitude to the Braeclaws and their family for your safety."

"Where's my father?" I asked. I was being slammed with an info dump, and I felt the clock ticking away. "Maybe he can help me get my mother back."

"Your father was the first immortal ever murdered by the darkness the Maddison coven created. Your father was your mother's first victim."

"I think I'm going to barf."

"You're stronger than that," she insisted. "Now, listen to me. You must return to the academy. Dean Edgewater serves the Maddison coven. It is his job to ensure no one questions anything about that school or escapes it. He is the one who selectively picks immortals to be used to give your mother more power. The dungeons you've been warned about do not exist. Tales about the dungeons were only created to cover up the fact that immortals were going missing. The school is a very, very dark place. Do you understand me?"

"Yes. There are shadow creatures that walk through the dorms. I've seen them," I offered up.

"I don't doubt that."

"Why are Dominic, Ethan, and I the only ones who haven't been affected by whatever these witches have the dean doing to everyone at the school?"

"Ethan, come here, child."

Ethan stepped around the corner and smiled at me. "Jenna Silvers."

"E?" I looked at him, shocked that he was here. "Why are you here? How did you know about this lady?"

"Jenna, do not be rude. Your godmother has helped me protect you. Thank her."

"Thank you," I said with fear. "What do I do? How do we stop it all?"

"Everyone who has fought the Maddison coven has been delivered to the beast in the water. No one is strong enough, not even my owl friend."

"You and Dominic will one day destroy the beast, Jenna. Not now," Ethan said in his matter of fact tone.

"I can't let Dominic go back there then. I have to get help and get the kids out of that place."

"No one can leave unless they die. A dark spell is injected into the supernatural being, liquefying their insides, and then they are fed the immortal to the beast in the water."

"Ethan, I get it. We have to stop that. We have to take out the dean then. We stop him, we find this coven of witches, and we all work together to destroy them and send them back to hell where they came from."

"It is not an easy event. Child, so many have gone up against this coven. They cannot defeat them without being drawn to them by their own alluring spell. Your friend—Vannah, is it?"

"Yes," I gulped, "What about her? Can her coven help?"

"How is she faring at Immortal Academy?"

"Stoned out with the others. Maybe we can get her coven to create something to snap her out of it."

"Her coven has merged with the Maddison coven. Every single supernatural who has fought these dark witches has fallen victim to them. You, the Rossi shifter, and Ethan are the only ones who have not. There is a reason for that."

"Lusa fell to the academy on the blood lust quest. She drank the blood with the curse of the academy in it. These spells I can help reverse, but we cannot just so easily wage war with a coven and risk you—unprepared—being lured into their world. Don't you know they believe that one day you will try to come for them? Do you think it is worth that risk?" Ethan said.

"No." I grit my teeth together. "How do I prepare to take them all on?"

"Dominic Rossi said something very interesting before you took it upon yourself to wander dangerously out into these woods, looking for an escape. Do you remember what that was?" the woman asked.

"Fight them together. Stay with my friends and not leave."

"The boy is wise. Now, you will do as he suggests. Once the

dean is exposed for the deaths of the children, he must not be killed. He must not die at that school. The beast in the water—your mother—will take his dark energy and gain more strength."

"How do we expose the dean when we can't leave the school without dying? How do we do any of this?"

"I am sending a group from House Braeclaw, House Mage, House Draugar, and House Fae to Immortal Academy. We meet in a day from now. As soon as you went into the water with your mother, I knew it was time to call the headmasters of the houses. You will expose the dean with evidence of his dealings at the school, and we will remove him. The Maddison witches will not know anything has happened until your mother—the beast in the water—is starved. Perhaps this will be the end of her and her feedings. She will die peacefully, and I will work with House Mage covens to ensure your mother's spirit finds rest."

"And how do we expose him?"

"You must stop him, child. Find a way to get him to unlock the trees that harbor their secrets. Enchant House Fae to reveal all that's transpired. He feeds a starving monster once a week now. It will soon come down to once a day."

"The dean is already hunting for us. We're his fugitives." I said, defeated. "Why can't I just kill him?"

"Taking out the darkness that fell on the Immortal Academy years ago doesn't happen by snapping your fingers. You must keep your true identity a secret. This is why you are a Silver from House Silvers, the extinct monarchy in the supernatural realm. You must work to remain hidden from all beings until you are ready to defend yourself from any one of them should they get greedy and take you and try to turn you dark. If that happens, all of this was for nothing."

"I am not sure how to do any of this."

"When I send you back you will return to a time period where you can work to stop the dean from taking the younger immortals' lives such as he has done this year. He is turning as dark as the school and must be stopped. Do not think for a second he hasn't already reported you to the Maddison coven. He was too excited about the miracle that happened between you and the Rossi shifter."

"So we're going back in time. Will everyone remember..."

"You and Ethan will be the only ones who remember, but Dominic will help you. He knew something wasn't right during that time. He also was starting to fight his wolf feelings off for you. The moment you didn't answer his alpha, his wolf knew you were his. Ethan will work with him, and Dominic will work with you. You will also need Lusa Rossi to help as well. This will not be an easy takedown. No one should be trusted at that school. The darkness will reveal itself easier to you now that you carry some of Dominic's power in you."

"Dominic will sense you carrying his wolf powers, Jenna," Ethan reassured me. "He has never loved anyone. Dominic and his wolf love you and will know you even if we go back in time."

I half smiled at Ethan. "Okay," I said, feeling totally tripped out and trying not to think but one step at a time. "After the dean's out, when do we kill the monster in the freaking water?"

"Like I said, you don't carry all your power yet. It will take time. Do not rush this, or you will fall victim to the Maddison coven and give them all the power they have ever wanted. You must promise me that you will climb this mountain slowly. If you rush it, you will doom much more than just the students at that school."

"Got it," I said. "Take me back. And then," I looked at her, "I want to know more. I need you at that school or something."

"You do not need me at the school." She smiled. "Though I am always keeping a watchful eye on you. Trust your wolf. You haven't been listening to her or following her lead. Trust your newfound powers, and don't fear them. Above all, trust yourself, and have patience in this endeavor. All humanity and supernatural of all kind are depending on you to have patience. Once the dean is gone, you will remain at the school as its protector. Dominic Rossi will be your protector, and Ethan will protect both of you. As your relationship moves deeper, you will both get stronger. You must understand that."

"I feel like the weight of the world is on my shoulders, and now I get to pull Dominic into this crap with me. It's my evil mom who has caused countless—"

"Dominic is your mate. His memories of you may stay when she brings us back to before Jess's death. Do not begin to direct his fate, Jenna," Ethan demanded. "His fate is with you."

"Take out the dean. That is your objective," she said.

"I will be helping to guide you, Jenna."

"I hope so, Ethan Carter. This is the most you've said since I've met you, you know. If Dom isn't with me due to time travel memory loss, I'm going to need you."

"We'll fix this," he promised.

"Now, let's get you all back to the day of the Ageless Ball."

*Wait...*It was too late. The info dump, Jenna's entire life is a screwed-up, dark lie conversation abruptly halted, and I was walking into the Ageless Ball dressed in the Queen of Sparta's outfit I swore I would never wear again in my life. Oh my God, how was I going to pull all of this off? I needed to know where Jess was instead of marching the steps with my best friend into the dean's mansion. Damn it, I had no idea where to start.

# CHAPTER THIRTY-SIX

"Dude, I have to pee," I said to Vannah, knowing I needed to break away from her.

"Seriously?" she laughed. "We just got here."

"I drank too much water."

She eyed me with a smile, "You're too much sometimes. I'll see you inside."

"Alright. Don't be too surprised if I manage to weasel my way out of this too. I'm not really down for this ball thingy or this revealing outfit."

"You're not chickening out on me, girl. Get back here."

"You'll forget about me once you see your man."

"True," she gripped my arm.

"Yeah," I managed with the best smile of encouragement.

She gathered up her dress and walked up the steps like Cinderella, heading off to meet her prince. Students passed me as I swerved my way away from the Dean's mansion, looking for clues of where the heck to start. I knew I was on a time crunch and had a sneaking suspicion Jess was already in trouble, if not dead.

I had to find those buildings that were hidden from the enchantment of the alluring buildings at the front of this place. I stopped in my tracks. Lusa and Dom seemed to show up late, and Ethan never made it to this ball, which was why I'd initially thought Ethan was mixed up with the deaths. I had to find him, maybe he was already tripping out, and Lusa and Dom had him somewhere.

I raced back to my dorm and heard a noise before I turned the corner. I had no idea where Dom's room was, but I was guessing that the loud *Shhh's* and the chants going off in the far corner were coming from Ethan, Dom, and Lusa. This might be where Ethan was compelled to calm down due to what had happened or was currently happening to Jess.

I walked toward the door, seeing shadows moving in the light underneath it, and I knocked. The silence and feet shuffling stopped.

"Just get the door," I heard Dom say in a hushed voice.

Lusa opened it, and her eyes widened when she saw me.

"Jenna," she said in shock. "Why are you here?"

"I was looking for my date. Someone told me he was here."

"Scott?" she answered. "That's shocking."

"Don't know what's so shocking about it," I said, trying to see around Lusa as she stood guard at the door. I shoved the door open and moved into an immaculate and massive corner dorm room. *Nice suite, Dom!*

"What is she doing in here?" Dom had his hand covering Ethan's mouth, and he kept it there as he looked past me to Lusa. "Don't you have manners?" he glared at me. "You think you can just bust into—"

"Let Ethan go," I said, walking over to my frantic friend.

"He's tripping out. You shouldn't be here. We need to calm him down, or he'll shift," Dom said.

I sat next to Ethan, where Dominic had him on the couch. "E, it's me, Jenna. Do you remember what we need to do?"

"Danger. Immortals will die," he chanted out before Dom covered his mouth again.

He sternly looked at me. "What are you talking about? You're making this worse. Lusa?" he called to his sister who was walking in behind me. "You need to compel him and calm him down."

"No!" I demanded. "We need his help. Don't you remember?" I asked Dominic, feeling that weird void as if I lost the guy I had just connected with.

"Remember what? If you have something to say, say it and then get out of here."

"Jess is in trouble. Ethan knows it. Whatever darkness is at this school is screwing with his mind. I need his help, and I need your wolf."

"You know nothing about this school, Ethan, or my wolf."

I'd forgotten what a jerk he was in the beginning. "I know your wolf feels mine. I know your wolf is sensing more right now, just looking into my eyes." I felt a strong alpha force in me. It was the connection I took with me from him. "Your wolf is urging you to accept this, but you won't because you're an arrogant, stubborn jerk. I need you to get over yourself and trust me."

"You're talking crazy."

"Please," I reached for Dominic's hand, and we both froze. I absorbed the feeling I got from being in contact with him again, and I could sense that he was shocked and trying to process the feeling of being shot back in time. "Just trust me, if I'm wrong, you can move me off your unit, or make me do pushups until you feel I've been punished enough."

Dom's eyes narrowed at me. "What are you doing to me? Why do I feel like you and I have made this connection before? It's like Deja Vu or something."

"I don't have time to go into all of that. All I have time to do is convince you that bad stuff is about to go down…if it already hasn't."

Dom looked at Lusa. "Find a way to make some dumb excuse as to why I got sick tonight," he grumbled.

He looked at me, his eyes still trying to figure out what he felt with my touch. I could sense it coming off of him, and it's only because I took that part of him with me before that Godmother of mine sent me back to this moment in time. "Tell them I am dealing with my sick cousin if they ask my whereabouts. Just pull off some coverup as to why I'm not showing up at this ball tonight."

"I'll come up with something." She looked at both of us. "Are you two experiencing the same thing my instincts are trying to tell me?"

"Yes."

"No," Dom said.

"I'll explain later." I looked at Dom, "We need Ethan." I ran my hand on Ethan's arm, "I need you to remember what that godmother lady put in your head. You're my only hope, Ethan Carter. Dom doesn't remember."

"You and Dominic are true mates."

"Gah," I said in frustration. "No. Not about us, Ethan, I'm talking about Jess and what they're going to do to her. It's what you're flipping out about. You have to take Dom and me to her. We have to save her."

"Save her from what?" Dom snapped.

"It would be better if you trusted me and let me take the lead. I know you're sensing that in me. I know your wolf is begging you to do it, so do it. Stop arguing with me and asking questions, or I won't be able to get Ethan to focus."

"How are you doing this?" Dom growled.

"Getting pissed isn't going to help either. I'll explain later."

"The black buildings, the quiet places," Ethan said. "Boilers, the furnace."

"I don't know where that is. Can you take us there, E?"

Dom rose us up, "I'm going with this, only because my wolf is ready to shift and follow your commands." He looked at Ethan, then me, "after we figure out what the heck is going on, both of you are going to tell me why this is happening. I have better control over my shifting abilities—"

"Where are the buildings, Ethan?"

"Follow me," Dom said. "I think I know what he's talking about, and if we get caught there, we're all in the dungeons."

"Yeah, I'll tell you about those later," I rolled my eyes, knowing now that the freaking things didn't even exist.

"Let's go."

We marched out of the dorms. Lusa split to the left, heading toward the ball, and we followed Dom toward the library. We snuck off to where I saw the black buildings and the body bag with Kat in it.

"Are these the buildings, E?" Dom asked his cousin, who had become silent once we got on the trail to hopefully saving Jess and catching this dean in the act.

"Through the basement doors," Ethan said.

We stepped down steps, and all three of us molded into the brick walls of the musty place when we heard feet shuffling. Dom went into some *commander of the supernatural army* mode and motioned for us to duck while crossing over to another hall. We ran through wet floors and turned up concrete steps that led to a closed metal door.

"This place is the ultimate creep show of this whole school," I whispered.

"That's why students don't come to the abandoned buildings," Dom retorted.

"Through the door, to the right. She is dead now. Immortals dead."

"What?" I seethed. "We're too late?"

"We must go now," Ethan ordered and shoved his robust cousin out of his way.

When we walked into some chamber, we saw Jess's lifeless

body lying on a white bed with metal legs. Her arms had rubber tubes coming out of them with green fluid being pushed into them. A soft whimper came from her final breath.

Dom rushed to her side, gently trying to rouse her awake by tapping the sides of her face. "Jess. Come on, you stay with me." His voice was cracking, in shock. Who knew, maybe he lied and did have feelings for the girl. Instead of getting jealous, I was actually heartbroken, knowing he and Jess had a little kissing fling. Now, here she was...dead.

Dom turned back to me, eyes severe. "Who the hell are you, Jenna Silvers?" he growled. "How did you know about her? How did you manipulate my wolf? What the hell is going on?"

"I see you have finally learned the truth of the unique shifter. Yes. We wondered if she was the one who killed this innocent girl. Immortals don't die, yet here is a dead shifter."

I looked back, seeing this whole rescue mission backfiring on me. Mistress Sirena slowly approached from behind. None of this made sense to me. I thought this was the dean's doing.

"I didn't do shit!" I snapped at the eerie look on the lady's face while three black, faceless demon men stood tall at her side. "The dean did this, and now you? How many more are involved?"

"Get the dark shifter child out of here. Put her on the machines. She gets to experience what it's like to die an immortal death, just like the poor shifter she killed."

"What!" I looked at Dom, "Stop them! Dammit it, you're smarter than this."

"You won't stop us from seeking justice. You loved this shifter, you both were just too young; isn't that right, Dominic Rossi?"

"Dominic and Jenna are mates!" Ethan shouted, mainly toward Dom who fell under some weird hypnosis the witch had hit him with.

Ethan shifted at that moment, and his owl tore into the black, faceless men, his large talons turning them into dust particles where they once stood. Ethan swarmed the room, but a large green energy swirled around his owl. My only ally was suddenly gone, and I felt a needle get stabbed into my neck. Slowly, the room blurred, Dom's face was blank, and I dropped.

Everything was dark, and all I heard was the crashing of metal objects, a shriek, a growl—Dom had shifted—and then it was game over for me.

My insides started burning, my lids became too heavy, and the next thing I knew, I was floating above my body. How was I supposed to help any of the kids at this school as Casper the ghost? I needed a restart on this. I needed godmother granny to give me another shot at this. This is not what she was expecting to happen, or was she? Maybe she was the trap the entire time, sending me straight to the evil witch who was obviously doing the dean's bidding to get me killed.

I seemed to be in spirit limbo, and if I was still lurking around like a ghost, staring at my body crashed out on the ground, then where was Jess in this limbo of death world I was floating around in?

# CHAPTER THIRTY-SEVEN

The spirit world had me tethered to the real world, and it was frustrating not to be able to punch a black demon in its face. I swung at one of the black faceless entities after Dom's wolf was pinned by two of those things. I heard him call out in pain, so I lurched into it only to swoosh in spirit form right through the thing.

I had no sensory perception by not feeling mass and being in this state. My wolf was present with me, but her eyes were set on the black wolf—her other half—and that's when I felt something real. She wanted to join his wolf. I had no idea if it was possible since the Dom of the past hadn't accepted her yet, but maybe because of the feelings of the strong wolf I still carried from our kiss it would work.

Dom's wolf had three of those respawning, undying things smothering him. All I could hear were his growls, then one of the faceless creatures disappeared, and another back to take its place.

He needed something, and my wolf was pretty sure her power could help. I wasn't going to argue because if I didn't act fast, then Dom would be with me—or wherever Jessica's fox shifter spirit went—and nothing would be left to save this school from the crazy witch clan that took it over.

I sank down and found Dom's wolf snarling in the corner he was trapped in. I had no idea how my wolf was going to transfer this energy she had to unite us, but she was in a crouching position and ready to pounce. She was ready, and I went with my gut instinct.

I crawled over to the snapping, vicious wolf and dove toward the massive alpha. I felt my inner wolf leave me, and for the first time ever, I couldn't feel my inner wolf...she was gone.

I slumped in spirit form against the wall, feeling like letting go and moving on. I couldn't explain this feeling of void, it was as if part of my soul was ripped from me. Dom's wolf seemed to jump into a more powerful action, and when he stood, slowly stepping toward the faceless demon things, they stepped back. They must have sensed the alpha charged up with more power—or they knew he carried death in his eyes.

The black wolf must have sensed my presence—or it was my girl working with him—because Dom's bronze-eyed wolf craned his head back to where I was watching and waiting. When I saw the wolf's eyes, I was blown away to see Dom's bronze eyes had been replaced by the blue eyes of what I knew was my wolf. Then in a blink, his eyes were his silver lined, bronze wolf eyes again.

*Show off!* My wolf sensed me and was relieved that I finally listened to her plans. Dom went to action, ripping those things apart and defeating them with brutal force.

Everything happened so swiftly from seeing my wolf to where I was now. The war was over, but I was still dead and couldn't find my way back to my body. I watched in disbelief as my surroundings changed. It was daylight now, and my body was lying out on the front lawns to the school's entrance.

Five black SUV's pulled up and followed each other down the driveway and up to the school. The school students all stood out, Mistress Sirena—the vampire who worked for the Maddison coven—was handcuffed with warded sigil cuffs and being walked out to one of those black cars.

A large group dressed in black suits and long black dresses worked the area.

"The owl won't leave her," Dean Edgewater said with a hand clamped on Dominic's shoulder. "We must take her and Jessica's body and…"

"No one is to touch the bodies," a short man with an authoritative voice said.

I looked over and saw my body lying there—in my Queen of Sparta costume, no less—with Ethan's large owl behind me. One of his massive wings was spanned out and reaching around my head, planted like a barrier in front of my body, reaching almost to my waist. His owl was enormous, and his owl was pissed. No one was going near the angry shifter, even Dom had a fearful expression on his face toward Ethan as his owl was in full predator mode.

"I see you have learned a little about this ancient school," a voice said to my right. "The darkness will soon lift, for now."

The school scene faded when I looked and saw a tall man with *my* brown eyes and short brown curly hair.

"Dad?" I questioned the familiar features I shared with the man.

His lips pulled together in a fine line and drew up in one corner, offering me a curious smile and nod. "Your mother was right, look at you, you certainly do look like me." He chuckled. "Although, I see so much of her in you too."

"Am I in shifter afterlife? How is this happening?"

"You're still needed on this earth, you won't be coming with me, Jenna."

I ran to hug him, but an invisible wall stomped me inches from contact. "As much as I long to embrace my baby girl, I'm only here in your spiritual mind."

"I'm so confused."

"I would think you were insane if you weren't," he said, eyes locked on mine. "Listen, we don't have much time before they take you from here. I need you to understand that you must always fight. The war may seem to be over for now, but until the creature is exposed and you find a way to destroy her and the coven that cursed our family, you must always watch and be ready."

"Ready for what? They just took that professor who was killing immortals out of this place," I said, my mind still blown I was talking to my dad. Naturally, I should've been skeptical that this was him, but it wasn't even a question in my mind.

"The darkness lives and breathes in the walls of Immortal Academy. Look at the school." He pointed back to where I once was, watching all the students as they huddled together and stared at House Draugar's headmaster being hauled off, my dead corpse positioned like sleeping beauty waiting for the prince to kiss her and lift her curse, and the dean talking to the army of people in black clothes.

I saw the brilliance of the charming school. I could see the alluring nature it projected and the fairies' magic sprinkled everywhere...the beautiful, majestic school that I hated even past its beauty.

"Look harder, Jenna. You have the ability to see past this façade. The school is spelled to allure students—to be everything they want it to be in a school. That's where it takes them and slowly digests them to thrive."

All he had to do is hit me with that cryptic message, and I narrowed my eyes at the school I hated...the creepy school that took my friends from me. That's when the façade dropped, and I saw the school for what it really was now.

It was dark gray, eerie gray. Thick brown twigs replaced the vibrant glittery vines that had bright blooms in a variety of gemstone colors. The lawns were brown and overgrown. The crystal clear water was a murky green and brown mudhole for the deteriorating fountains that graced the lawns. The trees were all dead, branches like skeleton fingers sprawling out from their massive trunks and reaching toward a greenish black sky. Everything about this school screamed death and darkness.

"It looks like death...like this has been abandoned for decades."

"Now you see what the evil has done here. Lift your eyes, but don't forget—this is what Immortal Academy truly looks like. Once the creature is destroyed, the coven of witches who destroyed this school will be gone with their creation, and the school will return to its natural beauty. Even more beautiful than what your mind sees in its façade."

"How do I do any of that? Apparently, my mother was part witch and part fairy. I have no control over the crazy powers when they hit me, but they seem to come in when I beg them to."

"You have to control that. Do not beg for the powers, but you should know that you have much more than just the powers of the fae and witch. You are the strongest shifter. Once you and House Braeclaw's strongest alpha are mated, you will begin to see your powers develop further. Until then, you must continue on your path of destiny."

"Destiny? Why can't I just help to free the kids out of this place? Why can't we just leave to save our lives?"

"If you all leave, the darkness will follow you out into the world, and Earth will look like this place."

"Why is this all on my shoulders? What if this all fires back up again and more immortals die?"

"Immortals will die, Jenna. You can't save all of them, even by freeing them. Every immortal at this school was selected to be here, and once here, they feed the beast. They feed the walls of that place. They are connected. The connection has been reversed by you and the alpha working together to destroy the darkness for now, but it's not left the school. It will always continue to feed until the coven, their spell, and their beast have been defeated. The time will come, but that time is not now."

"Then, when is *that time?*"

"You'll know. Until then, all you can do is work to help House Mage and the surveillance council that is at the school now to get rid of the ones who fall under its possession."

"Dean Edgewater. He is part of this, but he stands out there, free."

"Dean Edgewater has not been possessed by the school, not fully. His fairy genetics have kept the dark fight within him at bay. It was the vampire who fell, she dabbled in the darkness that lured her. She wanted more power, the school gave her what she wanted and took what it wanted in return. That woman will be locked away by the council."

"And if the Maddison coven finds out about her and what the surveillance council—those people dressed in black—did?"

"The war would come sooner. The Maddison coven knows there is one who can defeat them, they just don't know exactly who that is."

"This is all insanity."

"Evil is insanity, Jenna. That's why we took you away before they spelled you and hid you from them. They still believe you are the nineteen-year-old child, the oracle that you spoke with—"

"Fairy godmother," I offered.

He grinned. "Yes. She's protected you since the fire. We trusted her to protect you, to keep you from this place, but as she warned, your blood wouldn't be able to withstand the dark magic from sensing that you are all immortal. We'd hoped her spell would hide the fact that your mother and I were full-blooded immortals, but fairy and witch blood in your system kept overcoming it all. Now, you're at the age where she can't reverse your memories anymore. You will know and remember everything now."

"Hold up," I said. "My memories have been screwed with?"

"Yes," he said. "For your protection. There are so many people secretly working for Maddison coven that we couldn't take chances. There are also many working for us—for you—to help keep you protected. The oracle—your godmother—has stepped in more than once to erase your memories and to mute your abilities outside of being a shifter."

"Can't you all take us back in time, like she did for me to *unsuccessfully* save Jessica and stop Dominic Rossi and me from doing that connection thing?"

"Does your soul wish to be separated from him? We've already pulled your wolves apart once, we will not make that mistake again. It could have cost more than poor Jessica's immortal life."

"What the hell are you talking about?" I asked in a low voice.

"You and Dominic have already connected your wolves. That's when your powers came too early. You were too young. We questioned all of it, and we altered fates because of it. If there is one thing we won't do again, it is separating your wolves."

"When?" I asked him. "When did this happen? How many times have I had my brains scrambled by this oracle?"

"It was at your previous school. You and Dominic sensed each other's wolves. You were both too young for such a connection to be forged—he eighteen and you seventeen. We were sure both of you were in grave danger and not mature enough to fight off being mated for the power. It had to be stopped."

"So you all just came in and stopped us. This is why our wolves both sense more, but we mentally fight it off in our natural forms?"

"Yes," he said sorrowfully. "You must understand that no malice was intended. We're doing our best to protect you."

"But now it's okay?"

"Now, you both are ready," he answered.

I should've been angry that my memories had been tampered with, but I knew that it was meant to protect me. The more I heard, the more it made sense. Our wolves already knew each other. It's the reason I didn't cower to his alpha stuff, the reason I felt a pull toward him, and him towards me.

"Dominic doesn't remember me. Since that Oracle Godmother brought me back here, he doesn't remember our connection."

"Dominic will always be your mate. You'll just have to be patient. It didn't take long for you both to reunite, it won't take long again. Your wolves already know each other, just stop fighting them and their instincts."

"How do we beat this thing?"

"The school—your friends even—have been given a fresh start. Even now, they are working to ward off all the sinister spells that fell on the students; however, as I said, the school will lure them all back to it. It will slowly digest who they really are, and they will fall under the spell again. Some may be able to fight it. You should work with your friend, Vannah. She is a strong witch—a Woodson witch. You will need her, so don't lose her to the school again."

"I don't know how to warn her."

"There will be a new professor for House Mage, Joseph Ramirez, he's a Brujo—a powerful witch from Mexico. He will watch over her. He has no desire to dabble in the darkness of Immortal Academy. He'll work with Vannah, he's been instructed to. It will be like killing an enemy from the inside out. The more talented and powerful immortals you can keep from succumbing to the evil of the school, the better the chance you have. This is the only way. There's nothing we can do. I tried, and you see where I am."

"Yeah, if you hadn't noticed, I tried too, and I'm here with you."

He laughed. "Your powers have kept you tethered to your body. The brujo is working with House Mage to purify the school, and then you will be brought back. Their memories will be lost on what has happened here. It will be like your first day of school again."

"Oh God," I sighed with frustration. "The only thing cool about the first day at this place was having my bug and my map... which I totally forgot about my little buddy. That was it. Well, that and the pie."

My dad laughed again. "You have your mother's personality and my love for pie. Listen, I said it would be *like* the first day of school...when your friends were normal. Jessica is at peace, and you will be the only one who remembers her death. You and the owl shifter, Ethan. Ethan will not whisper a word of it to anyone. Other than that, it will be just like any other day at the academy. You will see the difference, not the others."

"This sucks. Dominic won't even remember how he worked to kill off all those things? He practically saved the school while I died."

"Dominic will only remember what your wolf spirit lets him remember," he said.

I felt a heavy weight pulling me away from my father. "It's time you go. They're bringing you back now. I love you, Jenna. Always know I am proud, and when your mother's cursed spirit is at rest, she will be just as proud."

"Wait. I'm not..."

My eyes snapped open, and I was staring at my dorm room ceiling.

"Get out of bed sleepy head," Lusa's voice said with a laugh. "My brother is going to blame me for you being late to his training."

"What day is it?" I asked. I sat up, thinking maybe Dom and I were back, "Wait. Why would he blame you for me being late?"

She looked at me and laughed. "Because you're my dorm mate? He's got this weird thing about you not answering his alpha, and it's starting to bug me. He acts like his ego can't take it, but the Dominic I know would usually admire a chick who could possibly kick his butt."

"Oh, so we're back to that again."

"Back to what?" she looked at me curiously. "If I had to guess, I'd say you look bummed out that he would question you. You two have something going on the side?" she teased.

"You would think," I accidentally said out loud. "I mean—"

"What?" she asked. "You know, you and Dom act like you annoy each other. Although, last night at the ball showed me you two are actually the perfect match. The outfits were priceless," she laughed.

"Right," I said, blinking a few times.

Okay, so it was a day after the Ageless Ball. Lusa was friendlier than ever. Did I have my friends back? The thought of getting them back sounded terrific, but the void of Dom and me having to restart, me remembering him, but him not remembering me totally sucked.

*Why didn't you let him remember us?* I internally scolded my inner wolf. She pranced around like she had nothing to be sorry for. She helped Dom save the world, she knew his wolf was her true mate, and she taught me my lesson.

I had to really get Dom connected with me again. I felt stronger with him, and even now after my wolf had jumped into him, I was losing his strength. The truth was I needed him, and I was not one to admit I needed anyone.

# CHAPTER THIRTY-EIGHT

It was a roller coaster of a month. The good news was that I had my friends back. As for Tanner and Emma, that was an interesting breakup. Tanner moved on, and I wanted to feel bad for the sprite, but after the spell had been lifted and everyone had their original personalities, it didn't take long for her to realize their relationship wasn't going to work. His love 'em and leave 'em side was more than she could handle, but they managed to stay friends. Oddly enough, Vannah and blue-haired Nick managed to cool it as well, knocking their relationship back to friendship.

This was normal. Vannah was scared to commit in a relationship, and if it felt too serious too fast, she pumped the breaks on it. Tanner was a player and was already eyeing some vamp chick I hadn't met yet. My friends were themselves again for the first time since we got to this place.

Normal was good. The heavy darkness that clouded the school had been lifted, and it literally felt like the sun came out from behind dark clouds—to me at least. Everyone around me had no idea the crazy spell they had been under. No one knew the bizarre fact that this school was turning them into something

it wanted and slowly eating their personalities—their souls—
alive while being here.

We were back to normal class sessions, learning about all the
Houses and the history of each of the immortal beings at this
school. It was a breath of fresh air. As much as I hated sitting in
lectures, I had to admit, the normalcy of everything outweighed
me being bored in class.

Dom returned to Master Dominic with me, and that was the
hardest part of the new normal at this school. I gave up hope on
the *Dom and Jenna are fated mates* part a few days into the school
being straightened out. The dude was all over my butt and
singling me out during training, and it was starting to piss me off
instead of making me long for the Dom I felt a surreal connection with.

I was under the dude's watchful eye, and I swear I was getting
busted at every turn I made with the guy. It was annoying and
frustrating. My wolf was pissed off at him too, but I had my
friends back, and from what I remembered about my out of body
experience with my dad, I had to make sure I didn't lose them to
this school again. There was a looming battle hanging in the air,
and we all needed to be ready for it.

"Mind if I have a word with you, Silvers?" Dominic's voice
interrupted me as I savored my hot apple pie.

My eyes lifted to the table he was once at, and I smiled at all
the hateful expressions and arched eyebrows directed toward me.

"What did I screw up now?" I asked, remembering our
morning drills and using the skills I had learned from him before
the spell was lifted from the school. Throughout all the madness
of the school being a bizarre trip, one thing I took away from it
all was learning to fight—like Dominic. I held it all back, trying
not to upset the balance of everything being reset.

"Jenna," Vannah startled me. "Quit being so rude," she laughed.

I looked over at her, then back to Dominic. "Sorry, my brain
kind of goes dead once I start in on my pie."

"All I need is a minute alone," he said in a low voice.

I twisted in my seat and looked up at him. "Alright." I stood. "What do you need?"

He guided me over to a corner in the lunchroom. "Today. The way you fought." His dark eyebrows knit together as he studied me. "How did you learn that technique you used to drop Jon and pin him?"

"You taught me that," I answered. "Remember?"

"No, I don't," he answered sternly. "That's my own personal technique. I've never trained anyone on that."

"God, Dominic, I just dropped, let him come in for the fake pin, spun around, and took him down by the knees with my feet. Anyone could do it, but you're the one who taught me how to do it and when it would work best to my advantage."

"Are you some kind of a mind reader?" he asked.

*Crap. Did I just use a technique he taught me out on the quest?*

"No," I answered in the same rough tone. "You taught it to me. Sorry that you don't remember doing it. Maybe with all your, *'I'm going to break you and your wolf and have the best shifter unit at this school'* talk, you forgot you gave up your technique. Why? Am I in trouble or something? I finally do something that should be approved by you, and you act like you're pissed off about it."

His lips tightened, and I ignored the lustful thoughts that wanted to take over when his arms crossed and his bulging biceps tried to remind me of the guy I fell for.

"No. You're not in trouble for anything except for your foul mouth that is directed toward your instructor," he shook his head, and I could tell he was fighting a smile, "again. You really need to work on that. I'm getting sick of you throwing language around at me like you and I are friends. You're my trainee, and I expect you to respect that I'm your instructor. The next time you think you can use foul language toward me, I'll make sure you don't get your shifting time in for at least a week."

*What an asshole! Dude practically hates me now—damn this school.*

*I knew it was driving its evil to tear Dominic Rossi and me apart.* If it weren't for me knowing this school had it out for us, I would seriously hate this guy. God, I should hate him right now for interrupting me eating my now *cold* apple pie.

"Sorry about that. I need to keep my frustration in check when I feel I'm being singled out by my master."

"You're not being singled out. I was curious, that's all. I never share any of those skills with my new recruits. It wasn't something you made up either. The timing, the reason, and how you did all of it, that's something I came up with."

"Well, I'm sorry I stole your special little fight move. Is there anything else?"

His eyes were severe. "No," he managed in a low voice. "I'll see you this evening in wolf form."

Great, that actually sounded like a threat. Dom being up my butt for a month was getting old. Now, this hatred he'd developed for me was just making it all worse, and I was over it.

"What was that all about?" Vannah asked when I got back to my abandoned pie. "What'd you do to upset your master now?"

"I guess it's pretty obvious he and I don't get along, eh?"

"Obvious is an understatement. If I had to guess, the dude hates you to cover up the fact he most likely likes you. You shifters are weird like that."

I smiled at Vannah, a month having her back to her normal self again still felt like I just got my bestie back. "You're probably right. We're destined to be together. A strong alpha like him with a wolf that doesn't follow his haughty alpha commands...a match made in heaven," I teased.

She giggled—the Vannah, low and in control of herself giggle—and rolled her eyes. "Well, it's just a hunch."

"Oh? You using your witchy skills outside of school rules?" I asked.

Vannah's eyes dropped to her plate, where she was finishing

her cheesecake. "You ever get the feeling this school is watching us?" she asked in a hushed voice.

"Are you serious? Are you picking up on something? Because last time, you..." I stopped myself. My God, what was wrong with me today. It was like everything I had held in about what the school was like before the reset was coming out like crazy.

"Last time I what?" she looked at me with curiosity. "Jenna, if you know something, you need to tell me."

*I so wish I could.*

"I feel the same as you. I get the creeps here, but you knew that already. It's just me being upset I had to come here, I guess."

"Possibly. Don't tell anyone I said that."

"Never," I answered. "You know you can tell me anything, right?"

She smiled. "You've always been my most trusted friend. Of course. Just watch your back. I have a weird feeling that things might get crazy at this school."

"Then use your secret protector spell on yourself," I ordered her. "Seriously. If you're sensing something, then go with it."

"I think I might."

"Promise me, you will," I urged.

She looked at my hands, gripping her arm. "Easy, Jenna." She looked around. "I can't do anything if you have the entire school watching us. Like I said, it's just a hunch, nothing more."

"When did you start feeling this way?"

"Last night maybe?" she questioned herself. "But last night was such a blur I hardly remember it. Maybe this morning, who knows. I just want you to be watchful and try and follow the rules."

"I will."

I closed my eyes, remembering how last time it was just Dom and me left to fight this. I looked over at his table, and he turned his head to hide the fact that he was watching me with those brown eyes that once saw straight into my soul and connected with it.

"He will remember."

I looked to my left to find my favorite owl who always sat next to me, yet said very little these days.

"Hopefully, soon," I whispered.

"Soon enough," Ethan smirked.

"I've got to get out of here," I said, getting up. "I'll see you at free-time tonight," I told Vannah.

"Okay. We need to study that Lore of the Fae stuff for the final."

I walked out of the lunchroom and went to the closest restroom. I felt like a dam of emotions was about to break on me, and I was overwhelmed with everything slamming into me all at once. Why was this happening? I couldn't lose it or let this school start screwing with my mind. I had to stay the course and do my part to make sure we were ready to take out this evil when that day came.

# CHAPTER THIRTY-NINE

I was sound asleep when my wolf ears heard the soft tapping at my door. I looked over at Lusa, who was sound asleep and snoring. My wolf drew me to the door with confidence, thinking this might be Vannah wanting to let me in on what she was sensing at the school, and letting me know she threw on the protective spell magic.

I opened the door, and the big brown eyes of Dominic Rossi met mine. He was wearing a simple shirt and sweat pants, not his usual master clothes.

"Jenna," he said in a hushed voice. "I think we need to have a talk."

"What time is it?" I said, trying to figure him out.

"Close to three in the morning, but I can't sleep. Will you trust me to take you somewhere?"

"The rainbow trees."

"How do you know about that place?" he scrunched his forehead like he was in pain with what I'd suggested.

"Word gets around. Hold on, let me get my hoodie."

I slipped on my Dark Water Academy hooded sweatshirt and

met Dominic, who looked pale and was rubbing his forehead like he had the worst headache of his life.

"You okay?" I asked, trying to keep up with his long strides.

"No, I'm not," he answered.

We got to the trees, the moonlight being our only light, and it reminded me of the first time he brought me here.

"What's up?" I asked, watching him pace.

"You," he answered. "It's been driving me insane since that stupid ball."

"Why, because your cousin thought it was cute to dress us up as a couple?"

"No." He was stern. "I can't get you out of my head, and I don't know why. You're just a new shifter at this school. I'm not looking for a mate. I don't want this."

"What the living hell are you talking about?" I snapped.

"My wolf," he growled. "Your wolf. Do you sense it, or am I losing my damn mind?"

"All I sense is that you've been nothing but an asshole, and I did nothing to deserve you singling me out and trying to beat my spirit down as my instructor."

He reached for my hand, and I watched his eyes widen as he felt the electric jolt that surged through me before he dropped my hand like I'd burned him. He glared at his palm and then looked at me with different eyes...the old Dominic eyes.

"What is happening between us?" he said in a low voice. "Who are you, really?"

"Listen, I don't know why you're feeling anything, but that's between you and—"

My lips were captured by his, and my breathing stopped entirely. His firm lips pressed against mine, and I jerked back, feeling all of those emotions flood through me again. Dominic's eyes were silver lined now. His wolf was present and obviously drove him to kiss me. He let out a breath and cocked his head to the side.

"That felt familiar," he said softly. "I'm sorry. I didn't mean—"

Now, I cut him off. My emotions, my wolf, and my hormones were taking the wheel and urging me to kiss him like the last kiss we shared. I reached up to his brawny shoulders, stood on my toes, and nipped at his bottom lip.

Dominic sighed, framed my face with his hands, and shamelessly indulged us both in the kiss we shared the day I left him. My head was spinning, my body floating as our tongues reunited in desperation. I heard a low groan come from Dom while I pressed my body against his. His hands were tighter on my face now, and our kiss ended as fast as it began. Instead of pulling completely away, Dominic let his forehead rest against mine while his hands came down and he interlaced his long fingers with mine.

"Hold very still," he whispered.

I was frozen like a statue. His grip tightened in my hands, and all I heard was his breathing. I had no idea what was going on, but my wolf seemed to be on full alert.

Dominic's thumbs rubbed against where they rested on my hands, making a warm sensation wash over me. It was a feeling of comfort and completion I hadn't felt since Dominic lost all memory of what happened.

When he rose up, he had a smile I had never seen on his face before. He reached for my face and ran his knuckles along my jawline. "How could I ever forget us?" he said with a smile of love and adoration.

*He remembers!*

"A lot of crazy shit went down, and unfortunately, after you kicked ass and saved this wicked place, you didn't—"

"No," he said. "More than that, Jenna." His eyes were bronze again. He let out a sigh like he remembered a whole lot more crap than I had locked up. "We go farther back than this school. How could you just let me treat you like crap while I fought off my own selfish emotions?"

"Because I didn't want to wake the sleeping evil in this place. And trust me, you didn't treat me like crap, I would have cussed you out and requested another unit if I'd thought that."

My breath hitched in my chest when he shook his head. "I remember it all. You and me at Dark Water," he laughed. "Our wolves embraced their fates and forced us at such a young age to accept it all." I stood in silence and shock at *this* memory highlight reel he was having and watched his expression grow sad. "I promised you I would never forget. I swore it to you when they took our memories to protect you."

"Okay, I'm completely lost now. As far as I know, I never met you until I came to IA."

He shook his head. "It was my senior year, your junior year. The supernatural magic you used on our quest brought in an older woman. She took me, you, Ethan, and Lusa. Professor Matthews was concerned for your safety, and they never explained why you had that magic or how you used it. They just told us that they needed to pull our memories of the event and of each other to keep us safe. That one day, it would no longer work on all of us, but they had to. You don't remember any of it?"

"All I remember is you and me figuring out this school was killing immortals. Then I went into some spirit world...just the stuff from here. I didn't know you and Lusa went to Dark Water."

"That was part of the cover-up. They impressed in our minds that we went somewhere else. My wolf hung onto everything and just showed me our history. Who we are—you and me."

"Why were Lusa and Ethan involved?"

"You and Lusa were best friends." He laughed. "My God, they took everything, and it didn't even really protect you. I remember everything that happened here too. How your wolf jumped into mine will always be a mystery," he took my face in his hands again, "but you've always been more than just a shifter, Jen, that's why they pulled us apart like this. To protect you. To protect our strength because they knew this school would catch on."

"What do we do now?" I asked. "I mean, I don't remember us at Dark Water, but I still have feelings for you."

"How strong are your feelings?" he asked.

"Well, they were a lot stronger before. After a month of us being separated like this and having to suppress everything, I haven't let myself feel them. It's almost like regressing."

"I'm not losing you again. You are my soul, Jen Silvers. You may not remember the bond we formed at Dark Water, but I do. My wolf does. I won't pretend I don't love you like I did before and still do now that I remember us."

"Hey, I'm not sure exactly how much of my past I'm missing out on here, but I *hate* when people call me Jen," I said, getting a little nervous as to what the hell he was remembering and what exactly we might have done.

"I know." He smirked. "You would never let anyone call you Jen, so I took it upon myself to call you only that. You eventually didn't mind anymore...I think."

"So we had a healthy, loving relationship that I'm completely unaware of at the moment?"

"It looks like it, yes," he said with a huge grin.

"Okay. I guess." Now, I was the one with the nagging headache. "What do we do? I mean, I felt a bond with us, our wolves knew it before we did, right?"

"Yes. Our wolves remembered even when they took our memories of each other away for the *second* damn time," he growled. "Whoever in the hell is doing this is starting to piss me off. The first time they tore us apart to protect you, I was certain our love and devotion would overcome the spell, but it didn't."

"The people who did this seem to be on our side, but by the tone in your voice, I'm guessing you think they're not?"

"I think you and I are a pawn in some witch and dark magic

voodoo artist's game. I don't trust anyone. You said you were dead…"

"Yes. And I saw my dad."

His eyes grew severe, and he reached for my hands, "Your friend Vannah is a powerful witch, they took her in first before they wiped out our memories. She said she had a spell to shield our power, we need her."

"Maybe that's why Vannah fell so easily into the school's trap here."

"It's exactly why. Same as Lusa. I'm not sure, but that may not have been your dad," he said somberly. "I know you don't remember who we were or why it all happened, but it did. We will have Vannah cover up our bond. We'll have her do it now so that as the bond strengthens, we don't have the memory erasers screwing with our lives again. I'm not losing my girl ever again."

I felt more love pouring out of this man than I had ever felt, and it made me angry to know that we went back even farther than this school, but I couldn't remember it. I was angry that hearing him tell me he loved me sounded foreign because I couldn't remember. He was recalling memories of us—memories I might possibly never get back.

"I'm so sorry that I don't remember us," I said, hugging him, needing to feel his strong arms and smell his woodsy and spicy aroma.

"I'll make you feel the love we felt before, I promise you that. I'll get you back, Jen, if it's the last damn thing I do. Then we'll get Vannah up to speed and have her cover our butts so no one comes between us again. You and I are fated to be together for more than one reason. This school is just a small piece to a larger puzzle. A mystery is being kept from us, and every time these people get into our heads and screw with our memories and minds, it keeps them all a step ahead of us."

I looked up at him, needed to feel the connection his powerful and tasteful kiss gave me. "I want to remember us like you do."

He ran his fingers through my hair and his eyes glistened, "I would give anything to have you remember who we were, babe, but maybe it's safer like this for now. You will remember, and I will be patient until you do."

"My gosh, Dom," I said, seeing the sadness in his eyes. "I love what we are when we're close like this."

"I do too," he answered. "Just know I will kill all of them. I know the time isn't right, and we're not ready yet, but I will spend every day we are at this school until it is time to take them all out, finding out who these people are and ways to destroy them."

"We'll take them down together," I said, trying to reassure him I was with him, even though I hadn't made it to the *love story* chapter of our memory loss book just yet.

"You and me," he smiled, "Forever."

I licked my lips, "Will you tell me about us, you know, from before?"

He glanced behind me and then his eyes met mine. "I'll tell you absolutely everything, but right now, we have to get back to the dorms. If Vannah can't help us, then we're on our own. I'll get us the hell out of here and on the run if I have to, I'm not losing you again."

"We can't leave the school, Dominic. Death is the only way out."

"We would find a way, Jen. For now, we play the game."

I laughed. "Play the game. Seems like famous last words to me."

Dom smiled the smile that captured my heart, body, and soul. "It just might be if we can't take out what's after us. I will die before I lose you again—since we both know immortals can die, you can probably sense how much I'm done with people screwing with you and me."

I walked back to the dorms, Dom's hand holding mine in a tightened grip. I glanced at the enchantment of the school, then tried to let my eyes see it for what it was. The façade didn't fade, and I felt my heart rate pick up. My head grew fuzzy, and I had to wonder if I was falling victim to this stupid school and the evil that could have just sparked up because of Dom's memories coming back to him.

It felt like we just woke up the sleeping, evil school, and we were going to be lucky to make it past this year. What happened to just going to freaking school and majoring in something you loved? What happened to the basics of studying Fairy BS 101? Not here, not at Immortal Academy, and apparently not even at the school I loved and trusted—Dark Water Academy. We were not just in a supernatural school system, Dom and I were literally locked up in some supernatural prison that wanted us either dead or doing its bidding.

"Jen!" I felt Dom pull me into his arms.

I rocked my head up. "I think we just pissed the school off, and it's—" I stopped when I saw a dark orb over me and then shoot into my stomach, making me almost barf all over Dominic.

Oh my gosh, this wasn't happening. As Dom took off in a sprint, I felt my veins heat up and hoped that maybe it was my inner fairy-witch genes killing whatever darkness had just entered my body.

The last thing I remember, I was being rushed into Vannah's room, her roommate freaking, and Vannah's eyes as wide as silver dollars while Dominic ordered her to help cleanse whatever darkness had jumped me and was about to have its way with everyone.

"I can only do so much," Vannah said.

"If you don't, she'll be powerful enough to take me with her next, and then every human and supernatural are screwed! Lives depend on Jenna and me *not* going dark, Sahvannah!"

"How did you remember her?" Vannah asked him while I was internally fighting a battle between good and evil inside my aching bones.

"How do you know I remember her?" Dominic seethed like he was staring at a demon.

"Because I'm not Sahvannah," the voice sneered.

"A shape-shifter? Who are you!" Dominic said with panic in his voice.

"You're going to find out, Dominic Rossi. Now, I have you both, and it's up to me what I'll do here at Immortal Academy, then I will work my way through the rest after that. Taking out all of the human race isn't exactly a snap your fingers kind of routine, these things take time. So you will sit there silently and paralyzed while you watch me encourage your little wolf mate to accept the darkness that found her. Sorry that your reunion had to be cut short."

After that voice faded—that familiar voice—I went under and was suffocating in darkness. Things just went from bad to worse, and all I had now was hope...hope that Ethan would stop this and give Dom and I the chance we needed and deserved.

It was the last hope all of us had.

# CHAPTER FORTY

As I was sucked deeper and deeper into the darkness, my mind called out to Ethan, begging him to come and take out the shapeshifter who was threatening Dominic and me. Something deep within me knew I had gotten to Ethan telepathically, and if I truly had, that evil soul sucker was about to be ripped apart by a pissed off owl.

As soon as I let my mind face the darkness, an instant feeling of reassurance washed over me. I might not have known how to get the darkness out of me, but I knew I could control and contain it.

It was a strange situation. One second, I felt like I was drowning in darkness, and the next, I was in a void inside my mind, facing one of those shadow creatures. It was up to me to juice up my magic and lock this sucker down. I took control of my mental state, knowing this was a foreigner in my body. It was possessing me, but I could control it.

It had no face, so I couldn't get a read on the thing, but I felt its consuming power, and I was screwed if I didn't shut this thing down. I looked around when this creep shifted my mind to another location. The void had transformed into the creepy room where they'd killed Jess.

This was a stupid move on its part. I had no idea how to lock this thing up, but it'd just manipulated a memory of mine, and I was going to build on that. I was going to lock it up in this room. I stood there with the creature facing me, floating inches off the ground in the black looking suit it wore. It was taunting me, this is where it must have thought it was going to lock me up in my mind, so it had full possession of me.

Hell no, I was beating this SOB at its own game.

I felt it grow stronger, and I felt a sense of being trapped here. I had to stop overthinking this and draw on the magic I had inside me. *Time for the trap.* I ran over to the area where they had the needles that killed my immortal fox shifter friend. The demon spawn moved toward the needles, but my mental will to get there faster beat it.

The thing squealed like a pig—good it was pissed. Anger is a weakness. I took the needle we both went after at the same time, stabbed it into its neck, and magically imagined the thing being restrained on the same bed as Jess when they killed her.

Feeling like I was somehow exacting revenge for Jessica's murder, my desire for retribution grew. I looked at the machine that the needles were connected to by tubes and pushed every freaking button on it.

Nothing.

*We're in your mind, Jenna, you have control. Turn on, dammit!* I scolded myself. As soon as I mentally willed the machine on, the spawn started shaking, and then all grew quiet.

It was struggling, fighting the invisible restraints my mind put it under, but it wasn't dying. The good news was that I felt myself regaining control of my mind, and that was a positive sign. Time to lock this SOB up and wake the hell up.

I walked to the door, knowing I was locking this creature away in my mind, giving me myself back. So long as I could keep in contained, I would wake up, and I would figure out how to get something to spell this crap out of me. Right now, I had to wake up. Period.

I walked to the door of the realistic room in my mind, the demon thing still squirming and fighting, but I had control. This was my body, my mind, and I was in control of the evil that tried to screw me. I stepped out of the freaky room and imagined using my hand—my witchy magic—to seal up the door for good.

As I sealed the door, I felt my body again. I was back, I just couldn't open my freaking eyes right now.

I heard shuffling in the room around me, I tried with all my power to open my eyes, but failed. I had no idea what was happening. What if Dominic was also possessed? That thing that we thought was Vannah said it was taking him and me. I had to fully wake up.

"You okay, Sahvannah?" I heard Dominic's oddly out-of-breath voice.

"Yes, what happened? One minute you're walking into my room, the next minute I'm waking up to…" she paused. "Oh my gosh, Jenna!"

"It took her down hard. Ethan said the darkness who jumped you was a straggler, left behind after the cleansing of this school. Ethan's owl killed it, but one got into Jenna." I felt his warm palm running across my forehead and over the top of my hair. "I can't lose her."

"Jenna will be fine. She locked up the evil inside her." Ethan's voice rang through my head, and his words blanketed me with relief.

"What are you talking about, E?" Dom asked.

"She's waking up. She will come back."

At that moment, my eyes finally let me see the face of my god-like man. I drew on his wolf that he had opened up fully to me.

"Dom," I said, reaching for his face, "I think we did it."

Dom's hands were on my face, his eyes searching mine. "Oh

my God, Jen." He looked back at Vannah who was behind him, trembling with tears in her eyes. "Vannah, I need you to pull it together. I need you to cloak us now. Can you do that?"

Vannah was frozen in some fear and relief state when Ethan stepped toward her. "You must cloak their power. The evil is locked in Jenna. The school is safe from all of it now. If you don't, the evil will come back."

"Okay," she stammered. "Oh, God, okay."

"Vannah," I smiled, sitting up, Dom's hand supporting my back and holding my hand like he was never going to let me go. "You've got this. Cloak us, and it will all be over."

Vannah swallowed and nodded. "Ethan," she looked at the owl shifter, "I saw you when you came into my mind and fought that thing, I felt your powers. I need them. Can I draw on your owl's energy?"

"Yes." Ethan nodded. He gave her his hand, "Use our physical connection."

"Maybe I can help?" I offered, knowing I had some fairy juice still left.

Ethan's eyes were sincere when he looked at me. "Jenna, you have to reserve your powers to keep the evil from taking over again. You can't use it on anything but fighting what you have locked inside you."

I exhaled, "You're right."

"God, just do this shit, right now," Dom growled. "If you two can cloak us, get to it. We're wasting time."

Vannah instantly starting chanting, Ethan's eyes went white, and I felt a cold breeze blast over my face. After that, green, magenta, and purple energy were like swirls in the room, surrounding Dominic and me.

Dom held me close, and I absorbed that sense of completion his energy gave me. Our wolves appeared to both be silent and still, knowing we were being shielded by good magic. We needed this, the school needed this, and I had to hope it would work.

"Done," Vannah said. "Your energy isn't even recognizable."

Ethan released her hand and smiled at Dominic and me. "You both have a great amount of power. It is hidden. You cannot use your power, or you will breach the shield cloaking it. You must get through without it."

"What does that mean, E?" I asked. "We have to stay away from each other?"

"No," he said as he shook his head. "You can't use any supernatural power that is new to you. Dominic will give you his power unknowingly because your wolves have bonded. You will sense his strength, don't draw on it. Ignore it."

"This is such BS," Dom said. "And me?"

"You feel her power too. Don't draw on it. It is simple, you both were strong enough before your phenomenon took place."

"True," I slid my hand onto Dom's lower back, bringing my man even closer. "We managed before without this awesome wolf power thing. We can do this."

"What if we screw it up?" Dom asked. "My memories are hit and miss with what happened at Dark Water, but I do remember that when this hit us at first, it was hard and fast. If we gave into those emotions at the time, we would've let the merge happen between the wolves."

"You are too young to mate, Dominic Rossi," Ethan scolded him, and even though I was back to wondering what the heck happened between us at Dark Water, I couldn't help but laugh.

Vannah giggled. "They say abstinence is the way to go, you know. Besides, I'm not sure this college is okay with their students sneaking off and—"

"I'm serious," Dominic said, "Our souls were practically driving us to merge the wolves and unite ourselves, not giving a crap that we were too young for all of that. Jenna is my life—my other half—it is difficult not to follow through with what my soul is calling me to do."

"You both are strong. You need to help Jenna," Ethan said. "She will need your help as she fights the darkness in her."

"I have that thing locked up," I said, irritated that Ethan was implying that the mental cage I had that thing locked away in could break and the darkness could come after me again. "How do we just get it out of me?"

"There is no one who has that ability at this school." Ethan said. "A Woodson witch like Sahvannah may be able to do it, but it will take a lot of spell magic and research for her to do this for you. Right now, she's too young. The spell magic will take her life."

"We don't want that." Dom said. "I'll help my girl. We'll fix this. For now, let's finish this school year and get on our virtual summer break."

"Well, you're quick to make this all easy," I teased Dominic.

He draped an arm around me and kissed my temple. "It's all we can do. As long as whatever evil that is lurking in this school is waiting for us to spark its interest again, I say we go back to normal. This time, I'll have my memories and my girl."

"We all still need to be cautious," Ethan said. "I sense no evil, only what Jenna has contained. The school is safe. The staff is normal again, and we must return to normal with them."

"Normal? Normal sounds amazing! I'm all about doing that and finishing this year out," I said.

"Come on, babe," Dominic said while encouraging me to get up. "You feeling okay?"

"Oddly enough, like nothing ever happened."

"Alright guys, let's get this all settled, finish the year out, then summer break will be our reward."

"The blue waters." Ethan smiled. "The trees with large leaves."

Dom laughed. "Yes, buddy, I'm taking you to a virtual ocean. You deserve it."

"A virtual ocean?" I asked.

"Yes," Dom smiled, and his eyes soothed my soul right then

and there. "Care to lay out under a warm sun, in velvety soft sand, listening to relaxing sounds of waves while you relax next to me?"

"Can we go there now?" I said with a laugh.

Dom's lips were at my ear, "Trust me, if we can't complete the bond that you will soon feel is so powerful, you're going to want time to prep for our summer break I'm planning."

His voice was husky, and his eyes swirling with an energy that made my entire body tingly for more than just a kiss right now.

Dom laughed, "Yes. That feeling you're getting right now? It's the same one that had us not giving a crap about gossip or talk, it's you feeling what needs to be done between you and me. And it's not just simply mating," he brushed a finger over my nose, "it's much more intense than that."

"Wow, this really is going to be hard," I said with a smile.

Dom smirked, "Seeing you in a bathing suit on the beach may just screw the entire school again. I won't be able to resist you."

I rolled my eyes, "I'm wearing regular clothes."

Dom surprisingly picked me up, and I locked my legs around his waist, staring down into his eyes. "God, you're beautiful," I admitted to him.

He licked his lips. "I love you, Jenna Silvers, don't you ever forget that. It's you and me, babe. Forever."

"That's if we all survive the next two and a half years," Vannah said, obviously judging Dom and me who were about to kiss, clearly not caring what anyone thought about this moment we were having.

"Thank you for cloaking us," Dominic said to Vannah before he looked at Ethan. "Thank you, bud, we won't ruin what you both did to help us."

"And the school," Ethan added to the gratitude pouring out of Dom.

Dom chuckled and brought his eyes back to mine. "And the school," he said in a lower voice. "Let's get the rest of this year over with, I want some time alone with my girl. We need some fun time anyway."

"Agreed," I said.

I framed his face with my hands and brought my lips down onto his. We both groaned in satisfaction of this connection. The deeper and the more passionate Dom made this kiss, the more I worried we were going to blow it and just finish off this nagging bond that was pressing us to mate.

For now, it had to be narrowed down to these kisses, but I knew deep inside that Dom and I were going to want to take this all further, but for the sake of everyone around us, we needed to control ourselves.

We could do it. I think.

I was going to set my mind on other goals. Finishing this school year out with my friends back, my man at my side, and sweet Ethan watching over all of us was priority number one. Priority number two? Getting on the all too awesome, virtual reality vacation that Dom was already planning for our summer break. I'd never done the virtual reality stuff, but from what I was told, it was freaking awesome. We could pick any place, and it was like we were there and really living it. Even though it was all virtual, you supposedly couldn't tell the difference.

If Dom thought seeing me in a swimsuit would make it hard on him, heaven help us all while I laid out under the warm sun with this dude shirtless and in swim trunks by my side the entire time.

Good God, we better not blow this over lustful crap—we were stronger than this.

We were practically halfway through the year, the school's darkness was cleaned up, and I had my other half consuming me in a kiss. It was all so very worth it, every last bit of horror I'd experienced my first year at Immortal Academy. I survived it, and I was going to survive the next two years.

# AFTERWORD

The journey continues late summer or earlier at Immortal Academy.

Click here to preorder and enroll for your second year with Jenna and the gang at Immortal Academy. Plus, a nice virtual summer vacation awaits in Immortal Academy: Year Two.

While waiting, if you'd like to check out the prequel of Jenna at Dark Water Academy, you'll learn a little about what Dominic just revealed to her before the unexpected happened.

Thank you for taking the time to download and read Immortal Academy: Year One. I had a blast writing this book and am counting down the days to get you all back with these characters as they finish out the first year (if they finish out the first year ;-D) and go through their second and third years at the school.

Hang in there with me, there are a lot of distractions at Immortal Academy and my little owl, Ethan, is only giving me these stories little at a time. He's my sweetheart, but he needs to understand we don't like cliffhangers and we just want the next book. He's definitely a wise owl shifter...maybe he's got a reason he's revealing these stories to me one month at a time.

Again, thank you for taking the time to read. A review is always appreciated and is the biggest thanks an author can receive.

Also, a debt of gratitude to all of you who shared in my excitement of releasing this new series. I haven't been this excited about hanging out with characters since Levi, Reece, and Harrison in my Ancient Guardians novel series.

My love and best to all of you.

Stacy "S.L." Morgan.

# ABOUT THE AUTHOR

S.L. Morgan is the USA Today Bestselling & Award winning author of the Ancient Guardians novel series.

Being a storyteller at heart, Morgan loves creating worlds, characters, and tales that will bring readers into a escape unlike any other.

Morgan is the author of:

- The Ancient Guardians Series (A four book completed novel series)
- The Dragons Curse Series (Completed Trilogy Series
- The Rift (Unfinished co-authored series with Ella Avery)
- The Guardians Novella Series
- The Immortal Academy Series

You can follow her on Facebook book, Instagram, Pinterest, and twitter for updates on new releases.

Sign up for her VIP mailing list on her website www.slmorganauthor.com

## ALSO BY S.L. MORGAN

The Ancient Guardians Novel Series:

A novel series that is praised for the enchanting realms and other world romance that serves as an escape read. This series has been praised by avid Harry Potter fans, and compared to Outlander. Readers are addicted to the characters, their lives, and have difficulty stepping out of the book and back into reality.

The Ancient Guardians Series is a completed series:

- 1. Legacy of the Key
- 2. The Uninvited
- 3. The Awakening
- 4. The Reckoning
- Special Christmas light holiday read: A Christmas at Pasidian Palace

The Dragon's Curse Series:

Dragon's curse can be read as a stand-alone series, but is in the same universe as the Ancient Guardians series. It, as well, is praised for its unique world building.

- 1. Cursed
- 2. Marked
- 3. Dragon's Fire

The Rift:

(Currently only one book is available. This first book follows the good and evil angels in their battles for one human's life. It takes readers into the rift, where they follow the main character as she navigates through a new world, wondering if modern day was the dream-world, not this mystical enchanting realm with a new family she never wants to leave.

The Guardians:

This is a spin-off prequel to the Ancient Guardians series. Due to fans wanting to learn more about Levi and Harrison, and their love for these two characters. This prequel series began. It starts with Twin Paradox: Levi and Harrison's first assignment as human guardians.

The Immortal Academy Series:

- Year One
- Year Two
- Year Three

Follow me on Amazon and be notified as soon as my books release. Or follow me on BookBub where any book I am about to release is submitted to my followers for their consideration.

38284334R00180

Made in the USA
San Bernardino, CA
09 June 2019